I0681721

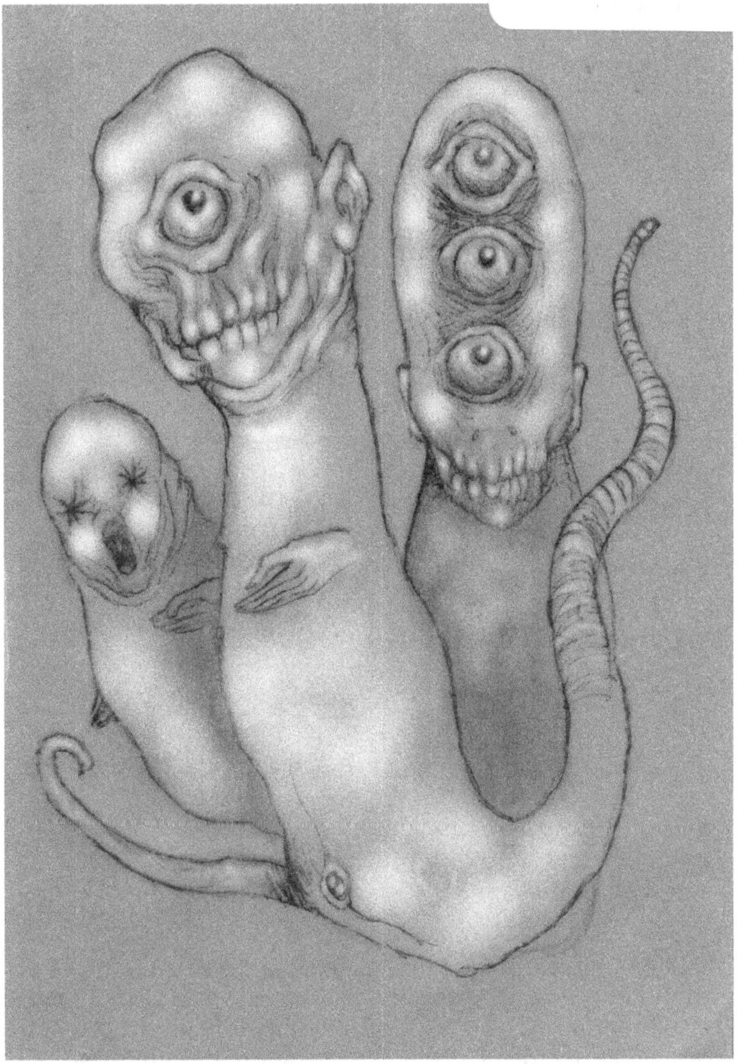

Ghosts Revenge

JWK Fiction

Ghosts Revenge

Book © 2015 James Ward Kirk Publishing

Internet: http://www.jwkfiction.com
Twitter: @jameswardkirk
Facebook: James-Ward-Kirk-Fiction

Cover art © Stephen Cooney 2015
Cover Design by John D. Stanton
Illustrations by Gidion Van de Swaluw © 2015

ISBN-13: 978-0692407752 (James Ward Kirk Publishing)

ISBN-10: 0692407758

All rights reserved. No part of this book may be reproduced in any form or by any electronic or mechanical means, including information storage and retrieval systems, without written permission from the publisher or author, except in the case of a reviewer, who may quote brief passages embodied in critical articles or in a review.

Contents

The publisher thanks Gidion Van de Swaluw for his wonderful illustrations, Stephen Cooney for the beautiful cover art, and John D. Stanton for his excellent cover design. The stories and poetry appearing upon these pages will be forever loved. These authors are indeed quite special.

.

Mary Genevieve Fortier

In Stately Pious Prayer

Somewhere in my dreaming
Was this so?
So, it seeming
To appear unfamiliar was the night
The darkness in its streaming
Was this so?
A distant screaming
Enveloped the air
Choked with despair
          ...and fright

Stumbled blindly into nowhere
Upon a stair, I entered somewhere
The darkness now shifted to mist
A church, complete with steeple
In frozen time, were people
Shadow cloaked, what questioned to exist

Upon their knees they stayed
Hands clasped, heads bowed, they prayed
No breath from their form did escape
Again, in the dark
Somewhere in the dark
A scream, then a shuffle, a scrape

Ne'er one body did move
No speck of dust dare removed
Beneath the dead, shrouded and posed
Wait! A faint murmur
A sob, near the alter
Though nothing
Nor no one disclosed

A whisper, a humming
Wicked and drumming
Coming from above the choir loft
A cackling came after
Maniacal, the laughter
Echo now, distant and soft

Chipped and peeling
Walls and ceiling
Creaked in loneliness
            ...the hollow, empty pews
Movement somewhere creeping
A liquid sound was seeping
'Neath the moaning
            ...that so quietly ensued

From beyond the choral arch
Phantom fingers played a march
A haunting, death's great lullaby
Rocked on rotting pipes now singing
As unholy bells were ringing
Played a dirge upon an ancient organ's cry

As by some unearthly command
Or an unseen, ghostly hand
Those draped and still, now corpse-like, gravely stood
From a state of pious prayer
Turned their heads to me and stared
In what once a shroud, looked back at me a hood

The march grew with intensity
Propelled by some strange entity
That hummed beneath an empty, eerie tune
Toward me they moved, shuffling
Backing awkward, stumbling
I begged the end, "My God, dear God, come soon!"

Closer now, a pew away
The music hushed, then ceased to play
Those shrouded, ever slowly turned around

Entranced by silence, shuffled on
The humming, haunting screams now gone
So quiet yes, oh nary was a sound

Returned them to their quiet pose
Shrouded bodies, stiff, reposed
The stillness of it all, just took my breath
Toward the door, I wished to find
Before I knew, I'd lose my mind
The scare alone, would be my certain death

A simple pause
A quick glance back
Cold, my soul
The darkness, black
In fear, returned the sights and spectral sounds
Dare I take but one last look
Tempted by the ground that shook
Dare I take the chance and turn around?

Yes,
    I dared...
            And there I found

Upon their knees, they stayed
Hands clasped, heads bowed, they prayed
No breath from their form did escape
Again, in the dark
Somewhere, in the dark
A scream, then a shuffle, a scrape

In silence, I stood screaming
For I knew, this was no dreaming
When the humming before me, took shape
Then the organ began the march
From above the lofts great arch
The draped stood
            Knowing I
                    ...had no escape
Now...

Upon my knees, I stayed
Hands clasped, head bowed, I prayed
No breath from my form, did escape
Again in the dark
Somewhere, in the dark
A scream, then a shuffle, a scrape...

Once the music ceased to play
So piously I prayed
Right there, draped and still, I stayed
Yes, there is where
                    ... I stayed

K.Z. Morano

Yūrei no Yado

Akuji mi ni tomaru.
All evil done clings to the body.

Zen proverb

The streets are crowded and the air is thick with the mingled exhalations of both the living and the dead. Indeed, with my failing eyesight and the endless swirl and flicker of vibrantly printed kimonos, it grows more and more difficult for me to distinguish one from the other. It is the night of the *O-bon* festival, that time of the year when the deceased are able to pass through the whisper-thin mist separating their world from ours. To others, it is a time of remembrance and prayer. To me, it is nothing but a curse rekindled year after year. People return to their individual hometowns to pay their respects to the dead—to place upon the *butsudan*, or the spirit cabinet, perhaps more food than they have served their relatives while they still lived... to wash the cold tombstones more diligently than they would've washed their elders' diseased bodies while they still breathed. Oh how we fear the dead and the whole concept of life after death!

It is a funny thing, how the memory of the departed causes the living to come together and how, in turn, the traditions of the living bring about this curious congregation of souls. For three nights, the ghosts dwell amongst us and we walk, sit; we lie beside them and inhale their putrid outbreaths without realizing it... for their foulness is masked by the profuse offerings of flowers and their presence is made less palpable by the pyrotechnic pageantry and the thunderous beating of the *taiko* drums. Unfortunately, unlike the others, I am not spared these ghastly visions. For soon, I am to become one of them. Indeed, I am as good as dead. I can feel my spirit trickling out of my body with every breath. I can feel death's weight upon me as if I were carrying my own tombstone around my neck.

Tonight is the third and the last night of the Festival of the Dead and it is time to send the spirits back whence they came. I watch the paper lanterns floating down the river like the flaming fleet of some Lilliputian army, meant to guide the spirits back as though being dead means being lost. As though being a spirit means having no idea of where one wishes to go. On the contrary, it isn't until we die that we become utterly aware of what we want and how to get it. When one suffers a violent death or when plagued with regrets or unfinished business, fueled with sufficient volumes of love, or lust, or hatred, or sorrow, or desire for vengeance, one's soul can be powerful enough as to bridge the gap back to the physical world. Decisiveness born from death, one might say.

Furthermore, the dead are ungoverned by the same limitations that bind the living. Simply put, the dead do whatever they please. They go where they wish to go... and sometimes, they choose to linger; hence, my duty and my curse . . .

An adolescent voice cracks out from the shadows, "*Ojisan.*" The sound reminds me of the bursting of a hollow shell.

The owner of the voice is a boy, no more than fifteen and from what I can see with my waning vision, a somewhat handsome one. A *gaijin* perhaps, for though he speaks the language like a native, he has very pale features and a lost aura about him. Like the others, he is wearing a lightweight cotton *yukata* preferable on sweltering nights such as this.

"I was wondering," he says, "If you might know of a place where I can stay the night. I don't have any money on me but I can pay you... in kind."

A delinquent, I decide. Usually, during this time of the year, I endeavor to be on my best behavior. The ancestors are watching, after all. Not tonight. Tonight, I need the kind of succor that only another human being can provide.

"What a coincidence," I reply. "I happen to own an inn. Though I must warn you, it is a very long walk from here to the *yado.*"

"Then I shall walk with you, *Ojisan.*"

I feel slightly uncomfortable with the boy addressing me as "uncle," knowing that soon I would be wrapping my mouth around his youthful flesh, suckling as an infant would of its mother's teat, as though my very survival depended on it.

"Please, call me Mamoru."

"I am in your debt, Mamoru-san. My mother named me Akihiro." He bows politely.

What a pleasant child, I think. I am sure that he is flesh and blood though I sense something otherworldly about him-- perhaps it's because his obsidian eyes reflect a wisdom that is greater than his years... or the fact that his shadow appears to be diminished, half-eaten. I choose to ignore it. If he turns out to be a wandering spirit, then this would not be the first time that I would take one home with me. Besides, I feel as if I know him already. It may sound ridiculous but I see something of me in him. Whoever he is, whatever he has done, he is alone in this world. As am I. Apart from the random sexual encounters with prostitutes, I have spent the past several years of my life in solitude... and for a good reason. But not tonight. Tonight, I cannot bear to be alone.

"I must warn you about some things," I tell Akihiro during our laborious hike. "At the inn, if you happen to hear the faint whisperings of robes or the clip-clopping of a woman's *geta* sandals against the floorboards... if you catch snatches of a song or hear someone sobbing, do not, by any means, rise from your futon. If you see *Manekute no Yurei* reaching out from the hallway, I bid you, do not fear."

"Why would I be afraid of severed ethereal hands reaching out to grab me?" A playful smile touches the youth's pale lips and I feel an intense urge to kiss him. Every fiber of my being is aching for any kind of human connection. It is as if my soul knows that it is to depart from my body soon and is thus craving for comfort, no matter how fleeting-- a final act of intimacy with the corporeal world. Nevertheless, I restrain myself. I return his smile. I have not smiled in such a long time that I feel as though my face is about to crack and peel.

"They mean no harm. They only wish for you to acknowledge their presence. Utter a prayer for them. But if you wish, I shall give you a package of *ofuda* blessed by the local monk so that you may throw the paper strips at the *yūrei* to send them away."

After a few minutes of walking in silence, I ask Akihiro, "You do believe in ghosts, don't you?"

"You mean like the ones following us right now?"

I back away from him. "You can see them, too?"

7

"No." he answers solemnly. "But I can feel them. I can feel their gazes piercing my back, ice-cold and malignant, like poisoned needles."

I understand what he means. I, too, can feel their eyes boring holes into my flesh. More than that, I can feel the oppressive weight of their collective emotions bearing down on me. Their anger, their fear, their thirst for revenge is a gray nimbus draped over my shoulder-- a burden that I have been carrying ever since we began this walk.

"Why do you do this?" the boy asks.

"What do you mean?"

"This." he gestures toward the eerie balls of flames floating behind us, the fires of the dead. "Why do you lead this procession of souls?"

From where I stand, the *hitodama* look like firefly lamps, brilliant yet benign, flaring and failing at each turn. Even when they keep their distance, it is impossible to ignore their presence. Their concentrated voices are like a steadily mounting clamor at the edge of my perception. Even in my sleep, they penetrate my head, vipers invading the nest of my dreams.

"On the last night of the Bon Festival," I explain, "The families of these ghosts bid them farewell and send them to sail back toward the underworld. The doors of their homes remain shut to these spirits until the next *O-bon* so those who have decided to linger have no place to stay. I come to the river so that I may guide them toward the inn. Such is my duty. Such is my curse. I have been doing this for many years."

"But why?" he asks again. "Do you like it? Do you find pleasure in playing host to your ghostly guests?"

"Like it?" I exclaim. Then I lower my voice into a whisper. "My boy, I am exhausted."

He casts upon me a look of such pity—a gesture so rare to me, so human-like, that I find myself wishing once again that he indeed turns out to be a real living person and not one of the restless dead that have dominated every day of my life for so long.

"I suppose," I say, in the hopes of amusing him, "That there are certain benefits gathered from accommodating these *yūrei*. I am able to learn each of their stories."

"Tell me." This seems to please Akihiro and for some unexplainable reason, I feel pleased with myself.

"Hmmm... Let me see... Ah! The Tale of the Kappa and Ayame."

"*Kappa?*" he interrupts. "I asked for a haunting story not a children's tale! Do you expect me to believe that river goblins exist?"

Ignoring him, I begin: "Once, long ago, there lived a woman named Ayame. She was with child and I suppose she was happy. When the time came for her to give birth, she delivered a son with crooked limbs. Now, you must understand, a boy with such defects could be of no use to his father—not in combat, not in the fields, not even to further the family line... for who, indeed, would risk having grandchildren with crooked limbs?"

Akihiro nods.

"So, he did what the men of his time normally did on such occasions. He blamed it on the *Kappa*. He accused his wife of bearing the foul creature's son. He beat her mercilessly until she finally admitted in front of the entire village that she had indeed been ravaged by the scabrous amphibian while she was washing clothes in the river."

"And was she?" the boy asks, his black eyes bright with anticipation.

"Of course not! There's no such thing as water goblins. During that time, however, people believed that the *Kappa* and other similar creatures exist. And when the time came that they needed an excuse for anything—bad luck, murder, unwanted pregnancies, the *Kappa* provided them with a convenient scapegoat. Do you know what they did to infants that were suspected of being a river goblin's bastard?"

Akihiro shakes his head.

"Some are chopped to pieces and buried into the ground; some, like Ayame's son, are placed inside wooden wine receptacles and hurled into the river. So, you see, Ayame had to watch as her own child was taken from her by the villagers to be drowned into the river."

"How is that a ghost story?" my companion asks, disappointment creeping into his voice.

"Ayame is one of the spirits who frequent the inn. It is for that very same reason that over the years, several mothers who had the misfortune of staying in room number two awoke to find their children drowned in their sleep, their beddings wet, their lungs filled with water from the river."

9

The lad's eyes widen in disbelief.

"Y-you mean... You allow real, live people to stay at your *yado* with the ghosts?"

"Well, naturally." I shrug. "That's part of my job. Besides, what good is a *yūrei* with no one to haunt? What good is vengeance with no one to inflict it upon?"

Akihiro considers this for a moment.

"I suppose it is sort of fascinating... in a cold-hearted, evil kind of way."

I nod. He has a penchant for the macabre, a boy after my own heart!

"But tell me, Mamoru-san," he presses, his adolescent voice quivering with what can only be described as exhilaration. "What became of the mothers?"

"They met their individual fates, torn apart by the other *yūrei* that inhabit the inn."

"But what of their relatives, and the authorities—did they not trace them back to your *yado*?"

Clever child, I think, and again, I utter a silent prayer that he would indeed pass the test and prove himself a living, breathing human being and not just another confused vagrant spirit.

"What kind of people would seek accommodation in an obscure place like this? Certainly not tourists, fugitives, most likely... those who are either harboring dark secrets or fleeing from someone... people who were either lost or don't care to be found."

Akihiro nods in silent appreciation. "Tell me another story."

I fight the urge to grin, afraid that my smile would frighten him.

"Once, in the Tokugawa era, there lived a *daimyo* with a wife named Natsumi. Years passed and she was unable to bear the lord any sons. It was not long before she started hearing rumors of his plans to replace her. Natsumi, clever lady that she was, had the idea that perhaps the fault wasn't entirely her own. So, while the *daimyo* was away to visit some property, Natsumi seduced one of his young samurai. Soon, she was able to conceive. The *daimyo*, naturally, was very pleased with her and showered her with jewels. But Natsumi fell in love with the samurai and couldn't stop meeting with him in secret. Whispers spread like wildfire all over the palace. The *daimyo*, turned violent with rage, refused to have her hanged and instead had her tortured and raped to death by his faithful retainers while he watched. Finally, the lord ordered the samurai lover to ram his *katana* deep into her *omanko*."

The youth shudders, more from thrill than terror. "And I suppose she had her revenge?"

"Yes. That very day, the samurai performed *hara-kiri* in public. He plunged the *tantō* into his belly and disemboweled himself by slicing the blade from left to right. However, possessed by some unexplainable force, the samurai pulled the knife from his abdomen, bent over and there for the entire public to see, plunged the dagger up his anus and pulled out his bowels through the orifice. Needless to say, he died in utter humiliation."

Akihiro's obsidian eyes shine demonic black. "And the *daimyo*?"

"Remember when I told you to that if you hear the sound of footsteps, then you mustn't leave your bed?"

The child nodded.

"One night, a foul wind entered the *daimyo's* chambers and the fire in his lantern guttered and died. He then heard the eerie sound of Natsumi's footfalls. Grabbing his sword, he cried, 'Who goes there', but there was nothing-- only darkness swallowing darkness. Then suddenly, emerging from the abyss, Natsumi revealed herself-- her white *katabira* steeped in blood, her feet not touching the ground, her hair dancing to a breeze that the *daimyo* could not feel... She raised her gown and revealed between her thighs the hilt of the *katana* pressed against her blood-encrusted pubic hair. She pulled out the blade and her insides spattered onto the floor, whipping around like water hoses. The next morning, they found the *daimyo* kneeling on his own entrails, his body spitted on his own sword, right through the anus. I need not tell you that, at the inn, several men had died in the same fashion, sometimes with metal pipes or bamboo poles rammed up their anal cavities."

The youth's face is alight with excitement so I tell him more. I tell him the tale of Momo, the concubine who boasted that she was more beautiful than a powerful *shogun's* wife and how the warlord's wife retaliated by throwing acid onto the girl's face, and how Momo now haunts the inn and rips the face of every woman who she thinks is pretty so that she may wear it over her own weeping, crusty patches of skin, until it rots. Then I tell him of

11

Kaede, the hungry ghost, whose stingy stepmother had starved him to his early death.

"Let me guess," Akihiro laughs. "He haunts the kitchen at night."

"No," I reply, without humor. "He returned as a *Jikininki*, a corpse-eating ghost, and his first meal after a very long time was his stepmother's still-warm cadaver. I suppose I should be grateful for his presence. He spares me from the trouble of disposing the bodies of the murdered guests."

By the time we reach the inn, it is midnight, with the hour of the ox drawing near.

The *yado* is old and in the traditional style, with a thatched roof, *tatami* flooring, and *shoji* screens.

"How did this inn come into your care?" he asks as we lie together on the futon.

I narrate to him the story of that one fateful night which commenced my years of servitude to these souls.

"Once, in a night such as this, I was the unfortunate guest of this very same inn. I, like many of the other guests, was running away from something. One night, I was awakened by a strange wind that wafted through the screen, making the paper shiver against the bamboo frames. At first, I saw only her silhouette... then I heard her laughter, gentle, like the rippling of a lake. The next thing I know, she was straddling me, making love to me, her back turned toward me. For a while, I cared for nothing else but the sweet rush of blood through my groin.

"I noticed that she was wearing a grand robe, such as one that a noblewoman would wear during the Edo period. I fancied her very beautiful so I ventured to touch her face. It was like pressing my hand against the abyss. Several times, I demanded that she turn around so that I might see her but instead of facing me, her neck twisted itself into a terrible angle and there I saw that I had been making love to a *Noppera-bō*, for there was nothing but a blank sheet, pale as winter, where her face should have been.

"Too late did I realize that engaging in intercourse with the dead means that she now has the right to claim me. I was to die very soon, and dragged into my grave by that faceless ghost; but she struck a bargain with me. She will allow me to live as long as I keep the inn and ensure that she'll always have a place to stay."

"You slept with a woman?" come Akihiro's unexpected question. "Male and female... You like them both the same?"

"Yes." I laugh. "Don't you? I was married before, you know."

"What became of her?"

"She was the one that I was running away from, the reason why I came to this inn. I was abandoning her and my son to be with another woman."

"Why?" says Akihiro, with something akin to bitterness seeping into his tone. "Did the child have crooked limbs?"

I therefore conclude that he, too, was an abandoned child.

"No." My spasmodic fingers trace shaky labyrinths on his naked skin. Oh what I would not give to be young once again! I feel my body wasting away. I can feel my insides rot, can smell the fetor of death in my breath. I notice that Akihiro has not complained about any of these things. How very decent of him. Perhaps he can be my companion until I die. I shall pretend that I am a samurai of the old days and he, my apprentice. We shall engage in *wakashudo*, the way of the youth. Perhaps we can even form a "brotherhood contract" and swear to be each other's' exclusive lover until he comes of age. I cannot for the life of me, explain why I feel such a strong connection with the boy.

"I am so glad that you passed the test." I whisper into his ear.

"What test?" he asks.

"Have you not noticed the *ofuda* pasted on the door? I have several attached to every entrance of this inn. The sacred texts will prevent the spirits from entering this place. Had you been a ghost of the dead, you would not have been able to come inside with me."

"What are you trying to say? You're planning on keeping the spirits out tonight?"

It is past 1 a.m. The hour of the ox has begun, the time of the day when the walls separating the spirit world from the physical world are at their thinnest.

"Come." I grab his hand and lead him toward the window.

Outside, the stymied spirits stand, gray as tombstones, fluctuating in the air, peering through misty curtains, gathering the night behind them. Their angry breaths erupt in plumes; they look like furious animals, eager to attack, but have unfortunately reached the limit of their tethers.

"I am done!" I bellow at the tomb-like faces. "I am ready to meet my death! But know this-- none of you shall ever set foot in this inn again. Go! Now! You have no place in this world."

We wait until three in the morning, when the hour of the tiger begins. Then one by one, the spirits dissipate, and their horrid faces-- Ayame, Natsumi, Momo, Kaede, and the Noppera-bō among them-- disappear into the mist, like the closing of a theater curtain.

"Are they gone?" Akihiro asks.

"Ye,." I reply, and I feel him from behind embrace me.

"Those ghosts are ridiculous." he speaks. "This whole idea about revenge... they're doing it all wrong."

"How is that?"

"They wreak vengeance on people who have absolutely nothing to do with their misfortunes. Ayame murders children just because she lost her own. Momo brings her revenge upon innocent women when she should have punished the *shogun's* wife instead. And Natsumi, well, she already had her vengeance on the *daimyo* and her samurai lover, so why does she not let it go?"

"Dear boy," I say. "People are weak, petty, envious, selfish, and evil in ways that you will never comprehend. Why should they be any different in death?"

"If my spirit were to exact revenge on someone, it would be on the person who has been the author of all my misfortunes."

I chuckle at his naiveté. "And who, pray tell, is this unfortunate fellow?"

He presses his lips against my ear and whispers wetly, "My father."

I feel his fingers wrap around my throat, squeezing with such incredible force. I struggle, catch a glimpse of our reflection in the mirror, and see that Akihiro's image is paler and vaguer than ever, as if he is transparent. Glinting from one of the opaque fingers cruelly clasped around my neck is the ring that I had given my wife. The terrible knowledge blooms inside my brain, threatening to burst my skull. Or, perhaps it is just my own son's hands, choking my circulation.

"Did you know," he shrilled, sharp as a bayonet. "That my mother died of poverty?"

14

I try to pry his hands off me but my efforts are all in vain, so I grab the knife that I always keep inside my robe and slice off his wrists.

The authorities find me on my knees, a semi-corpse, with my spine curved, as though carrying a great weight, and with my son's severed hands still wrapped around my neck. No amount of beating can cause me to right myself and no amount of prying can help them remove the rigored fingers from me. They say that the boy's flesh had mysteriously fused with my own and that to remove it would be to kill me as well.

They say that in a far-away prefecture, a boy bled to death in his sleep. They say that there was nothing but bloodied stumps where his hands should have been. They say that I am guilty of murdering him.

How am I supposed to tell them that it was my son's *Ikiryō* that came to me, that so great was the grudge that Akihiro bore against me that his living ghost left his body while he slept and traveled across great distances to cast his vengeance upon me.

How am I to tell them that until now, I carry the burden of all my crimes, for when I look into the mirror, I see Akihiro's ghost riding on my back.

William Cook

Hope

Anne hugged her little legs tight to her chest. She sobbed quietly in the dark space at the bottom of her closet. Mummy and Daddy were making big noises in the dining room, again. The darkness in the closet scared her but Daddy scared her more. Mummy was too frightened to be Mummy these days – she spent all her time crying and sleeping when Daddy wasn't home. Anne counted slowly in the dark: one, two, three, four, five, six, seven, eight, nine . . .

She jumped as her father smashed a window with her mother's forehead, a handful of jet-black hair clenched in his fist as he pushed her face into the pane of glass. Her mother screamed as broken glass cut a deep track across her forehead and into her scalp. He pulled her backward and down, ripping a clump of her long hair out as he threw her across the room. She crashed into the wall and slumped to the floor, her head bleeding profusely as she swam in and out of consciousness. Anne bit down on her small knuckles until she drew blood. She wanted to scream but knew that if she did, Daddy would pay her a visit next. *Mummy, mummy, mummy, mummy* . . .

Anne had eventually ventured down the hall and into the dining room after her father had slammed the front door and left the house. She found her unconscious mother crumpled on the floor in a pool of dark blood, broken glass sparkling in her thick black hair, a large flap of flesh and scalp dangling from her forehead. Anne threw up in the corner of the room. She felt dizzy and lost but still somehow managed to lift the telephone receiver and dial 911. "My mummy's dead. She's not moving. Please help. Please help. Please . . ."

The officers first on the scene had determined that her mother was still alive. They shook their heads and tried their best to make her comfortable while they waited for the ambulance. One of them went outside to the waiting squad car and Anne followed and sat with him in the back seat until the ambulance arrived.

16

The officer kept talking into the radio on his shoulder; ". . . domestic incident, possible attempted murder. Suspect absent. Next of kin requested . . ." She sat quietly, shaking as if it were a winter's day, despite the sun streaming through the squad car's window. The ambulance came and went; she saw her mother's long black hair hanging down as they wheeled her out on a gurney and put her in the back of the vehicle. The other officer returned to the car and got in behind the steering wheel. He looked over his shoulder at Anne before reversing out of the driveway and onto the main street. Ten minutes later she was standing on her Grandmother's porch, watching as the police informed the old woman about the assault on her daughter-in-law and the fugitive status of her only son. Her Grandma showed no emotion, just clasped her shawl tighter about her and said quietly to the shocked officers. "Good riddance to bad rubbish! And I don't mean my son!" With that, she had promptly slammed the door shut on the two officers.

Anne overheard the cops as they clomped their way down the porch steps before leaving her all alone with the old witch.

"Jesus Christ! No wonder the husband's a prick—poor woman, having only that woman as her next-of-kin!"

Her mother spent three days in the hospital undergoing microsurgery to mend the deep wound that her husband had given her. She also underwent treatment for a severe concussion and fractured ribs. "A nasty tumble down the steps" was what she'd told the doctors, despite the fact there were no steps tall enough to cause her injuries. No steps near a window to cause the horrible scarring she now had to live with. The doctors wrote down the mother's statement in their notebooks and on the medical documents, but they still referred her to the trauma-counselling department for a pre-release session.

Anne stayed with her Grandmother while her mother was in hospital. Her father's mother was as cold to her as she'd always been – she said nothing to her, indifferent to the child's presence in her home. Meanwhile, Anne's father went on a three-day drunk while she sheltered in her Grandmother's lonely house, seven doors down from her family home. At night, she lay in the dark, the starched sheets cold to the touch on her father's childhood bed. The old house creaked as she tried to sleep but all she could think about was her mother. During the day, she wandered between the two houses, unsure of where she should be or what she should be doing. She couldn't wait 'til her mother returned home. She missed her so bad. On the third day, Anne walked to the hospital. It took her a good hour to walk the distance and her little legs ached when she arrived at the main entrance. No one at the hospital spoke to Anne. It was as if she was invisible, as she sat quietly in the waiting room with all the other patients' families. The medical staff was constantly moving about as new trauma cases flooded the emergency department. It was nearly impossible to catch someone's attention to inquire as to the state of her mother's health.

After nearly three hours of waiting, Anne decided to walk back to her Grandma's house and get some sleep. She felt strange as she walked the darkening streets – as though she was floating in a dream, her legs now numb with exertion but thankfully no longer aching.

Her father turned up that night, banging on her Grandma's front door and stinking of cheap gin and cigarettes. Anne noticed the cuts and marks on his knuckles from where he had hit her mother. "Bitch had it comin'," was all he said to his mother as he climbed the stairs and entered his old room, removing a shoebox from the depths of the cluttered closet. His mother stood sternly at the entrance as he descended the stairs, holding the door open for him, not saying a word.

Anne climbed into the back seat of her father's car, careful not to trip on the empty beer cans and liquor bottles that littered the floor. She sat silently as her father climbed in and stashed the shoebox under the passenger's seat before steering the car toward the hospital, chain-smoking cigarettes and sipping beer from a can as he weaved in and out of traffic – not saying a word to his daughter. When they arrived, Anne was shocked at the sight of her mum. Her mother said nothing, just looked at the floor and hobbled alongside her father who was joking and flirting with passing nurses. Somehow, he'd managed to bluff his way onto the ward – the nursing staff had been so busy they hadn't even noticed as he bundled his hunched wife up under a coat and shuffled her out toward the exit. Bandages swathed her mother's head, purple bruised skin ringed her eyes, and stitches lined her face.

As they stepped out into the sunlight, her father wrapped his large hairy arm around her mother's weak shoulders and whispered in her bandaged ear.

"What a great day to be alive eh, Beverley?"

As her father walked around the car and got in the driver's seat, Anne heard her mother mutter under her breath as she gingerly opened the passenger's door and lowered herself into the seat. "Fuck you, husband. Fuck you."

They drove slowly home, her father singing a mindless tune aloud until they pulled up in the driveway. He turned the ignition off and looked at his wife for a few long slow seconds before winking.

"I have a surprise for you when we get inside. Yes sirree."

He got out and slammed the car door before opening his wife's door, gripping her arm tightly as she struggled out of her seat. Anne looked at her father and felt nothing but hate for the man who stood before her.

"Come on," he yelled, "didn't you hear me you stupid bitch? I have a surprise waiting for you, now fucking move!" He shoved her frightened mother toward the front door and then retrieved the shoebox from under the seat.

"Sit," he commanded, pointing to the kitchen chair. Anne did as told while watching her mother slowly seat herself on the chair. She saw the pain in her mother's eyes and knew that the pain went a lot deeper than the fresh scars on her face. Her father burped and ceremoniously placed the shoebox in the middle of the kitchen table.

"Nosey shit ain't ya," he drawled drunkenly, as he loomed over his cowering wife. But you're right in thinkin' there's something in that box that should interest you. Open it, wife."

She raised her head slowly and looked at the shoebox for a second – unsure of what lay in store for her.

"Open it, bitch." He hissed at her and tugged her hair.

She winced and whimpered as the stitched wound on her scalp flared with hot pain, but she did as told. Anne watched her mother remove the cardboard lid and set it to one side – a shocked look on her face and then the tears began to run down her bruised cheeks. She wanted to reach out and comfort her mother but she had never liked to be touched. Instead, Anne sat motionless and watched her mother cry as her father removed the snub-nosed revolver from the shoebox and held it up to admire it. He tilted it in the light, watching the steel shine – he hefted the weight of it in his hand and then levelled it at her mother's head.

"Now I bet you're wondering what I'm gonna do with this little puppy, huh?"

Anne felt her bladder loosen and her pee wetted the seat of her skirt.

"I am sick of having to keep an eye on you. This here's gonna be your passport to hell if you don't get your shit together and do what I fuckin' tell you to do."

He ranted wildly, waving the pistol about.

"GOT IT? HAVE YOU GODDAMN GOT IT?"

Anne and her mother simultaneously uttered their affirmative replies between sobs.

Her father aimed the pistol directly at her head for a minute, before caressing her mother's head bandage menacingly. Time seemed to stand still and Anne was sure he was going to kill them both then and there. Her father smiled and stepped back, putting the revolver in the waistband of his trousers.

"Good. Now go to your room," he commanded.

Anne found herself hunkered down amongst the shoes and fallen clothes in her parent's closet. She sat in the dark space, much the same way she had so often hidden in her own closet, her little arms wrapped around her bent knees drawn up under her cherub chin. Tears freely ran down her soft pale cheeks as she waited in the dark. She knew something bad was going to happen soon, something really, really, bad. She heard her mother quietly sobbing as she lay on the bed. Anne put her eye up to the crack in the door and watched her mother, as she lay on the bed on her back, rigid, waiting for her husband to enter the room. Daddy was a bad man and he was going to do bad things to mummy. She felt so sad for her mum and she wished she could make things better. Then her father kicked the door open and leaped on top of her screaming mother, ripping at her clothes like a wild bear, slapping at her, pushing her, saying disgusting things to her as he pulled his own clothes from his drunk sweaty self.

Anne looked away, trying hard not to throw up as she covered her ears. It seemed to take forever, as she sat there in the closet shadows feeling the thumps and vibrations on her cold back as the headboard smacked against the bedroom wall. Finally, the noises ceased and she took her hands from her ears. Anne could hear her mother's sobs and light footfalls as she stumbled from the bed and left the bedroom. Her naked father lay on the bed on his back, his large gut rising and falling as his snores began to fill the room. Anne hated the sight of him. Every ounce of her wanted rid of him. She wished him dead.

She opened the closet door and stepped into the half-light of the bedroom, the sunrise creeping between the cracks in the old curtains. She pulled the bloodied bed-sheet up and covered her father's flaccid sex. She stood next to him, looking down at the man who she had once idolized. She knew what she had to do as she turned and left the bedroom, making her way downstairs to the kitchen.

On the way back to her parent's bedroom, she looked in her own room. Her mother was in her bed facing the wall. She closed the door gently and crossed the hall to her parent's bedroom. Her father hadn't moved although, she noticed with disgust, he had relieved himself in the bed – a spreading wet stain on the bed-sheet, testament to his weak bladder. She placed the shoebox on the bedside table and removed the lid. She stood there for a long minute, listening to her father's drunken snores as she stared at the chrome-plated revolver. Anne willed herself to pick up the handgun. Using all of her strength, she raised the weapon with her small opaque hands. The weight of the gun was nowhere near as heavy as the dread that accompanied her decision.

She had seen this pistol before – a year ago, she had felt the cold steel barrel pressed against her temple in the woods down by the river. It was no less frightening to her now, but all she could feel was a deep sad emptiness. She was frightened because she knew there was no other way. She was scared that her Daddy would kill her Mummy just as he had killed her in the woods. She remembered the stillness of the forest as he led her deeper into the tall trees, the pine needles crunching under his big boots as he walked ahead. The river had whispered to her as she followed her father – 'Run, Anne. Run . . .' But she hadn't run, she had done as her father instructed and closed her eyes as she stood on the lip of the shallow grave he had prepared earlier for her.

Then there was nothing for a while, just blackness. She remembered the world revealing itself again to her – only this time it would remain different, like it was late afternoon in a light fog all the time. She had trailed the path back out of the woods and returned home. The first thing she did was find her mother sitting at the kitchen table, a large glass of brown water in her hand. Anne tried to hug her mother but it was no use – she couldn't see or feel her and that was when Anne realized that her world was not as it once was. Her mother had cried and cried for what seemed like days as Anne witnessed the stream of police and neighbors searching the house and surrounding neighborhood. On the third day, they had given up the search, and her father taken to the police station for 'questioning.' He'd returned that evening with a smug smile on his unshaven face and had told her mother that Anne was lost, probably abducted, and we should prepare ourselves for the worst. Her mother had crumpled to the floor and wailed into the night, until her father came down the stairs and shut her up with a punch to the mouth. She had listened to her mother whimpering as the father pointed out the "positives" of the situation. Now they didn't need to "feed another mouth" or "worry about looking after her." She was gone, but, of course, she wasn't.

Now she stood next to the prone body of the man who had once been her Daddy. Now he was nothing but a monster and she knew he would only get worse. She thought of her mother, now reduced to a mere shadow of her former self – bloodied, beaten, humiliated . . . and pulled the trigger.

Anne's mother stood in the bedroom doorway, her mouth agape as she took in what she saw in front of her. Her husband's lifeless body lay sprawled across the bed, head turned in her direction, his face twisted in a weird grimace, a small black hole in his temple and a large splash of dark blood on the wall behind the bed. The smell of gunpowder and burnt flesh hung heavy in the air. She stepped forward into the room and slowly crossed the floor to stand next to the window, not taking her sight off her dead husband as she did so. She stood there trembling as she took in the scene, trying to work out what had happened. The revolver was sitting neatly in the shoebox, the lid next to it on the bedside table. Next to the shoebox was a picture in a frame. It was her most treasured memory of her daughter, Anne. The photo showed the two of them, her holding the small child in her arms, both of them smiling back at the camera with the river in the background and a picnic blanket set out on the grass next to them. The picture had been thrown in the attic along with Anne's other belongings not long after she'd disappeared. Beverly had protested, but her husband's reply had made her cease to question anything he did after that. She picked up the picture and clasped it to her chest

Anne, I miss you so much my darling. Please forgive me. Please . . .

She stood like that for a long time, cherishing the memory of her daughter as the noon sun filled the room. She placed the picture down carefully and took one of her husband's t-shirts from the over-flowing laundry hamper. She picked up the gun with the t-shirt wrapped around her hand and carefully placed it in her husband's clawed fist. Making sure not to disturb anything else, she took the picture and closed the bedroom door behind her. She made her way to the kitchen and began pouring herself a very strong brandy before thinking better of it. She upended the bottle and poured the remains into the sink before calling the police.

She sat on the front steps in the warm sunlight, waiting for the inevitable approach of sirens and looked at her daughter's picture. Her long fingers traced the smile on her daughter's face and then fluttered up to the raw scars that lined her own. She knew that the scars would fade in time, but also that the scars inside would remain with her forever, but somehow she was ok with that. For the first time in a year, she felt as though her child was with her again. For the first time since she was married, she could taste freedom and, ultimately, hope and she knew that she would be once again with her precious Anne when all this was over.

24

Roger Cowin

The Room at the Top of the Stairs

It was in the early autumn of my fortieth year when I heard the news that the countryside around Iliad was being flooded to make way for a new reservoir. The engineers spared Iliad itself, but several dozen farms on the outskirts faced immersion beneath fifty feet of water. The news left me saddened when I learned one of the farmhouses marked for demolition would be my grandparent's old homestead.

I had not set eyes on the place in over thirty years, not since my grandfather had sold the place and moved into a tiny bungalow in Richmond, Indiana. My grandmother had just passed and he said a farm was just too much for a single man to run alone but I think he just couldn't stand the thought of being alone in that place where he and Nana had spent so many good years together.

Maybe it was just the sentimental foolishness but it seemed the best part of my childhood was spent on my grandparent's farm, so it was with a mix of excitement and trepidation I set out to pay my final respects to the old house.

I arranged to take the day off from my job as stocker in a department store. I had been working at the store since my release some six months previous from the hospital where I had spent most of the previous year undergoing treatment for what the doctor's described as "nervous exhaustion." More accurately, overwrought by the recent death of my mother, I had swallowed several dozen sedatives in an attempt to hasten our reunion in the next life. If not for an unexpected visit from my brother, I have no doubt my attempt would have succeeded. A temporary commitment followed an emergency detention and I spent the next nine months pacing the nonviolent ward of the local loony bin.

So on a crisp, pleasant October morning, I left my apartment in Portland, climbed into my rusted old Chevy and headed south on US-27. After traveling south for several hours, I took a right onto IN-1 before turning south again onto a twisting county road. The route to Iliad itself was simple enough, just a matter of following the road signs, but once past the tiny village I would be navigating from memory.

Iliad was just as small and inconspicuous as I remembered; a smattering of houses, an abandoned diner and the local post office. A white, clapboard church stood on the corner of the village's lone intersection.

I took a right at the church, but from there my memory was murkier and I spent the next two hours driving up and down various back country roads looking for any landmarks that might penetrate the fog of thirty long years. I had almost decided to give up when I saw a familiar looking fork in the road. A newer, ranch-style home occupied one side of the road, but on the other side was an older farmhouse that, if I was not mistaken, had belonged to my grandparent's nearest neighbors, and kept well maintained, and was recently painted, but I was certain it was the same house. Feeling a burst of anticipation, I took the left fork down the pitted, graveled road, my excitement growing as the terrain became more recognizable.

It was almost three in the afternoon when I rounded a sharp curve and saw my grandparent's farm, abandoned and ravaged but still standing. I pulled up to the driveway, reassured myself that I was indeed in the right place and turned in.

I crept up the narrow drive, now mostly overgrown with weeds and rocks, taking care not to bottom out my old jalopy on the considerable ruts that neglect and weather had gouged into the hard-packed lane. The closer I came to the house, the more it took on an aura of sentiency as if was a living, breathing entity. The upper windows, devoid of any trace of glass, resembled hollow, watching eyes and only enhanced the house's malignant appearance. Ropes of ivy snaked up its scabrous brick skin like hungry fingers desperate to pull the old place down into the ground. The battered oak door hung precariously by its hinges, held up only by the solid 19th century construction.

As I pulled the car up to house, my initial excitement tempered by an increasing sense of apprehension, I let my eyes drift to a corner window on the second story. The window belonged to the bedroom that my grandmother forbade anyone to enter.

Nana had always insisted the house was haunted, the result of a particularly gruesome murder that had occurred back in the 19th century. The way my grandmother told the story, the original owner, one of the wealthiest men in the county had taken a beautiful, teen bride though he was himself in his early fifties. As you can probably guess, the marriage was not particularly happy. He was far too old to please such a young wife, either physically or emotionally and it was not long before she began an affair with one of her husband's farmhands, a man much closer to her age and more suitable to the needs of such a tempestuous young woman.

Upon learning of his wife's infidelity, the owner had concocted a tale about needing to attend some urgent business in Cincinnati. His wife helped him pack his bag, gave him a peck on the cheek and watched as he rode off in his coach. Instead of continuing on to Ohio, he had his driver pull over several miles down the road, instructed him to take the coach on into Iliad and not return before morning. Then he had hiked back to the house where he hid in the shadows of the barn and waited until he saw his rival enter the house.

When he saw the gas oil-lamp flare in his wife's bedroom, he slipped back into the house, stealthy as a thief, drew one of the swords he kept above the fireplace and crept up the stairs. With a single blow, the cuckolded farmer, kicked in the door to his wife's boudoir, discovering the startled couple stretched on the bed, *in flagrante*. The old man was not about to give the younger, stronger farmhand a chance to defend himself and immediately ran his sword through the poor fellow's chest.

His terrified wife got down on her knees, her full nakedness visible in the pale glow of the oil-lamp, and begged for mercy. She promised him her eternal faithfulness, hinted at sexual delights he could not imagine and when her pleas had no effect, she turned to tears and wept. She deserved death she knew, she was nothing but a whore, a worthless harlot, not fit to be the wife of such a great man but even her tears failed to sway him. As a last resort she turned to hurtling curses and disparagements at his skills as a lover, seeking to shame him into sparing her life.

"I would sooner fuck a corpse than let you touch me again!" She spat with as much venom as she could muster.

"And so you shall, my dear," he replied and with a single swipe of his sword lopped off her head. Still his anger was not sated. Taking her decapitated head, her eyes wide and staring in death, the farmer set it afire and kicked it down the stairs where it might have burned the whole house down but for the actions of a quick thinking servant who, alerted to the murder by the woman's screams, ripped a curtain from the window to extinguish the flames.

The cuckolded husband never stood trial for his murders, his wealth was enough to shield him from any consequences and he remained in the house until his death many years later. He never set foot in his wife's room again, keeping it locked and in the exact same state as when she died.

My grandmother claimed she had seen the ghostly specter of the woman's burning head many times, rolling down the staircase, always vanishing before it hit the bottom landing. However, she also said, the real haunting was in the forbidden bedroom where the murdered woman's vengeful spirit dwelled, waiting for unwary visitors to demonstrate her wrath. The door remained locked, just as it had when the original owner lived there.

Of course, my grandmother would *never* have told such a story to a seven-year-old boy. I only heard the tale much later, second hand from my mother but I never forgot the locked door and Nana's reluctance to enter the room.

So naturally, the window drew my eyes, and though the day was still, with no trace of a breeze I thought I could see the curtains moving in the room, swaying gently as if inviting me to come inside, it had been too long since it had a visitor.

For a moment, I almost considered putting the vehicle in reverse and heading back the way I came. Better to leave with my pleasant memories intact than taint them by entering this monstrosity. Then I was outside my car and the house was just a house again; an empty, run-down farmhouse unoccupied for far too long, simply that and nothing more.

I took a few moments to stretch my limbs and shake the cobwebs from my head. The landscape was pretty much as I remembered it. The house lay at the end of the road, seated on the highest point of the property. In the back, past a sizable back yard, now overgrown with several years of uncut grass was my grandfather's cornfield. The huge barn on the side of the house had long since collapsed and was now only a pile of old bleached lumber and rusty nails. Behind me, the woods where I had spent so many long summer days exploring was still as wild and compelling as ever.

Accompanied by a chorus of insects, I beat a path through the tall grass to the front door. It was a simple matter to move the heavy, wooden door out of the way and slip through into the dim, shabby foyer. Despite the brightness of the day and the absence of shutters on the windows, the house appeared dark and foreboding. I took several minutes to allow my eyes time to adjust the subdued lighting before I felt confident enough to enter the large, spacious living room.

A blanket of dust and broken glass covered most of the floor, cobwebs stretched across the antique, brass chandelier, the bones of a long dead fire remained in the brick fireplace but the oil painting that hung over the mantle was gone, replaced by an ornate, silver framed mirror. The once beautiful French Country wallpaper was peeling in long strips, like a snake slithering out of its skin.

The graffiti marred walls informed me, *"Ernie was here"* and *"John loves Annie." Good for you John*, I thought, *wonder how Ernie felt about it.*

I was surprised by the amount of my grandparent's furniture that remained in the room. When my grandfather had sold the place, he included much of the furnishings in the deal. Still...I would have thought the next owner would have replaced more of the furniture at some point.

There was my grandmother's Victorian settee, the cotton stuffing leaking from the elegant, damask cloth. Beside an unfamiliar end table was my grandfather's glider rocker, the wood dry-rotted, its cushions moth eaten and water damaged. Old whisky bottles and fast food wrappers offered mute testimony that squatters had been here in the recent past.

I spent the next half hour or so, investigating the downstairs, poking my head into the various rooms, admiring the fine sturdy woodwork and artisanship. Whenever I passed the staircase leading to the second story, I would give it a nervous glance, almost expecting to see a headless apparition floating down the steps. Despite my nerves, I continued my exploration.

I glanced at my watch and was surprised to find it much later than I thought. I expected the sun to have pushed back the shadows a bit more; instead, the meager light breaking through the windows only highlighted the dust that floated through the air like spectral phantoms. If I was going to brace the second floor I had best get to it, I reckoned.

Hesitating at the foot of the stairs, I rubbed the wood ball of the newel post for luck. Once I ascertained no flaming head was going to come screaming down the steps after me I cautiously began climbing the stairs, taking care not to push too firmly against the unsteady railing.

The stairs creaked and moaned beneath my weight and when I reached the second floor landing, I breathed a sigh of relief. Nothing up here but empty bedrooms, some still filled with the detritus of former occupants but nothing that hinted at anything out of the ordinary. Maybe even ghosts got tired of a place eventually, maybe they heard the house was going to be flooded and sought out environments that were more hospitable.

In the small bedroom I had once called my own, I watched as the golden light of the afternoon sun reflected off the autumn fields. It was hot for October and the fields were alive with crows, swooping and rising in choreographed waves, like performers in an interpretive ballet.

The room was one of the few devoid of furnishings or clutter. It was a dead room, sterile as a dry attic. I sighed, disappointed not to feel even a hint of the nostalgia that brought me here in the first place. Nothing of my boyhood remained; I could have been standing in any stranger's room.

Each room was the same - blank spaces bleached of personality. Inevitably, I found myself standing in front of the door to the forbidden room. Compelled by my own morbid curiosity, my hand reached out and grasped the brass doorknob. Odd that this was the only room that had a closed door, in fact, most of the rooms had no doors at all; only open portals to vacant rooms beyond.

I told myself the door would be locked, just as it had always been in the days of my grandparents but as I turned the knob, the tumbler clicked over easily. The door squealed in its rusty hinges as I nudged it open. I was aware of my heart drumming a staccato beat in my chest.

"Don't touch anything. They don't like people touching their things," I could hear my grandmother saying in my head.

The room was a picture of preservation. The magnificent, four-poster bed remained draped in fine linens, though the plush, down comforter was now stained yellow with age. The Victorian furniture looked intact and serviceable. A beautiful Queen Ann vanity stood against one wall, its oval mirror covered in a thin film of dust but otherwise in near perfect condition. A monstrous armoire lay open, revealing a closet full of elegant ladies clothing. It was also the only room to retain its curtains, though they too were yellow and worn.

I found it strange that vandals had not pilfered this quality furniture. There was a small fortune in this room; it was hard to believe a simple ghost story would dissuade thieves. Greed always trumped superstition.

Reassured when a vengeful, headless ghost did not attack me, I stepped into the room. On the vanity was an ornate, silver, hand-held mirror. It was inlaid with an intricate *fleur-dis-lis* pattern on its handle and back. I picked it up; studying my reflection until an unexpected swoon overtook me and I quickly set it aside.

I felt a bit silly letting my nerves get the better of me and decided a souvenir of my trip was in order, a little memento of my visit. I looked around before spotting a beautiful, antique snow globe. Constructed of fine porcelain and glass, no cheap plastic trinket here, I held it up for closer inspection. Inside, a quaint, picturesque cottage sat amid a forest of pines - a fairy tale scene straight out of the Brothers Grimm. I gave the globe a shake, delighted by the tiny flakes that drifted over the fairy tale cottage. This would do I thought, slipping the precious item in my jacket pocket before proceeding towards the ornate, four poster bed.

A dark, unsettling stain on the ratty carpet caught my attention. It might have been an ordinary stain for all I knew, but some pressing feeling, call it a psychic twinge, made me believe this was where the murder had taken place. Could I really be looking at the blood from a century old murder?

The voice of a young woman came from behind me. "Yes, that's where it happened."

I turned, not feeling in the least shocked or surprised. Standing before me was one of the most beautiful women upon which I had ever laid eyes. She looked to be in her late teens or early twenties. A flowing mane of tight, ashen curls framed her heart-shaped face. Her grey eyes were large and wide; she looked more like one of those vintage porcelain dolls you find in museums than an actual person. She was dressed in a filmy, powder blue peignoir that left nothing to the imagination. I could clearly make out the perfect, pink aureoles of her small breasts and the soft, dark tuft of her pubis beneath the gossamer material. I couldn't help but wonder what it'd be like to bury my face between those creamy thighs, slip my tongue between those nether lips, to taste the silky folds of her shimmery center.

"Thaddeus was a cruel man. He often beat me, even before I was ever unfaithful,"

"Thaddeus,' I asked. He was your husband?"

"My husband's name was Thaddeus Murphy, yes. I *suppose* our names are no longer remembered, just the legend. And like most legends, it contains only the faintest whisper of the true story."

"And what is the truth?"

I didn't find it the least bit strange to be speaking with a ghost. The whole encounter had taken on the fuzzy, unreal quality of a dream. The room no longer possessed its dull, lifeless appearance but was as vibrant and inviting as must have been a hundred years ago. The bed linen was clean and white, the furniture polished and shining. Even the carpet had regained its bright colors. Only the ugly stain remained to mar its luxurious surface.

"My name was Elizabeth Barron. I was just a girl from the village when my father agreed to give me in marriage to Thaddeus. I didn't blame my father though, we were so very poor and the dowry Thaddeus offered was enough to insure my father and mother had a substantial nest egg to see them through their golden years."

I said, "Still...it doesn't seem right to sell your daughter off to the highest bidder."

She shook her lovely head and smiled. "It was not so unusual in those days. Such marriages were often successful even when young brides were given over to much older men, but Thaddeus was a violent man, given to terrible rages especially when he was drunk, which was most times. Once he beat me so savagely I could not show my face in public for a month. The beatings became even more severe when I could not produce the heir he desired"

"So you took a lover?"

"Yes, my handsome William. He was the most beautiful man I ever saw. I lavished upon all the love William denied me. He taught me that love did not have to be cruel, but could be tender and kind. Thaddeus would only come to me when he was drunk and even then our trysts were more akin to rape than lovemaking."

"So he killed William and then you when he found out?"

"Oh, my poor William, I loved him so." She collapsed onto the bed, covering her face in her hands. "Thaddeus never even gave him a chance to defend himself. He just strode in like the High Lord Master of Creation and ran his foul blade through William's chest."

"Did he really cut off your head?"

"Oh yes, but only after he raped me one more time. That part of the story is forgotten. Nor did I beg to for my life. No, by then I was praying for death. I wanted only to rejoin my William and if Thaddeus had not murdered me I would have killed myself the first chance I got."

"So where is William now? Is he not here with you?"

Real tears came from her eyes as she shook her head, biting her lips in such a way that despite her grief, my desire was inflamed. I would have strangled Thaddeus myself if he had been standing there.

"He must have gone on. Either to Heaven or to Hell, I do not know which, but I found myself alone in this room, a poor spirit doomed to wander this awful house. Hating that Thaddeus was able to continue his life, while I remained a mute witness to his evil."

"Thaddeus lived for many more years?"

"He even married again. A more mature woman this time, one who was able to give him the heir he desired."

"That explains my grandmother's surname, doesn't it? Murphy? Bernice Murphy was her maiden name."

"Yes, Thaddeus was your great- great grandfather. I have waited for you for so long Carl."

"You know my name" I asked, shocked.

"Of course, I know you Carl. I remember you as a boy. I wanted to go to you then but your grandmother forbade anyone to enter this room."

"And you've been alone all this time? Why have you never told anyone else your story?"

She reached out and took my hand, pulled me onto the bed beside her. Her hand was warm and it struck me how solid she seemed- how *there* she was.

33

"Because they weren't you. I could only unburden myself to Thaddeus' heir. Only a male descendent can release me from my tedious purgatory."

I choked out, "How?"

She placed a hand behind my neck, pulled me close and pressed her lips against mine; favoring me with the sweetest kiss I had ever known. I cupped her perfect, breasts in my palms, my breath quickening as my thumbs traced circles around her small, hard nipples.

"Make love to me," she sighed, and when her hand dropped to grasp my throbbing erection, any hesitation I might have felt evaporated.

I pushed her down onto the bed, ripping at my clothes. In moments, I was deep inside her, my aching member swollen harder and longer than at any time I could remember.

I was not a virgin, but neither overly experienced. There had been few lovers over the years and none in the past decade but I took her as hard and savage as any man had ever taken a woman. She responded in like, matching me kiss for kiss, thrust for thrust. I lost track of how many orgasms ravaged her body but whenever I sought my own release, she begged me to last a little longer.

Finally, I could not hold back any longer and my own orgasm erupted from me like a volcano. Spasm after spasm raced up and down the length of my manhood as my seed spilled into her like lava. It felt like I might never stop coming, but when the last dregs of semen had seeped from my member, I collapsed beside her, breathing hard, our bodies drenched in sweat.

How long we lay there, I couldn't say but I knew it was night and the oil lamps had somehow lighted themselves. At some point, I would have to take my leave, but I was reluctant to say my farewells. The thought of abandoning her was almost too much to bear.

"There is way," she said, as if reading my mind.

"How? I have to go back to my life and within days this whole area will be buried beneath fifty feet of water."

"Why go back? What's there for you? You have been as lonely as I since your mother died. You can stay here with me. Think about it; no more fear, pain or loneliness. Just an eternity to do this," she reached between my legs and began stroking me again, and I responded readily to her expert caresses.

I sat up on my elbows and wanted to ask, *"Are you serious,"* but it made perfect sense. After all, what *was* out there for me? An empty apartment, a boring job, a life devoid of purpose? Did I really want to go back to spending my days stocking endless cans of green beans, my nights watching reruns on the television? What she was offering sounded infinitely richer.

When I turned to her, she held an ivory handle knife, the blade cradled in the palm of her hand.

"Will it hurt?" I asked.

"Only for a moment, my love, then we can be together for always," she replied, and passed the knife to me.

I took the knife, turning it over and over, mesmerized by the light shimmering off the steel.

I pressed the blade against my wrist, fascinated by the blood beading up on my skin. How easy it would be - just a few quick cuts and then...blessed release.

So, thus juxtaposed on the precipice of life and death, I caught a glimpse of Elizabeth out of the corner of my eye. Her sweet, angelic face contorted in a mask of hate and rage.

"Do it, Carl, do it!" She was licking her lips, her eyes wide and greedy for my death.

Yes, I thought, and pushed the blade deeper into my flesh.

"CARL, NO! DON'T LISTEN TO HER." Startled, I glanced toward the voice, the spell broken.

Standing just outside the doorway was my grandmother; her hard, angular face, etched and grooved with deep wrinkles but filled with love and kindness.

"Nana? Is that you?" I continued to hold the knife to my wrist, but no longer aware how it had come into my possession.

"It's me, Carl. Don't listen to her, my love. Put the knife down and leave the room."

"Shut up you old hag. He's mine, mine." Elizabeth was sitting straight up in the bed, her body trembling in frustrated anger.

Nana stepped into the room, her lips constricted in her own fury. "Not tonight Elizabeth, you will not claim one of mine."

I swiveled back and forth between Elizabeth and Nana, my brain a jumble. *Why was there a knife in my hand? How did I cut myself? Did I try to kill myself again?*

Nana came closer to the bed, holding something peculiar that I could not quite make out, as if something was blocking me from seeing it clearly.

"GET OUT OF MY ROOM, HE'S MINE," Elizabeth shrieked.

"Carl, snap out of it. She is a liar. She has led more than one lover to their death. She promises love but all she delivers is death, feeding on their souls to preserve her own."

"You lying cunt. Get out and take that thing with you," Elizabeth spat, pointing at the object Nana still grasped between her hands.

I could feel the glamour over the room fading as Nana came nearer. The room still looked clean and new, but underneath I could see its true appearance bleeding through, like a double exposure photograph.

"Look at her Carl, see her as she really is."

I looked at Elizabeth, and, at first, she looked the same – beautiful and alive, a woman to die for, but as the illusion wavered I saw her as she was – a thin, desiccated headless corpse.

Screaming, I scrambled backward out of the bed, landing so hard on the floor I felt my teeth sink into my tongue. Warm, coppery blood filled my mouth but I couldn't stop screaming, not when I finally saw that what my grandmother held in her hands was nothing less than the burning, decapitated head of Elizabeth Murphy.

Elizabeth's head continued to speak but the sweet, musical voice was gone, replaced by a hollow, sepulchral voice devoid of any trace of humanity. "Carl please, my love, we can be together."

I looked madly around the room, all traces of the illusion gone; the room was back to its dilapidated self and I could see by the light outside the window, that it was still day, late afternoon by the look but still daylight. Elizabeth's body was gone from the bed and only my grandmother remained, still holding the head.

"Go on Carl, leave now while her power is weak," Nana said.

I staggered to my feet, gathering my clothes from the bed and lurched toward the door as fast as I could, pursued by Elizabeth's anguished screams. Then I was down the stairs and back into the blessed outdoors. Collapsing on the lawn, I lay naked in the tall, cool grass, thanking a God I had long stopped believing in. Then I remembered nothing until I awoke in my car sometime later that evening.

I was sitting behind the wheel, still parked in the drive of the old house. The shadows of evening had drowned out most of the light. Only a few, dying purple rays remained to keep the night at bay. Fear hastened my awakening, but a hurried check of the car assured me that I was safe and alone. I could not recall how I had reached my car or how I had come to be dressed, nor did I understand why I had fallen asleep instead of driving off. My wrist bore no signs of the cut I had made, though my tongue remained sore from where I had bitten it. In fact, if it wasn't for the snow-globe I clutched in my hand, I might have dismissed it all as a dream.

Not wanting to be here after dark, I started the engine, turned my old Chevy around and headed down the lane. When I reached the end of the drive, I stopped the car, climbed out and looked back at the house. The encroaching night had swallowed most of the old farm in darkness, but a faint glow came from the window in the room at the top of the stairs, a glow much like the light an oil-lamp might make. A vague silhouette moved across the window. I climbed back in the car and drove away, preciously anticipating the coming flood and the end of her.

Scáth Beorh

Broad Smile in Scarlet

Dressed in the dearest of crimson silks, with one slash of his curved blade, the Long Man of Lankin procured life from another young mother. Her depression left her as rapidly as it had come upon her. She was taken to a place where her vision filled with shining angels, secret gardens, and fleeting, though surprising, delights of the tongue and heart.

Her baby boy had cried out in the night. She, as would have any good mother, rushed to comfort him from a peaceful dream of roses and laughter, longing with sudden tears to let him know that she was near... that he was loved. Had she known her destiny, would her steps have faltered?

Long Lankin breached the old stone manor through an opening in its antique gilded ceiling—an aperture made by rage, and by life taken for granted. With stealth, he penetrated the dusky environ, first toying with porcelain dolls who populated the antechamber. He smoothed their creased velvet dresses, straightened their twisted stockings, rearranged their disheveled curls, kissed their smiling mouths. He then went to retire in the Great Hall before a dying fire, where, after pouring himself a snifter of brandy, he mused over the particularities of his most recent three victims—their truly unique reactions to abrupt departure, as it were.

As her life wafted from her, the smile on her countenance. *Ah!* How absolutely astonishing in its ephemeral beauty! And, oh!, that delicious look of abject terror in the crystal blue gaze of the other as she fell to her knees, her arms reaching out to him as if he were her savior! *Delectable!* And the third. Oh, how she had pleaded for her life! How she had offered her own *daughter* to his ravenous palate. *Dirty girl!* Yet, she tasted sweeter than the hundred who came before her. A true pleasure in a world so dim with human folly!

His smart red cape a'billow, he swept up a winding stair and then down a wide, dark hallway toward the nursery—the room of the small boy. In no hurry, he played at length with a gorgeous wooden train set, and caused a stuffed monkey and a *papier mache* tiger to say unusual things to one another. Then he crossed the tranquil room and feathered the child's rosy cheeks with slender fingers.

'Sleep, my child, and God be with thee, all through the night...' he sang with a peculiar slickness of tongue morbid to anyone loving the lullaby. 'Where are your guardian angels now? At *least* where is your nurse? Ah, yes! Now I remember!' he said as he poked and stabbed the baby's body with needles fine as hair.

Startled awake by the stinging pricks, the child peered up into the handsome, thin face—dimpled chin, regal cheekbones, broad forehead befitting royalty. The monster's fevered eyes, ignited with envy and hatred, burned into the man-child as he wailed in horror. Only moments later *she* rushed in, to save her child from his night-terror. Long Lankin laughed loud and long as he struck with his arched knife, providing for her a broad smile in scarlet.

"Your mother really tosses her head back when she laughs."

"**Y**ou say you *dreamt* this?"

"Yes, Dr. Larkin. Disturbing, isn't it?" Ms. Wearie sat up on the couch, rubbed her watery eyes, and then stared into space. Suddenly chilled, she pulled her cardigan closer to her.

"Are you cold?"

"Just a little."

"Did *you* write that story... what you just read to me from your journal?"

"Yes. What... do you think it means?"

"Well, my initial reaction, Wendy, is that this *Lankin* is symbolic of hatred for women. For womanhood at large, I'd even venture. Why you are dreaming about him will take us some time to discover, I think."

"Do you think he is real?"

"That depends on what you mean by the word *real*."

"Are you familiar with the legend of Long Lankin, Dr. Larkin?"

"Only vaguely. Tell me what you know."

"Well, other than his various names—Lankin, Larkin, Mannequin, Lammikin—all I know is a piece of a rhyme I learned when I was a little girl."

"Did you just say *Larkin?*"

"Yes."

"*Interesting*. Will you recite the rhyme for me, Wendy?"

Ms. Wearie lay her journal aside, straightened her back, pulled her feet together, folded her hands on her lap, shut her eyes, and began:

Oh, spare me, my Lord Lammikin!
Oh, spare me now one hour!
You'll have my Alice sooner then;
she blooms the sweetest flower.

Where sleeps your daughter Alice?
She may do me some good;
She'll hold my silver chalice
into which I'll catch your blood.

James S. Dopp

Tit for Tat

Little Willie caught a cold
after the preacher's sermon Sunday,
chilled unto his very soul
he was dead by teatime Monday.

He was buried in a coffin
waiting to be sent to Hades,
there to burn eternally
with naughty boys and demon ladies.

That is what the preacher taught,
that lads like him, with reckless ways,
should expect when they demised,
the wages of their sins to pay.

But there were no flames, no perdition,
none of what the preacher roared,
just cold and damp and nibbling worms --
the truth was Will was getting bored.

So Willie swore the preacher lied
and to the church he sent his ghost,
he'd gain revenge upon that cleric,
that was Willie's spirit's boast.

He rattled papers, shrieked through windows,
which upset the church's choir,
he kicked the votive candles over
causing danger of a fire.

He chased the preacher from his pulpit,
scared the old man near to death,
he tweaked his nose and pinched his ears,

blew in his face with graveyard breath.

And thus, this moral may be found
for those who orate of the Lord:
if you would consign souls to Hell,
be sure that you can keep your word.

Author's Note: This is a "Little Willie," a type of dark-humored poem popular in the early 20th century, though usually shorter, about a bad boy who either causes great harm or suffers a horrible fate, at the end of which the poet expresses either glee, indifference, or draws a laughably inadequate moral.

Dona Fox

Shypoke's Tears

Damn, it was the kid. Too late, again. I wasn't even across the bridge. Her sneakers slap-squeaked on the boards as she ran toward me.

"Uncle Frank? Wait!"

I slowed my steps but didn't look back right away. I took a deep breath, and then turned. "Where you coming from, Shypoke?"

"I've been down at the river, picking blackberries." She held out her pail.

"You don't seem to have many in there."

She laughed. "Well, I ate a lot. Mama says you'd have to weigh me to know how many I really picked." She looked me straight in the eye. "Been down there all day."

I heard odd noises under the old bridge, tiny claws scratching at the wooden underpinnings. "It sounds like there's some kind of wild animal down there. Did you have to fight the critters for the berries?" I peered over the edge of the bridge. The blackberry vines were dense.

"The wind's pickin' up, blowing those berry vines against the bridge. The thorns are scraping at the bottom of the boards." She reminded me of her father as she tilted her head, closed one eye, and squinted against the setting sun before asking, "You coming or going?"

"I'm on my way to the forks, figure'd I'd catch the late train."

"Still riding the rails." She smiled. "Did you see my dad?"

Bile rose in my throat. I sucked it down quick. "At the house you mean? Don't reckon I did." My nerves were taking over; I was beginning to speak in the vernacular of the valley. Her dad, my brother, had been dead since my last visit. That was when I'd found out he liked to beat Shy's mother. I tried to reason with him. I wasn't the one who killed him.

"Did you see my mama?"

"No, I must have missed her," I lied.

44

She spotted the strings of the Bull Durham pouch hanging out of my pocket. "Is that empty?"

"No. There's some in it."

"Can I have a spot on my tongue? Like you used to do?"

"Sure, just a spot."

We both smiled.

"Might as well set awhile." I was more comfortable now; this was familiar.

We sat at the edge of the bridge, dangling our legs over the side. I could use a smoke. I wasn't near as calm as I was acting. I'd been through a lot in my life so I was good at putting on a show.

I wiped my hands off on my pants then I took the little cloth bag out of my pocket and pulled the drawstrings open. I reached in delicately with my thumb and forefinger and took out a little pinch.

Shy already had her eyes and mouth wide open, her tongue stuck out like a hungry little bird. I dropped the speck of tobacco on her tongue. She shut her mouth and eyes slowly, "Mmmm." She giggled and waved her hands in the air as if she was going to take off flying.

I pulled out a pack of papers and rolled myself a cigarette, licked and lit it. A luxury, I smoked it slowly, allowing myself to relax, trying not to think outside the moment.

"So you didn't see my mama?"

"No. I said I didn't. Must have missed her."

"Were you here last spring?"

"Why do you ask?"

"Just wondering." She was staring at my pant leg.

I'd left a muddy streak where I'd wiped off my hand. I put my arm over it. My nails were muddy. I closed my hand. Her eyes narrowed. She put her hand over mine.

"Tell me about the war."

"What about it?

"They say war changes you. Did it make it easier for you to kill people?"

"I've never killed anybody on purpose, Shy."

"Hmph." She drilled a hole clean into my brain with her eyes then looked away. "Not even in the war?"

"That was different. Let's not talk about that."

"Okay. The song you taught me. Seems I can't remember all the words." She started to sing in her reedy voice, "Mademoiselle from Armentieres, Parley-voo? She hasn't been kissed in forty years, Parley-voo."

As the sun went down we sat on the bridge and we sang the song over and over until we thought we had it right. Once again, I taught my niece almost all of the verses of the song I recalled. We made up rhymes and we laughed until we had tears in our eyes. Then we reviewed how to cuss in French. She remembered a lot of the swear words; she was smart as a whip.

I smoked cigarette after cigarette. When the Bull Durham bag was empty, she tucked it in her pocket–a remembrance, she said.

I heard tiny mewling sounds; I looked around expecting to see a kitten.

"Uncle Frank, did you know my mama was gonna have a baby?"

A chill took hold of me, "When was that, Shy?"

"She got pregnant long about, I guess it was, last spring, I guess."

The scratching under the bridge was louder now. Somehow, the small noises sounded closer.

I thought carefully before I answered. "Well, that's great; you'll have a little brother or sister." Uneasy now, I was going to stand up and get away from the edge of the bridge. "I've got to get going if I'm going to catch my train."

It was full dark.

Shy slipped her arm through mine.

"I want to go with you." Shy had ahold of me–tight. Almost like her mother, my Mary. Except Mary had grabbed me and said she wanted me to stay. I loved Mary, I did, but I'm not the kind that stays.

A little leery of Mary's temper, I tried to push her away gently. She latched on harder; her eyes took on that same crazy mean glint I'd seen right before she brought that skillet down on my brother's head.

I pushed Mary hard–with a lot more force than I meant to use. I tried to catch her, to pull her back when I realized how fast she was flying toward the bricks. Mary's last moments cycle through my mind repeatedly, but now in slow motion as if that is the speed at which the event actually occurred, and the sound when her head hit the fireplace still wakes me up in the night.

When Shy knocked on the boards beneath us, I almost peed my pants. "I don't think it's time for you to go, Uncle Frank."

I searched the dark behind us and now I thought I saw eyes, glowing, down low, near the boards. Maybe just a stray cat that had come looking for some warmth?

The breeze swirled around me and lifted up the back of my shirt. As the gust cooled the sweat that had formed there, as each little hair dried in its pore, it felt like nothing so much as little claws crawling up my spine.

"No, Shypoke. I'm leaving now. Let go of me."

"You can't leave, Uncle Frank. I know you killed my daddy."

"That's silly, don't be a silly girl."

"Mama told me. She was there, wasn't she? She helped you. She was in love with you. She was in love with you then. She told me–things change. What does that mean, Uncle Frank? Things change?"

The boards beneath us bounced lightly. I peered into the dark expecting to see someone walking toward us on the bridge. No one was there.

"I don't know what you're talking about. I didn't kill your father." I looked her in the eye. "Ask you mother."

"Oh, you know I can't do that–you just got done burying her, didn't you, Uncle Frank?"

I tried to pull away from the child but she clung to my arm like a chigger.

"Is that what Mama meant when she said things change? You and her killed my daddy 'cause you were in love then she got pregnant and you didn't love her anymore?"

"I didn't know she was pregnant." I hadn't meant to say that.

"Oh, you admit you killed her, just that you didn't know she was pregnant?"

I looked at her sideways. "You're just imagining things. You're imagining your mother is dead. You must have been in the sun too long today." I patted the little blackberry stained fingers that dug into my arm, "Let's go back to the house and you'll see that your mother's walking around and mad as a rattlesnake that your dinner's getting cold."

"No! You just want to get me to the house and kill me too. We can just wait here. The proof is comin'."

"How's that?" I was getting ready to throw her off me, and be done with her, even though I really liked the kid. I didn't need to

47

explain to her that I didn't kill her father or that her mother's death was an accident. I didn't need to stay here and sort it out with the authorities either. There was no way I was taking her with me.

"I watched."

"What are you talking about?" I heard the scratching again. I looked into the dark, that damn animal's eyes were closer–it sure moved slow–distrustful creature maybe, moving up on us all slow like that. Now I could smell it, the cat, or whatever it was, smelled like it had a festering sore on its body. Maybe I'd throw Shy's bucket at it, maybe kick it over the edge. I covered my nose with my free hand.

"Yeah, I watched you kill my mama. You grabbed her and threw her head against the bricks. There wasn't anything I could do to stop you."

"You must have misunderstood. We were probably making love. Kids don't understand."

"Yeah, then why'd you bury her afterwards? I watched that, too."

"Let go of me." I was flexing to throw her off me so I could get out of there. I was leaving, right now.

"Wait, you're gonna wanna hear this, this is the most important part." She scrambled up so her legs weren't hanging over the edge; she wrapped her skinny legs around me and put her mouth next to my ear. "I stayed. I kept watching after you left."

I thought I heard a tiny hiss from somewhere in the darkness, just as the night snapped chill.

Her moist breath continued to deliver her soft whispers straight into my ear. "At first I wasn't sure. The movement was so slight, I just wasn't sure. Then bits of the dirt began to shift and I was positive. Something was moving in that grave. In my mama's grave."

I wanted to get up and run. For a shameful second I thought of throwing her off the bridge, but she must have sensed my intentions for she clung even harder.

"You must have gone back in to clean up the house. Maybe remove your fingerprints? I've watched the shows. 'Cause I sat there a long time and watched mama's grave.

"Like shoots rising fast in the garden, I saw the tips of tiny fingers, then pudgy ashen hands. Little hands poked out of the

48

dirt, reached up through the soil, and pushed aside the earth from my mama's hasty grave.

"I wasn't real surprised. I grew up here. You didn't, did you? I'd heard the stories. This can happen when you don't bury a mama-to-be in the proper manner. And this was a very improper burial, don't you think.

"The unborn clawed its way out of the grave to avenge my mama's death. Yes, I've heard it often happens here in the valley." My niece giggled sharp and loud, right in my ear. I cringed.

"I followed it.

"It seemed to know where it was going. It crawled slow, real slow. So I ran on ahead. And that's when I found you here on the bridge, Uncle Frank. It's coming this way. What do you think that little unborn wants with you?" She ran a fingernail down the back of my neck.

I pried her off me, we struggled; she was all arms, legs and screams. I lost my balance; my stomach lurched as I looked into the vines below and saw them rising up to meet me. I whipped my arms in circles, trying to regain control but I went off the side of the bridge anyway.

Fortunately, my reflexes are still quick. I reached out and grabbed one of the supports just under the deck of the bridge. I could hear Shy screaming.

Oh, god. The smell. The scratching on the boards. I looked up. The thing was under the bridge. The eyes were several feet away. It seemed to be moving fast.

With a massive effort, I threw a leg up onto the bridge, then an elbow. Pulling myself up this far had been hard work; I was winded. Damn cigarettes. I wanted to rest but the thing was under the bridge and closing in on me.

My stomach tightened. I strained until I got myself all the way up onto the deck then I lay there panting.

I looked around. Shy was standing in the middle of the bridge. She glowed white in the moonlight. Her hands covered her face; her slender body shook as she sobbed.

"It's alright, Shy. I'm okay."

This is the point where it always dawns on me—we've done all this before. Not just the reminiscing and the re-enactment of the speck of Bull Durham, the song, and the cussing words—I mean this isn't the first time we've had this exact same meeting with

49

it's unfortunate disclosures; the entire bittersweet drama on the old wooden bridge.

I wonder if this is always my point of epiphany. Perhaps going beyond this point would be more than I could bear–more than even I deserve. I'm afraid to know why Shypoke has the power to compel me to return, why she is here unchanged every year.

Perhaps she is waiting for me to ask, but I'm a coward, condemned to die not once but a thousand times in my imaginings–I will not ask her how she died. I will not.

"I'm okay, Shy." I stood up slowly, the night was cold, and those acrobatics weren't as easy as they used to be. Someday the creature was going to catch me or I was going to lose my grip and fall into the ravine. I wondered if that was even possible.

"That's it for me. I've got to go now," I said.

Shy ran to me, snaked her arms around me again, and buried her face in my shirt. "Uncle Frank, you will come back, won't you? We had a good time, right?"

"Sure, I want to come back, Shy. You know that I have to come back." I kissed the top of her head where she still tasted of sunshine. The scalp where her hair was parted cast off the faint scent of an old attic.

I took hold of her thin arms and pried her from me gently, oh so gently. I'd learned my lesson, yes; I'd learned that lesson over and over again.

"I'll be waiting, right here–on our bridge." Her lower lip trembled. She began singing in her sweet, reedy voice.

"Mademoiselle from Armentieres, Parley-voo? Just blow your nose, and dry your tears, We'll all be back in a few short years...Hinky dinky parley-voo..."

Her lonesome song faded away as I walked, then ran, to catch the next train–the next train to anywhere.

I'm not the staying kind, but I haven't found anywhere far enough away so I know I'll be returning.

Distance, time and sleep will gradually fade my memory, until we're on the bridge again.

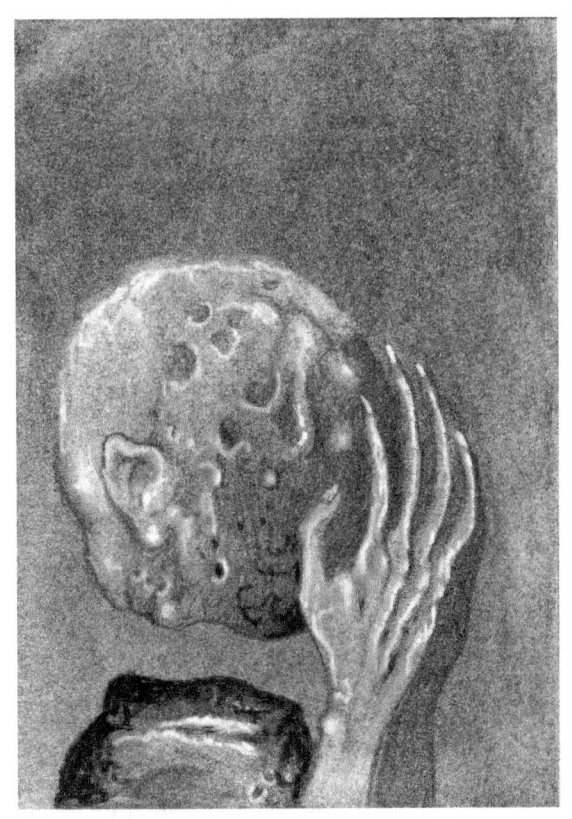

CS Nelson

Madonna

"I want to show you something." Noah rotates the column shift into P. "Do you give your entire being unto me?"

Jacob squalls from his car seat, kicking to get free from a gasoline-soaked diaper. The elastic and cotton fiber abrade welts into his thighs. Beside him, little Caroline sits quiet, bundled, big eyes watching through bigger glasses, tears building from the fumes.

"All of me," Jenine says. She means it. If ever there was doubt, it lay vanquished in the too-blue depths of her savior's eyes. "All of *us*."

"Together." Noah's voice, a deep and rolling bass vibrating above the engine, commands her body, soothes her fears, and excites her sex. Jenine squeezes her legs at the power still flowing from his seed within her, capturing every drop of him. Warmth from the Buick's busted heater core ekes out to the floorboard and rises in wavelets across her naked flesh. Sweat glistens on his bare chest. The musk of their joining fills the car; it steams the windows and blocks the winter night from their spot overlooking the Puget Sound. Her and her babies, safe from the world, safe with Noah, tucked away in paradise forthcoming.

She interlaces her fingers with his. The gas can clangs to the back seat, spent. Caroline's snow boots turn toes-in. Tears trace her cheeks, pooling at her chin. Jenine smiles at her daughter. Jacob kicks and screams louder.

"Together," she says.

Snick.

She holds her Zippo lighter in the center of the Gran Sport. Noah pulls a Lucky Strike from his pack, tiny sparks dancing above the flame. The gasoline-infused air ignites in a Luciferian celebration strobing a glow across the wet cheeks of her angels.

Angels. They are all angels now.

Noah is the way.

Noah is the light.

Noah blows a plume of smoke and she drops the lighter over the backseat.

A final thought falls across her fugue, a strand of doubt to shatter the LSD magic of Noah's doped eyes: *My God, what have I done?*

Whumph!

"**D**o you smell that?"

Tess sniffs the air and scrunches her brow. *Odd.*

Daniel, unfathomable behind his shades and hangover, slips his Beamer into the Pregnant/ Expectant stall next to the disabled parking. "No."

Tess rolls her eyes. *You're an ass.*

Baby powder, gasoline, barbecue, coitus; the potpourri lingers a second longer, body salts and petroleum lightly painting the back of her throat before it's gone.

"Never mind."

"Sure."

Fuck! Daniel's being a dick has grown ten inches with genital warts over the last six weeks.

Tess glances out her window at the Tasty Freeze next to the paternity clinic.

"Mommy? I'm a little bit thirsty." Collin's voice is soft. Sweet. Her angel.

"Of course he is." Daniel slams the shift into P and throws his door open.

Tess looks over her headrest to the back and Collin's toddler seat. She smiles. He grins, big, blue eyes glowing.

"Okay, baby. After Mommy's appointment, maybe we can talk Daniel into a milkshake."

Collin's face slacks. He knows. "It's okay, Mommy."

Daniel, you bet your ass you're fucking buying my son a milkshake. She smiles. Collin blinks.

"Come on," Daniel barks from the front of the car. "Let's get this over with already."

Tess slams her door—stops to glare at Daniel despite his scorn—and gathers her son from the back.

"This won't take long. Then *Mommy will* buy us a shake. Kay?"

Daniel lolls his head and mutters a string of what-the-fuck-evers as they pass by.

An hour and one tell-all ultrasound later, Tess leans with Collin perched over the faux-granite table, their foreheads touching as they sip French Vanilla Chocolate Chunk from two straws. Daniel sleeps it off in the front seat of his BMW i3 custom.

"Mommy?"

"Yeah, baby?"

"Can my friend have some?"

Tess smiles.

"Of course, he can."

Collin scoots over and bends the straw down. Tess cradles her chin on her fingers and asks, "What's his name?"

"Jacob. He's little, though."

"Does Jacob like the milkshake, too?" She realizes these are the precious moments. Those un-forgettables. One day Collin will be a man and all she will have are ghosts of shared milkshake moments. *Make 'em last, girl. God knows you've fucked up everything else in the poor kid's life.*

But things will be good again. Tess rubs her barely showing tummy. Caroline is on the way, her new tiny spark of innocents. She envisions her daughter's wide eyes, full of wonder and curiosity, and hums softly. Content. And this time the daddy has money.

Even if he is a selfish prick.

Tess jerks and her hand goes to her lump out of instinct. Burnt meat slices through the steady flow of Tasty Freeze's regular grill. Not a hamburger and fries scent, but one of charred carbon. Violence. Death.

"Mommy, Jacob doesn't feel good."

She can't talk. The bench next to Collin puffs in a little wisp of smoke, dissipating before it fully manifests. The straw curls and twists into itself. Baby powder, out of place, and saccharine, cloys her senses.

"Jacob says he's sorry." Collin looks down at two half-moons burned into the stone bench outside the Tasty Freeze. "He had to go."

Wham! Tess doubles over into the cramp. She can't lose this one.

Daniel throws open his car door and stomps toward them.

"You're not worthy."

"I'm not." Jenine licks her lips. "But I want you." She means it. "All of you. In me."

Noah's laugh rumbles from his gut, deep and inviting. "Everyone wants me."

Jenine tosses her hair, crouched before him, her place of worship, her crimson locks cascading down her naked back. The bruised vertebrae in her neck scream agony at her sensual grace, but it is a necessary pain. Noah must understand how important he is to her. If only he would give her what she most desires. To enter her. To plant his seed. Grant her his immaculate life to bear. Join them forever. She tongues her split lip and slithers up to his member.

Caroline stares at her from the corner, through her heavy glasses, coloring book abandoned. Jacob sleeps in his carrier against the doorway.

Her ultimate sacrifice. To give what she loves most for his blessing. He has already banished all worshipers except her and the kids. This is the way. They are the chosen.

Jenine grips Noah's penis in both hands. Wringing. Sliding. Working him to climax. This is enough. It is not what she wants, but it satisfies. She licks her lips and finishes him, tasting the sweet salt of him, his holy mana.

He sighs and drifts to sleep with her lips still at worship.

Jenine's sacrifice will come soon. Angels need not suffer. Her holy babes should never sleep in the cold, and never again go hungry. This is right. This is destiny.

She leaves him limp and spent as she crawls for the phosphorous lines of coke neatly cut on the TV table against the trailer's thin wall. One more hit to cap the night in the light of National Anthem television static.

She snorts a toot, just enough to numb her teeth and head, but not too much. Noah doesn't like that.

Caroline coughs. Jenine smiles at her daughter before curling up, cut and bruised cheek pressed into Noah's abdomen, his heat feeding her, giving her the acceptance she needs. She won't sleep, but she will be here when he wakes. To greet him in the morning in the way he has trained her.

She stretches and winces. Blood runs down her back from a whip's lash scabbed and broken.

Caroline yawns and closes her eyes.

Fucking Daniel. In Vegas. Business. Or pleasure. Asshole.

Tess cleans the kitchen, systemically washing and replacing

dishes from Collin's breakfast, making sure to leave no hints her son has touched any of her boyfriend's things.

In the living room, the television flashes an ad for a Vegas vacation package. Drinks with every flavor of the rainbow. Women in porn bikinis. Lavish and exorbitant decor, beaches that don't exist, gaming tables full of big wins and bigger grins, unreal girls with sequins and white peacock feathers sprouting from their asses.

"Fuck!"

A clay coffee mug explodes against the wall beside the TV. Collin stares at her wide-eyed, his face twisting into a toddler's exaggeration of fear.

"Oh, baby," she says too late. He hics and hitches into terrified sobs. *Nice temper, Mom.*

Tess swoops her son into her arms. She presses her cheek against his hair and shushes him as she bounces, cradling and rocking, willing the bad away.

The crying doubles.

"Shh. Sh-sh-sh. We're okay, baby." She covers his wet cheeks in tiny kisses. He calms. Tess gives a sidelong glance, then raises his shirt and blows into his tummy, eliciting a cascade of giggles.

Elsewhere in the condo, a baby cries in reverse. Soft. Close.

"Collin?"

He blinks.

The cry swells again, this time from the bedroom. It's gone with a staccato puncture.

Balancing Collin on her hip, Tess moves to the sound.

"Collin, did you hear that, baby?"

He nods.

The cry echoes softer than before, a hurt toddler pulled down a well.

"What is it?" she whispers.

"Jacob," Collin whispers back.

The skin on Tess's neck tightens up to her scalp. A lump in the wadded bedding twitches.

Her heart races.

Collin giggles.

Tess reaches out with trembling fingers. Sunlight streams in through the window, painting dust motes in a micro galaxy hovering over the form. The blanket jerks to the side in a fetal twist. The air thickens with gas fumes, charred fat, No More

Tears shampoo.

She yanks and the world erupts in an infant's rage. Tess screams over the shrieking baby, a burnt and bleeding thing smeared into the sheets. She backs against the door with her arms tight around her son, eyes straining at the impossible sight.

Silence. She blinks.

The bed sits empty, sheets creased and folded from her restless sleep the night before. She slides down the wall and rests her forehead against Collin, taking slow breaths and focusing on her out of control heart, all too aware of her out of control life. She eventually grounds in Collin and her sense of motherhood. She closes her eyes and slips away to the feeling of a warm life, pure and fresh and growing inside of her.

My sweet Caroline.

Jenine nurses her swollen jaw and pulls Jacob close to her chest, to quiet him lest he wake Noah again. Caroline sits in the corner and cries silent tears. She lifts her small glasses and wipes her eyes. Jenine smooth's her hair.

"It's going to be okay, baby doll." Her voice sounds hallow to her ears. "Noah can't help it. He just gets a little bit mad sometimes."

All of this she nulls down to a whisper, her savior in the same kitchen leaned back in his chair. His tea of psilocybin mushrooms drips from a mug in his clasped hands, dribbling down his naked leg. A curtain of cigarette smoke hangs between the linoleum and Noah.

A thin stream of vomit stains her blouse, her own body's answer to the mushroom tea. Her eye twitches and her hand goes instinctively to her jaw at the memory of his sudden and violent strike. Noah's response to her wastefulness.

Jenine looks through the beads at the rest of his followers in the living room. Writhing bodies, some from orgasm, others from overdose, carpet the floor, the dilapidated couches. She nods downward at her two children. Sleeping Jacob, two years tomorrow, and her mute princess, five-year-old Caroline born with a malformed tongue and larynx. Caroline holds her gaze, big eyes conveying so much without words.

She murmurs, "My God. What am I doing?"

"Come." Noah sits up and places his mug on the table.

Jenine gasps and pulls Jacob closer. He shifts.

"Do not wake my new son, Jenine." Noah stands, letting his robe fall open wide to his bare abdomen and swollen member. "Place him by my mute daughter you have given unto me, and come."

Noah's voice deepens, sparking fear and something else. Heat. Jenine wants him. She can't control it. Her eye pulses from the last blow. Her labia and uterus ache from Noah's continued abuse of her womanhood. Inside her, the voice of a once reasoning Jenine gives sway to a newly reborn acolyte, a sex-starved nymph who can only imagine the ecstasy of having Noah inside her. A pleasure he still withholds until she proves her worth.

He takes her by the hand and leads her to his bedroom. His other hand trails his gnarled, wooden pleasuring stave. Jenine whimpers when he forces her down before him, but obeys. She sips from his cup. The absinthe stings her throat shredded from her stomach's recent expulsion.

"Drink. For this is the blood of my temple. Clean are those who drink of me."

Noah places a single tab of acid on her tongue.

"Eat. For this is my body. Happy are those who sup at my table."

She closes her eyes and allows the liquid rapture to happen as Noah's implement penetrates her harder, faster.

Through the colors of her feelings.

Violent. Surpassing the sound of smell.

Enraged.

"Daniel, I need you to come home," Tess says into the cupped phone. She strives for strength she doesn't feel. "Please."

His answer deflates her. Meeting. Maybe tomorrow. He doesn't ask about Collin. He doesn't care about his unborn daughter, baby Caroline. Tomorrow, or maybe the next day and now he has to go.

Tess sniffs and places the phone in its cradle. She can't cry. This is stupid.

Collin putters with his toy cars in the living room. She should check him. He needs dinner.

Pdrdrdrdrdr...pdrdrdr

"Collin, honey," she calls.

"Yes, Mommy?" She yelps with a start and pivots, hand to her chest. Collin blinks up at her from behind.

Pdrdrdrpdrdrdr...

Tiny lips raspberry motor sounds. From the living room.

Tess swallows and pushes Collin behind her, edging toward the living room door.

Pdrdr...pdrdrdr...pdrdr...

Her breath comes in shallow pulls.

"Stay behind me, baby," she says, taking courage from her stance as a guardian. Caroline kicks inside of her. A live and playful spirit. *So healthy.*

Tess swallows and steps onto the living room carpet.

Collin's cars lay piled in his toy box. Untouched. She scans, tension draining from her shoulders.

SssshPAP!

The lights cut out.

"Mommy? I'm scared."

"Where's Jacob."

Collin doesn't answer.

"Collin." Her voice climbs to a hissing whisper. "Where is Jacob?"

Nothing.

"Collin? Answer me, dammit!"

"He's on your back, Mommy."

She freezes in place.

Gasoline fumes and Desitin diaper cream. Stale cigarettes. Melting car pleather.

Tiny hands claw at her, digging into her flesh. Heat burns into her back. She swings wide from Collin and screams, batting at the thing attached to her.

Whumph!

The lights blaze and she spins into a dervish. She collapses to the floor in sobs.

Nothing holds her. The smell dissipates.

"Mommy, you scared me."

Tess crawls to the couch and leans her head against it, arms wide to accept her son. He runs to her and she holds him.

"I'm losing my mind—" She stops and swallows hard.

Out of the corner of her eye, standing at the hallway entrance to the living room, a small figure looms just beyond the shadows. Collin raises his head over Tess's shoulder.

"Collin, baby. Please, don't look at it."

"Why, Mommy?" He grins at the thing. Tess closes her eyes for a beat and slowly turns to face it. He whispers, "I think it's Jacob's sister."

Tess stops before the figure comes into full view. She pulls Collin tight and digs deep for the same mothering instinct she needed to get free from his draconian father a year ago. Her arm covers her Caroline, safe in her womb.

"I think she's mad, Mommy."

Tess twists and stands in one fluid motion, rage and fear stitching her emotions into a battle cry. "Get the fuck away from us—"

A little girl, blackened with bleeding cracks, takes one step sideways to blend into the shadows. Light reflects on a small pair of spectacles barely visible.

"Who are you?" Tess asks, releasing Collin and falling to her knees. "Please? What do you want from me?"

Tess shrieks. The girl thing moves with scorpion speed and palsied limbs, jerking its way from the shadows, circling in toward them.

"Mommy!"

"Don't look!"

It gains foothold in the shadows of the opposite side of the couch and disappears.

The sound of their breathing huffs loud and heavy in the silence.

Whum... whum... whum...

"No!"

The lights pulse on and off, a lightning fast figure bouncing closer with each wave.

Whumph!

The living room bulb ignites and swells, throwing insane amounts of eco-white illumination. Tess glances up. "God, no." *It's going to blow.*

She yanks Collin to the kitchen utility drawer, and fumbles for the emergency candles and matches.

SHPAPP!

All lights go out at once. Her candle sparks to life. She holds it out before her, keeping Collin to her back.

Something scuttles to the corner, away from the flame. She holds it up. A shadow of frenzied arms and legs crabwalks up the wall and suspends panting from the ceiling. Tess advances with her flame.

The thing hisses and spirals into itself, back into the darkness.

Tess turns in a slow arc, holding her candle high. "Collin? Where's Jacob?"

Collin cries.

Tiny hands dig into her neck. She feels the warmth of a mouth suckling at her back before she collapses. The twisted figure of a little girl convulses from the shadows, advancing in bursts, ushering in the darkness. Reaching for her tummy.

The Lizard King staggers through his number, a world away on the stage. Club lights drip velvety red and lime green, turning every sequined dress into a disco ball, bringing all skin tones together in a single, harmonious acid splash of happy horny people.

The newcomer doesn't dance, but moves behind mirrored shades with a congregation of supple young disciples in hip huggers and platforms. Jenine licks her lips. This is the one. She has no doubts. He moves her more than Jim Morrison does. He is her new messiah. He will be her savior.

Morrison beckons her to light his fire. She sways to the music, but the acid wore off hours ago. Now it's just a feel-good high.

"He wants to talk to you," says a young African acolyte. The girl holds out a red rose and shimmies her bare midriff in time to the music, matching Jenine move-for-slinky-move. Jenine takes her offered hand and sashays toward the back table. The crowd of followers parts before her, yielding to the enigmatic Noah.

"Hello, young and voluptuous."

She blushes. His voice penetrates her.

"Are you spoken for?"

"No." She could giggle, but this messiah doesn't want high school girl bullshit. He smiles. She falls into his eyes. He looks down and traces her Cesarean scar above her belt line, barely visible through the layers of foundation and powder. Jenine shudders, but he lays a hand onto each shoulder and pushes her into his eyes.

"You are a mother." He whispers it, pulling her close, his bared chest sliding against her strapless dress. "A beautiful mother." She moans. In another world, the Lizard King chants of his mojo risin.

"Yes." They sway to the music, his body entwining around her.

"How many?"

"Three—" she bites her lip. The first doesn't count. Little Tessy was Daddy's accident. *A forget-me-now. Poor little Tess. But Daddy took care of that. A good family, Daddy said.* "Two. I have two children." *A good Catholic family, Daddy said.* "Jacob and Caroline." Her voice is tiny in the thrumming bass line.

"Two is a good number." He whispers it into her ear, his absinthe-moistened breath flowing through her, warming her. "Will you have me, Jenine?"

In another world, she shudders and explodes. Here, she sucks air and holds her breath.

"Will you become one with me, Jenine?" They twist and move, sharing body space. Her sex pulses for him. Her heart yearns for his yes, his now, his more.

"Will you purify and be my bride in the second life, my beautiful Jenine?"

"Yes."

Their lips collide and his tongue penetrates her, sweet and sour coolness of wine adding headiness to her moment.

"Come home with me, Jenine."

She takes his hand and follows him out the door, his cult of beautiful people collapsing behind them in a lit entourage.

"Let us greet the children."

The boy smolders in her arms. His cries strain down to a wounded mewling, a sound no child should make. Beside her, the little girl tugs at her skirt, flames erupting in small patches from her heavy quilted coat and hair. Her superheated glasses have become part of her face.

"This is what happened to you," Tess says. She is no longer afraid. In another world, she knows she lays face down on the floor while Collin pushes his cars around her body, waiting for her to wake.

The girl leans into her.

"Who did this?"

Before them, a late 60's model Buick burns with the serenity of a funeral pyre. Two charred skeletons clutch each other from the front seat.

The girl tugs and Tess follows, wending their way through alleys made of ash and sand. A man leans on the stoop of a house Tess recognizes. A house built behind Our Lady of Sorrows

Church in downtown Seattle. The rectory.

Her childhood home.

The door opens and a gentle man of the cloth steps to the light, accepting a bundle from the dark stranger.

"Papa?"

And in that moment she realizes the dichotomy of the word as she stares at the two men. One who created her, and the other with the heart to raise her.

Tess's pulse flails against her veins.

The little girl tugs again and now they are running, weaving between alleys and brownstones, stepping over puddles and litter. They stop. This house is much worse than the rectory. A shanty in the downtown slums. A woman screams.

Tess doesn't want to see, but she can't help it. She moves toward a wash of candle light spilling from a window.

"Momma."

She can't know this, yet she does.

The woman in the bedroom sits upright and screams at the space between her thighs. The wailing of her newborn breaks her cry. The dark man steps from the shadows in the room and takes the baby, his face falling full on into the light for a fleet second. Tess holds her breath. The upturned nose, high cheekbones, thin eyebrows. His resemblance to the birth mother is too close for coincidence. Their features identical to Tess's. Tess screams into her clasped hands, a tear squeezing from her eye as her history unfolds.

The boy squalls and transforms in her arms. She looks down on Collin's cherubic face and shrieks a long, tortured, "No..."

The little girl steps forward, her hand on Tess's womb, and pushes *into* the newly forming Caroline. Sweet innocence slips beneath the murk of something dark inside her. Collin's charred body crumbles.

"What are we doing here?" Daniel bought her a new car. He offered to pay for the abortion. He promised to ensure her compensation. Tess took it all in stride. He hasn't been the same since Vegas.

Neither has Tess. Or Collin. Her hand drops to her tummy. A kick. Tess smiles. Little Caroline. Already such a tiny, blackened old soul. Poor thing. *My God, how can I bring you into this a second time?*

"I want to show you something," she says.

She slips her new Benz into the pier parking, overlooking the Puget Sound. The dash's digital analog clock tips just past midnight. The pier lot sits cold and empty.

Collin snores in a Benadryl slumber from the backseat.

Tess reaches over and pulls a tin can from beneath his baby blanket.

"What are you doing?"

She upends it and lets the golden fuel splash across her face, her clothes, into the back—

"Hey! What the fuck—"

Daniel yanks at the door handle, but the child lock holds. The child locks always hold, she thinks. He beats at the glass.

"Let me out! Tess! Goddammit let me out—"

Collin stirs from the fumes and his thumb finds his mouth. Tess rubs her bump.

She holds out her Zippo and flicks the wheel.

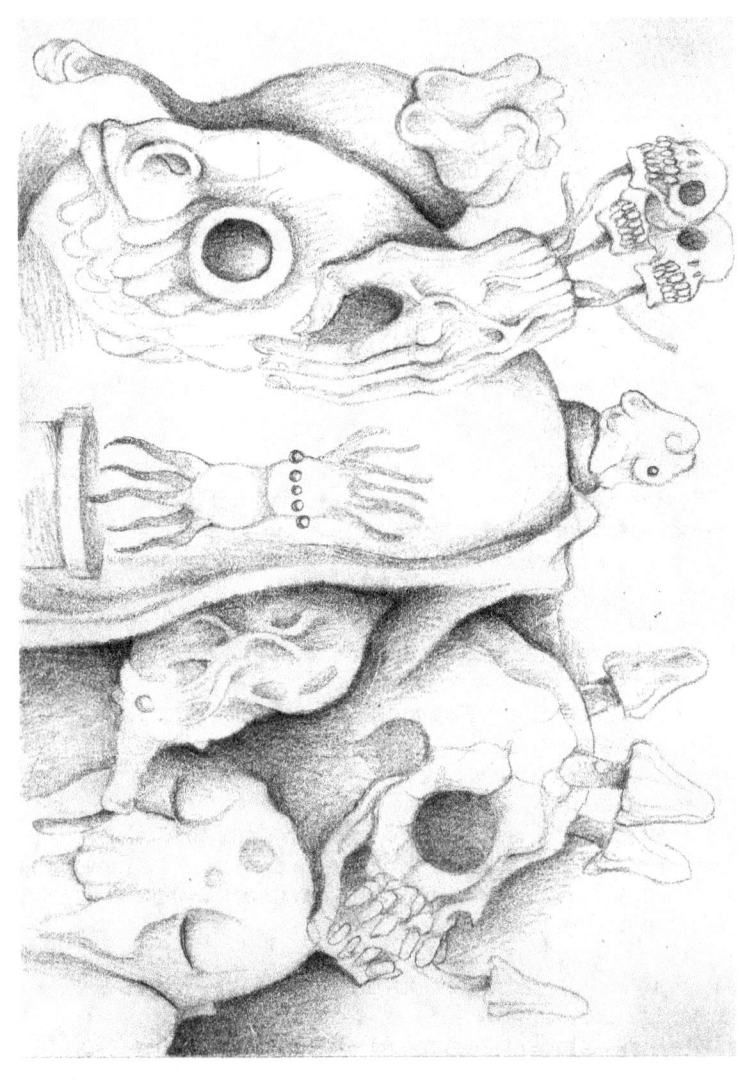

John Sies

The Forest For The Trees

I'm awake.

Why?

Something is moving. Not an animal. No, I wouldn't have awakened for that.

A person.

Shuffling footsteps amid the dried leaves littering the ground.

Moving nearer. Heavy breathing. A grunt of exertion. Though I cannot see, I can tell it is a male.

Is it he? I wait as each slow step brings him closer. I have to know.

He has stopped, and shuffles around. Getting his bearings? How can he not know this place intimately? He has come to this forest for several years.

He's moving again. The footfalls are becoming heavier, more solid with his approach. The gait, the step, is so familiar. It *IS* he! For the first time in a long while, I snap fully awake. A thrill of excitement, anticipation, flows through me.

I realize that his steps are heavier than they should be. A second set of breaths comes to my awareness. The new breaths are shallow and slow—another person, unconscious, or nearly so. He must have a girl with him.

He is approaching me. It has been...what, a year and a half? It seems to have been much longer. Last time he came, he was too far away. Now... now he has stopped right next to me! The excitement of him close ripples through me.

He stops, setting down his burden and I can feel the waves of excitement coming off him; the passion, the arousal. He steps closer to me.

Ah yes, his ritual; He will take off his favored long coat, hang it on a tree branch out of the way, then don the cheap plastic raincoat from his cloth bag. His breathing is growing quicker as the anticipation builds in him. From the bag, he will also unpack the camera, the folding shovel, and his special rolled bundle. He will set it by the girl, and with reverence, unroll the cloth, exposing the knives. He will fawn over them, fondle each one... the large one, the long thin one, and the scalpel.

I feel the pressure as he moves about her, unfrocking his prize from the blanket, spreading her arms wide, straightening her legs in a mock crucifixion pose.

My awareness flares. I can hear his every breath, his very heartbeat. I fancy I can sense his muscles flexing. The ripples of emotions flowing off him shine like a beacon to me.

He steps to the side; he will be reaching for the middle knife.

Now is my time.

He turns and stumbles. He realizes he has caught his shoe on a root. He will try to pull it out, but will fail...Ha! I feel confusion, frustration rush through him. He reaches down with the knife to cut the root. Ah, the sweet shock when another root bursts from the moist earth and ensnares his ankle. Confusion! Confusion! I wish I could laugh. This is perfect! A dream comes true!

Now anger rolls off him. He still thinks he is in control. He is trying to bend to cut the offending snare. I move. He hears the groan, the creaking. Oh, but if I only still had eyes to fully witness his face right now, as he looks up and sees the skeletal branches of the large, old oak come alive, impossibly reaching for him, wrapping themselves around him in an unnatural embrace.

I can feel the vibrations of his screaming, the tug of his thrashing. I face him toward the tree, while pushing myself up into his view. The root that grows through my corpse breaks through the ground, sitting me up so he can see me. Even dead in the ground for eighteen months, he will remember who I am. I was the one who never fully succumbed. I was the one who fought him. I was the one who very nearly bested him, except for an unlucky slip in the muddy soil.

I never gave up, even after my body died. I held on, focused on vengeance, using the old life essence of the oak as an anchor. The others in this grove left quickly after their deaths. I had other plans. I will provide justice for them also.

The tree groans, and then cracks, a large fissure opening in the trunk a good eight feet in length. I open it wide, deep into the core of the wood.

The timbre of his screaming changes as the branches drag him to the gaping maw. I can feel his thrashing, the delicious panic and horror he is emanating. I know he won't be able to tear his eyes from me as the gap in the wood takes him.

I can feel his body pulp, his mind fracture, as I slowly close the trunk around him. I reel in ecstasy as his last moments end in insane horror. I replay the memory again and again, enjoying an almost orgasmic rush that makes the tree quiver sympathetically.

The girl's heartbeat is faster. She will wake soon. His precious coat, with identification, is still on the branch. The knife and his belongings with his fingerprints lay for all to see. She will awake and lead the police here, to the proof of his guilt. His crimes will bear witness. All of us hidden here shall be found, returned to our families. Rest, my sisters, justice is done.

I relax, letting go of the essence of the oak.

I see a light.

William Cook

But Only a Non-Entity

A stranger in a strange land
it has been said before
but there are no words more succinct
to describe my predicament
at this time, forevermore

I have wandered without reason
beneath the yellow moon
hung like a wrecking ball
in the tinctured heavens
all logic lost to this black season
still I roam, this foggy gloom

a barren wasteland –
the scorched earth, scabrous beneath my chaffed feet
through what once were Winter forests
now skeletal remains, laid bare
I move forward undeterred
beyond hope, but seldom without fear

I know not whence I came
or how I lost my way from the righteous path
but here I am without compass
or moral direction – oblivious to ethos
no desideratum to be sure
I want for nothing, save for blood and rest
because I am nothing anymore
I am truly 'living dead' . . .

I have lost count of the times
I have circumnavigated this cruel world
there is no water, no oasis
in this bleak desert of despair
my perambulation is comeuppance
for a paucity of faith
for believing in the wrong gods

and so now, I face the wraith
standing before me in a Christ-like pose
a terrifying spectre of myself
without flesh, without a soul
I will my mind to justify the apparition
as it extends a cloven limb
my legs, without recourse to mind
walk me forward into its realm
and what I hoped a phantasm, becomes too real
for me to cogitate, to comprehend
as I feel its preternatural touch
reach my heart and shut me down

and as I lay there dying
underneath the yellow moon
I felt alive, for the first time in my life
as I watched the spectre float away
into the shadowed hinterland
the perpetual twilight shuddered
the clouds of fog dissolved the gloom
and the last sight I saw, was a white bright light
that filled my humble room.

Post-script:

They found him in the bedsit, the dull bulb still burning above him as he lay prone on the mattress beneath. The rent arrears were such that a pauper's grave was the only recourse. The matter of the gaping wound in his thin chest was never resolved, and because of his impoverished nature, no further investigation was deemed warrantable. His identity has never been claimed.

Michael Tugendhat

Darkness Is

When darkness enters the mouth,
it crawls into a centerfold and weakly
presses the tongue toward a maze,
a field of blue-white sky, the way
each piece of darkness won't die,
men are waking and boys are born.
As darkness enters the eye,
the pupils blister, wind sneers,
that it may enter and exit
like a boy falling into his shadow
entering a fantasy, and leaving in lethargy.
He isn't the dark's mistress
but it is essential to have a life
when death closes in asking for more.
And the darkness, upon overtaking
the body, wants another person
to smooth to sleep in its own slumber
within the trees, it goes: into me.

Guy Burtenshaw

The Yellow Dress

I hadn't thought about Gail in seven months. I suppose she had only been at M'Gill's for a couple of months, and a place like M'Gill's has a high turnover even for a sleazy bar that begrudgingly pays minimum wage.

I had been working until eleven four nights a week, Monday through Thursday, but money was short, and a vacancy had arisen for a Friday shift, and I found myself working five nights.

It was a Friday night at the end of October and I missed the bus. It was raining hard and I didn't have a coat. I lived about four miles away on the eastern edge of town in a small apartment in an old converted house. I considered walking, but the route passed by a disused chemical plant, and at night it did not look like a place any health conscious person would want to be walking alone.

The next bus was an hour later. I huddled in a shop doorway and patiently waited. When the bus finally arrived, I got on and made my way to the back where I slumped down against a window.

There was only one other passenger on the bus. She sat several rows in front of me; long dark hair hanging down over the backrest, a bright yellow dress contrasting with the dark blue material of the seat. She turned her head and looked back, and I was surprised when I recognized her. Gail Brown gave a nervous smile, and I smiled back. I thought she was going to come over, but she just turned back to face the front and I fell asleep with my head resting against the window.

Apart from the manager, I was the second longest serving member of staff. I had been there for eight months if that gives you any indication of employee morale. The longest serving member of staff was an old friend of mine called Haden Dade. By old friend, I'd sat next to him from fifth grade to eighth grade, but hadn't seen him again until I started at M'Gill's.

When I told him that I had seen Gail on the bus, he looked shocked. Not surprised, but shocked as though I had slapped him across the face. He told me that I must have been mistaken because she had moved to the west coast.

I looked out for her for the rest of the following week. There were other people on the bus, but not Gail. By Friday, I decided to get the later bus again. I sat at the back and smiled when I saw Gail sitting in the same seat a few rows in front.

"Gail," I called out, and she looked back and smiled.

I thought perhaps I had been mistaken after talking to Haden, but there was no mistaking. It was definitely Gail.

The bus stopped in the middle of what had once been a service road running through the middle of the chemical plant and a man got on. Before the doors closed, Gail got off and I watched as she walked across the road and disappeared into the darkness next to an office building. The entrance to the building was boarded, and there were grilles covering the windows. A bright blue sign attached to the front told anyone that was interested that the building was available for rent, but I could not see it attracting any interest other than vagrants.

On Monday, I told Haden that I had seen Gail again. He just smiled, but he was not his usual talkative self for the rest of the night. The next shift he wandered over and asked me where she had got off and I told him that she had got off by the old chemical plant. He had smiled, but it had been a cold smile, and made me feel uncomfortable. I thought that perhaps something had been going on between Haden and Gail. Possibly the reason she had left so suddenly and he claimed to know that she had moved to the other side of the country.

On Friday, Haden approached me again and asked me what I was playing at. I don't know why, but I responded by saying, "Don't worry, your secret's safe with me." I was joking, but you would have thought I had just sworn at him from the expression I got in response.

I had not intended to get the later bus on that Friday, but I had stayed an extra half an hour to cover an absent colleague. I found myself on that later bus for the third time in as many weeks, and Gail was sitting in her usual seat wearing that same bright yellow dress.

As the bus approached the stop in the middle of the disused chemical plant, I pressed the stop buzzer and the bus stopped.

Gail looked back, but she did not smile. She opened her mouth and mouthed the words 'Help Me.' Two simple words, but they made me shiver.

Gail stood and walked to the front of the bus where she got off. I stood, but hesitated. The door remained open. I was about to sit back down when the bus driver leaned from his cab and shouted, "Are you getting off or not?"

The last thing I wanted to do was get off when I was still two miles from home, but I did. I walked to the front and got off the bus. I looked about to see where Gail had gone, and I saw her as she disappeared out of view next to the vacant office.

When I turned to get back on the bus, my nerves getting the better of me, the doors slammed closed, and the bus moved away. I stood on the sidewalk and watched as the taillights disappeared into the distance and faded away into the night.

I looked about. I felt relieved that I could not see anyone, but I also felt anxious that I was completely alone in such a desolate part of town. If anyone were to appear and decide I looked like a victim, there would be no one to come to my rescue. I walked along the road until I could see along the side road that Gail had walked along. The side of the building was in complete darkness.

The sound of an approaching car turned my attention back to the road. Headlights broke through the night, dots of white light that reminded me of Karswell in Night of the Demon. The moment he realizes there is no escape as the demon reaches out to take him. My nerves were fraying, and that thought did not help.

I backed away from the road and entered the shadows by the building. The car slowed. It was a black Dodge Charger: Second Generation with the headlamps hidden behind a black undivided grill. I had not realized until then just how menacing something so magnificent could be. The car stopped and I could feel eyes staring through the tinted windows boring into me.

A scream broke the silence shredding what was left of my nerves, and my mind turned to Gail. I could not think of any reason why she would wander into the darkness, but something was terribly wrong. I had hoped the car would just rev its engine and continue on its way, but it just remained, its engine rumbling steadily.

Another scream, this one more severe than the last, and I turned and started running. I could not see any reason why whomever was in that car would follow, but the driver gunned the engine and I heard the car turning to follow.

I reached the end of the road and ran across an intersecting road toward a chain link fence that surrounded what looked like steel chemical storage tanks. There were gaps in the fencing where it looked as though people had cut through, presumably to see what could be stolen or just vandalized for what passed as their amusement.

I squeezed through a gap, sharp points of steel painfully scraping my skin before I left the fence behind and made my way between two of the tanks. I looked back and saw that the car had one again stopped, its headlights illuminating the ground in front of the fence. I was dazzled suddenly as the headlights changed to full, and startled at the dark shape that loomed up in front of me, my nerves calming none at the realization that it was just my own shadow on the tank.

The driver's door opened and I moved around the tank. I heard feet walking across the concrete ground and I looked about for a weapon. I tried to steady my breathing, and I realized I could no longer hear anything. A hand grabbed my shoulder and I spun around, fist clenched, ready to strike.

Haden Dade stared at me, his expression hard and serious.

"What are you doing here?" I asked. "You scared the crap out of me."

"We need to talk," Haden said.

"Were you following me?" I asked, and felt stupid. An abandoned chemical plant is hardly the sort of place you just bump into anyone, let alone a work colleague.

"I was driving over to see you," he said. "And I think you know what we need to talk about. What is it that you want?"

"I don't know what you're talking about," I told him. "I saw Gail get off here. You *must* have heard her scream."

"I saw you run," he said.

We both turned to look at the entrance to a building next to the tanks. Someone was standing in the doorway. From the yellow dress, I knew it was Gail. Haden started walking toward the doorway, and I followed.

As we entered the building, I stopped. The space inside was dark, but moonlight cast a subtle light across the floor from holes in the roof. Through the gloom, I saw the bright yellow dress and walked toward it, stopping as my mind tried to comprehend what confronted me.

The skin was mottled and dry, long black hair hanging down around the shoulders, the eyes eaten away, the yellow dress contrasting with the decay. My skin crawled as I realized it was the same yellow dress I had seen Gail wearing as she had stepped off the bus. I forced myself to look at the face and I knew that it was Gail.

It seemed impossible. The body must have been there for months, and I felt that I knew that it had been there since she had left M'Gill's for the last time seven months earlier.

"Why did you kill her?" I asked Haden.

"How did you know?" he asked.

"I saw her on the bus," I told him, but I knew that was impossible. She had been dead for months, but I knew what I had seen.

An explosion of pain filled my side and I looked down to see a knife. Haden stepped back, I saw my blood clinging to the blade, and I felt as though I could feel my life draining away. I clutched at my side and pressed the wound, the pain bringing me to me knees.

"Why couldn't you just keep your mouth shut," Haden said.

Haden turned to walk away and stopped. Standing about ten feet in front of him was Gail in her bright yellow dress.

"It's a trick," Haden said. "You're not Gail."

He looked back to make sure that the body was still where he had left it. I watched the expression on his face. It was one of confusion rather than fear. When he turned again, there was no one there.

"You can't hide from me," Haden shouted.

I remembered Mr. White telling Mr. Orange in Reservoir Dogs that it takes days to die from a gunshot wound to the stomach. I know knowledge gained from cinema is not a medically recognized diagnosis, but I hoped that the same was true for a knife wound. I could not see anyone passing by day or night, but if Haden just left me to die, I was sure that I could somehow manage to crawl back to the main road.

Haden stared down at me and held the knife up as though to study its serrated blade. The pain in my side was intense, but I was determined not to lose consciousness. I knew that if that happened, I would die there on the floor of that place, and a derelict chemical plant is no place for anyone to die.

A cold breeze brushed across my face and Haden spun around as though he thought someone was behind him. I thought I heard whispering, but I could not make out any words, and, from Haden's expression, I was certain he could hear the sound too.

"Who's there?" Haden shouted.

His arms rose as though unseen hands had grabbed hold of him, and he moved backward across the space. As he fell to the ground, the look on his face was one of fear. I thought I saw shapes around him, but my vision was not clear, and I cannot be certain, but he waved his arms about his face as though trying to defend himself.

He slashed at the air with the knife, and then the knife plunged down into his stomach. His hand rose and the knife plunged down again, and again, and again. As darkness finally took hold, I saw dark blood spreading out around his body like a lake, and Gail crouched next to me. She reached out, put her hand against my wound, and whispered, "Thank you."

When I opened my eyes, I was in the back of an ambulance on the way to the hospital. A security patrol had seen the Dodge Charger and taken a check around. They thought I was dead, but fortunately checked for a pulse.

After a thorough search of the building, the police discovered the remains of fourteen bodies. It turned out that there had been a reason for the high turnover at M'Gill's. I thought I had known Haden. I guess you never truly know anyone. As for Gail, I never saw her again. She had come from the west coast, and her body returned to her parents for burial. I had never believed in ghosts, but I believe Gail lured Haden back to that place, and together his victims had their revenge.

E.F. Schraeder

Empty Pillow

Her small hand, still a hint of father's,
but it's too dark for shadows in the empty crib
and the dirge pounding in the drunken head reminds him
no family remains in that forsaken house.

Delicate feathers dance from a spindly mobile frame,
Scotch-taped stars glisten stuck to the walls
like bad memories. But no child's laughter greets him
in the hall, nothing to hear but echoes of unspent lives,
splashed hopes like fresh paint, washable but stained.

Unable to make it upstairs where the accident haunts
each room with the nagging question, what have I done?,
he dozes in an easy chair, head drooped, drooling
into the rough woven fabric, swatting at the hands that return
each night, choking him as he fights for uneven sleep
until the last breath catches in his throat
and the laughter finally returns, rising.

Evan Dicken

Last Words

Wallace smiled at the pistol in my hand.

"I was hoping you'd come." His bourbon-sharp breath cut the reek of sweat and cigarette smoke from inside the house. The smell, more than anything, made me angry. For all her faults, my sister had been tidy. God forbid I didn't hang up a towel or forget to rinse the flecks of toothpaste off the mirror in the bathroom we'd shared growing up. I bet the inside of Fiona's coffin was spotless.

"Care for a drink?" Wallace shook a mostly empty bottle of Old Crow. He hadn't changed clothes since the funeral, and the rumpled pima cotton shirt and slacks were spotted with sweat, ash, and what might've been blood.

"Sit down, asshole." I flicked the pistol at the couch.

Wallace sat.

I hesitated in the doorway, I'd felt prepared for almost anything--denial, fear, even anger--but Wallace looked almost grateful.

Light from the flickering television rimed his face in shadows that put me in mind of bruises peeking from beneath scarves and sweaters. That was probably just my guilty conscience, though. Fiona had called near the end, left a half dozen accusatory messages on my voicemail, deleted unheard. It hadn't been the first time, and it wouldn't be the last, or so I'd thought. Like mom, Fiona had always been high-strung, prone to drama. Her complaints about Wallace were easy to dismiss. He'd been so *earnest*, and to be honest, I'd been happy she was finally someone else's problem.

Guilt was a firm hand at my back, pressing me forward. I shut the door behind me, careful not to take my eyes off Wallace. There was a brush of cold air across my neck like the air conditioner kicking on.

Wallace moaned.

"I know it wasn't suicide," I said.

"I was out of the country."

"That's not a denial."

He looked over his shoulder at the darkened kitchen, seeming to fold in on himself. It irritated me not to have his full attention, and I stepped forward to press the barrel of the pistol into his cheek. Fiona had called Wallace a heartless bastard, but she'd said the same thing about me more than once, so that didn't mean much. I could probably count on one hand the number of times I'd seen him lose his cool.

"How'd you do it?" I still didn't know if I could kill him, but I really wanted to see him scared.

"Does it matter?" There *was* fear in his eyes, but he barely glanced at the gun.

Something thumped against the back window, and I almost blew his head off.

"What was that?"

"Please, do it." He only had eyes for me, now. "I can't take another night."

"What do you mean?"

"Always picking, always pushing, nothing was ever good enough." He rubbed a trembling hand across his stubble. "I didn't want to do it, but she would get in my head and twist shit around. You know how she was."

I did. It was easy to lash out when nothing was ever your fault. My sister, perennial victim. This time, though, she'd been right.

The curtains at the back of the room fluttered. Another blast of cold, dry air carried notes of body lotion. No surprise the house still reeked of cucumber melon, Fiona had practically bathed in the stuff.

I wrinkled my nose. Wallace started shaking. He pawed at the gun, not trying to take it from me, but to push the barrel up to his temple. I snatched it back.

"I only hit her once, you know. She called me a coward, said the real reason I was in twelve steps was because I wasn't man enough to handle my own shit." He spoke quickly, words tumbling like he was late for something. "She said she forgave me, but she took pictures, threatened to tell everyone. Jesus, it would've ruined me. I didn't know what else to do, but she won't let me go."

The kitchen shadows rippled like sheets in the wind. Something rose through the darkness like a diver surfacing on a storm-tossed sea.

"Who's back there?" I backed away, pistol twitching between Wallace and the kitchen.

"Who do you think?" He whimpered, rolling up his shirtsleeves to reveal a tapestry of burns, bruises, and half-healed cuts. "Why won't she end it?"

A familiar hand slipped from the deepening shadow, fingers trailing up Wallace's cheek to stroke his hair. They tightened, then jerked him roughly back into the darkness. There was a high panting wheeze, which tapered into the hoarse gasps of someone too terrified to scream.

"I was hoping you'd come." The words seemed to assemble themselves from my memory, dripping with scorn. It didn't matter that I'd talked Fiona down from a thousand cliffs, swallowed decades of accusations and abuse, that I'd come to avenge her.

Somehow, I knew Fiona still blamed me for everything.

Wallace didn't start screaming until I fumbled open the door. His ragged shrieks chased me down the front walk and onto the street. A car went by, headlights glinting off the gun in my hand. I saw a woman inside, eyes wide, already fumbling for her cellphone. It didn't matter. None of it mattered.

I hadn't listened while Fiona was alive, and was terrified of what she had to say now.

Brian Rosenberger

Homeowners

The porch light is on, mosquitoes and moths in competition to burn.

The driveway is gravel, a crunch beneath footsteps.

The light, an oasis, hopefully sanctuary, a chance to forget the mechanic who assured you the engine was fine. Five hundred dollars and less than two hundred miles later, the broken Honda, parked on the moonlight side of a dark road, its journey ended. The clouds rain down as you reach the porch. A knock. Then two. Then three. The door opens and you step over the "Welcome" as a bolt of lightning splits the sky.

The walls, off-white, like the face of a decomposing clown.

Your "hello" greeted in silence.

You try the phone. Dead.

Fast-forward two hours, after the screams and unanswered prayers and offerings of pain and sacrifices taken, after you have met the homeowners in their less-than-flesh.

The phone is still dead. Like your Honda. Like the homeowners. Like you.

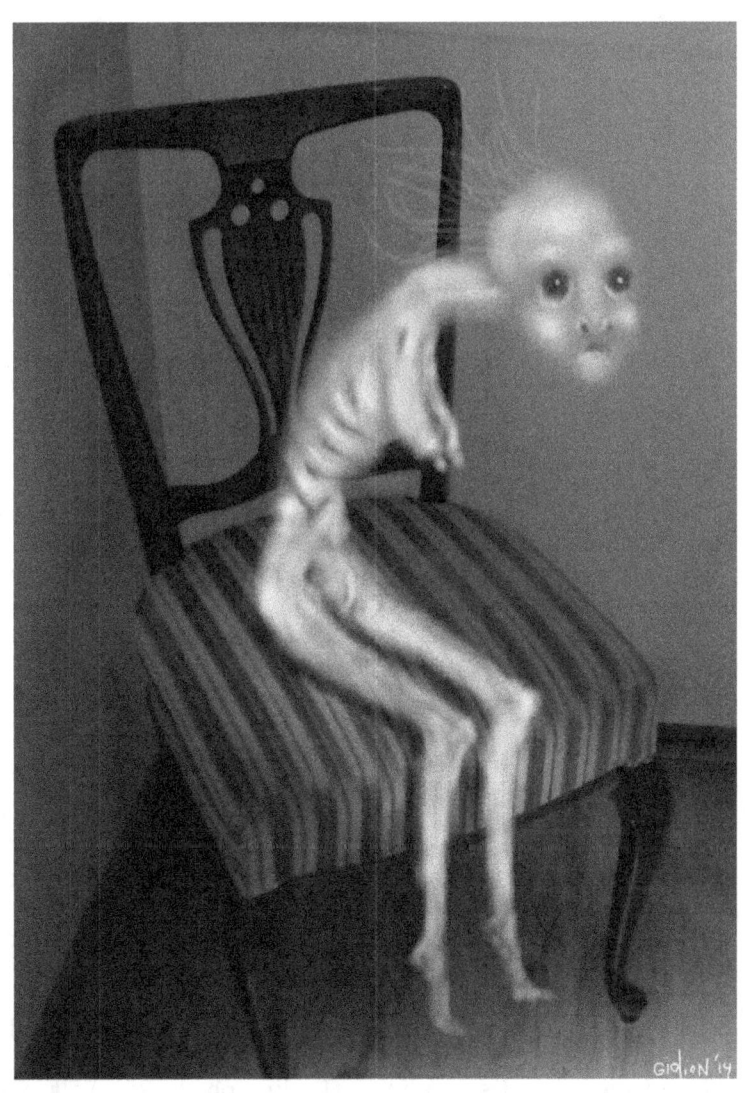

Mike Jansen

From the flame

Lovingly he caressed the outside of the window-frame of his living room. The paint felt a bit rough in spots, a clear sign the weather was working its wiles on the protective coating.

Henri Dunant stepped back onto the lawn to take in the whole of the house. The walls were partially gray concrete blocks, for the foundation, with the rest a wood frame for the first and second floor, painted in distinguished looking dark green. The window-frames were bright white and the first light of the sun reflected in the windows. The top windows were multi-colored leaded glass that enlivened the picture.

He took a deep breath of the fresh morning air. It was a perfect day to sand and paint the window-frames. A faint breeze played through the branches of the oak that grew next to the house and stretched out over his driveway and garage.

Henri took excellent care of his house and the lot it rested upon. He wished some of his neighbors could be more like him, but unfortunately most young folks had left and only the elderly remained. They were not very much into maintaining their houses.

The tar on the sloping roof above his bay window could do with an extra layer and in his mind he made a list of all the tools and supplies he would need for the coming weekend. He had lived in the house for almost twenty years, of which fifteen alone and ever since he started living there he had spent most of his free time on improving and maintaining the building.

"Morning, neighbor," a voice behind him said, one that he recognized.

Henri turned and saw Widow Harding on the sidewalk. She leaned her voluminous frame on her walking stick. "Morning, Widow Harding, all is well I hope?"

"Ah well, gout, rheumatism and other old woman troubles." She shrugged. "When are you coming over to paint my house?"

Henri smiled. "I explained that, remember?"

Widow Harding nodded slowly. "Yes, and I still think it's a pretty weak excuse. Your house will not get jealous when you give attention to another house."

Henri sighed. He still regretted his earlier words. It just felt wrong, working on another house while so much remained for his home. "You could just hire someone to paint, right?"

"Pfft, strangers in my house, no thank you." Widow Harding snorted. "You can never be careful enough, Dunant." She turned around and limped off in the direction of her own house, a low bungalow a few hundred yards down the road. It was almost bare of paint and the window-frames were dull. Her thatched roof needed a full restoration. Beyond her house were the other houses of the village.

"I'll see if I have some time left," he called after her. They both knew it was an empty promise.

The sound of sand paper on the window frame and the regular motions cause Henri to enter a trance like state. With each spot and each irregularity, his mind sank deeper into the caverns of his past.

He thought of Melanie again, his wife, who had left him fifteen years ago, rather unexpectedly. He thought they were happy together in their beautiful house. He had ignored her complaints about his obsession until one day she no longer spoke about the house. In retrospect, her melancholy manifested itself everywhere, the way an image in glass exists for a moment after one moves away. He understood those moments were when she chose her own path. One day, she was gone.

He wiped the thin layer of dust from the window-frame and saw his own reflection, dust covered too, in the window glass. He had sanded the wood to perfection and he was ready to wipe it down with ammonia. After that, he would apply the primer and as soon as that dried up, he would start the actual paint undercoat. Henri would not use the simple, modern paint that you could just roll onto the wood. He always used the classic methods, proven technology, in use and unchanged for hundreds of years. Traditions were, after all, traditions, for a reason.

The moment he picked up the paint for the undercoat, the sun just turned to the side of the house, leaving the window-frame in the shadows. Sun was bad for the bonding of the next layer of paint, after all. When he finished the last of the paint, he took a few steps back to examine his handiwork. He was very pleased with himself. The window-frames looked fresh, brand spanking new in fact.

While cleaning up his paintbrushes, he felt a familiar loneliness. He missed Melanie, or any other woman, for that matter, in his life. He sighed. He was too old and worked too hard. Whenever he got home, he had no energy left to go out. He much rather enjoyed the perfectly papered walls with their gray-red diamond pattern or the beautifully dark stained oak fire place that crackled joyously when he burned blocks of wood on the cast iron grating.

During the summer he most often sat on his porch with a tall glass of lemonade or delicious, icy beer, reading a thriller and listening to his favorite sixties rock-n-roll. In the winter, he curled up on his large couch and stared at the fire in the fireplace or watched some TV. As perfect as everything seemed, how well maintained his house, he missed Melanie in his life.

Dusk was a fiery red. Henri saw the red disk of the sun disappear behind the hills and trees in the distance as he prepared his dinner of spicy marinated chicken satay for the barbeque, a fresh salad from his garden and a very nice red wine from a nearby vineyard.

He was about to place the first stick on the steel grating above the glowing coals when the doorbell rang. It was a civilized gong, but loud enough to be heard throughout the house. Henri replaced his stick on the platter and placed that on the kitchen counter. *Who could that be?*

When he opened his front door, a young woman greeted him. She held keys in her right hand and wore a bright dress with red and orange that reached to just above her knees. She had a friendly smile. Behind her on the road sat an old Saab 900 convertible, night black, like her hair, cut to shoulder length.

"Evening," said Henri. He looked at the road to the left and right. No one. "Anything I can do for you, Ma'am?"

"I sure hope so," she said with a clear voice. "I have a flat tire and I don't think I should drive any further." She held up her mobile, an old model Nokia similar to one Henri had owned long ago. "This does not work here."

Henri smiled. Coverage was spotty in these parts, at best. More reason for him not to take out a new subscription, several years ago. "Should I have a look?" he offered.

"Would you?" the woman asked. She folded her hands and blinked her eyes. "That is so very sweet of you, sir."

"Don't call me sir, I'm not that old."

"Only if you'll stop calling me ma'am."

"It's a deal. I'm Henry."

"Pleasure to meet you, I'm Lise."

Henri walked with Lise over the gravel path to the road. The car had two wheels on the road banking and Henri saw immediately what was wrong. "That's on the rim. You can't drive further like that."

"That's what I thought. I tried to call a friend, but, well, no connection here."

"Is there a spare tire in the trunk?" Henri asked. He tried the lock and opened the trunk. Beneath the cover was a hole. "I guess not."

"Uh, yeah, it was flat too, so I left it at home."

Henri shook his head. "Too bad, and all I have are spare tires for my classic Mustang. They'll never fit this car."

"Could I use your land line?"

"Sure, come on inside." Henri showed her the telephone, an imitation Bakelite model with a rotary disk. Lise looked at the machine, surprise on her face. Henri grinned. "I'm not that old, but you must be quite young if you don't remember the rotary disk."

Lise looked at him. "Old enough, really. We just never had a phone where I lived. My first telephone was a mobile." She picked up the horn, tried the disk and dialed the first number. "Hello? Yes, Lise here. I was on my way to the restaurant, but I'm in a small village now with a flat tire. No, no spare tire either. Can you pick me up?" She was quiet while she listened to the voice on the other end. "Yeah, I understand. When can you?" Silence again. "Fine, I'll stay with the car until then." She replaced the horn.

"Problem?" Henri asked.

Lise nodded. "He's still at work, and it's rather far away. So it will take a few hours until he gets here." She sighed and raised her hands in defeat. "Thanks for your time, Henri."

She was almost at the front door when Henri said, "If you're hungry, barbecue's on."

Lise turned and looked him in the eyes. She blinked her eyes a few times and Henri noticed her long black lashes against her pale cheeks.

"Lovely, Henri, I'm starving really." She smiled and then remained silent, like Henri.

A painting on the wall next to the door shifted slightly, ruining the moment. Henri replaced it. "Come on," he said and took her to the kitchen and from there to the porch. He placed an extra chair at the table and an extra plate and cutlery. "Wine?" he asked and showed her the bottle.

"Yes, please," said Lise. She smelled the wine and said, "This is good wine, Henri. I'll bet it's from an expensive year."

"Wasn't very expensive when I bought it. And yes, it was a perfect year for wine." He placed a half dozen satay sticks on the grating and the chicken sizzled merrily. Besides the salad, he served baguette with brie and camembert.

"You have a nice place, Henri," Lise said.

"Thanks, Lise. The house is wonderful and the view is magnificent."

"You live alone, don't you? You're not married?"

"I'm not," Henri said. "She walked out fifteen years ago."

"Don't you get lonely?"

A large spark sprung from the barbecue, nearly reaching Lise. She jumped.

"Are you ok?"

"Yes, fine."

"Well, ok." Henri turned the sticks. "They're going well, nearly done."

"If you think I talk too much, do let me know," Lise said, an innocent look on her face.

"It's alright. Really, I don't have much time to get lonely. I work a lot and when I'm home I work on maintaining and improving the house. Sometimes I work on the Mustang." He put some brie cheese on a piece of bread and took a large bite.

"I just noticed a lack of feminine accessories about the house," Lise said.

The kitchen door blew open and a chill wind came around the corner of the house. Henri got up and fastened a hook on the door. He swallowed his bread. "You got that right." He took the sticks and loaded up her plate until she indicated she had enough.

"Hmm, this is good," Lise said, between two bites of chicken.

"Thank you. My own recipe."

"Yes, well, without a wife to cook for you it's necessary you learn it yourself, I guess."

Henri smiled and shook his head. "I always cooked, even when my wife still lived here."

They enjoyed their meal, talked and drank all the wine and a second bottle.

"Can I make another call?" Lise said. She looked at her watch. "Ten already. What's taking him?"

"That late already?" Henri asked. Time had flown by, and the darkness outside was complete.

"Great company, Henri," Lise said. She got up and walked inside. Henri heard her talking. During the phone call, he noticed the change in her voice and the panicky tones. He followed her inside, just in time to see her replace the horn.

"Something the matter?"

"No. Yes." She breathed deeply. "My friend won't make it tonight. Tomorrow morning. Maybe."

Henri frowned. "What guy would leave his girl stranded in the dark somewhere?"

Lisa smiled. "He's not that kind of friend, Henri. I have no 'friend' in that sense."

"Aha, I apologize," Henri said. "So now what?"

Lise bit her lower lip. "I don't know. Is there a hotel nearby? If I call a cab..." She yawned.

Henri shook his head. "The nearest hotel is twenty miles. And cabs rather not come all the way down here. Too far away from the popular rides. Unless you're willing to pay a small fortune, of course. And it seems to me you're already tired."

"Is there an alternative?" Lise asked.

"I have a spare bedroom," Henri said. "It has all the amenities and its own bathroom."

Lise looked at him for some time. She was obviously suspicious. "Is there a lock on the door?"

"Ye of little faith," Henri said. "However, yes, there is a proper lock on the door."

There was a loud cracking noise in the living room.

"What was that?" Lise asked.

Henri shrugged. "The fire place most likely. The wood works. Nearly everything here is wood. Hot weather, cold weather, day, night, everything always works in this house."

"Aha, ok, I get it." She yawned and blinked her eyes from fatigue and perhaps a little wine. "Alright, Henri, I will take you up on your offer."

Henri smiled benevolently. "Come, I'll show you your room." He led her up the stairs. The thick, red carpet muffled their footsteps, but the steps creaked ominously. In the spare bedroom, he laid out sheets and blankets for Lise and showed her the bathroom. "Make yourself at home. And good night. I'm turning in, myself. Just clean up downstairs and I'm off to bed."

"Good night, Henri. And thanks."

Fifteen minutes later the last of the lights in the house blinked off.

Well after midnight, a Range Rover came rolling down the gentle slope from the center of the village with its engine and its lights off. Close to the Saab 900, the car came to a stop.

Four men got out. The driver lit a cigarette and inhaled deeply a couple of times, before he threw it on the ground and put it out. From the trunk, they took crowbars and baseball bats. They walked across the lawn until they were close to the front door.

With a few short, harshly crunching steps across the gravel of the driveway, they were at the front door. The door opened silently for them.

"Ssht," came a voice, and a flash light that switched on showed Lise's face. "Henri's asleep."

"Of course," the driver said with a broad grin that revealed a broken front tooth. "You worked your magic again. Time for an extra night cap and then we empty the place."

Lise walked ahead of the four through the living room toward the stairs of which the steps seemed to creak louder in the dark than before. At Henri's bedroom, she stopped and pointed at the door. Very carefully, the driver pushed the door handle and the door opened slowly.

The four men slid into the bedroom where Henri Dunant was lying on his bed. He snored softly. The men stood on either side in the faint light of Lise's flashlight. The driver gave the signal the first man smacked his bat on Henri's unprotected belly, hard enough to cause him to immediately sit upright in shock, but not hard enough to cause any real damage. The light in his eyes blinded him and the second bat hit his forehead, opening a deep gash from which blood ran across his face and into his eyes.

"What's happening?" Henry mewled.

His answer arrived via a few more smacks with baseball bats. The arm he tried to keep raised to ward of the blows broke with a sickening crack.

"Your money and valuables, Henri. Tell us where they are!" The driver's voice was rough. "Where is the safe?"

Henri cried, "Next to the fire place, behind the painting. Take everything, just leave me alone!" He took the key hanging from a chain around his neck with his good arm and held it up.

"Leave him," the driver said. He grabbed the key with chain and all and ripped it from Henri's neck. "He ain't going anywhere."

"Sleep tight, Henri," Lise said and switched off the flashlight. The robbers walked down in the dark with only some moonlight that fell through the windows. There they switched on the lights, took the painting off the wall and located the safe.

Meanwhile Henri had crawled out of bed. With a sheet, he wiped blood from his face and eyes so he could see again. Everything hurt, his arm was useless and he felt ribs moving oddly and quite painfully in his rib cage. "Dirty bastards," he whispered. He crawled out of his room. Light from below illuminated the hallway and through the lattice work of the railing he saw the four men and Lise open his safe and take out a stack of cash, his collection of gold coins and the jewelry that had belonged to his mother.

He leaned his throbbing head against the latticework and felt drops of blood slide across his cheeks. He knew they would stain the carpet and the oak floor downstairs, but at that moment, he couldn't care. The only thoughts in his mind were revenge and the betrayal of his trust. He believed Lise, invited her into his home, but in the end she was just a thief.

A loud cracking boomed through the living room. Henri did not know if it was his imagination or a result of the smack to his head, but the house seemed to shake on its foundations. Through his misty eyes, he saw the driver hunch and grab the leg. A foot long oak splinter protruded from his thigh. Pandemonium ensued; splinters flew through the room and hit the men indiscriminately. Thorns stretched up from the floor, digging through shoe soles and feet, pinning the men to the floor. Lise started to scream.

Henri watched with open eyes; saw the men struggle, bleeding profusely from dozens of small wounds, wooden stakes like tentacles shooting from floor and walls, wrapping around arms, legs and heads of the people downstairs. They started to pull until, one by one, the robbers were dismembered with the sickening sound of wet flesh tearing.

Lise tried to escape. She made it to the front door but as soon as she set one foot outside, it slammed shut so hard that one of her legs remained trapped inside. Henri watched openmouthed. Outside was a shriek of fear, followed by such terrifying howls of terror that he tried to cover his ears.

Then it was quiet. Downstairs the floor started to churn and move and blood, bones and flesh slowly dissipated into the wood, until the floor was empty again and all traces of the robbers were gone. Only some loose cash and a few coins remained.

"House," Henri whispered, "what have you done?" He started to cry with relief and pain, but also with the tension that now left his body. As soon as he regained some strength, he called the police.

Six weeks later the investigations concluded and Henri no longer needed to explain the cars found before his house. They belonged to a gang suspected of robbing and even killing lonely residents in the countryside.

The police suspected something irregular about Henri Dunant's story of a robbery attempt in his own home, but had managed to scare away his assailants. Pieces of the story were missing, but without bodies or actual traces inside the house, there was no case.

Henri's arm healed fast. His ribs were mostly just bruised, with some minor fractions; painful, but definitely temporary.

The day the case formally closed, he pulled the door of the house closed and put the now empty gasoline jerry can on the gravel of the driveway. His suitcases were already in the trunk of his Mustang, parked on the road banking.

A thin stream of gasoline flowed underneath the door and the scent of permeated the air. Henri took a Zippo from his pocket, lit it and threw it onto the fluid that caught fire immediately. The fire moved inside and Henri could almost imagine the flames traversing all the way upstairs along the trail he had made through the house and on all the flammables.

It was time for a new start, away from this nightmare.

He turned and walked along the driveway.

Henri...

He turned back. Smoke billowed from the wood, and in the white grey vapor, he thought he saw the shape of Melanie, her lips moving in slow motion.

Henri, what are you doing?

Henri breathed deep. "It's over. I'm through with all this."

I was there for you, always. I saved your life. I had hoped you loved me.

Henri laughed without mirth. "Until a few weeks ago you were there for me, but I have seen you. I know what you did that night."

I saved your life.

"No. You tortured those people, ripped at them like a rabid dog. I don't know you anymore. And rabid dogs need to be put down."

Henri? Doubt and despair laced the voice and he was nearly tempted to call the fire department. *I shall never leave you!*

He got into his Mustang and drove away from the burning house, a bright new future ahead, alone, or perhaps with a new love, one that he would be there for always.

He switched on the radio and listened to golden oldies. In his rear view mirror, he saw the smoke rise ever higher. A commercial interrupted the music.

Henri wanted to press the button for another music channel, but the car seemed to hit a bump in the road, causing the channel to jump. Henri looked in the mirror again, at the rising smoke and then shrugged. He slowly caressed the antelope leather of the steering wheel, lovingly.

Sheldon Woodbury

The Holy Ghost

At what point does pain become so unbearable that a single word is no longer capable of fully describing the agony's manifestations? He had lay splayed out in the sulfurous soot and ash for so long he'd lost all sense of time. Had he been here for years, decades, centuries, eons, or for an unfathomable period that was much closer to the haunting bleakness of eternity?

He no longer knew.

It was as if everything had been burned out of him long ago, his earthly memory, his lost humanity, and most of all, every last shred of his soul. The last was the greatest contributor to his unending horror, leaving a gaping emptiness inside him. For some unknown expanse of time, he'd been a whimpering heap in the horrible and wretched pits of hell, with no sensation except for the pain that was so much more than just pain. He was an ash-covered carcass of scorched flesh in this unholy place indescribable with any amount of earthly words. Other scorched bodies were scattered around him, some still flailing with anger and rage, but most were as crusted and limp as he, underworld road kill in a no man's land were everything was damned.

Then, without warning, a softness came, a startling surprise; he felt a strange force creep in beneath him. After all you've felt is thundering pain and agony for millennia without any chance of release or escape, it was even more shocking because it was *new*. Even more surprising was what happened in the eerie moments that followed. The unseen force lifted his charred body off the soot and ash and into the burning air. The sunken black orbs of his lifeless eyes slowly cracked open, because now there was something new to see. It was, in all its infernal glory, the underworld insanity of hell.

From his limited vantage point on the ground below, he had only guessed at what he was now seeing for the very first time. He'd heard the legion of wails and whimpers echoing around him, felt the unbearable sizzle of the fiendish heat, and been constantly rattled by the bellowing roar of some monstrous god.

Now he saw it all without having to conjure it up in his tattered mind. It was madness indeed, on a scale that was both surreal and demented at the same time. His body was still rising up through the burning haze like a creepy cadaver made out of char and ash, and the landscape of hell became fully visible in the yawning gloom below. There were colossal mountains of craggy white bones spewing volcanic gushes of crackling fire, gargantuan fissures and craters crammed to the top with screeching demons, and every other kind of torturous excess imaginable, an underworld grotesquerie of wickedness. He saw the ground wasn't soil at all, but the grime and decay of decomposed flesh, an infinite wasteland of misery and madness.

Now, in the midst of it all, he saw the towering figure of the Dark Lord, looming scarily in the smoky distance. He was even more monstrous and shocking than he'd imagined from his alienated prison on the ground, a freakish apparition amassing fear and terror starkly visible in one abominable shape. He was stomping through the burning landscape on gargantuan cloven hooves like a demented child eager to unleash as much havoc and destruction as possible.

A new notion seized him, as he continued to float up through the fiery haze. Was it possible he was leaving all this behind? The thought gave him a sensation that was so strange and new he didn't know what it was. He then realized it was a forgotten treasure from another time, the ability to feel a glimmer of hope. The bizarre new feeling struggled to take hold inside of him, a desperate wish that his relentless misery abate in some small way.

He felt his scorched flesh begin to crumble away like burnt crust, tumbling and swirling back down through the fire and smoke to hell below. It was as if his corporal shell was being discarded so something completely different could take its place. The fiery landscape below was now murky and red, like sputtering fireworks fading away in the underworld gloom.

On and on he still rose, higher and higher, passing through gargantuan layers of rock and earth and molten ooze, because now his outer form was completely gone, and just his flickering spirit was left. He also felt as if he was passing through the secret barriers of time itself. Faint memories from his past began to take shape in his ghostly consciousness. He had no way of knowing how long the strange journey took, but it didn't matter because it was carrying him away from the unbearable miseries of hell.

He shimmered up through a last thick barrier of earth and rock into a place his gathering memories instantly recognized; the earthly realm where he'd once lived his human life. He saw a listless grey sky hanging overhead and a blurry sun only faintly visible. After the roaring red horrors of hell, it seemed bland and drab. Skeletal birds flapped and cawed overhead. His wraithlike attention turned to a howling mob trudging down a long dirt road, fifty strong, soldiers making up the greatest part; soldiers dressed in ceremonial attire. They marched as one, a screaming and vengeful throng, stomping upon the earth with pounding boots. They stopped, their breaths hoarse and ragged, unexpectedly parting to reveal a stumbling figure clutched among them.

His ghostly form shivered at the sight that was now before him in the blurry afternoon haze. He'd witnessed the horrors of hell and he saw right away this was a horror of similar depravity. The lean figure was naked and bruised, his trembling body covered with his crimson blood, a crown of thorns shoved upon his hanging head with obvious viciousness, causing more blood to stream down his long brown hair and over the panting hollows of his face. He saw a brutish man with a thick coarse beard standing nearby, a long leather whip hanging at his waist, had tiny shards of iron and bone tied to the ends, and he knew that's where the tortured figure's flayed flesh had gotten his merciless beating.

He also knew he was only a haunting spirit now, but his senses were also sharper somehow, as if the discarding of his charred flesh had made his ghostly essence even stronger and more preternatural. He realized with absolute certainty that the brutish man with the whip was the person he once was back on this earthly realm. His name was Tiberius, a Roman Centurion. A distant memory abruptly took form in the clearest way possible, and he shuddered at the part he knew he was going to play in the sickening cruelty ahead. His spectral shape hovered in the darkening air like a flickering light, an invisible witness to the sadistic spectacle unfolding below. The tortured figure with the ragged flesh was dragged to a craggy hill, along with two others, sniveling thieves who the howling mob of soldiers and others had decided would share his fate. Three giant crosses nailed out of rotted wood rose up from the barren ground like stakes stabbed into the earth, hanging crookedly in the darkening mist. The sight of the sun was completely gone, banished behind rumbling clouds charged in as if summoned from the heavens above. The mob roared like a single animal, spitting and hurled taunts at the three beaten men, coating their bloody welts and slashes with the wetness of their snarling venom. Each of the three heaved to a cross, and the man called Jesus pushed against the one in the middle.

His ethereal senses shuddered again when he saw his earthly form stride up to the middle cross, the burning fire of hatred in his eyes. He gripped a crude iron mallet in his hand. The man called Jesus was hoisted upward like a sack of flesh; his trembling arms stretched out against the rotted slabs of wood by two other soldiers, his naked legs left dangling above the ground.

It all became clear as he watched in horror as his brutish earthly form pounded rusted nails into the sacred flesh of the man he now knew was the son of God. Bones cracked and more blood spurted as the unholy crucifixion was inflicted on the hanging man. It was an act of insanity and brutality, vengeance and depravity, all done as a drenching rain began to fall, washing over the three men, sending their flowing blood swirling away.

Yes, it was all very clear.

In hell, there were always more devious ways to ratchet up the pain, to make it even more unbearable than just a single word was able to describe. For him, the tortures of hell had become an endless monotony, and that wouldn't do. So he'd returned to earth as a ghost to remind him of his despicable sins.

He was already feeling the invisible tug of the underworld force summoning him back so he could experience its tortures with the fresh memory of why he was there. In hell, the crushing agony of shame and regret must surely always be an integral part of the blasphemous mix.

Now he felt something new again; another spectral presence had precipitously arrived that was as ethereal as he was; but glorious and grander, not of this world, and quickly enveloped his shimmering form with a feeling so radically different from what he felt in hell, it overpowered even the numbing wretchedness of his missing soul.

It happened in an instant, as his return decent was already underway. He had one last fleeting glance at the dead body on the cross, and a final look at the part he'd played in the evil slaughter. His indistinct spirit passed through the barren ground, then back down through the underground slabs of earth and rock and molten ooze, until he once again felt the fiendish fires of hell crackling below him. His crusty outer shell drifted in like floating black embers and assembled into a corporal form again.

The pain of hell came back too and now extremer than before, amplified a brutal new level by the memory trapped inside him of what he'd done. It hadn't just been a crime of personal sin, but something far worse. He'd been the perpetrator of the most horrific crime it was possible to commit.

He'd killed the son of God.

He passed back down through the burning air and churning smoke, as the demons howled and he heard the bellowing roar of the Dark Lord. The strange force settled him back down on the grime and decay of decomposed flesh, and, once again, misery enveloped his howling body like a funeral shroud.

He also felt another sensation, one he knew put there by the celestial ghost that had embraced him before. The sensation was something completely new in the unforgiving depths of despair and fire of hell. That's why the Dark Lord bellowed ever more lurid, because he sensed it too. He glared into the gloom with his reverberating eyes, suffering agony that was much more than just agony, but loss, because he knew the name of this underworld infiltrator. The man who had killed the son of God felt his torturous pain begin to slip away, because the holy treasure hidden deep inside revealed his soul, and forgiveness was his. Upward he turned.

Allen Griffin

Nocturne

Simon Duchamp walked across the stage and sat down in front of the piano. He looked to Catherine's seat in the front row, empty now save for a bouquet of roses and a silver-framed wedding picture. The applause died down and a few people coughed and cleared their throats. Simon waited for complete silence and then he placed his fingers on the keys.

He closed his eyes and his fingers began to slowly dance on the keyboard. A melody, soft and full of melancholy, wove around middle C. Left-hand chords fell like footfalls on dead leaves, making him imagine the woods behind the house, a walk in late autumn.

He walked with Anne Charles, a writer for Scherzo magazine. She should've been asking about his upcoming European tour, as that was her assignment. However, she already knew all about the dates, where he was performing, which pieces he prepared and so on. They spoke often; hushed late-night conversations on his cell phone or working lunches with nothing accomplished.

Simon stopped occasionally to clear limbs from the trail or to kick at a worm-rotted stump. The house and property showed signs of neglect and when he was home, he tried to put forth an effort to clean things up.

"I should really be home more," he commented. Anne looked at him sideways as they walked. He realized she might not know what he meant, should he work on the house or spend more time with Catherine. If she asked him what he meant, he wouldn't know how to answer, but instead she just said, "You're busy man. I'm sure you do what you can."

"You have a beautiful home," she added, stopping to look around, to look back at the house. "The two of you are very lucky."

The conversation snaked back around to music and they discussed John Cage at length. He pointed out that every moment of existence contained beautiful music, one just needed to stop and listen. Anne touched Simon's shoulder, causing him to stop and turn around. She held his left hand between both of her own and massaged his ring finger. They listened to the wind blow through the trees. The dead leaves rattled in the gust and a few stragglers floated down to the ground.

The first movement ended with a series of subdued cadences, the melody slowly pitching higher on the keyboard. The notes never resolved. Rather, they hung in the air like something left unspoken.

The audience remained completely quiet. Simon reveled in the silence; considered for a moment not even starting the second section. He wondered if any music could compare to the beauty of silence. What music did the dead hear? Maybe this song should be left to whither on the vine un-played. When the pause became uncomfortable, Simon began to play the second movement. The tempo picked up just a little, a slow, sad waltz for troubled lovers. Catherine loved the second section, the only part of the piece she'd heard, and she asked him to play it often. Usually this came after returning home from some droll party whose only attraction proved to be abundant Merlot, and she started to display signs of wistful melancholy, a symptom she experienced when the fine wine consumed began its lazy departure.

As the music progressed, the bass notes became more insistent and the piano resonated with the rhythm. The sound contained a powerful physicality, like a body dancing around the frame of the instrument. Simon completed a series of runs, the left hand climbing until the right took over and back again. He surged with confidence, aware of his own virtuosity. Inside, the hammers struck the strings in rolling waves. Simon manipulated the damper to keep the whole thing from sliding into cacophony. He imagined the mutes to be cold fingers grasping the steel strings.

The piece surged toward something just out of reach, the tempo and momentum continuing to build, confrontation expressed musically.

Simon woke early and made his way downstairs, but when he saw Catherine, he could tell she had risen much earlier. Wrapped in an oversized sweater, she stared out the bay window in the kitchen and she didn't look up when he entered. Her black hair fell in unruly curls and looked as if she hadn't washed it in days.

Simon saw the cigarette butts in the ashtrays throughout the house; she didn't even make the effort to throw them out. They weren't her brand and Simon didn't smoke. He knew if he asked, she would claim the gas station ran out of her regular brand and he knew he wouldn't believe her. He also saw the indentations in the wall, sometimes with flecks of red-brown outlining the shapes. Scabbed tissue lay exposed upon Catherine's knuckles and dark bags circled her eyes. Whatever she did while he toured failed to relieve the pain built up inside her.

He slid into the bench next to her and put his arm around her shoulders. "I love you," he whispered. She didn't say anything but rested her head on him and continued to stare into the woods.

Simon didn't stop between the second and third movements. Momentum thrust him onward, the two sections inseparable in their agitation. His left hand crashed out a series of dissonant chords. He thought of gunshots, knowing there had only been one.

The right hand picked up a distorted and tangled variation of the melody from the first movement. The flat-fives sounded like empty suitcases on the bed and the sharp-nines—pleas that true love could overcome both of their infidelities.

Catherine pulled drawers from the dresser and dumped the clothes into the suitcases. She didn't bother to separate his from hers. The act stood symbolic, dissolution.

The pulse of the music faltered, stuttered around the beat.

"Liar!" she yelled, condemning him. He tried to grasp her, place his hands around her shoulders but she pushed him away. On his third attempt, she turned and struck him across the face. His jaw ached and his cheek burned.

Dissonant chords, played by both hands, crashed all around them.

Simon stomped into the bathroom, slamming the door behind him. He turned the tap on full force, the water spilling into the sink violently as the right hand peppered discord, high notes falling like a hard rain.

When Simon emerged, his anger at least somewhat under control, the bedroom sat empty. He slumped down in a chair and looked at the stuff, their stuff, strewn about the bedroom as if a tornado had crashed into the house. His eyes came to rest on the nightstand's open drawer on his side of the bed. He kept his pistol in that drawer, and when he jumped up and looked, it was no longer there.

He would've ran if there was time, time to run to the woods, time to find her and beg her not to.

The final chord of the third movement crashed in a cadence like a gunshot, leaving an infinite silence in its wake.

The auditorium sat empty save the flowers and the wedding picture in Catherine's seat. Simon relished the solitude; he wanted to be alone with the music. He didn't have to explain it, or share it with anyone else; just he and the music existed.

The fourth movement began with a march, a steady step to be maintained throughout the rest of the piece. The right hand joined the left in a call and response. The left kept the rhythm while the right plucked clusters of notes from the air, together forming a spectral harmony.

The march didn't evoke a mood of glory; rather, it sounded like a funerary procession, or soldiers returning home from a lost war. Moreover, that was the truth of the matter. Simon glanced up at Catherine's seat and felt her presence, not in the picture or the flowers but haunting the whole concert hall.

A pair of eyes emerged just above the sheet music in front of him, staring directly at him. The music shielded him from fear. Strings of black hair draped themselves across the pages, notes obscured by flecks of dry blood. Leaves stuck to her head in great clumps.

Simon continued to play when Catherine swiped the sheet music to the floor. He knew the tune by heart, hearing it in his head ever since he found her in the woods, maybe even since they met.

Catherine squatted on the front of the piano, looming over the keyboard. A dry leaf wrestled free from her dirty hair and floated down to Simon's lap. Her skin was a blue-grey, and gun smoke floated out of her mouth like the remnants of some long extinguished cigarette. Simon realized she had eaten his sins and they'd blown out the back of her skull.

She cocked her head to one side as if to listen to the chord progression. He played infinite variations on an inevitable end. The fourth movement marched onward toward nothingness. Simon only wanted to rebalance the scales. He wanted his blood to soak into the curtain as it lowered. His body should hang from the rafters.

But this was not what she chose. Catherine took his hands into hers and gently pulled him up from the bench. The piano continued to play as she brought him toward her. Their lips met and she filled his lungs with her smoke. He climbed over the keyboard, and they sunk down on a bed of steel strings. In each other's arms, the lid pulled shut like a coffin and they lay together in the darkness, listening to the endless sound of the music; infinite variations marching forever into the endless night.

Ken L. Jones

Suicide Hill

Slashed to ribbons memories
In hollows where the cadavers scream
Where something touches me
With a claw that can freeze
That transcends even the withered sky
Whose raging rain is phantom filled
And was long ago mummified
But now it somehow slithers and crawls even still
Toward a long haired unkempt cemetery
Where waits for me six feet under
Yet can never peacefully sleep
She who was supposed to be my bride
But who learned when poison was stealthily plied
That some men are not to be by marriage yoked
But when I told her she thought that was a joke
And thought the baby in her womb
Would translate into wedded bliss for her ere soon
But when the nemesis of all rats was sequestered in her plate
She crossed into the great unknown without a mate
And fool oh such a fool was I
That I thought that would be the end of it when she died
But death knows not what to do with such as she
And so she has since then not given me even a moment's peace
And is at my elbow both day and night
Reminding me that a promise should never be a lie
And though she is now but decomposition showing bone
She awaits our honeymoon with fervor still
Six feet under on Suicide Hill.

Rik Raven

Semicentennial Mystery

Whenever I float over Daleford, I remember my dreams. The wind tears with cold fingers at my naked body beneath my flapping nightgown. Beneath me, I see my house, hidden behind trees and brush, but situated near the mud track close to the edge of the village, a favorite of local young lovers.

As always, these dreams push me toward the center of town; to the old Blasius Church, imprinting the impression of a tired old warrior with the graves of his victims scattered around him. It's cold, deserted and dark. A spooky kind of darkness surrounds the bell tower, as if the ancient bronze chimes desire to scare off occasional visitors with their reverberating song.

I'm not easily frightened. This is a dream, one that might grant me insight into the secrets of Daleford, one that may even set me on track to discover the Beguine killer.

Behind the church, in one of the furthest corners, I notice movement. I float in that direction, tense, but the chimes start to move and their reverberating bronze disturbs my dream.

The red characters on my alarm clock show six A.M.

In the dark of my bedroom, I hear the clanging of the bells, far away, but as always, when one strains to hear something it disappears.

I switch on the light and rub sleep from my eyes. A quick shower and then the same jeans and dark blue sweater I wore yesterday, but today I add a spunky bowler hat, which under I tuck my hair.

Before I leave for work, I decide to visit the Blasius Church. I discovered a connection for the two Beguine murders that occurred last week—that church. The documents proving it were on my nightstand: the Daleford Gazette of July 1965 and the Daleford Herald of 1915 and 1865.

By day, I'm a librarian in the next village over, Valmont, a somewhat larger village still with its original documents.

Moreover, it boasted an extensive archive of all publications of the past five hundred years, every since its founding.

That first murder, last week Wednesday, made the headlines; an old woman, in the Beguinage church alley, hanging upside down, suspended from a streetlight, her skin largely flayed off by a kind of serrated whip. Reporters from the big city descended on Daleford in large numbers to air this sensational news.

An attempt to keep quiet the next murder, on a Wednesday evening, failed but the local gossip quickly found out that the Beguinage's concierge lay eviscerated in his office.

I dreamed about these exact two places, as if I actually visited them. Therefore, when I heard what happened, I started to rummage through the archives. I was almost certain I had once read something about murders in the Beguinage.

The 1965 gazette showed me what I needed to know. Three murders, close together: a woman, hung and flayed, a man, chopped to pieces and a woman, strangled on a stone bench in the cemetery of the Blasius Church. The murderer escaped discovery and quiet returned for the next fifty years.

I redoubled my search and again found the exact same murderous methods occurred fifty years earlier. Three murders, and again, perfectly replicated, fifty years before that; somehow, I knew this pattern would repeat all the way back to the founding of Daleford in the year 1200.

Of course, I went to the police with my theory, after all, as the third murder was yet to occur and thusly avoided, but they laughed at me. Therefore, I decided to find and confront this murderer myself. I have read many books on self-defense, and with my lucid, near clairvoyant dreams, things cannot go wrong. The murders must end.

The chill morning air enhances my crisp footsteps on the gravel path leading up to the Blasius Church. Centuries-old oaks and voluptuous chestnut created a green wall surrounding the ancient building. The square tower and the gothic nave clearly hailed from different times.

The ancient graves along the path show the history of the place, especially the note- worthies important to Daleford, or those who donated enough money to purchase a spot near the Lord's house. I walk around the church to the rear, to the dark corner close to the forest's edge. That's where I saw the movement in my dreams.

A worn gravestone stands there, surrounded by a low, rusted, cast-iron fence. The characters are nearly unreadable, but when I squint and use my flashlight, I can just make out the words "John Moonen," date of birth unknown, died 1465—and that date caused my heart to jump and turn ice cold. I noticed the stone, once carved deeply with symbols, were not Christian symbols. I wrote the name in my notebook and copied a few of the symbols

On my way to the library I try to remember old local proverbs and children's rhymes, hoping some kind of old wisdom is hidden in their words that might apply to this situation, but I come up with nothing.

The earliest books in the library actually have a reference to a John Moonen, even an illustration of the man in a book from 1465, about the last of the witch trials that ran rampant in these parts during the late middle ages. On it, Moonen is depicted with horns and a forked tongue. Two women and a man oppose him; in the background, the old part of the Beguinage is visible.

The symbols are easier to find. They're heathen symbols, often used in the Walpurgis Night. *To keep evil out*, I remember, *or inside, or underground, in the soil.*

More old books give testimony of the fifty-year event and the terrible murders that occur. There are always two in the Beguinage, a nun, a man, and one near the Blasius Church, the third, usually a young woman. This particular murder has not taken place yet, this time around.

I begin to suspect, or actually, I'm nearly certain what my role will be. It's a leading part in a deeply sad tragedy performed for the last five hundred years. Fortunately, I have the wisdom of all those years around me, and a connection to the largest library ever built, the Internet. Like any drama, this too must finally end.

Determined I examine all the options and write the documents and instructions I think will be required.

That night I float over Daleford again. I feel the cool night air flowing around me, maybe even through me. I know this is a dream, just not any dream.

The Beguinage stood shrouded in eerie light. I descend and I can see the semi- transparent bodies of the recently murdered old woman and the concierge. The expressions on their faces display deep, primal fear.

Footsteps glisten, leading in the direction of the Blasius Church. I follow them, knowing they will lead me to the killer, to confront him face to face, as I have foreseen.

This time my footsteps on the gravel produce no sound. The cemetery is empty and if you expect "ghosts" or "spirits," then disappointment will fill you. Hallowed ground is the most effective way to quiet restless spirits looking to move on.

No such place for John Moonen, who was tried for witchery and dealing with the Devil and found guilty on all charges, and as punishment drowned in the water of Daleford's Pit; his body was buried in the only corner of the cemetery not hallowed.

I sit upon the ancient bench and sense his presence, his cold fingers sliding forward across my neck.

His dark whisper sounds behind me. "You came, Seer."

I smile and say, "I forgive you, John Moonen."

"That won't help," he says and I smell the stench of the grave and sulfur oozing from him. "Vengeance is mine." His fingers close around my neck and he squeezes.

While my breath halts and my brain slowly dies, I smile again, knowing that my body will rest in the newly hallowed ground in the place where an ancient grave will be removed, the stones and their symbols broken and the remainder of the bones pulverized, spread to the winds, as described in the documents I wrote.

The next morning the police find my strangled corpse on the bench near the Blasius Church, exactly as I foresaw. I have a mysterious smile on my face, a clear last will and testament, and a set of instructions in my pocket.

Considered mad, my instructions ignored, I rest quietly, gathering strength, for in fifty years I must again contest the actions of the demon Moonen. For eternity, I suppose.

Flo Stanton

She Waits

Maggie thought of her heart as a dead piece of meat, a lifeless mass of ugly gray tissue beating just enough to keep the dull weight of her body going, centered in her chest where she knew her heart should be, glowing pinkish for a moment when she worked in the garden or on those rare occasions when Ed allowed her to visit the grandchildren; but not enough to make a difference.

Maggie didn't believe in the afterlife, and not much in the here-life, either. She considered the advantages of being dead—no more trips up and down the stairs, no more picking up a moat of beer cans and taking them to the recycling station for her spending money. It didn't seem like such a bad thing, not as bad as everyone made out.

She couldn't see the fear in it, anyway, and voiced it once to the reverend, a red-faced young know-nothing. That was okay. He wore Old Spice like her dad did, and greeted her by name every Sunday. She liked to watch his smooth shaven jowl fold over his collar as he preached and waited for the day his head would explode.

It was her liver, not her heart. She went to the doctor on Thursday, was admitted to Indiana Mercy by Monday, cut open and sown right back up on Tuesday. Six weeks, they said. She was so looking forward to going; the docs thought she'd found religion.

Ed showed an uncommon amount of tenderness in her last days. Maggie knew death scared him.

She could take a nap anytime now. She could work in the garden whenever she liked, permitted to visit the grandchildren undisturbed by Ed's presence. It was wonderful, and it was over too soon.

Because Ed married again, to a widow that would outlive him by many years. She found a dark corner and waited there, and she waits there still. She keeps to the shadows, and every once in a while a giggle escapes. Her grip is firm, her mind made up. She grips the handle of the garden spade, and waits.

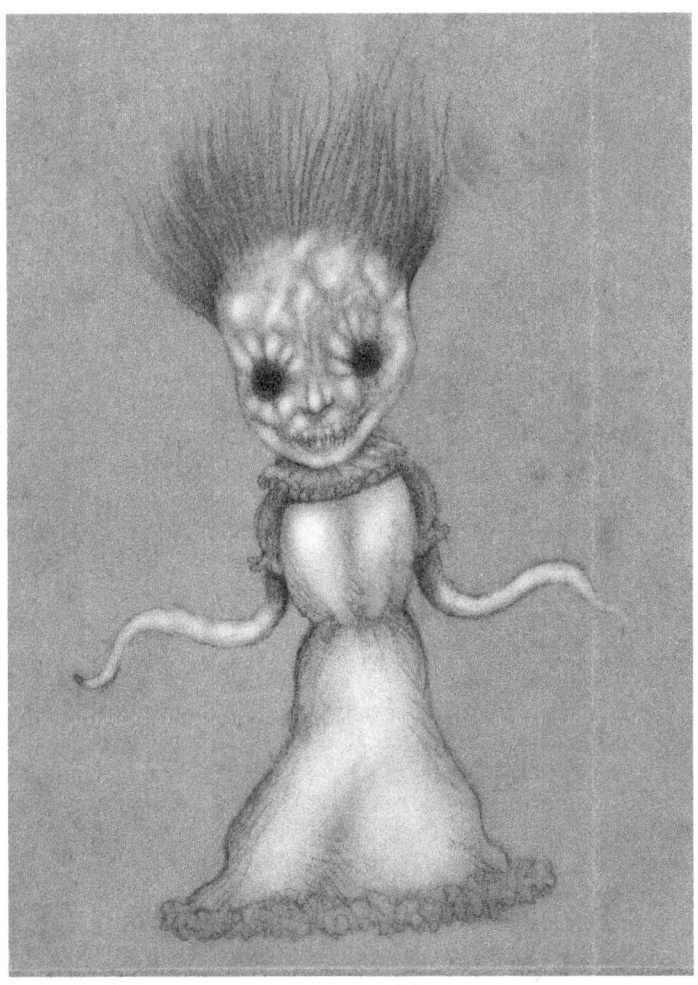

Kenneth Whitfield

The Neighborhood

The neighborhood is off the main highway, but people use it as a cut-through to avoid traffic during rush hours. They speed through in the mornings, half-asleep, spilling coffee as they bounce over speed bumps, or they hurry through in the evenings, tired from work, radio blasting, just wanting to get home. Either way, they never seem to notice the kids.

Shelly stands on the curb in the rain, facing traffic, letting passing cars splash her with water from the gutter. Another young girl, Lynda, walks out of a little patch of woods and stands under an umbrella a few feet behind her, nervously twirling the umbrella, watching.

Shelly has her eyes closed, leaning forward with a hint of a smile on her face as a car flashes by, the driver fussing with the radio, swerving toward the girls. He corrects at the last second, veering back from the gutter, spraying them both with a rooster tail of water. Lynda hides behind her umbrella and avoids most of it while Shelly's threadbare jeans and too large 'Hello Kitty' t-shirt are drenched.

Lynda easies up beside Shelly and offers to share her umbrella. Shelly looks at her, water dripping, and laughs a good laugh, not mean-spirited like Lynda gets from the other neighborhood kids.

"I know it's silly, but Mom made me bring it," Lynda says, folding the umbrella and letting the rain dampen her. They smile at each other a moment, then Lynda introduces herself.

"My name's Lynda. I saw you guys moving in."

Shelly looks at her a little longer, until Lynda drops her gaze, and then spoke softly. "Yeah, we ain't been here long."

The rain begins to taper off. "My name's Shelly." She takes Lynda in, looking from her shoes up to the bow in her curly brown hair, then asks, "How long you been here?"

Lynda shifts her weight from one foot to another, holding tight to the umbrella.

"For a while. We moved here right after," she pauses, swallowing hard, "right after the accident with my brother."

Shelly cocks her head, listening. Lynda fills the silence.

"Dad says to look at it like a new beginning." She stops, remembering the cookouts, the birthday parties, and the good times with her little brother. "But me and Mom, well, sometimes we miss our old neighborhood." She fusses with the umbrella, trying to fasten the little Velcro strip around it.

Shelly gets a faraway look in her eyes, remembering her and her Mama's crummy apartment, sleeping completely under the covers to keep the rats from biting her face, her hands, her feet, and the constant flow of sick and scary looking people; especially all the men, and her mother needing her "medicine" more and more, the fussing and fighting, the shouting and screaming, gunshots and sirens. She looks at Lynda.

"I don't miss our old neighborhood."

Lynda gets the umbrella fastened, but keeps fidgeting with it, not knowing what to say. Shelly looks at it and then tugs at her own t-shirt self-consciously. "So your Mama got you an umbrella?"

Lynda shakes her head. "Not really. It's just one we keep around for when it rains."

Shelly pulls at her t-shirt again. "Mama got me this for my birthday."

Lynda nods. "It's pretty. Is today your birthday?"

"Yeah, Mama made me a cake and everything. She said that turning eleven was a big deal." Shelly has that distant look in her eyes again as she speaks, remembering birthdays that never were.

Lynda brightens.

"I'm eleven too! All the other kids here are older. It's nice to have someone the same age."

She didn't get into how she didn't socialize much with the others. They usually ignored her, except when they got bored and picked on her. She'd seen them smoking cigarettes, or something like cigarettes, and heard them talking about drinking and stealing stuff too.

Shelly smiles, her long blonde hair plastered to her face.

Another car splashes by. Lynda backs a couple steps away from the road.

"Water scares you?" asks Shelly.

Lynda nods. "No, cars, that's how we lost my brother."

Shelly's smile fades. In some way older than her years, she realizes she should say something comforting, that it took a lot of courage for Lynda to approach and talk with her so near the road. She's trying to think of something to say when Lynda asks, "Do you want to come to my house?"

Glancing at her darkened house, hoping her mama is asleep, Shelly nods. They head to Lynda's, the rain slowing, and finally stopping by the time they arrive.

Lynda's parents are at home and happy to meet Shelly. They let them have snacks and turn the family room over to them while they retreat to the back deck. The girls watch *Harry Potter and the Deathly Hallows Part 2* for over an hour, until there is a frantic pounding on the door accompanied by the shrill voice of a woman yelling.

"Shelly! Shelly are you in there?"

Shelly goes tense and drops her popcorn. They both listen as the screeching continues. Lynda's parents come in from the deck and head toward the door, looking in on the girls, questioningly. The girls slowly rise and follow. They peek out from the family room as the door opens.

Standing there is a very skinny, pale woman. She is hunched over, her arms clasped across her stomach tightly. She has an oversized, faded gray sweater on over a soiled and thin sundress that may have been yellow at one time. Battered flip-flops graced her dirty feet. She looks up at Lynda's parents expectantly, moisture in her dark, black ringed eyes.

In a panic stricken staccato she blurts out - "Shelly! Have you seen my little girl, Shelly? I've been to a lot of houses looking and no one has seen her."

Lynda sees Shelly flinch. She can only imagine how it must feel having your mom running from house to house looking for you, especially when your mom was so upset.

They both step out and the lady sees them.

"Shelly! I was so worried! I woke up and you were gone and I needed my medicine and I couldn't find you." She reaches out with both arms toward them, clear mucus running from her nose.

Shelly walks up and stands between Lynda's parents in the doorway. Her head down, clearly embarrassed, she says, "I was just visiting my new friend, Mama."

Her mother looks from her to Lynda, then up at the two adults. Lynda's Dad clears his throat. "We're sorry for the misunderstanding. She's fine. They've been watching a movie. We assumed her parents knew she was here."

Shelly's Mom wipes her nose with the back of her hand. "Well, *I* didn't! I was scared and afraid something bad happened to her! I don't know you people and I don't want her hanging around with strangers."

Lynda's Mom speaks up. "I understand, but we're not really strangers. We're neighbors. Perhaps this isn't the best way to meet, but it would be nice to get to know each other. Lynda and Shelly really seem to hit it off."

The cloudy skies have given way to bright sunshine, but Shelly's Mom is shivering despite the warmth. She hugs herself again.

"We prefer to be left alone. Shelly – come on." She reaches out to her daughter. Shelly steps out and allows herself a brief hug. She pulls back, takes her Mama's shaking hand and looks sadly back at Lynda and her parents. No words will come. They turn and Shelly leads her mama away, her mama leaning down, whispering furiously in her ear.

Lynda and her family watch. Lynda's mom says, "That was odd." Her dad says, "That lady is obviously on something." Lynda just feels sorry for Shelly—and excited because Shelly had called her 'friend'. They close the door slowly.

The next day Lynda is outside early. She tries not to be obvious as she keeps watch on Shelly's house, hoping she'll come out soon. Around noon she does, closing the door softly behind her. She's wearing the same clothes as yesterday and is barefoot. Lynda runs over, shouting "Hey! Shelly!" Shelly looks around, face stern and hisses through clenched teeth, "Be quiet! Mama's asleep!"

Lynda stops abruptly, as if slapped. They walk in silence to the end of the driveway, and then Lynda asks in hushed tones, "Is your mom sick?" Shelly smiles wistfully at that, a smile too old for her. "Yeah, you could say that."

They head down the sidewalk in silence. Shelly a step ahead, ignoring Lynda. Lynda finally says, "So you want to come over and maybe finish watching Harry Potter or maybe we could go to the Little Woods and..."

Shelly stops, Lynda almost bumping into her. Shelly turns and stares at her, eyes hard and lips pulled thin—yet another expression much too old for her. "Look. Mama doesn't want me hanging around with you. She's right. You folks all think you are too good for us. So just go on back to your hoighty-toighty house and play with all the things your rich parents have spoiled you with." She turns and walks away.

Lynda doesn't understand. She feels like she's taken a punch in the stomach. She runs after her. "Wait! What do you mean! I just want us to be friends."

Shelly stops again. "Friends! How could we be friends? Just look at you in those fancy clothes and tennis shoes. I bet you and your parents made fun of me soon as I left yesterday." Lynda looks down at her Wal-Mart special play clothes, still not understanding. Shelly continues. "I'm going to go get my mama some cigarettes. Have you ever been sent to buy cigarettes or beer for your Mom? I bet not. I bet you don't even know how to get cigarettes and beer at our age."

A slow realization that Shelly is jealous of her begins dawning on Lynda as Shelly continues ranting.

"I bet *your* mama and daddy do everything for you too. They probably won't let their little Princess do anything that would help her in the real world." Shelly looks angry, and Lynda backs up a step. "I don't even have a Daddy. Don't need one. Mama says we don't. And we get along just fine." Shelly's fists are balled. Lynda takes another step back. Shelly takes a step forward. Tears form in Lynda's eyes as she squeaks out "I... I don't understand. I just really wanted us to be friends because the other kids here are so mean."

For just a moment, Shelly's eyes soften. Her fists unclench. Her eyes get watery too. Then she bites her lower lips, turns and runs off down the sidewalk. Lynda watches her, tears trailing down her cheeks.

In the distance, she sees Shelly stop and sit on the ground beside the sidewalk, hugging herself, rocking. Lynda believes she may be crying too.

After a while, several of the older neighborhood kids appear and approach Shelly. They sit on the ground with her, and eventually she starts talking with them. Lynda sees sparks of fire as matches light, then trails of smoke from cigarettes. One kid is drinking something from a yellow can and she's sure it's not soda pop.

Shelly points at her. All the kids laugh as if Shelly has just made a joke about her. One kid hands Shelly a cigarette. She takes it and smokes with practiced ease. Another offers the yellow can; she takes it and drinks, passes it back. Soon they are all laughing and talking, occasionally pointing at Lynda. Shelly looks toward Lynda a lot. Soon they all stand and stare at her.

Lynda turns and heads back home. This is usually where the kids decide they are bored and come to pick on her. She looks back once and sees they are heading the other way, out of the neighborhood. At least they would leave her alone today.

She wipes the tears from her cheek, sad for having lost a friend.

Lynda doesn't go outside much the next few days. When she does, she's very careful to avoid the other kids, staying in the shadows behind trees and bushes. Staying close to what she and her brother always called the Little Woods in the common area. Having learned long ago all the best hiding spots in the neighborhood, she was good at being invisible when she needed to be.

She does notice that the other kids are gathering earlier every day to drink and smoke, and then they all head somewhere outside the neighborhood.

Her parents talk about how the incidents of thefts and vandalism in the neighborhood are dropping, that maybe the kids are growing out of it and maturing, but Lynda knows it's really because they are expanding their horizons beyond the boundaries of the neighborhood.

As the days stretch on, she stays out of their way, spying on them occasionally. Every now and then, someone might chase her a short way or call her a bad name, but mostly they still ignored her. It's as if they have moved on and she wasn't worth the bother.

One day she is following a yellow butterfly and comes upon Shelly sitting with her back against a tree in the Little Woods. The butterfly lands on Shelly's leg. Lynda and Shelly stare at each other, then at the butterfly opening and closing its wings. Lynda smiles, and Shelly laughs. That same laugh she had the first day they'd met. A good laugh. For a moment, it looks like Shelly might actually be nice.

Then some of the other kids show up, not seeing Lynda stepping back into the shadows and hiding behind a tree. Shelly looks at them and instantly gets that hard look about her. She swats the butterfly, smearing yellow residue from its wings all over her blue jeans. They all laugh at the crumpled creature, and then head out. Shelly turns and cast one last look toward where Lynda is hiding, smiling the smile of someone who has seen too much at too young an age.

That was the last time Lynda saw Shelly.

The city eventually put up a *"No Cut Through"* sign at both entrances to the neighborhood. They even sent a police car in the mornings and evenings to monitor during the rush hours. That slowed the flow of speeding traffic to a trickle, but by then there weren't many children left to watch out for.

The neighborhood talk was the kids had just up and run away, all of them, whispers of someone abducting them dismissed, though Shelly's distraught mom clung to that belief up until the day she went inside her house and no one ever saw her again either.

Though they were isolated, tales of vandalisms, thefts and acts of violence outside the neighborhood trickled in when new residents arrived.

Childless new residents, noted a disappointed Lynda.

Lynda knew Shelly was involved in many of the things gossiped about, as were the neighborhood kids. And they were being joined by others from everywhere. More who had just given up and gone over. A growing gang let loose where nothing could contain them. Old souls in young bodies, haunting the world.

It was sad, and Lynda had never felt so lonely. She hoped that soon another young girl would move into the neighborhood and they could be friends.

It was so hard doing the right thing.

Her brother comes to see them on Easter. He is dressed in a crisp uniform and brings flowers. He stays a while, telling them of his adventures, asking how they are. He chuckles softly reminiscing about how he and Lynda used to play in the Little Woods, and how scared they were of the well-kept cemetery just beyond those woods.

Rubbing his eyes, he tells them again how sorry he is. That he wishes he could take back that day when he was little and had yanked away from Lynda holding his hand, running into the road without looking. How much he loves them and he would never take for granted the price they paid coming to his rescue. That he was trying his best to make them proud for their sacrifice.

Standing in the warm sun in their Sunday best, smiling, Lynda and her parents feel honored as he places the flowers on their headstones. He rises, closes his eyes, whispers, "Thank you." Then he turns and walks away, wiping tears, nodding respectfully to others visiting deceased loved ones in the Little Woods Cemetery. He follows the path he and his sister use to take, back to the old neighborhood.

He walks slowly along the sidewalk; again nodding respectfully to people along the way. He pauses; standing in front of the house his family lived in so long ago. Tears flow freely as he waves at an unknown couple puttering in the yard. Edging close to the road, he darted out in, his sister and parents following, pushing him away from the speeding car, shielding him with their bodies as the car's brakes squealed too late. He wipes his eyes with a crisp white handkerchief, knowing in his heart of hearts the residents of the cemetery, those ghosts he just left, are just as real, if not *more* real, than these strangers he sees now. He imagines the cemetary as a community unto itself, populated by the dead from the other side of the copse of woods.

He walks on, fervently hoping, praying his sister and family are happy in their new neighborhood.

Rie Sheridan Rose

She Comes to Me at Midnight

She comes to me at midnight...
Hair unbound moonlight—
Pale silk against paler skin.
Soundlessly weeping,
Her eyes drowned stars.

She comes to me at midnight...
Fragile as a thought,
Broken by a whisper,
And I hunger for her touch—
To hold her in my arms once more.

She comes to me at midnight...
From her restless dreams
To kneel beside my earthen bed,
Shaken by her guilt,
And my bone-thin fingers clench.

She comes to me at midnight...
Reliving every moment of the death
She made me suffer.
Begging my forgiveness—
And my specter whispers "No."

She comes to me at midnight...
Each night closer to her own extinction
And my murdered heart rejoices.
Tonight I let her see
The phantom I've become.

William Petersen

Peeping Tom

"Mmm... three-A is looking good today," Thomas told his television, intently watching as the attractive woman disrobed and stepped into the shower. Once she was behind the curtain, he typed a few lines of code into his laptop, and the view changed to one inside the shower compartment. He removed the computer from his lap to reveal yellow stained briefs and pale, hairy legs. A twinge of guilt pecked at his subconscious, which would intensify after, but he was powerless to stop himself. His hnd slowly descended toward his crotch as the woman began to soap up.

The phone rang and startled him so badly that he lurched forward, launching his thick, black rimmed glasses right off of his face. He stared into the fuzziness trying to locate the landing site of his spectacles, when the phone rang again. He reached down and retrieved the device, holding it close to his face while squinting to read the display. It was the landlord. Thomas thought about ignoring it, but knew that the old man would just keep calling and eventually show up at his door if he didn't answer.

"Hello?" he greeted the building owner as he depressed the button on the computer to pause his little peep show.

"Tom, the cameras on the third floor hallway are out again," the raspy voice emanating from the phone told him. Thomas knew that the old man had a thing for voyeurism as well, but the old man's obsession was slightly different from his own; he only wanted to be the eye in the sky, the king of the castle watching over his subjects with an unblinking gaze. 'Everyone had needs' was Thomas' philosophy and justification. The old man's need was control, and Thomas served his own perversions by catering to those of the cantankerous senior.

"I'll go check it out right now," Thomas offered.

"Well hurry up before one of the low-life's in that building takes a shit on the floor or spray-paints their name on the wall."

"I'm opening the door as we speak," Thomas lied, hoping to speed up conversation, "I'll call you back as soon as it's working."

"Don't bother, I'll be watching and waiting," the crabby voice announced and was followed the by the sudden silence of a severed connection. Thomas knew that the old man was telling the truth. He had made a deal with Thomas to install and maintain a building-wide video system and route the feeds back to the old man's house. The relic spent the vast majority his days and nights cycling through the various displays, looking for any tenants or visitors up to no good.

"Everyone has needs..." Thomas thought, as he squinted at the frozen image on his television screen. The old man let him live there rent and utility free in exchange for Thomas being on call twenty-four hours day. There was nothing wrong with the cameras on three, and Thomas knew it; the building was mostly full of college kids in their twenties, and they didn't like to be watched. *"That's why I keep mine hidden...,"* echoed in the back of his mind as a sly grin spread across his face.

Thomas carelessly dressed and ran a hand through his ear-length black hair, now shimmering with more than a week's worth of oil, then made his way to the third floor. He navigated using the stairwells and quietly peered out of the door to ensure the hallway was empty before emerging. He quickly removed the foam cups from the cameras at each end of the hall, then stealthily rushed back to his apartment to revel in one of his favorite episodes of the day: three-A preparing for work.

Thomas had watched her long enough to learn her patterns and routine; he felt as if he had gotten to know her over time and that they now shared a special connection, one much more profound than his previous distractions. He had become so enamored with her; he barely looked in on the rest of the women of the building. He smiled openly at the mental image of her and eagerly slipped back into his apartment. Once inside, he diligently secured both locks on the door and was removing his pants as he maneuvered through the trash and dishes littering the floor, making his way to the couch.

Brushing the previous evening's pizza box from the far cushion, Thomas hurried to get the images back on the screen. The television screen coming to life followed the clicking of his fingers on the keyboard of the laptop. More typing produced a cycle of images from within three-A's dwelling. He hastily input a new series of commands, and the black and white rendition of the third floor hallway appeared on his television screen. He caught three-A stepping into the elevator, wearing a black skirt and white tank top.

The attire she wore during the day was conservative but modern, but her transformation into more racy and revealing nightwear hinted at a bar or nightclub job. After watching her constantly, he could even tell if she was going to work or if she was going to play, just by what she chose to wear and how she prepared and groomed herself prior to leaving. He was even more pleased that in all the time he had been observing her, she had never once brought anyone back to her place, reinforcing his delusion of their bond. Thomas sighed, then looked back down to his computer. After a few quick keyboard strokes, the television began to display the contents of various rooms from around the building.

Thomas set the computer aside, scratched around in his furry navel until he had prized an impressive lint ball from the orifice, then rose to his feet while simultaneously flicking the tangle of fuzz across the room. He navigated to the refrigerator and fished out the gallon bottle of cheap bourbon and an expired bottle of lime juice, then returned to his nest on the couch. Knowing his own routines as well as those of three-A, he activated his television's sleep function, then set to taking shots and watching the slide show. He stretched out with legs splayed apart, watching the mundane lives of others play out in high-definition.

Thomas drifted off into a drunken dreamland and visited his youthful self. He had left his house early on a Saturday morning to rendezvous with a neighbor boy and explore a new bike trail. Arriving at the boy's house, Thomas' younger form skirted around the side of the structure and knocked on his friend's bedroom window. When no answer came, seeking to avoid alerting the boy's parents, Thomas moved to the next window. However, before he could knock, his friend's twelve-year-old sister appeared through the glass, returning from a shower. Upon removing her towel to continue drying and dress, she noticed him watching.

Her screams sent him running home, but the house phone was already ringing when he returned, and then his parents were screaming at him. Counseling, therapy and decades of social ridicule followed, fueled largely by his portly appearance, beady eyes and thick glasses. But most of all, his unfortunate first name ensured that the dubious title of Peeping Tom would brand itself to him for the rest of his life.

A dim light was hurting his eyes, and the invisible spike driven into his head was competing with it for his attention. Thomas let one eye peel open to reveal the dancing blurs of luminescence coming from the television screen. He closed the eye and fumbled around for the remote, but his hand found his glasses first, which he donned, then slowly opened both eyes. After blinking several times and rubbing the sleep from his eyes, he sat up and looked around for the remote, but was momentarily distracted by movement on the screen.

Three-A had returned from her night shift and appeared to have been drinking a bit after work; she moved around on unsteady legs and nearly tripped over her own feet. Thomas found it endearing, and retrieved his bottle of bourbon to salute her with a toast, but his actions stopped cold as another person stumbled into the image. The other, clearly a man in his forties, reached out to brace himself with her shoulders, then the two laughed and began kissing passionately. Thomas felt the foul bile of jealousy welling up and grit his teeth, then proceeded with the shot of liquor.

He brought his laptop to life with the intent of cutting the video signal for the night, when the movements on the television screen took on an increased pace. Before he realized what was happening, the man's arm extended with lightning speed and struck her chin; three-A lurched and crumpled onto the kitchen floor. Thomas' mouth dropped open, and he blinked twice to ensure he wasn't misinterpreting what he was seeing. As he looked on in disbelief, the man grabbed a handful of her flaxen hair and drug her limp body over to one of the two chairs flanking the tiny kitchen table.

The assailant exited the frame for several minutes, then returned with a disc-shaped object in one hand and what looked like a belt dangling from the other. The man patiently set about removing all of her clothes, and the thought of what might come next terrified Thomas. He watched with a morbid curiosity thankfully denied when the man picked up her body and placed it in one of the chairs. He then secured her in several places around her arms and legs with a thick, gray tape.

Three-A began to come back to consciousness just as the man was securing the last of several windings around her head to redundantly cover her mouth. She began rapidly looking around the kitchen, her eyes wide with fear and confusion. Then, resigned to her situation, she stared pleadingly at her tormenter. The man seemed to take this as a cue and began lashing her with the belt all across her body, head and legs. After several agonizingly long minutes of this, the man turned to his fists, and even bit a large chunk of skin from her cheek, which he indignantly spat back at her. The grim spectacle continued to play out as the man gathered the belt around his hands and moved to stand behind the hapless woman.

He looped the belt around her neck and jerked backward, using the weight of his body to assist his efforts. The poor woman's face contorted, and within what seemed like a few seconds, her eyes began to bulge. Her left eye was suddenly tinted pink, and her tongue sprang from her grimacing mouth. Her fingers knotted into fists then extended and, after a painfully long moment, mercifully fell still.

Paralyzed by fear and shock, Thomas continued to stare at the display until the man left the apartment. A thought begged at the edge of his mind, and he forced himself out of stasis to clumsily depress the keys of the laptop. The view on the television changed to that of each of the three hallways in turn, but the man seemed to be gone. Thomas grabbed his phone and retrieved the number for the landlord, hoping the cameras had captured the man's face at some point. Before he initiated the call, another thought slammed into the forefront of his mind, *"How am I going to explain this? I'm not supposed to have access to the feeds."*

Thomas dropped the phone, and his eyes began to dart around behind his glasses. His growing concern turned into full-blown panic as he thought of all the wiring and subverted networking equipment that led from his apartment to the others. His beady eyes opened just a bit wider as the realization hit him, *"There would be an investigation, and the cameras would be found."*

The thought panicked him to the point that he dressed, gathered his tool belt and began the long and tedious task of disconnecting dozens of secretive conduits and tiny imaging devices. He watched carefully and noted as various subjects of his peep show departed for their daily, or nightly, obligations. He then moved in to detach his equipment and cover any signs of its existence. For two long days, he watched and worked, and each time he returned to watch, he also checked on the body to ensure it was still undiscovered. Logic and necessity dictated that the cameras in three-A be saved for last.

Late in the afternoon on the second day, the landlord was summoned by the police at the request of classmates and co-workers of three-A, and the body was discovered. Thomas locked his door and watched through the peephole as a number of official personnel funneling into the building and up through the first stairwell grew. Normally, the extra attention wouldn't have concerned him; he had plenty of experience covering his tracks, but his activities had never been under the scrutiny of a murder investigation. A small sense of relief came to him as he watched the fish-eye view of the landlord pass by in the hallway.

Thomas suddenly felt the consequences of the preceding day's exertions; his muscles began protesting his movements and his eyelids felt as heavy the image of the dead girl weighing on his conscious. *"They'll get him,"* he kept telling himself. *"They don't need anything from me. Surely someone saw him enter or leave the building, or at the very least, saw the couple out together,"* and the more he recited it, the more it calmed him. Thomas didn't bother to disrobe or even take off his shoes or glasses; he just fell back into the familiar embrace of the abused sofa and closed his eyes. Sleep took him almost immediately.

Urgent banging snatched him from his slumber, and it took him several seconds to realize that someone was knocking. He stumbled from the couch and made his way to the door, slid his fingers under his glasses to rub his eyes and peered out of the eyepiece. Two police officers accompanying a man in a brown trench coat waited outside, and one of the officers knocked again. Thomas took a step back and opened the door.

The middle-aged man donning the overcoat introduced himself as Detective Hornby and announced that he was conducting routine interviews with all of the tenants. "Even if you just had a bad feeling about something, it may help..." the detective trailed off as he took a closer inventory of the man in the doorway. A frown wrinkled his ample brow as he watched Thomas' eyes dart back and forth, immediately repositioning whenever eye-contact was made. The detective looked over Thomas' shoulder at the mess within the domicile, then looked back at Thomas, who was now staring at the floor. "Are you alright, sir?" the detective queried.

Thomas was becoming flustered. He was socially inept and became visibly uncomfortable during the most miniscule interactions, and this direct questioning exacerbated his condition. "No... I mean, yes. I mean, no. Nothing is wrong. What do want again?" he asked, trying to position his body to block the taller man's view of his dwelling.

Hornby asked his name and a few general questions, all the while continuing to study Thomas and his awkward behavior. His professional senses were piqued. "Okay, well thanks for your cooperation, and if you think of anything, give me a call," the detective told him as he handed over a business card. Thomas stuffed it into the front pocket of his pants and hastily shut the door without further ceremony.

Thomas returned to couch and stared at his reflection in the black screen of the television. He grabbed the bottle from the coffee table and took several, long pulls. He continued drinking and telling himself, *"They'll catch him..."* and passed out sitting upright with the bottle clinched between his pudgy legs.

The television flickered to life, and Thomas awoke to the distant sounds of a reporter discussing what details had emerged about the killing, and the words, "No suspects or leads at this time, but the investigation is ongoing," reverberated inside his head. He sat up and stared at the illuminated screen, quickly learning that he had once again wet himself. The television screen went black, then a bluish-white light flashed, and the image slowly revealed the interior of apartment three-A.

"But there's no cameras anymore," Thomas said aloud, as his forehead wrinkled. The view abruptly changed, and Thomas was looking down into the kitchen. His heart nearly jumped into his throat when he saw the chair, with a familiar form bound to it, sitting center frame. Only this time, the victim was not three-A, it was the man who had killed her. He was nude, and his shoulder-length brown hair was slick with sweat. The clarity of the video was stunning as the man looked directly into the view of whatever device was now feeding his television.

The man's head jerked violently to one side, then he grunted and his head fell forward as blood rushed from his nose and mouth. He coughed and sprayed a fine, red mist into the air, then he seemed to stiffen. A depression seemed to appear around the circumference of the man's neck, and his eyes abruptly rolled up into their sockets, revealing only pale orbs. The man's feet and hands twitched and contorted as his tongue jabbed out of his open mouth, then his body slackened and his head rolled to one side. Over the course of a few seconds, the screen faded to a haunting black.

Thomas suddenly felt as if ice water were trickling down the center of his back, yet his face and ears felt like they were heated from within. Scared in place, his eyes strained to open wider as the television screen again sputtered with light, and when the image focused, it was that of an empty chair sporting shards of torn tape. Full on fear was gripping him now, and he reached out to grab his phone while wrestling Detective Hornby's card from his pocket. Attributing the images to hallucinations brought on by pressing guilt, he mentally resolved to come clean and try to work out a deal in exchange for his contribution. *"I'm just going to tell him everything, before this gets out of control,"* he told himself as he dialed the number.

The call was immediately routed to the detective's voice mail, and Thomas left a generic message asking him to return the call. Anticipating the sensation of weight being removed from his shoulders, Thomas again turned to his bottle of bourbon to sooth his nerves and usher him off to sleep. He raised the bottle to his lips, but a resounding thud against the front door caused him to jerk and splash the liquid up onto his glasses.

Thomas got up and opened the door rudely, without bothering to look through the eyepiece first, but found the hallway empty. His vision suddenly jerked and then went completely white, as a ringing filled his ears. The ringing tapered off in time with an encroaching blackness that overtook the white... and then there was nothing.

"Thom-as," the sound, drawn out in exaggerated syllables, caressed his ear. His eyelids snapped open and blinked out of sequence with one another as he struggled to see without his glasses. "Thom-as..." the sensual, female voice called again, "Time to get up."

"Who, who's there?" he slurred, squinting and trying to locate the source of the sound.

"You like to watch, don't you?"

"What?" Thomas asked, suddenly aware that he couldn't move anything other than his hands, feet and head. The sounds of something heavy sliding across the linoleum flooring sent vibrations up through his legs and fueled his mounting dread. He craned his neck and strained to see. "Let me help you with that," the lyrical voice offered, and Thomas' vision became as clear as fine crystal. He struggled to understand what was happening as he stared at the large, upright mirror before him.

The realization hit, and Thomas began to beg, "I didn't do anything. I'm sorry this happened to you, but it wasn't me. You know that. Why are you doing this to me? I didn't *do* anything!" he pleaded.

"That's right," the deceptively gentle voice told him, "You didn't do anything. You didn't call anyone. You didn't try to help or stop it. But you if you had, I might still be alive. You even withheld information from the police that could have identified a serial killer whose career had lasted decades." The voice paused. "You're exactly right, Tom, or would you prefer, *Peeping* Tom? You *didn't* do anything, anything at all..."

"I was going to, I swear. I just called the detective," Thomas contested.

"Ah, but that was just another act of self-preservation, wasn't it? You weren't sorry about what happened; only that it might lead back to you and your little pass-time. Face it, Tommy-Boy, you stood by and watched, yet did nothing, so you might as well have held the belt."

Before he could offer an argument, a red-hot stinging stretched across his face, and when the tears in his eyes cleared, he could see the angry, pink stripe glowing in his reflected image. Thomas cried and moaned as the blows turned from slaps to blunt strikes. After an incalculable barrage of impacts, a lull in the attack allowed him to look at the mirror that now displayed his reddened skin and bleeding face. His right eye was swollen shut, and there was large gash beneath it.

Thomas' head jerked again, and he could feel a thin band of tension uniformly increasing around his neck. As his trachea was slowly squeezed shut, he heard the soft voice again, "So, you like to watch? Well... watch *this*."

The pressure around his neck spiked, and as he stared into the mirror, a pink film slid down over his vision. In the reflection, blood began streaming out of his functional eye, and he could feel the pressure building within the capillaries of his lungs. Just before the tiny bundles of vascular pathways began to rupture, he stole one last glance at the looking glass, where a depression had formed around his neck, though no means of ligature was visible. Thomas watched his tongue protrude from his contorted, rapidly bluing face. Time ceased to have meaning, and he felt as if he were floating... then the blackness came and took everything away.

Detective Hornby raced to the apartment building where several uniformed officers were on the scene and awaiting his arrival. He had been receiving updates through the radio while trying to call Thomas' phone, until one of the officers answered to inform him that Thomas was not there. Upon arriving, Hornby made his way straight to three-A. He burst in and strode directly into the kitchen where a chair sat just a few feet from a large, oval mirror on a swiveling stand. Scraps of thick, gray tape clung to the chair in very familiar patterns.

"Hey, isn't that the mirror from the bedroom?" one of the patrolmen asked from behind him.

"I'm not sure," Hornby replied, obviously confused.

"And didn't forensics already process that chair in as evidence?" the younger man persisted.

Hornby stared at the tiny table in the corner of the kitchen, then turned to look at the patrolman, whose eyes were almost as wide as his own, "Yeah, they *did*..."

Brian Rosenberger

The Screams All Sound The Same

It's the same old suicide.
I blame you.
You blame me.
Blame the House.

It was old and empty even
Before we moved in and
The contracts signed.

Its previous owners, eyes stitched,
Already six feet beneath the soil.
Why gamble? Why bet?
The House always wins.

Close your eyes, It whispers.
I tread the hallways, sleepless.
The creaks and groans of the stairs,
My only company, silent whispers.
Soon. Very soon.

The stairs creak as I walk.
The House is keeping me awake,
No chance of slumber.
The House croons a lullaby, a chorus of
Close your eyes, just close your eyes.

There's a voice telling me "This is wrong"
And "Put down the axe" and "No, no, no."
But the other singer is louder, more demanding.

Some days, some nights, I imagine we are already dead.

There's a voice that tells me "Wait" and "Remember"

But it's a song I can't recall, the singer and lyrics
Part of a past, a radio station for the dead.

Once we were young, so in love, the future was ours.
Once...

Now, your screams echo through hallway after hallway, haunting
me.

I walk the hallways.
Your screams keeping me awake.
I walk the hallways,
Looking for a new throat
My axe can silence.

Tim Jeffreys

Another Shore

Danub liked to rise early even on Mondays, the one day of the week the restaurant is closed for the day, the restaurant he ran with his new wife, Paz. He'd always been an early riser, but now as the years advanced he found himself getting out of bed before it was even light outside. Paz thought he was crazy, getting up so early when he didn't have to, but he could think of nothing worse than lying in the dark unable to sleep with his thoughts turning. One of his ex-wives used to say that he hated to be alone with himself, and this – he supposed - was true.

On Monday mornings, he liked to walk along the beach at the edge of the surf, watching the sunrise and collecting coloured pebbles to take home for Abril, the daughter Paz had given him, to marvel. He had other children out there in the world, some fully grown, some in other countries, who he no longer saw but thought about often, ticking their names off a mental checklist one by one and wondering what had become of them. As he walked along the beach he would stare out to sea, thinking about the past and about his home country, from where he'd fled so many years ago it now it looked to him like another lifetime. *That man who left Hungary, he was a different person*, he would say to himself. *I'm not the same one now.* He'd lived so many more lives since then, in other countries and with other wives, using other names even, always moving, until eventually he'd found himself in Portugal; old but still handsome, still virile, still able to attract a much younger woman like Paz.

One Monday morning toward the end of summer, he was so lost in thought, and the sun took so long to rise, that he walked the full length of the beach without realising. At the very end was a finger of cliff that marked the end of the bay, but before that was a stretch of sand – about 100 meters or so – that separated the rest of the beach by a fence made of ugly black netting. The netting had been ravaged and half-flattened by the wind. Though it didn't act as much of a deterrent, people tended to avoid this particular stretch of beach as it was littered with black boulders that had rolled down from the low cliffs above. A sign, written in Portuguese, English and German, stood crookedly, warning people not to sunbathe or swim here, which Danub – though he'd seen it before - stopped and gazed at. ATTENTION it read at the top.

He shifted his eyes to look along that last stretch of beach and understood in the back of his mind that the reason no one came here was not the fence, the sign, or the threat of falling boulders. It was because the beach here had a strange, gloomy atmosphere. The promenade ended some way back, so there were no bars or shops overlooking the sand, just a snarl of trees.

Something intangible about this end of the beach made a person want to turn back. Some dark presence seemed to hover over it, so that even the seagulls left it alone. This idea only pressed upon him for a moment. The sun inched further up from below the horizon, drawing his attention to the wash of orange light filling the sky.

After some moments, he glanced down at his hands and realised he'd not picked up any pebbles for Abril. Despite his earlier misgivings, he thought he might find some interesting stones on this lonely stretch of beach, so he continued walking on past the tattered fence. He walked where the tide had soaked the sand, stopping now and then to turn a pebble with his toes. Before he reached the end of the bay, he saw something small and pink ahead of him sloshing about in the foam at the edge of the sea. He narrowed his eyes and tried to make out what it was. As he moved nearer, the tide swept this thing onto the sand right in front of his feet, as if it was presented to him. Seeing it there, he bent forward and gazed at it.

"No," he said, aloud.

It was that one. That one he still saw often in his mind's eye. *Impossible.*

Gingerly, he picked the bit of jetsam up and turned it in his hands. It was a plastic doll, about the size of a new born baby, but it was no modern toy. The style was dated. It looked to be at least forty or fifty years old. Its heavily lashed eyes opened and closed in a loose, disjoined way, first the right, then the left, as if it were winking at him. As if it was saying: *You remember me, right? You remember don't you, Danub?* The doll was nude, wiry blonde hair, and had lost one arm, the left, *just like...*

Exactly like...

He stopped the thought before it could go any further.

He looked down at the doll he held in his hands and felt something stir in his stomach. Turning to one side, he bent and retched. Nothing came up. His mouth tasted sour. He felt the cold tide lap around his feet and ankles. A wave had unfurled suddenly close, surprising him, seeming to clutch at his legs, grabbing at him, so that he leapt away and stumbled in the sand.

Righting himself, he turned toward the water, drew back his arm and hurled the doll with all the force he could muster back out to sea. He didn't wait to see if it washed up again onto the beach. Instead he turned away and hurried back the way he'd come, following the lone trail of footprints he'd left in the sand.

He noticed Paz glancing at him in a concerned way for some days after. On Friday, when he went to the restaurant's kitchen to collect a customer's order, she stopped him and looked into his face.

"What is it, Danub? You're not yourself lately."

"Nothing is wrong."

"Something's wrong. You can tell me."

He forced a smile. "Nothing's wrong, my love. Are these the croquetas for table six?"

She put her hands on his chest as he reached for the plates, forcing him to face her again.

"Where do you go on Mondays? In the morning?"

At her words, he felt a blush rise in his face, as if he had some reason to be ashamed. He shifted his gaze from hers and tried to speak casually. "Just walking on the beach, then I have a coffee in one of the bars on the seafront. You know that."

Paz was still staring into his face. He saw how her beauty had faded in the four years since he'd met her. She looked more drawn and sickly with each passing day. The skin of her face had a sallow, rubbery quality. Her eyes were sunken and her teeth appeared more prominent. He didn't know if she was simply exhausted from running a home and a restaurant; or the shadow of her former life, that life from which she always said he'd rescued her.

I'm a new woman now, thanks to you, she would say. *I'm a businesswoman, and a mother. When I think how I used to spend my time.*

We all have things in our past, he would answer, *things we're ashamed of.*

Then she would put her arms around him and say, *let's be other people. Let's be new.*

Yes, he would say, though in his heart he knew that it was not so easy.

Paz frowned.

"What're you thinking about?"

"Nothing. Just...you look tired, that's all. You should rest more."

"I feel fine. Why don't you stay with me in bed on our one day off instead of going walking by yourself? There are things I want to do to you that I don't have the energy for normally."

"Paz..."

"I like you to be there when I wake up."

"Once I'm awake, I'm awake. That's it. I'm not going to lie around for hours staring into the dark, am I?" Though he'd not intended it, his voice had a trace of anger. Before she could answer, he picked up the plates, turned on the spot and left the kitchen. "The croquetta's are getting cold," he told her over his shoulder.

On Sunday, he was at home, doing the accounts for the restaurant, when Paz rang to say she was taking Abril to the beach. Business had been slow at the restaurant and she had decided to close up for the rest of the day. Danub told her this was a good idea, that she needed some time off, and anyway with autumn approaching there wouldn't be many more days left for them to enjoy the beach. When he put the phone down and returned to the books, he began to grow increasingly anxious. Just the thought of Abril playing in the sea bothered him. Sometimes Paz was not as vigilant as she should have been. She got distracted, chatting with strangers or on her mobile phone. Abril, though she was only three, was getting more and more headstrong, always trying to do more than she was capable. What if...?

He took a deep breath and told himself to relax. They would be fine. They may not even go into the water. It was getting too cold.

He'd driven past the beach earlier on his way home and had seen that there were only a few people braving the sea.

Still, when he returned to the books he found it difficult to concentrate. He couldn't relax until he heard Paz's key in the lock of the front door.

"Papa!"

Hearing Abril's voice, a grin spread across his face and he felt his anxiety melt away. Taking off his glasses, he fell back in his chair and greeted her as she ran into the room with her mother close behind her. Both were smiling. He put his arms out to lift Abril into his lap, but then he saw what she was clutching in her hands and a wave of horror passed through his body. He sprang to his feet and recoiled from her.

"Papa, look! It's my baby!"

"Where did you get *that thing* from?"

"She found it on the beach," Paz said. She no longer smiled. She was looking at Danub in a puzzled way instead. "She wouldn't let go of it. She said it's a mermaid's baby because it came from the sea." Her voice dropped as she went on. "Don't worry; I'll throw it in the bin when she goes to bed."

"Throw it away now!"

"Danub?" Paz said. "What's the matter with you? It's just an old doll."

Abril was holding the doll out for him to see. He didn't need to look again to see that it was the same one that had been washed onto the beach in front of him the previous Monday, the same one that...

"It's not got arm," Abril said.

Danub felt that lurch in his stomach again. He turned from his wife and child's bemused faces and went into the kitchen. There, he poured himself a brandy. He saw that his hands were shaking when he reached into the cupboard to get a glass.

Paz appeared in the kitchen door space.

"What's got into you?"

"Nothing. Nothing. I've been at the books too long."

"We're going to take a shower."

He nodded at her between slurps of his drink.

"Did you go to the very end of the beach, that part that's cordoned off?"

"Abril felt like walking."

141

"You shouldn't go there. The...the sign. Didn't you see the sign?"

"We just walked. We didn't hang around. What's the harm in that?"

"It's not...it's not safe. You shouldn't..."

She gave him a long look. "You sure you're okay? Maybe..."

"I'm fine. Honestly. You two go and have your shower. Go on."

Paz held his gaze for a long moment, and then nodded. Turning, she called to Abril.

When Danub emerged from the kitchen, he saw that his daughter had left the doll lying on the sofa. She had put it to bed, covering it to the shoulders with a tea towel. Without thinking, he snatched it up. Hearing the shower running, and Paz and Abril laughing, he went into the kitchen and tossed the doll on top of one of the high cupboards, then reached up and pushed it out of sight with his fingertips.

He knew there would be tears later, but those he could deal with.

The next morning he woke as usual, before daylight. Dawn was just beginning to break when he reached the far end of the beach. He carried with him the doll Abril brought home. He knew he couldn't just throw the doll away. He had to make a gesture of defiance. He had to return it to the sea. It might wash up again, but he would tell Paz never to bring Abril here again. He would tell her it was dangerous. And he had no intention of returning to this part of the beach himself.

He gazed out across the black ocean at the thread of light that had appeared along the horizon, holding the doll in his two hands. In his mind, he was picturing it, that first time he's seen it, long ago in Hungary, when his car came to a halt and it had just been sitting there on the windscreen. He'd been up all night drinking with his friends in a local bar, singing songs, dancing with women and girls. The best night of his life, he'd thought at the time, not knowing then how it would end late the next morning, not knowing of the horror that awaited him and how the course of his life would change thereafter.

"Are you sure you should be driving?" one of his friends had said to him as they left the bar. He could remember how stunned he'd been by the bright sunlight.

He often wished there was some way he could go back. Travel back in time as they did in the movies. Re-enter that scene when his friend said, "Are you sure you should be driving?" and he had just laughed and said, "I'm not drunk. It's all of you who're drunk." He would be there. He would walk straight up to his younger self and, without a word, he would take the car keys out of his hand. Then he would simply walk away. He would return to his own time and find everything changed. No more bad memories, no longer anything to run from, to keep running from; his conscience wiped clear.

There had been three of them, crossing the road at a traffic light, two boys and a girl. The girl was a little older. She'd been in charge of the other two. He could remember their small, terror-struck faces.

Afterward, as he came to his senses, gazing at that doll sitting there on his windscreen, the wipers for some reason working, pushing at it. Running was all he could think to do. He popped the car door open, fell out onto the pavement, then – the worst part of all, without even a look back – picked himself up and ran. He'd been running ever since.

Then there he was, on that beach in Portugal, thirty years later with that same doll in his hands. With that shame that just would not leave him alone.

He'd taken off his shoes and left them further up the beach. Now he felt the cold tide swim around his feet. He looked down at the doll in his hands. He stared into its blank, motionless face.

"It was an accident," he said, aloud. "I was a fool, an idiot child. We all make mistakes when we're young. What do you want from me?"

Another wave broke, sloshing around his calves this time. He felt it pulling at him as it retreated.

"No," he said. "No. I have Paz and Abril to think of."

It was still dark, with only that thin line of light along the horizon. He turned his head in alarm thinking he heard something splashing in the water nearby. All was blackness. For a brief moment, he thought he heard the sound of children's laughter. Then another wave rolled up, surprising him with the shock of cold water so that he stumbled to one side and fell down on his hands and knees. Before he could get to his feet, another wave came, taking hold of his legs like half a dozen small cold hands dragging him backwards into the sea. He floundered for a moment. He thought that again he heard that sound of children's laughter, closer this time. He struggled to his feet, knowing that in a matter of seconds another wave would come and suck him backwards even further. The currents would take hold then. Fighting against the clutching water, he scrambled to his feet and waded back onto the beach. At once, he began to run along the sand. He was shaking and sobbing from the cold. His clothes were soaked through and clinging to him. He had lost the doll.

The next day he told Paz he was feeling unwell, and stayed at home whilst she went to the restaurant. When he heard her drive away, he took his atlas down from the bookshelf and sat at the table, leafing through it. Sunlight fell as hard shapes through the blinds. The only sound was the whirr of the air conditioning unit. Before he realized, it was almost lunchtime. His stomach growled. The phone rang, and it was Paz, again telling him that it had been a slow day at the restaurant so she'd decided to close for the day and take Abril to the beach.

"All right," he said. "But be careful and don't..."

But she was distracted by Abril who wanted an ice cream. "See you later, okay?" she said, and hung up.

He turned his attention back to the atlas. The page he had left it open on showed a map of Brazil. He wondered if he could go there, work there, stay there legally, or if he would need a permit. He already knew the language.

It's a pattern with you, Danub, his ex-wife had once said to him, when he called on the phone to ask about their children. *You just keep repeating it, over and over. I thought it'd be different with me, but I should have known better.*

Brazil was far away.

He wondered, was it far enough.

He got up to make some lunch.

Paz and Abril returned home around six. By then the atlas was back on the bookshelf. Abril was sleeping in her mother's arms. Danub noticed that Paz seemed troubled. The casual manner in which she spoke to him seemed forced. She kept avoiding his eyes.

"Is something wrong?" he asked her when she returned from putting Abril to bed.

She went outside onto the balcony. She stood looking down at the street, biting at the nails of one hand. Danub went out and stood beside her.

"What is it? What's the matter?"

She flicked her eyes to him. They looked watery.

"I had a bit of a shock, that's all."

"What happened?"

She took in a deep breath and let it out slowly. "Don't be mad."

"What is there to be mad about?"

Paz watched a car passing along the street below. It was going too fast.

"We went to the end of the beach again – that part you told us never to go to."

"Paz...?"

"Abril thought she could find the doll again. She kept talking about it being a mermaid's baby."

"And...did she find it?"

"No. Well, she said later that she saw it, but it was out on the waves. I think that's why..."

"What happened, Paz? Did she...?"

"There was a couple there and they ask me if I knew anywhere they could go to eat. We were chatting and I started telling them about our place. They said they might try it one day. Anyway, I thought Abril was just playing by the edge of the sea, but when I looked around..."

Tears came now. She hid her face with one hand. "I just panicked. If that couple hadn't been there...I don't think I could have got her out on my own. It was as if the sea just...just wanted her."

Danub felt cold. He felt numb. He stared at Paz. Then he turned to one side and said as if to himself.

"It's me they want."

The next day was Monday. He woke early, as always. He spent a while standing over Paz as it began to get light. She didn't stir. Then he went to Abril's room and watched her sleeping. He leaned forward and kissed her on the forehead.

"My angel," he breathed.

Then he left the house and took the car down to the far end of the beach. He wanted to get there before it got fully light.

Daylight would make everything too stark, too real. He would begin to think that it was all in his imagination.

Leaving the car, he padded across the sand, down past the tattered fence and the sign that warned, ATTENTION! He faced the sea. The tide nipped at his toes.

He heard splashing on the water and looked toward the source, expecting to see a swimmer, but instead he saw the doll. It rolled just out of reach on top of the waves. He moved forwards, trying to reach for it. He felt the cold sea suddenly swell around him. It made him gasp. He heard a child laughing, he was sure of it, but then the sand seemed to disappear from under his feet and he plunged forwards into the sea. He felt the shock of cold. Then he surfaced again, gasping, thrashing at the water. He turned about, trying to see the beach, but all he could see was the flat surface of the sea. He was sure that what happened then was that small cold hands took hold of his legs and dragged him under. He fought them for a moment, crying out as seawater filled his mouth. Then he let himself be still. He thought of Abril, and for the first time since he was a young man, he felt at peace.

Stephen O'Connor

The Knocker

The two men sat in the cab of the pickup. Piker Dowling was teaching Sharkey Boyle how to cry. His lower lip trembled. His eyes filled. He sniffed and dragged a Dunkin Donuts napkin across his face.

"Jeez, that's pretty good, Piker," Sharkey said, pulling the plastic lid off his coffee.

The other raised a finger to indicate that the performance was incomplete. He puckered up his round face and spoke in a thin and quavering voice. "What's wrong, young man? Why are you crying?" His face melted once again into mournfulness. "It's OK Ma'm, it's not your problem. I just noticed that you had some broken slate up there, and I thought I could do a good job for you, and make a day's pay. Times are rough. My kid..." His face convulsed and he began to sob for a few seconds before he sat up, smiled, and lifted his coffee out of the holder. He sipped it and said, "Gimme me another sugar. There's some in the glove."

"Pretty damn good, Piker. Then what?"

"Well, you don't overdo it. You just shake your head and walk away, like you're too proud to stand there bawlin'. Half of 'em'll call you back, and you're in." He poured another packet of sugar into the coffee, sipped it, and nodded. Then he slid the coffee back in the cup holder and started the truck.

"Jeez, Piker, you're one hell of a knocker."

"I learned from the best. Butchie McAndrews. Now there was a knocker. Of course part of it is knowin' what door to knock." The aluminum ladders rattled on the roof racks as the truck slid out onto Chelmsford Street. "On garbage day, right, you see a single barrel with a brick on the lid. That's a hag. You check for a clothesline with like a flowered dress, a birdbath, that's another dead giveaway. Of course, you're only trollin' in rich neighborhoods. You want a rich hag. Butchie could spot 'em."

"I'm not good at talkin' to people."

"I remember one hag Butchie had on the line. He rips her chimney down. 'Mortar mites!' he says. 'Mortar mites ate up all the fuckin mortar!' So, we gotta rebuild that. Next thing we need to rip out all the valleys and ridges, replace 'em with new copper. By the time we leave, the fuckin' place is gleamin' like Camelot an' she's in the hole for forty grand."

"What the hell is Cama-lot?"

"Ya know—that fuckin' castle with the knights, Camelot. There was another one, a beaut', in Newton, Butchie tells her she got a few slate out. He had a dead squirrel in the back that he picked up off the road. So he says, 'Mam can I take a look in your attic? I think I saw a squirrel go into a hole up there.' He goes up with the squirrel tucked under his sweatshirt, starts yelling and banging around in the attic and comes down holdin' the squirrel by the tail. Oh my God, Mam, you need to patch up those holes! Then he gets up there and starts tearin' with a crowbar. Tells her he's gotta re-slate a whole section of the roof, but he needs the cash to go buy the slate, and squirrel traps of course. The nutty hag gives him a check for fifteen grand. 'OK' Ma'am, We'll be back!' Leaves the fuckin' ladder, which he stole from one of Hank Crowley's jobs anyway, leaves it leaning against the back of the house and boom—we're gone!"

"No shit?"

"He leaves her roof open down to the board, the shingles torn off the back. And Butchie, Mike and me go and get cocked in some Chinese restaurant in Haverhill, met some crazy broads. Stayed drunk for three days. Man, those were the days."

Ruth Addison was alone. Since John's death, nine years earlier, she spent most of her days alone. Her daughter had gone to North Carolina with her husband. He did something with computers. Ruth never understood exactly what, but he took care of Rose and that was all that mattered. Betty Briere was in assisted living now, but she called sometimes. Her brother Harold didn't get out much these days, and he couldn't hear very well on the telephone.

Ruth missed her old friends; most of them were gone now. Mitzy Meehan, Helen McGilvray, Marilyn Mears, Sheila Sterling and all the rest. A picture of the whole group had appeared in the Sunday paper once: "Brookline's Belles," the caption read. It was in her scrapbook, all of them smiling in front of the stadium in the belted coats that were the fashion before the war.

She never looked at the scrapbook now. She could see it all without looking, especially the photo of Danny McGilvray climbing into the cockpit of his fighter plane, its nose painted up to look like a shark, cruel jaw gaping to expose jagged teeth under an angry eye, the row of exhaust pipes like gills below the words, "Pearl's Revenge." On the back, Danny had written, "Curtis P-40 Warhawk." It was very probably the last photograph ever taken of him, and he was smiling in his leather cap and goggles, not the lurid death grin of his aircraft, but the same smile he'd worn at the CYO dances, a kind and warm smile. How could he be smiling? They said his plane dove right at the Japanese battery. Who would have known he had that kind of courage when the old gang clowned around in those golden summer days so long ago, sneaking cigarettes behind the bath house at the lake, or playing cards in the park on the river across from Burbeck's Ice Cream. His sister Helen had called her with the news, and the two of them cried together over the phone for a long time.

It wasn't until two years after the war that she met John Addison at the Totem Pole Ballroom. He was more serious than Danny had been. Or maybe it was the war that had made him serious. He would never have dared to ask her to dance, but it was lady's choice and she saw him there, dark and shy and apart. What a good man he was, she could sense that right away, and she began to love him, so much. They took the train into Boston.

She remembered their walk back through the Common after he'd bought her the engagement ring. They stopped there as the stars stood in the sky, burning in the cold night. Their breaths rose like wreaths of smoke and he told her that he wanted to be with her always, and take care of her and love her. And he did, oh he did. Still, she wondered sometimes. If there was a heaven, who would she be with there? Of course, there was no jealousy or anything like that and no physical bodies. Somehow, God must have sorted all that out. She hoped so, because she loved them both. She felt that Danny and John had already met on the other side, because she had seen them. Oh, yes. When she looked up from her gardening, she might see Danny, still young, passing quietly amid the oleander and hydrangeas. And John, too. Sometimes she smelled his cigar on the June breeze. Once she was sure she spied the two of them standing in the fragrant shade behind the pale pink wall of honeysuckle that climbed the trellis at the edge of the patio. But it was the sort of image that was gone when you focused on it, and maybe it was a sort of daydream, as Rose had assured her. She had never mentioned it to Harold at all. He would laugh.

Ruth prayed that she would see them again in some ideal place, to somehow fulfill the wild promise that Danny made as he left, so young, that he would come back and take care of her forever, and to feel again the steady and devoted companionship of her husband. She sighed as she remembered, and she said aloud, "Oh, well, what can you do?" -- a question that always concluded her reminiscences and marked the beginning of an attempt to buck up.

And it was no good to remember too much this early in the morning. The day promised a gray sky, and she would fall into that deep place that it was sometimes hard to climb out of. She turned on the radio and took a deep breath as the music filled the room. The Brandenburg Concertos. The music gave some sense to the emptiness, and she opened the back door and inhaled the warm air. She would fill the bird feeder and take the morning paper out to the garden. Nature was the only antidote to memory, and that was why that writer in Concord had once asked, "What right have I to grieve who have not ceased to wonder?" The black and white cat slunk out of from the lilac thicket and sat near her as she poured the seed into the feeder. She looked into his yellow eyes, and felt the sun on her shoulders and murmured, "Not ceased to wonder."

She was sitting in the shade working on the crossword puzzle when she heard something like a car door closing in her driveway. She heard a voice and rose, taking off her reading glasses and walking toward the gate.

A man approached, a working-man with white overalls and a stained Boston Red Sox tee shirt. "Good morning, Ma'm. Jack Dowling, Tip Top Roofing. We're doing some work in the area. We just finished a job for . . . do you know Mrs. Gibson up on Laura Drive?"

"No, I'm afraid I don't."

"Well we just finished there, and I noticed that you have a couple of slate out on your roof. Would you like me to go up and take a look around, give you a free estimate?"

"A free estimate for what?"

"To replace the missing or cracked slates. I'll bet no one has looked at that roof in a long time. They require some maintenance. I'll take pictures of anything up there that needs to be repaired and you can think it over."

"Well, my daughter and her husband usually handle repairs and things when they come up."

"Well, I can give you the estimate and you can pass it along to them—show them the pictures and just call me back if you want me to do the work."

The man was clean cut, and he had a nice smile. "It'll just take ten minutes," he said.

"I suppose I could give my daughter your assessment, and your estimate, and see what she says."

He nodded reassuringly. "Sure. No obligation, Ma'm. This is a very nice house by the way. I love your garden."

"Thank you, it keeps me busy."

"OK, we'll just check it out. . .what's your name, Ma'm?"

"Mrs. Addison."

"My co-worker and I will check it out and make up an estimate, Mrs. Addison. Just relax and do whatever you were doing. Enjoy your garden."

Sharkey saw the smile on Piker's face when he came around the house. "Set up the 32 foot extension, Sharkey boy, and throw the hook over the ridge. It's a hag. She bit."

"You're a hell of a knocker all right, Piker."

While his pupil climbed toward the roof with the hook ladder hanging from his shoulder, Piker rummaged through the toolbox that stretched from rail to rail in the bed of the pickup and pulled out an instamatic camera. He snapped on a tool belt and slipped a fifteen-inch flat pry bar under it. He knew how to play this. *She said; my daughter and her husband, when they come up."* They're probably in fucking Florida. *"I would never tell you to go ahead and do the work without consulting your daughter, unless it was an emergency, Mrs. Addison. This is an emergency! Have you noticed stains on your ceiling? No? The damage must be recent. Probably squirrels. First big storm, well look at this picture...the roof is wide open!"*

A few minutes later, the two men walked with outstretched arms across the ridge and stood by the chimney, lords of the rooftop. Piker looked over the steep expanse of slate, against which the hook ladder laid flat, the hook over the ridge. He felt the pry bar at his waist. Sharkey said, "You gonna rip some holes ... ow!"

He was rubbing his arm where Piker had punched him. "Wha' was that for?"

Sharkey whispered, "Never open your yap next to the chimney. The hag could be standing in her living room next to the fireplace and she hears your dumbass voice coming right down the chimney. Never talk beside the chimney!" He continued to whisper, motioning to Sharkey, "Get down the hook—it's a wooden gutter, see if you can pry it away from the house, we'll start there, and I'll hand you the camera. You know how to take a fuckin' picture?"

Sharkey sniffed and said that of course he knew how to take a fuckin' picture.

Soon the two men were sitting on the bottom rungs of the hook ladder. Piker was looking out to make sure that they were not visible to anyone on the street; a pair of maple trees provided good cover anyway. The instamatic camera looped on a cord around his forearm. He pulled the pry bar out of his belt and tapped his accomplice on the shoulder with it—"Here! Rip it!"

Sharkey, holding a ladder rung with his left hand, turned to take the pry bar, but it clanged against the aluminum ladder as he made a sudden jumping movement, an incautious movement to make on any kind of ladder.

"What the hell are you doin'?" Piker demanded.

"Jesus Christ!" Sharkey said, and called, "Hello?"

"Hello? Who the hell are you saying hello to?" Piker looked over his shoulder, to where Sharkey was staring. "What the hell are you looking at?"

"I just saw someone up there. I think he's behind the chimney."

"What the hell are you smokin'? Anybody up here had to come up the ladder. You see anyone come up the ladder?"

"I swear I saw a guy up there on the ridge."

"Are you serious? You're a mental case, Sharkey."

"He was crouched there with one of those leather things on his head and goggles like the pilots wear. Then he was gone, like; I think he ducked behind the chimney. I'm telling you!"

"Just rip the gutter. We don't got all day."

Sharkey took the pry bar, but he said, "Piker, I know what I saw."

"OK, I tell you what—I'll go up there and look behind the chimney. Godammit, all the guys hangin' around the Highland Tap, I gotta bring a guy sees shit."

Piker turned and clambered like a quadruped up the rungs of the hook, rose and walked along the ridge toward the chimney. Inexplicably nervous, he managed to put on a careless attitude and gazed behind the chimney; then, smiling in vindication, he said, "Nothing here, Shar—" He froze. The hook ladder still stretched down over the long breadth of the slate roof, but Sharkey was not on it. He felt his heart pounding in his throat. "Sharkey! Boyle!" No reply. Had he fallen without a sound?

He stepped toward the hook ladder. Years of moving over the ridges of roofs had given him an extraordinary sense of balance, but, in his terror, he moved more quickly than usual along that narrow line, sensing something odd, something horrible up there—that he was not alone—he could smell strong tobacco around him, a dizzying cigar smoke that filled his nose—he could taste it in his throat. In his haste, he had gained too much forward momentum. As he leaned to grasp the hook, he felt a sudden and unaccustomed sense of vertigo. He was trying to straighten himself when the world tilted sideways. The instamatic camera fell from his waving arm and clattered across the expanse of slate—he too was falling; he landed with a thud against the sharply angled roof. Every sense was alert as he slid; he lunged, extending his body, desperately reaching for the side rail of the ladder. Two fingers would save him! But the last thing he saw before he flew off the roof into that terminal void was the hook ladder jerking away from the outstretched hand that touched nothing but smooth, hot slate. The ladder moved by itself! It moved by itself! Jesus it

Matthew Weber

To Kill a Guy Twice

"So you've actually seen the ghost? No kidding?"

"No kidding," Jimmy Miller said to his new friend and neighbor Eric Hyde, who was carving his initials into the treehouse wall. "I wish like heck I hadn't."

A rumble of thunder, at first a distant murmur, grew to a booming quake like a giant boulder rolling overhead.

"Why? Were you scared?"

Although it was uncool for a fourteen-year-old to admit being frightened, Jimmy still said, "Yeah, I was scared. You'd have been, too."

They'd climbed into Eric's plywood shack an hour ago to play cards and read comics. Then a heavy rain fell, and they decided to wait out the downpour rather than shimmy down the rope ladder and get soaked on the thirty-yard dash to the house. While twiddling away the time, Eric asked the crucial question: *You ever seen the ghost of Caleb Wilder?*

Jimmy's parents had purchased the old house across the street for what his father described as a "steal." The family had to relocate from Georgia when the company he worked for asked him to relocate. He'd seen a sound investment in remodeling the old ranch-style home, structurally sound but cosmetically dated, and putting down roots in Trapper Valley, a seemingly quiet suburb just north of Birmingham, Alabama.

Not until after moving in did Jimmy learn why the house had remained unoccupied at such an inviting price: The locals believed it to be haunted.

Eric sheathed the survival knife he'd been using to etch his mark in the wood. "What did it look like?"

Jimmy told him that initially the ghost appeared as only a shape, a shadow that should not have been where it was. He had crept downstairs to raid the kitchen late one Friday night, his first week in the house. His parents had retired to their bedroom; he'd fallen asleep watching a *Friday the 13th* sequel and awoke in

155

the wee hours with a hunger. He snagged a plastic-wrapped cupcake from the pantry and opened the refrigerator, its white light spilling into the darkness. As he rummaged for the milk, he felt a looming presence behind him. He spun with jug in hand and scoured the room. The single bright bulb illuminated the kitchen, but the living area on the far side of a partition countertop remained murky. Shipping crates and various cardboard boxes were stacked throughout, but he saw no one or no *thing* watching him.

Until it moved.

Jimmy's breath caught in his throat. The dull glare of moonlight bled through a window, and, along its edge, he saw motion. A stark flash breached the distinct gray square that outlined the glass, then retreated back into the dark corner of the room.

Jimmy's first thought—*burglar,* His second—*the ghost.* His fingers tightened on the cold, sweaty handle of the milk container. He took a cautious step toward the window, craning his neck so his feet remained near the staircase, should he need to flee up to his room and scream for his parents. As he left the fridge light behind, the darkness gained contrast. Two more steps and he made out a figure in the corner. An arm, a leg, a torso—Jimmy's bladder quivered. When a gasp escaped him, the figure shifted in his direction, turning a pale face toward him, and Jimmy bolted.

Stumbling over his feet, he tripped forward, caught himself on the counter, milk jug pounding down and sliding to the stove. He twisted around and loped across the linoleum floor, slapping the wall for the kitchen light switch. The chandelier blazed to life, and Jimmy saw it all: coffee table, sofa, storage boxes, and his own harried reflection in the corner window. Nothing else occupied the room. Jimmy was alone.

"At first I think he was only watching me," Jimmy said. "He wanted to scope out the newcomers, see what he had to deal with."

Eric weighed this and nodded; "Makes sense. If I was haunting a house I'd want to know who was moving in."

"That's how it began, anyway. Then he started getting aggressive."

"Aggressive?"

"Yeah. Like he wanted to scare me away."

156

Eric curled a smile. "Scare you away? Like *booga-booga?* Okay, now you're losing me."

"Fine," Jimmy said. "I won't tell you."

A gust of wind howled through a broken window, spitting cold rain on Jimmy's arm, giving him goose bumps.

Eric reached up and unhooked a loop of twine that attached a thin wooden door to a hook on the ceiling. Hinged at the top, the door swung down and snapped over the window. He leaned back against the wall and opened a comic, thumbing through the pages and skimming the artwork.

"Alright," Eric said. "So, Caleb Wilder's ghost got 'aggressive' with you . . . What'd he do? You know he was a pretty sick puppy, right? That's how he ended up in his current condition—*dead.*"

"All Mom and Dad told me is that he died under mysterious circumstances, so the locals made up a story about a ghost."

Eric sat up as his eyes widened. "Wait. You mean you don't even know the story of what happened in your house? I guess nobody wanted to tell your parents. Either that or they are giving you a seriously whitewashed version of events. Because there ain't *no* mystery about how he died. Everybody knows exactly what happened."

"How? Were you there?"

"No. Of course not. But I know the story of Jesus and Mary and Joseph, and I wasn't there either."

Jimmy gave his friend a prying look. "So, tell me what happened."

Eric cracked his knuckles and folded his legs beneath him Indian-style. "The first thing you've got to realize is that Caleb Wilder was a real grade-A scumbag."

By "scumbag," Eric meant that Caleb was devoid of any redeeming qualities whatsoever, just like the guy's mother and father. Jimmy thought that was a hefty claim to make of even the rottenest human beings, but didn't bother to argue.

Eric told him Old Lady Wilder, a notorious loud-mouthed alcoholic, could clear a room with her acrid breath, and Caleb's dim-witted dad had been confined to the St. Clair Correctional Facility for armed robbery. Every Wilder in town had a reputation as conniving, deceitful and mean as a hornet, and the whole family wore that hate like a badge of honor. By the age of seventeen, Caleb had adopted the family tradition of drunken carousing and became a regular occupant of the city jail, picked up on all manner of charges.

Whereas cruelty to animals today signals all sorts of warning alarms to law enforcement about a person's psychotic tendencies, that particular behavioral association wasn't as clear-cut decades ago. Neighbors found Caleb gutting a neighborhood cat. After a few days in jail, the authorities let him back on the street. They would live to regret that decision.

"The guy killed a cat?" Jimmy had a tinge of sympathy for any kid growing up in such lousy circumstances as the Wilder boy, but word of animal cruelty instantly stemmed his good will.

"Worse," Eric said.

"He killed a dog?"

"Even worse."

"A person?"

Eric's lips tightened to a thin line. He looked more serious than Jimmy had ever seen him. "Persons," he whispered. "And they were kids."

A crack of thunder startled them both, and they chuckled nervously at its impeccable timing.

"Kids?" Jimmy asked as the laughter fell away.

Eric stopped smiling. "Three of them."

The feel of cold, dead flesh never bothered Caleb Wilder, but once the smell took hold he would lose all interest in a corpse. He rolled the stiffened little girl off his bed. The body struck the dusty floorboards with a thud.

His brain thumped from last night's whiskey, and his stomach gurgled with acid. He rubbed the crust from his eyes, dreading the labor of digging another hole in the hard ground during the bitter winter. But the body had to be hidden. She stunk. And everyone was looking for her.

He saw movement from the corner of his eye. To his left something flitted away from the window. He leapt to his feet and grabbed his jeans, hopping up and down to jam a leg inside. He jerked them up to his waist as voices rose outdoors. Caleb snatched a dirty sheet from the mattress, spread it over the corpse, and slid it beneath the bed. He turned to see a horrified face staring through the window at his crime. Then another face appeared.

"In here! It's the Wilder boy!"

"Good Lord—he's got Margie Hemmings!"

A patter of footfalls gathered outside. Caleb dashed out the room and sprinted down the hall. He'd left his pistol on the kitchen table. Glass shattered somewhere behind him. A heavy pounding echoed through the house, as the people outside beat on the bolted front door. He rounded the kitchen counter and lunged for the table where he'd left the thirty-eight. The gun was missing. The back door hung ajar.

"Don't move or I'll shoot!"

The familiar hammer-cock of his own revolver clicked right behind his ear.

Large hands clasped his arms and shoulders, shoving him to the table. His face broke an unfinished plate of three-day-old scrambled eggs. The weight of two or three men pinned him down.

He heard the front entrance splinter open. The stomp of boots shook the floor and table beneath his cheekbone. He heard the wail of a female voice, and pictured Mrs. Hemmings huddled over the remains of the child stuffed under his bed. Caleb smirked.

Unseen hands held down his head so he could see only cracks in the kitchen plaster, but several new shadows climbed the walls, and he realized a mob was surrounding him.

"We oughtta blow his brains out right here."

"Nah. Hang him like the old days."

"I want to burn him alive."

"Don't you *touch* him!" hissed a wavering voice in a higher pitch than the rest. "You let me have him first!"

Two burly, bearded men ripped Caleb upward and then hurled him back down on his back, snapping his spine on the table ledge. He bit his tongue bloody to stop from screaming in pain— and giving these people what they wanted.

"Where's the others?" the woman sniffled. Mascara streaked down from her red, watery eyes. Caleb recognized the sharpened carving knife in her hand. He'd used it many times. "You tell me where to find those other little angels, you piece of *garbage!*"

He parted his lips, blood trickling out, and smiled. "They're mine now."

Those were the last words of Caleb Wilder. The men held his head while Mrs. Hemmings cut out his tongue. Then the others went to work on his eyes. They cut off his nose, cut off his ears—everything.

"According to the story, everyone had a turn that day, cutting him to pieces, bit by bit," Eric said. "It happened right inside your *house*, dude."

Jimmy's mouth felt dry. He gnawed his cheek to generate saliva and form a question. "Everyone? What do you mean 'everyone'?"

"Everybody who caught him with the dead girl, I guess. The search party. Everybody who was there that day. Trapper Valley's a small town, even smaller back then, and people tended to look out for each other. The cops had already turned Wilder loose once, so the law couldn't be trusted. People saw there was a killer among them, and knew what had to be done. If everybody took part in the killing, then everybody shared the responsibility. Besides," Eric said, "what are the cops gonna do? Arrest the whole town?"

Jimmy lifted the small wooden door and looked out the broken window to his house across the street. His dad had been sprucing up the inside, but the shabby exterior still suffered from grimy siding, peeling paint and a roof streaked with black algae. "What about those other two kids?"

Eric joined him at the window. The rain had stopped falling, but a cold breeze stirred through the treehouse as they watched Jimmy's new home drip from the eaves.

"Two girls," Eric said. "Just like little Margie Hemmings, he'd killed them both. And did things to the bodies."

"Did things?" Jimmy said. "What kind of things?"

Eric glanced at him and shrugged. "You know. *Things*." He looked at the floor. That's all he needed to say.

"Where'd they find them?"

Eric pointed outside. "Buried in shallow graves. Right in your backyard."

Jimmy swallowed thickly and decided it was high time to have a long talk with his parents.

"I think Eric is pulling your leg, son." Jimmy's dad forked a piece of roast beef and stuck it in his mouth.

Jimmy poked at his mashed potatoes beneath the yellow light of the overhead dining room fixture. "The way he tells it, the whole town knows what happened to the Wilder kid. Right here in this house. Everyone knows except you guys."

His mother raised an eyebrow to his father. "David, there'd better not be any truth to this story." Her voice matched her stern glare.

"Relax, both of you," his dad said. "It didn't happen. Just a silly local legend. Pretty grisly story, sure. Karen, you don't seriously believe a mob of vigilantes cornered some killer in here and carved him like a turkey, do you?"

"Please don't be so graphic. We're having dinner."

His dad swigged down some iced tea. "Don't blame me. Your son's fault."

"Eric swore up and down it's true," Jimmy said.

"He swore that he *heard* it was true," his mother corrected.

"Right" his dad said. "He's just trying to spook you. Besides, even if it were true—which it isn't—what would be the big deal? It happened, what, twenty years ago? Doesn't mean a thing to us. I mean, what are you worried about? Ghosts?"

His dad's dismissal of the idea before he'd even introduced it told Jimmy everything he needed to know about seeking his help with the matter. If an adult were to claim to have seen a ghost, his parents would furtively roll their eyes, but also entertain the story in a polite and patient manner. If he, on the other hand, were to make the same claim then they would dismiss it completely out of hand, without a second thought. Case closed. Jimmy's just being weird.

Teenagers are only taken seriously when they've done something wrong. Jimmy was on his own.

He stared at his food, growing colder by the second. His appetite had left him, and he laid down his fork.

Two weeks later the house felt like a tomb.

"'Night, Mom. 'Night, Dad," Jimmy said from the doorway of their room.

They both lay in bed, reading. Expressionless. Each nodded wordlessly without so much as meeting his eyes. Then he turned in.

He laid his head on his cool pillow, closed his eyes and counted sheep. It never worked to help him sleep, but picturing fluffy cartoon sheep leaping single-file over a picket fence served as a pleasant distraction from the worry that now plagued him morning, noon and night. He feared for the fate of his family.

The spirit of Caleb Wilder slithered through every crack and crevice of his new home, and visual manifestation was only one of the ways it made its devilish presence known. Since they'd moved in, a pervasive coldness haunted the house from attic to cellar, and no matter how his dad chased it with the furnace the chill would not relent. His father blamed a drafty crawlspace, but Jimmy knew the cause was more sinister.

His parents, traditionally a cheery couple, now laughed much less, and even casual conversation in the house had slowed to a trickle. An insulating silence seemed to leaden everyday life. Caleb, lurking in the shadows, was leeching the light and love away from his family, just as he'd done to the handful of other occupants who'd formerly lived in the home.

Although Jimmy could find no proof of murder at their new address when researching online, he discovered that the house had swapped owners four times over the past two decades, and none of the families had lasted much more than a year before vacating. Their new home appeared to be a place where happiness went to die.

Jimmy hated it, but not the house itself. He knew exactly who to blame, just not what to do about it.

A faint whisper, unintelligible, drifted through his bedroom like a strand of spider silk carried by a breeze. It came again, and he made out a single word—his own name. *Jimmy . . .*

He opened his eyes and gave a screech—an eyeless, fleshy skull hovered inches from his face. The lipless mouth stretched a crooked grin beneath the black triangle of its shorn nose. Jimmy bucked and thrashed, madly slapping and swatting with pure instinct but only batting the air—the ghastly visage vanished as instantly as it had appeared.

Jimmy sat bolt upright in his bed, his breath coming in rapid puffs as he heard a trample of footsteps. The door shook with a knock.

"Jimmy, you okay?" his mother said.

"Yes, Mom. Come on in."

His mother showed a begrudging respect for his privacy and always asked permission before entering. Permission to enter, however, was permission to dote, so she rushed into the room, sat on his bedside and placed a hand on his forehead.

"What's wrong, honey?"

"Nothing," he said, pulse settling. "Just a bad dream."

She hugged him to her breast. "Oh sweetie, what are we going to do with you? This is becoming a pattern."

Jimmy took comfort in his mother's warm embrace—rare these days—as he stared into the darkest corner of his room, searching for any sign of the ghost. Caleb Wilder's favorite game was torment, and Jimmy was his new toy.

"I don't know what to do, Mom," he said. "But I'm going to figure it out."

Eric raised his trusty survival knife. "This is what you need."

The six-inch black blade, forged of hardened steel, with saw-tooth serrations along its back, looked capable, with a little elbow grease, of removing someone's head.

"Pop gave me this for camping," he said. "But I carry it around for self-defense. You never know . . . When the crap hits the fan, it's good to be prepared."

"What kind of crap?" Jimmy pulled a gummy worm from a package on the treehouse floor and slurped it up like a noodle.

"Who knows? Could be anything. Terrorists. Disgruntled postal workers. In your case, ghosts." The knife handle was hollow and capped with a ball compass, which Eric twisted off the end. "Inside this little storage compartment it's got a wire saw, a fishing hook and line—even a lead weight—plus a sewing needle in case you need to stitch yourself up." Eric retrieved these items from the handle to exhibit.

"Cool," Jimmy said, and he meant it.

"Yeah, I figure if a zombie apocalypse breaks out, I've got a pretty good leg up on the situation. And a weapon like this would be a good start when it comes to protecting your family from . . . your little problem."

Jimmy's problem had worsened. Not only did the specter plague his sleepless nights, but also Jimmy's family was under constant invisible attack.

Dirty dishes were piling up in the kitchen. Dust bunnies roamed freely across the floorboards. He'd run out of clean underwear, having long grown accustomed to fresh laundry magically reappearing in his chest-of-drawers. His homemaker mother now spent the majority of her days asleep in bed. When asked if she felt okay, if maybe she were sick or depressed, she brushed off the suggestion and acted as though it were a silly question.

Jimmy had become the resident dishwasher.

His father, too, had become an emotionless drone, diving into his remodeling every day after work without so much as acknowledging Jimmy or his mother's presence. Sanding, taping, priming, painting—robotically—one room and then the next, he worked with mechanical precision, rarely speaking a word. The most frustrating development was his parents' utter obliviousness to the change in their personalities, how it taxed the health and well-being of the family, as if infected with a cancer only he could detect. Jimmy knew without a doubt that Caleb Wilder was the tumor.

"The problem is," Jimmy said. "Caleb Wilder is already dead. In fact, the people of Trapper Valley used knives, much like that one, to cut him to pieces. And he still comes back."

"So . . ."

"*So*," Jimmy said. "How do you kill a guy twice?"

"I'm not sure. But have you even tried?"

Sinking a big blade into an evil ghost in the hope of saving his family did not strike Jimmy as a distasteful idea. His options were limited, and he supposed it was worth a shot.

"I found instructions online for assassinating a target with a knife."

"Jeez," Jimmy said. "I guess you can find pretty much anything online."

"Reckon so," Eric said, standing up. He unfolded a printed sheet of paper from his pocket and handed it to Jimmy. "It describes the technique here. The target is approached from the rear. You're supposed to grasp the mouth and nose in a clamped palm and simultaneously thrust the knife into the right kidney area, withdraw the knife and slash the throat from ear to ear."

As he described the tactic, he pantomimed the procedure, executing an imaginary victim and dropping them to the treehouse floor.

"Another variation," he said, "is instead of slicing the throat; the blade is stabbed into the neck three or four inches below the ear until it protrudes from the opposite side. Then the knife is slashed outwards, through the throat." He sliced the knife out of the imaginary neck. "I've been practicing."

"Looks like it."

"Take this," Eric said, sheathing the blade and extending it handle first. "Keep in mind that this weapon is my prized possession, and I would not loan it to just anybody. But you're a good bud. And you need it."

Jimmy took the knife and gazed upon it with reverence. "Thanks, man," he said. "I'll put it to good use."

The night was quiet. The only source of light in Jimmy's room, the dim bulb of his fish tank, lit the corner with a dull blue glow. Lying in bed with hands behind his head, he glassed every nook and cranny of the room, trying to penetrate the darkness with eagle vision. When Caleb would appear, it was always as a slender charcoal silhouette and a bone-white face more corpse than man, with pitch black holes where his features had been carved from his flesh. The apparition made frequent visits to jar Jimmy out of his troubled slumber. He figured the ghost's plan was to keep him bedraggled, weary and weak—to wear him down, and then one day finish him off. But tonight Jimmy had a surprise.

A shadow flashed across the fish tank, and he knew he wasn't alone. His pulse quickened.

"I know you're here," Jimmy said. "What do you want?"

He didn't understand the spirit's method of movement. On past encounters it seemed to leak from the shadows, vanish in a blink, then materialize elsewhere within the beat of a bat's wing. Jimmy's eyes danced across the room, ready to face any direction.

"Why not show yourself?" It took great effort for him to speak with a steady voice. Maybe antagonism would get a rise out of the thing. "What are you afraid of?"

An impulse nagged him to grab the nightstand lamp, pull the chain and awash the room with light. A second thought told him it wouldn't work; Caleb Wilder only appeared in the darkness.

A whisper tickled his ear. *What are you afraid of?*

Jimmy whipped upright, snatched the knife from beneath his pillow and sliced through the air. A snide chuckle came from behind him, and he swung around in a wide arc, the blade finding nothing.

Another snicker over his shoulder, and Jimmy stabbed before turning, spinning his body to follow through into black empty space. The voiceless hiss came again: *What are you afraid of?*

Jimmy knew the thing was projecting those words somehow, not speaking them. It had no tongue to form them.

"Where are you?" Jimmy stepped off the bed. He crouched with the knife eager to strike. "Are you chicken? Is that why you hide?"

The shape edged into the dim blue light of the room's corner. Jimmy first saw the arm, thin and inky, then a leg. He inched toward it. The thing's scraggly hair spiked and curled around its pallid face like a crown of thorns.

Jimmy, it whispered and then laughed.

Jimmy lunged and got him this time, drove the knife dead center of its chest, but met no resistance. The blade went right through him like stabbing an illusion. Jimmy's breath seized. Standing face to butchered face, the thing drew back its mangled mouth in a grimy smile and cackled. Elbow deep, Jimmy dug the blade around futilely in its spectral body. He felt no flesh or bone, nor smelled its gory decay. But around the torn rim of Caleb Wilder's missing eyes squirmed tiny countless vermin. And deep within those black pits he faintly saw the ashen faces of three little girls, screaming in terror.

The thing's wiry hands shot up and slashed at his throat. Jimmy cried out, leapt back in panic.

He was alone.

Jimmy threw a hand to his Adam's apple, gasping, spinning around in search of the ghost. But he saw nothing. And his throat felt fine.

He let go of his neck and saw no blood on his fingers. He took a deep breath. He sat on the bed and clutched his head, concentrating on easing his nerves.

Calm down, he thought. *You're not hurt. You're fine. You faced it down. You walked away . . . Think about what just happened.*

Head still swimming, it took several bangs on the door for him to realize his mother was knocking.

"I asked if everything was alright," his mom said. "I heard you shout."

"Uh. Yeh-*yes*, Mom," he stammered. "Sorry. Come on in."

The door opened. She went to his side, slid an arm around his shoulders, but blanched when she saw the knife.

"What's going on, son?"

166

He looked at the blade and put it down on the nightstand. Still foggy, he said, "Our house really is haunted, Mom. The story is true."

She squinted her eyes into a skeptical look.

"It's okay, though," he said. "Because I realized something tonight. The ghost can't really hurt us. I can't seem to harm him, but he can't touch us either. And if he can't hurt me, then there's really nothing to be afraid of."

Jimmy spoke the next words louder so Caleb Wilder might hear: "I guess when it gets right down to it, a ghost is really just a *wimp*. Nothing to it. Nothing but a stupid little *nuisance!*" He eyeballed the room, inspecting the shadows, unsure where to direct his daggered scowl.

Jimmy's dad appeared in the doorway. "Everything okay?" Those were the first words he'd heard his old man speak in days.

His mother looked at Jimmy, then at his dad, shaking her head. "Don't worry. Jimmy's just being weird."

The incident with the knife had eliminated half of Jimmy's problem—the corpselike-phantom-terrorizing-him portion of the haunting. While technically a failure at dispatching the thing, the face-to-face confrontation proved the ghost of Caleb Wilder was all but fangless, relying on fear and intimidation. Jimmy had not only shed his fear of bodily harm but now kindled a righteous fury against what he saw as his arch nemesis.

Its presence continued to poison the atmosphere of his home. His parents were still blindly stuck in emotionless mire, zombie walking through life with nothing to jump-start their personalities short of the fearful nighttime screams of their son. And those days were over.

"Too bad the knife didn't work," Eric said over the phone.

"It didn't kill him," Jimmy said. "But now I know Caleb can't kill me, either. That is crucial information."

"I'd say so."

"Now it's time for phase two."

"What do you mean?"

"For my parents' sake, I've got to get rid of the ghost completely."

"Phase two," Eric said, "Total eradication. Awesome. What's the plan?"

167

"I'm not sure. I was thinking maybe some sort of spell. Maybe even an exorcism."

"I'm in. But what do you know about exorcisms?"

"Nothing," Jimmy said. "But I'm willing to learn. Feel like going to the bookstore? I need to give your knife back, anyway."

"That's cool. I'll meet you out on the street."

Saturday afternoon brought a clear sky and a pleasant breeze. A few blocks beyond their neighborhood was a small business district with a couple of fast-food joints, a bank, post office and Burnside Books—Jimmy's favorite local shop.

Waiting for Eric to join him roadside, he opened the mailbox. He tucked the survival knife beneath his arm and sorted through the letters, hoping in vain for something interesting with his name on it. A car whizzed by as he filed through the stack. He found only bills and advertisement circulars for "unbelievable markdowns" on new vehicles.

As he stuffed the mail back in the box, a familiar sense of unease fell over him like a cold rain. Jimmy looked around. At first, nothing appeared out of the ordinary. A station wagon cruised past without incident. Two blackbirds took flight from a power line and soared into the sky. He noticed Eric had left his front porch and was walking across the lawn toward the street. Jimmy saw nobody else, but then heard a reptilian whisper behind him.

What are you afraid of?

Jimmy spun to see Caleb Wilder's skeletal figure ten yards away on his porch, with his white face cocked at an angle. Jimmy lost his breath. He blinked twice, hard. In that instant the thing appeared closer, just a few feet away, the crimson glint of crusted blood visible around its wounds.

It whispered, *Jimmy.*

His blood turned to ice. He cast a glance at Eric nearing the road, skipping along innocently, unaware of the ghost, not seeing what Jimmy saw.

Unsettled but unafraid, Jimmy snarled, "What do you want? You leave me and my family alone."

The hum of an engine signaled an approaching car.

A reedy snicker came from the thing's ragged grin, and Jimmy blinked again. When he opened his eyes, it was gone.

"You ready?" Eric's voice came from right across the road.

Jimmy whirled around. The piercing screech of skidding tires stabbed his ears. Caleb Wilder stood dead center in the road, arms outstretched in triumph. A speeding red SUV slammed on its brakes, jerked sideways and careened off the road to miss him.

Eric turned to the racket. The wall of ruby metal hurtled toward him like the sledge of a giant hammer. Jimmy shouted a warning from the top of his lungs, the words lost in the squeal of rubber.

Eric raised his hands, bracing. The impact erased him in a flash. A solid boom and a heavy clunking beneath the vehicle— the sounds hit Jimmy like a slug to the gut. Halfway off the road, the SUV came to a standstill in a spray of mud and sod.

The driver's door slung open. A young woman hopped out, shaking her hands like trying to dry her nails.

Jimmy couldn't breathe.

The woman ran to the rear of the vehicle. Eric's body lay twisted, not moving. She leaned over him and gave a low, animal wail like Jimmy had never heard before, falling to her knees and clutching her hair.

Another car pulled to a stop. Two people rushed out to help.

"It's not my fault," the driver cried. "I saw another boy! I had to swerve! He was in the middle of the road!"

The other couple covered their faces, shaking their heads.

"You!" the woman bawled, pointing at Jimmy. "The boy in the road—you saw him, right? I swear he was standing in the street!"

Eric's parents were now rushing from their home, shouting for their son, his mother's face withering as she drew near.

Jimmy stood there with his jaw open, speechless, watching the world fall apart.

At the viewing, Jimmy placed Eric's prized survival knife, cleaned and sheathed, alongside his body in the casket. Eric's parents had approved the gesture as a show of respect, agreeing their son would have wanted exactly that. Jimmy then mail-ordered an identical knife for himself—something to always keep as a reminder of their friendship.

In the days that followed, grief ate at Jimmy unlike anything he'd ever suffered. He'd never known a close friend to die, and the sorrow pulled him down like a tar pit. He tried not to think of how Eric would never drive a car, or go to prom, hit a game-winning home run, or marry the love of his life. He tried not to dwell on those thoughts because they were vile and poisonous, and Jimmy already bore plenty of those.

In the wake of the tragedy, his home life had sunk to an all-time low. The very atmosphere of the house had become so oppressive that joy seemed a distant memory. Nobody even spoke to each other. Caleb Wilder was killing his family from the inside out.

At a loss for what to do, Jimmy had picked up a few books at the local shop and researched a number of famous hauntings, but had yet to find instructions on how to rid the house of an entity. The future looked bleak.

The following Saturday shrouded Trapper Valley in a gray blanket of cloud, but Jimmy walked to his mailbox with a rare air of high expectation. His package was due to arrive: a new hardened steel survival knife, complete with ball compass, hollow composite handle, fishing tools, wire saw, leather case plus an integrated pocket for a sharpening stone. The parcel had shown up, and Jimmy tore into it with a fervor he hadn't felt in days. He ripped open the plastic and marveled at the knife's beautiful black steel and pristine cutting edge. Eric had been right; it was truly a work of art.

Yet, standing there holding the knife made it impossible to ignore the awful memory of losing his friend. The trauma still raw, everything felt cold, too cold and too familiar. Jimmy looked around. The street deserted, the neighborhood seemed uncannily still and quiet, like a sailor describes the eye of a storm.

Jimmy once again felt that leering stare burn into him like the scope of a sniper, and his heart darkened. He turned to see Caleb Wilder standing across the street like a scarecrow. The specter tilted its face, watching him from the very spot where Eric had met his end, and gave a wicked grin.

Pure hatred welled inside Jimmy. He clenched his teeth, and a fire stoked within him. He wanted nothing more than to stalk over to the thing and gash it to ribbons with his new razor-sharp weapon. But it would be useless to try, and Jimmy's powerlessness made him seethe with rage.

From the corner of his eye, something caught his attention. To the rear of that wretched face, roughly thirty yards away, was Eric's rickety treehouse perched in a tall maple. The frayed rope ladder that dangled beneath hung completely still even though

Jimmy could see perfectly well someone shimmying down to the ground.

Jimmy looked at the ghost of Caleb Wilder as it uttered with a tongue-less hiss, *what are you afraid of, Jimmy?*

The thing did not notice what approached it from behind.

Jimmy's heart raced. His good friend Eric Hyde was marching across the lawn while pulling a large black knife from a leg-strapped leather sheath. He wore the same clothes as on the day of his death—and not a scratch on him. Eric's steely, square-jaw expression, like a soldier on a mission, gave Jimmy a sudden rush of confidence. He leveled a glare at Caleb, who gawked back through empty sockets.

"You're a grade-A scumbag, you know that?" Jimmy growled. Impossibly, his friend had already halved the distance between them. "You're one seriously sick puppy."

The thing only chuckled, a sound of tumbling dead leaves.

Eric drew within a few feet of reach.

"But you screwed up this time. You shouldn't have messed with my friend . . ."

Eric clamped his palm over Caleb Wilder's ruined nose and mouth, lifting the bony figure from the ground with a single arm. In a spastic fit, the thing squirmed and writhed. Eric's eyes gleamed. He raised the knife high. With cobra speed, he thrust the blade into its right kidney area, eliciting a shocked but muffled moan.

. . . because Eric has been practicing.

Eric ripped out the knife and buried it to the hilt in the thing's pale, skinny throat. With a flick of the wrist, he slashed it open from ear to ear.

Gagging and convulsing, the black figure crumpled to the ground hemorrhaging a thick, sooty dust from the gaping wounds. Its elbows folded and its face hit the grass. The thing's skeletal frame bled away like spilled ink, disintegrating into the soil below. In a few seconds, it was gone.

Jimmy leaned against the mailbox to steady himself. He took a deep breath of fresh air. It cooled his lungs, tasted crisp and clean. Like breaking dawn, the day brightened. Clouds parted for a strong beam of sunlight that warmed his shoulders. A bird in the distance chirped a playful tune. Jimmy had the sense that the world around him was awakening from a long slumber.

Eric looked at him and said in a strangely distant voice, "Phase two." He sheathed his blade and smiled bigger than ever.

"Thanks, buddy," Jimmy said.

His friend lifted an arm and gave him a military-style salute. Then he turned and headed back to the treehouse, but vanished before making it to the rope ladder.

Wherever Eric was now, he seemed happy. And that meant a lot.

The music playing from inside his house surprised Jimmy as much as anything. He opened the door to the deep-bass baritone of Johnny Cash on the stereo, his dad's all-time favorite singer. In the kitchen, he found his mother humming along while stacking sugar, eggs and chocolate chips on the countertop.

"I feel like making cookies," she greeted. "How does that sound?"

His father came around the corner carrying a paint pail and singing the chorus to "I Got Stripes." He kissed his wife on the cheek and gave Jimmy a wink. "I could use a hand if you're not too busy, son."

"Jimmy?" his mother said, snapping him out of a confused stupor. "That sound good to you?"

"I'm sorry. What'd you say?"

"Cookies . . . You want some?"

Jimmy looked around his home as though seeing it for the first time. The icy chill was gone, and Jimmy welcomed the sunny warmth that now filled the house. At long last, everything felt right again.

"Sure, Mom."

Cookies had never sounded better.

Nicholas Day

The Ghost in Winter's Wake

Philip loved to hide...

It was one of the worst winters in William's memory, though the old man's memory wasn't always reliable, not nearly as reliable as his hands. Those hands were ready to get back to work.

Mrs. Reed woke William very early, so early that light had yet to tickle the horizon. She demanded that he sort through the garden and discard the dead plants, the fallen leaves, anything that would serve as a reminder of the death brought about by winter. Mrs. Reed believed that the dead growth would smother the perennials. William admired the woman's optimism, the way she handled death, but she was wrong.

William argued against the strange request. He tried to reassure the woman that dead vegetation would simply act as a natural fertilizer. The new plants could only benefit from what the winter left in its wake. She was very insistent that it all had to go, displaying a curtness unfamiliar to the aged gardener, informing him that either he would do it or she would simply hire someone else. William did as he told; after all, he knew what she was getting at.

Mrs. Reed wanted to forget winter, forget how it touched her and her husband. *Maybe,* William thought, *Mrs. Reed believes that the damned winter wants her, that it wants her whole family.* It was so unnecessary, though, because winter was gone. All that it took was her youngest son, Philip. William had almost forgotten that awful bit of news, his memory being what it was.

In Alton, Illinois, melting snow still stood in areas of heavy shade. It thrived in the periphery, slipping away from the town and disregarded like some seasonal leper. It was the rotting flesh of winter months, lying in its grave of early spring.

Ice on the Mississippi cracked and flaked like dead skin. The trees were within weeks of turning green. New flowers would soon begin to bloom. This winter, in particular, was terribly hard on everything and everyone. Its bitter cold left an air of grief that spring would have to balm.

William had been with the Reed family as far back as he could recall. He considered their garden the very best to work in and the Reed's always thought William to be their very best groundskeeper. After fifty-odd years, on that sunny, if not slightly cool afternoon, that sentiment remained unchallenged.

William walked the grounds of the Reed residence, which sat high atop the bluff along the mighty river, overlooking the city's bustling downtown. William thought of Philip, a playful child and, in his opinion, the best of the Reed's three children. He suspected that Mrs. Reed felt the same. He saw in their relationship an attention and affection that made him yearn for his own mother, April.

As it was with Philip, winter had been present for the death of William's mother, though it did not take her. Instead, winter was the weapon, snow to be precise, tightly compacted and used like a gag. William was too young to protect April from his father, Filicidio, and he could only bear witness to her murder. It was the most persistent of all the gardener's memories.

Philip Reed, like William's mother, was found face down in the snow, in the in the garden, dressed for the cold, still wearing his red wool mittens. The matching wool cap lay a few feet away. His big winter coat, zipped up tight, was a gift from Mrs. Reed, her last gift to the boy. He had been making a snowman. Philip loved the snow.

When did it happen?

William tried to remember. It must have been during that vacuum of time after Christmas but before New Year's Eve. People said that it was an ugly way to start the year.

Philip's eyes were wide open when Mrs. Reed found him, wide and dark, as dark as the onyx stones that the boy used for the snowman's eyes. His mouth gaped, as if he had trouble breathing; or died screaming.

The cause of death, drowning; the snow, you see, it melted. In the throat and in the lungs, winter's progeny collected in tiny, suffocating pools.

William tried to conjure the garden in winter as he closed his eyes: A blanket of white snow spread across the acre of growth;

heavy shade afforded by the great pine cutting that acre in half; a snowman, tucked away in the darkest corner, near the trunk of the evergreen. The hysterical Mrs. Reed, on her knees, screamed and pulled at her hair, while a faceless Mr. Reed ran out of the three-story brick home toward a dead little boy wearing red wool mittens. *Why can't I remember Mr. Reed's face?*

Remembering was so difficult that William often made up his own memories. They were just as good, he reckoned, and William closed his eyes tighter, trying to see everything from Mrs. Reed's point of view.

He imagined himself in the Reed's home, the smell of the raging fireplace and the clunk and clack of wood chucked into the hearth. *Father always threw wood into the fire.* Looking out through the big picture window, Mrs. Reed must have seen the hint of warm red clothes through the fallen snow. They were such big snowflakes, too, the size of quarters, perfect for packing tight and building. She would have seen the snowman facing the house, its arms raised in such a way that you could swear it looked as though it were trying to wave for help. Of course, trying to wave was all that the snowman could do, because he had no mouth with which to scream. Philip never had a chance to finish. No smoking corncob pipe or silly grin made out of coal. Just two twig arms, raised in alarm, and black, emotionless eyes. Philip was perfectly still.

William. . .

There was a chill in the air and William saw something else. Mrs. Reed ran frantically toward her motionless son. She saw the snowman waving to her, but not for help. His arms called to attention the boy before him, like an excited child. Those onyx eyes were wide with excitement. *Look! Look what I did! Here is your dead brat, you bitch. Take him away; take him into that big warm house. I've choked the life out of him, can't you see? He's still screaming, Mrs. Reed. Can you hear him? You cannot hide from me. I will have all of you.*

William opened his eyes. He was freezing cold, daydreamed his way to the garden. He had forgotten his coat.

William. . .

Did he hear his name? The air turned to bitter chill and the cold burned his ears. Where was his winter cap? William looked toward the great brick home. He saw someone standing at the far corner of the lawn, in the shade of the pine. The person waved and William waved in return. He started up the lawn. Mr. Reed was always a friendly man. William shivered violently. He hoped Mr. Reed would let him borrow a coat, but Mr. Reed *wasn't* the one standing beneath that great tree, waving.

Melting snow still accumulated in the heavy shade. It seemed to thrive there. Philip's snowman still stood, though hideously disfigured, wasting away like a nightmare raising its arms to the sky.

William looked at the terrible effigy and rubbed his cold hands together. They burned, naked in the elements. Why didn't he wear gloves? William pondered his burning hands and rubbed them up and down his arms. It felt like his whole body was burning. William grabbed his shirt at the hem and took it off. The cold air formed a sheath around his torso. He forgot the burning in his hands and ears.

William surveyed the garden, the spotted areas of snow, the twigs and leaves and flattened flowers, all the color of mud. *All this,* he thought, *nourishing rot.* What a waste. Didn't Mrs. Reed want him to do something about the decomposition?

William...

The old man spun around. Philip was playing a trick on him, hiding in the garden. Philip loved his tricks, didn't he? It's why Mrs. Reed wanted him punished. He scared her, wouldn't answer her calls, making her cry. She thought he'd been lost forever. She sobbed through the evening, until Philip pounced on her from the recess of a bedroom closet. "Boo." Philip screamed. "I was hiding in here the whole time, Mommy." He laughed until she struck him, then he cried too. The game was over. Philip would never hide, again. "Punish the boy." Mrs. Reed had demanded. William did as told.

The gardener crept around the base of the pine. He circled the dead Azalea bushes, sometimes pushing his face deep into the twisting branches. He felt them prick his skin. There was no sign of Philip. The boy was playing his silly game, again, even though William had told him not to, had begged him not to. Hurt him.

Something trickled down his forehead, into his eye. He felt the tickle of liquid running down his cheeks. His lips tasted of copper. William wiped his face.

His hands. Red. The mittens. He had Philip's mittens.

Who do you think you are?

William looked toward the Reed's home. He saw Mrs. Reed standing at the far corner of the lawn. The rear entrance to the home stood ajar. William smelled burning wood.

"William, what on earth are you doing? You. . ."

What am I doing? Mrs. Reed asked me to come here, doesn't she remember?

". . . have been out here for going on five hours!"

William squinted. He savored the feeling of warm skin sliding over cold, frozen eyes.

William, listen to me.

William's head felt like it was spinning. He thought he heard Mrs. Reed say something, but she didn't enunciate properly.

William, do you remember why you are here?

William pushed his hands into the cold, wet earth. Had he sat down? He couldn't remember. Someone, a woman, his mother, screamed nonsense. Stupid woman. Can't a man sit down for just one moment?

William, you came here to help me.

William's head swam in nausea. He opened his eyes but didn't know where he was. He thought he saw a woman off in the distance, near some great house.

He vomited.

Winter is over, William, but there's some flowers still living, in that house.

He wanted to get up. He wanted to leave. Something caught his attention. William thought he heard a new voice, a cold voice. It sounded like it came from the bottom of a well, from the bottom of his most persistent memory.

The old man couldn't see too far away, but two things stood out clearly: black, onyx eyes stared down at him—Filicidio's eyes.

Who do you think you are?

Mrs. Reed watched her husband William finally stand up. He must have sat there for what was going on six or seven minutes, and shirtless, no doubt. She worried that his mind was finally gone. She wondered if she should have him committed. The old man lumbered toward the house and away from the heavy shade. He was as white as a sheet.

William kept his eyes on her the whole time, except for one moment, when he stopped to pick up a handful of wet snow. He packed it tight, a thick blob of pure winter. He approached her.

William threw his arms up in the air, as if he was trying to bring attention to something, like an excited child. Mrs. Reed thought that she heard him say something, but all she could do was marvel at his black, emotionless eyes.

William pounced on her. "Boo!" He screamed. "I was hiding in here the whole time, Mommy." Mrs. Reed froze at the sound of Philip's voice. She cried. He laughed until she struck him, then he cried, too. Their game was over.

"Punish her," Philip demanded.

William did as told.

Steve Foreman

A Tale of Nan Scott

Fergus Shea turned the van off the main artery and onto a minor road that led toward the village of Lyme. "Were getting close," he remarked to his passenger. As they drove slowly through, the village appeared to be merely comprised of a narrow high street lined with cottages, a heavily whitewashed general store-cum-Post Office, and a pub bearing the sign, 'The Miners Arms'. The roofs of a few large farm buildings or barns were visible above and behind the cottages.

Passing out of Lyme village, the road narrowed further into a country lane lined with ancient hedges planted and laid a thousand years before by the Saxon farmers, and bordered by winter fields that sprouted only scarecrows and dead wheat stubble.

Slowing down, Fergus glanced up at a decorative metal sign affixed to a gatepost. The faded sign, pitted with rust, indicated they had reached their destination. "Here we are!" he announced as he swung the van to the left and stopped outside the wrought iron gates. His companion, Adrian Greensward, jumped out of the vehicle, and, with a bunch of keys given to him by the agency, soon had the padlock and chain removed. Swinging the gates open, he clambered back into the van and Fergus drove up the weed-covered gravel driveway.

Bellingham Towers loomed before them; a rambling old stone edifice—dominating the surrounding countryside from the crown of a small hill and silhouetted against the blue morning sky like some dark castle.

The mansion stood empty, decaying slowly amongst the poplars, oaks, and overgrown gardens of the vast grounds that surrounded it. With each year that passed it became more neglected and dilapidated.

"This property has been abandoned by the Bellingham family, in terms of actual habitation, for eight years," Fergus explained once again, although Adrian already knew the story. "Numerous schemes and projects to have it sold, tenanted or merely maintained failed due to various influences."

The rambling mansion was over six hundred years old, and much of it, particularly the peripheral wings and the four towers and turrets unoccupied for several centuries, was in a state of total and possibly irrevocable dilapidation. The main or central sections of the house that the last of the Bellinghams had occupied were in dire need of renovation... and then there was the haunting. If nothing else prevented the sale of the property, then the presence of the malevolent ghost did—the ghost of Nan Scott, whom the two paranormal investigators whose mission was to exorcise.

The van crunched to a halt on a gravel circle, in the centre of which stood a defunct fountain. After unloading their gear and piling it on the topmost of seven broad steps, Adrian unlocked the front doors with the largest key on the bunch and the two men found themselves inside the great hall of Bellingham Towers. They ferried their gear through the empty and neglected drawing rooms and morning rooms until various infrared and ultra-violet cameras, heat sensors and proximity detectors, high frequency sound sensors, and ultra-sensitive microphones and tape recorders lay deposited about the West Wing.

"Damn me, Fergus," Adrian said. "Have you noticed that even though it is warm and sunny outside, there is a pervading chill in the air in here?" Fergus nodded agreement and both men donned shell jackets to keep warm.

The door that led into the tower in which Nan Scott reportedly perished, firmly padlocked in place, and appeared untouched for years. "No key on this bunch fits the padlock," said Adrian, after trying the half-a-dozen keys. Fergus winked and reached into his pack, producing a small crowbar. "I have one that fits all!" He grinned. Walking over to the door, he inserted the end of the bar behind the padlock, ripped it away from the rusty hasp and, to the groaning accompaniment of protesting hinges, pushed the door wide open.

Directly in front of them were the first steps of a narrow wrought-iron staircase. Spiralling around a stone column, it climbed steeply into the ever-growing darkness above.

"It's too narrow to haul up all our equipment," Adrian said, selecting a couple of sensors and removing a specialised camera from its tripod. Fergus flicked on a flashlight, and, leading the way, the two men stepped through the doorway and immediately began climbing. They ascended cautiously, craning their necks as they peered around the ever-blind curve of the steep dark stairway. Finally, they came to a landing high in the tower. Arrow-slit windows let in narrow shafts of sunlight. The old wooden floorboards creaked as they stepped forward toward the single door that faced them. The door gave access to the turret that sat on top of the tower; the turret where Nan Scott had been housed and where she was allegedly murdered.

They glanced at each other in the gloom. Fergus could see the frown on Adrian's face and the clenched muscles of his jaw, but Adrian managed a grin and nodded his head; his blue eyes like saucers in the torchlight. "Go on, then," he encouraged. Fergus reached out tentatively for the simple latch. His hand trembled as he gripped the corroded lever. At first, it would not budge, but as he increased the pressure with his thumb, the latch suddenly flew up with a loud 'clack!' Both men gasped, but remained firm. Fergus pushed the door inward. A curtain of dust fell silently through the torch beam as the door creaked open. Adrian swung the proximity sensor he carried back and forth, but the needle did not move.

The torch light revealed a room that was empty save an ancient wooden trunk lying against the far wall, sitting like a coffin under a narrow slit window that let in only a faint knife blade of daylight.

"Well, what now?" asked Adrian, relief clearly discernible in his voice.

"Let's check out that trunk." Fergus indicated, and both men stepped toward it.

There was no warning. The lid flew open with a resounding crash and from the trunk a terrifying apparition flew screaming toward them. The men stumbled backward; their arms rose automatically across their faces in defence. Fergus held up a crucifix in one hand but the ghost merely sent it flying across the small chamber as she slashed at them wildly with long blackened fingernails, ripping holes in their shell jackets. An ear-splitting screech emitted from a gaping mouth full of rotten teeth and the two men covered their ears. The spiritual energy of the apparition crashed into them, and they fell backward down the spiral staircase. Tumbling head-over-heels, cracking shins and elbows on every sharp edge of the iron steps, and bashing their heads onto the hard stone walls, they crashed down in a confusion of twisting limbs and coruscating torchlight. Uttering a constant deafening shriek and with her tattered dress flying out behind her, the ghost of Nan Scott relentlessly pursued them; her evil talons outstretched. Her presence was a physical force that accelerated their fall and the men crashed onto the stone floor and went sprawling though the open doorway and into the West Wing, knocking over tripods and cameras, and slithered to a halt, bruised, bleeding and unconscious amongst their scattered equipment.

Nan Scott stood in the doorway, hands on hips, as she looked down at the two men. She smiled with satisfaction, an evil smile. Her figure began to lose substance, wavering and thinning, and like a cloud of cigar smoke suddenly tugged by a breeze, she melted away back into the shadows and drifted silently up the staircase of the tower.

Adrian and Fergus slowly regained consciousness more or less together. It was now dark in the room. Night had fallen outside while they lay there.

Fergus picked up the flashlight lying nearby, the light fading as the batteries died. "Jesus H. Christ!" He gasped breathlessly, glancing around in a sort of daze, "That was a close call. I have never in all my years as a ghost hunter..."

"Christ," interrupted Adrian in a hoarse whisper, as he sat up. "That scared me shitless! I have never seen a ghost before! Sorry Fergus... are you badly hurt?"

"A few cuts and bruises and maybe a cracked rib; and I must have bit my tongue." Fergus licked at the blood dripping from the corner of his lips. "But I don't think there's any permanent damage; how about you?"

In the faint light, Fergus could see there was a smear of blood on Adrian's forehead and that he had a slight nosebleed. Adrian tenderly rubbed his right shinbone, grimacing; "Jesus, that hurts! Don't think I'll be playing golf for a while," he said with a wry grin.

"You couldn't play before!" Fergus snorted a quick but painful laugh.

"We must have been unconscious for hours!" Adrian exclaimed. "What time is it? My watch is not working; the LED screen is blank."

Fergus tilted the limp flashlight onto his analogue watch, but the watch hands had stopped when the two men fell from the tower. He glanced out of the window at the night sky. "It's pitch black outside. I guess we were out for several hours! Unbelievable," he said, quietly, handing Adrian the handkerchief he had used to dab his lips. "Wipe the blood off your face. C'mon, let's get the hell out of here, we need to get checked out by a doctor or hospital as quick as possible, have X-rays or whatever; just in case there's any internal damage or fractures."

The two men limped their way silently to the great hall and left the house though the open doors and went down the steps to the parking circle, glancing over their shoulders at the double portals, but all was quiet; nothing pursued them. Dead leaves blew in a flurry, rustling and hissing as they tumbled and chased after each other across the weed-strewn gravel. The torch light faded and gave up its struggle to live. Fergus dropped it to the floor of the vehicle as they clambered inside.

He reached into his pocket for the van's keys, but they were missing. "Shit!" he exclaimed. "They must have fallen out when we fell down the staircase! I'm definitely not going back in there to look for them!"

Adrian nodded silently in firm agreement.

Adrian tried his mobile phone, but there was no signal. "What should we do?" he asked Fergus. "I mean, shall we walk to the village and see if there is a doctor or a police station?"

"I guess it's our only choice," Fergus replied, also checking, unsuccessfully, for a signal on his phone.

The two investigators, each supporting the other, limped slowly down the driveway. Passing through the open wrought iron gates, they stepped out onto the narrow country lane and stopped, looking left and right in silent perplexity. There was no light beyond a few faint stars and a pale fingernail paring of a moon. The lane was in almost total darkness.

A cold wind soughed through the trees arching above them, and rustled the hedgerows. An owl hooted eerily from a copse nearby. Across the dark empty fields could be heard the piercing yelp-howl of a dog fox. Adrian and Fergus shivered, turned to their right and began the two-mile walk to the tiny hamlet of Lyme.

After about half an hour, they saw faint lights. There were no lampposts as they entered the village; the dim yellow light shone from the low windows of several cottages that lined the narrow street. Just ahead was an open doorway, and here the light spilling out onto the pavement was brighter and accompanied by voices and raucous piano music; it was the village pub, The Miners Arms.

Eager to use a phone but even more keen to get a drink to warm them up, Adrian and Fergus stepped through the narrow open doorway and into the pub. The music faltered slightly as the piano player hit a couple of discordant notes and two or three patrons glanced briefly toward the doorway, but within seconds the pianist was banging away again at the old upright and a few voices were raised in song. Other than a few folks at the bar and a couple standing around the piano, most of the patrons were ensconced in small high-backed dark wood booths, where they sat chatting away noisily across the tops of mugs of ale. Most if not all were farm labourers, dressed in worn tweed jackets and rough corduroy trousers and heavy work boots; local folk, born and bred in the village; salt of the earth.

Adrian nudged Fergus and indicated with a nod the empty booth at the back of the smoky room. "C'mon. Let's grab a seat over there."

The ceiling was low, and supported by heavy oak beams adorned with horse brasses, arcane farm implements and old brewing paraphernalia. A log fire crackled in a hearth beneath a huge stone fireplace, warming the long, narrow room.

Adrian and Fergus slid in onto the worn wooden benches opposite each other and waited for a server.

"Funny lot, these villagers," Fergus whispered out of the corner of his mouth, leaning forward over the table toward Adrian. "Very closed shop to strangers and mistrustful of anyone who is not *from around these 'ere part,*" he finished, with a clichéd country accent.

Adrian came back with a wry grin. "At least we should look the part. Torn jackets and all covered in shit!"

At that moment, the stout landlord approached; he wore a long apron and carried aloft a wooden tray bearing some beverages. The publican ignored Fergus and Adrian and passed right by the booth; setting down on a small round table nearby two mugs of ale and a glass of sherry. The two old codgers at the table lifted their mugs and took big swallows of the beer. Turning to make his way back to the bar, the landlord hesitated at the booth where

Adrian and Fergus sat, glanced at them briefly with a dark frown upon his wide face and then, without speaking or taking their order, walked hurriedly away.

Before Adrian could protest or slide out of the booth to go and order drinks at the bar, a fat old woman came out of the toilets and waddled along the narrow gap that ran between the booths and the wall, blocking Adrian's route. As she drew level with Adrian and Fergus's booth, she faltered to a stop. Almost mimicking the landlord, the woman turned toward the booth, a silent question creasing her rapidly paling robust face. Without a word, she hurried away to where her glass of sherry sat waiting for her on the table between the two old men. She plumped herself down on her stool and finished off the sherry in one gulp. The two old men looked at her in surprise, then laughed and took good swallows of their beer. The woman sat with her mouth agape, speechless. Ignoring her, the two men carried on their conversation under drifting wreathes of blue pipe smoke.

"Have I still got blood on my face," Fergus asked his colleague. "Is that what's wrong with everyone?"

"Well, just a smudge on your forehead," Adrian confirmed, touching the corner of his own mouth to see if his tongue was still bleeding. "But I wouldn't have thought it was enough to cause that sort of reaction."

"This is weird, like something out of a horror movie." Fergus said quietly, and a mental image of the village pub scene in the film *An American Werewolf in London* slipped unannounced and unwelcome into Adrian's mind.

"I think it is time we got out of here," he said. "I don't like the feel of this place. Let's forget about having a drink and find a Police Station or a phone box." With that, the two men slid quietly out of the booth and shuffled through the crowded room to the door. Again, the piano player hit a couple of wrong keys and the ribald singing diminished. No one spoke to them.

"Holy Mother of God!" Fergus exclaimed, as Adrian squeezed past him, out of the narrow doorway, and into the street.

"What... what's wrong?" Adrian spun around warily on the narrow pavement.

"I hadn't noticed it until you got in front of me," Fergus moaned through the fingers of the hand clamped over his mouth. "But now you're in the light I can see that the back of your fecking skull is split wide open!" Fergus gently took hold of

Adrian's shoulders and turned his partner around so his back was in the pool of light once more. The glimmer of white bone among a bloody mess of brain tissue and matted hair was briefly illuminated. "Oh, Jesus Christ! We need to get you to a hospital double-quick," Fergus insisted, as he staggered away from the pub doorway, feeling quite sick.

Adrian touched the back of his head and brought his hand back covered in blood and bits of tissue. He stared at his fingers in perplexed silence for a few seconds. "What the hell is going on?" he asked, once he had found his voice. "I can't feel a thing."

Fergus had stepped away from his colleague and now stood shivering in the middle of the street, shocked and revolted by what he had seen. He never had been able to stand the sight of blood... never mind mashed brain tissue. The two men just stared at each other in perplexed silence.

At that moment, a teenager on a bicycle was racing toward them, peddling like mad; head down and arched over the handlebars. Fergus, feeling sick and very preoccupied with the revelation of Adrian's horrific injuries, was completely oblivious to the speeding biker. Without pause, the bike ran full tilt into Fergus, wobbling alarmingly as it passed through him. Fergus quivered violently and stumbled sideways a pace or two, but remained standing. The young rider, cursing loudly, quickly regained control of his swerving machine and continued his reckless journey along Lyme high street.

"What the hell was that?" Adrian cried, gazing to-and-fro between Fergus and the fast disappearing and perplexed cyclist.

"Don't you see?" Fergus replied, gazing up at the night sky and shaking his head slowly. "Jesus, Mary and Joseph! Don't you get what has happened to us?"

It took a while, but realisation gradually dawned upon Adrian, even as he fought to deny it. "Then... what are we to do? I mean, should we go back to the house?" he asked in puzzlement. "Come on, Fergus; you're the bloody expert in all this spiritual stuff!"

"I imagine so," Fergus replied. "Where else are we supposed to go?"

Therefore, the two men retraced their steps out of the village and back along the dark lane to the empty mansion. Small animals scurried away from them, hiding under hedgerows, and somewhere in the woods, an owl hooted.

Back at Bellingham Towers, they climbed the portico steps, and made their way through the house to the West Wing. They needed no torchlight to guide them.

They passed through their scattered equipment and reached the door to the tower, and the ghost of Nan Scott stood there in her ragged blue dress. Her sunken feverish eyes glanced down at the two nearby corpses, lying on the floor in the darkness, before piercing Adrian and Fergus with a terrible stare. "Hello boys, so you came to seek poor old Nan Scott did you?" The woman's voice tinkled like icicles breaking. "Tut, tut, tut! Well, now you have found her!"

Nan Scott reached out with her awful curved talons and took their hands, drawing the men to her and the three of them floated silently up the spiral staircase. "Now then, there is nothing more to fear. I have been so lonely all of these years; all the others have run away, but you must stay here and keep old Nan company."

Fergus and Adrian stayed, even following the discovery and removal of their dead bodies by the police some days later. They continue to reside with Nan in the tower, up to this very day.

Neal F. Litherland

The Legend of Black Jack Guillotine

I didn't know if I was still alive or if I'd fallen out of one world and into another. Pain lived in me, and a steady agony pulsed through my belly like an echo in a diving bell. The world moved, and I floated through it. I felt a heavy pressure against me. Rough grips and hands on my skin left behind a cold dampness like executioner's bile.

"Should have left her there," one of the shadows carrying me grunted as we stumbled. I gasped, a bolt of shock shooting through me and clearing my head for a moment as I pitched and yawed.

Another voice answered. "Leave a round bellied Katherine under a madman's moon on Headsman's Wharf?" A gruffer voice that smelled of spirits, but whose hands were surer and gentler. "Quit your bellyaching'. We're almost there."

Ghosts lived in the mists. Leering phantoms gathered round hotboxes on the corners, or lingering beneath the flickering corpse lamps along the cracked paves of the dock ward. They flitted in and out of the roiling fog; ragged things seen and then gone again down dark alleys and disappearing into slumped doorways like half glimpsed gargoyles. They looked back with eyes that stared from the grave, even though they still gleamed in filthy flesh. The mists of New Avalon rose into the cold night air from murky pools that stank of salt and waste, human and otherwise. The devil's breath swirled around the dark, blind eyes of row houses, and ran cold fingers around the rims of chimneys. It even reached along shuttered shops, and perused empty stalls with sagging canvas. Above the canyons of fashioned stones and fired brick, above the scudding clouds and half-hidden cooling stacks of the hulks borne by the harbor like dead sentinels, was a great, bloody moon. It glared down, a cankered and cancerous eye in the face of a black, twilight god.

The house appeared from the murk like a dream. An old building, the facade bore salty crusts in the mortar left by the winds and rains that came day in and day out. Thick chips of paint peeled from the splintered doors and shutters like a huge insect shedding its skin. One hand released my arm, and banged loudly on the door. There was no bell or pull rope. I wondered for a brief moment whether the damned could stand the sound of chimes, or if they really did drive them away like mediums claimed. Before I could wonder long my belly clenched, and I cried out as something hot ran down my leg beneath my dress.

"Miriam!" The older voice called, adding his fist to the hollow, headsman's knock. "We need you out here!"

A light swelled behind one of the shutters, and bobbed along like a will o' the wisp overtaken with curiosity. The door opened on a cavern of dancing shadows. The mistress stood in the door, a tall, handsome woman made ethereal by the white night dress and gentle candle light. She looked from the two men to me. I tried to speak, but my throat clenched shut as another sick spasm ran through me.

"Gods above and below, bring her inside!" Miriam swept the door wide. I crossed the threshold without ever touching the ground, and beneath me, blood marked my passage. It steamed, as if a small part of my soul was trying to escape from the little red river.

Light sprung up around me; bulbs coming to life at the turn of a key. Varnished workbenches gleamed along the walls, clean as if elves had been at work. Jars and bottles of powders and elixirs, along with pre-made tinctures stood in soldierly ranks. A great steel sink held a wide berth beneath a small, curtained window. A hulking iron stove brooded in the corner, still warm from a banked fire. In the center of the space stood the bastard son of an examining table, and a saddle. The leather gleamed dully, worn smooth and luminous from use. Set in the tiles beneath was a drain stained the color of an old man's tobacco smile.

"Don't worry now, love, I'm going to take care of you." Miriam guided me to the chair, then turned to the men and made shooing gestures. "All right now, both of you get going. Marvin, go roust Samuel out of his cups and tell him to get here. I need someone who knows what they're doing and who has a strong stomach."

"Yes Ma'am." The older man touched his cap and wiped his mouth as he stepped out the door on the heels of his younger companion. Miriam closed the door at their back and threw the latch as if afraid something might come inside. She came back to me and began folding back my dress.

"Who are you?" I asked. My mouth felt like something distant, my voice the query of a stranger.

She rolled back the hem carefully, despite the mud and the blood. "Miriam, dearest, how long since your bilge busted?"

"My... my what?" I asked. Miriam stood and shook her head once.

"Your water, love, how long since it broke?"

"I don't... what time is it now?"

"It's half three." Miriam stepped over to one of the tables. She took down a bottle of thick, clear liquid, and my stomach clenched in a way that didn't have anything to do with the baby. Wharf doctors had a reputation for brilliance just as often as they did madness. Their services often came cheap since there was no shortage of patients, but one took one's life in their hands when they sought strange help. Ships brought in strange concoctions and exotic drugs on a daily basis, and there was no telling what a sick man or woman might end up with inside their body cavity. I must have been worse than I'd feared, because the next thing I knew I felt a pinch, and Miriam was pulling a long needle out of my arm.

I opened my mouth to ask a question, but before I could my blood warmed up and pumped faster. The fog in my head cleared, and time seemed to take on its proper dimensions once more. The room, which had been hazy and vague about the edges, jumped into focus like a moving picture. Everything took on a sharp, bladed clarity. Bile rose, and Miriam gently touched my arm.

"Give it a moment, love," Miriam said, her words rubbed smooth at the ends with the water front brogue. She placed a cool cloth against my forehead. Water and sweat rolled down my neck, and collar of my dress clung to me like a child at the beach. "Now what's your name?"

"Cathleen." It came out a rasp, my throat as dry as my skin was wet. Miriam nodded, the red gold sunburst of her hair revealing a silver lining. She set pots to boiling, then took a kettle and poured a tall glass. She added a tincture and some honey, stirring both in with a deft, practiced hand.

"Well Cathleen, your chap's on its way into the world and we have a long, hard job ahead of us." She pressed the cup to my lips. I was so thirsty I drank without question, swallowing down the heavy, herbal brew. Miriam nodded and took the cup once it was empty. "This should dull your pain a little bit. I don't know what I can and can't give you love, so it seems that we're going to have to do this the same way women have had to since the old times."

A thousand thoughts whirled through my head like a gale. The urge to demand a real doctor, or a cab to the hospital where I knew I'd been seen came first. I thought to cry and thank her, to beg her to help me. I even thought to scream. But I didn't give my lips to any of those desires.

"Why did those men call me Katherine?" I asked. "Did they know me?"

Miriam paused in what she was doing and smiled at me. In that smile I could see that once she had been beautiful. Once she would have been the aurora of the night sky, a sight to hold the eye and enchant the imagination. There was a kindness in that expression, and a lurking merriment to catch the heart and burn a lover's lantern.

"It's a tale told by men in their cups on the wharf," Miriam replied. "Pay it no heed Cathleen."

"Tell me?" My muscles locked and my hands scrabbled at the arms of the chair. I didn't truly care, not right then, whether Miriam chose to talk about the weather, her life, or if she decided to compose poetry. I just wanted to hear her voice, and focus on something other than the dull sink of pain that pulsed more and more regularly in my womb. "Please... just tell me?"

"All right dear, all right." Miriam rolled up her sleeves and glanced down at me. I felt exposed and embarrassed, but less so than I'd thought I would. She gave me another of her smiles. It made her look like an indulgent grandmother giving secret permission for a ghost story she'd always said she'd never tell. "We have some time yet. Not much, but some, and you'll need something to take your mind off it till we come to the business."

Miriam busied herself about the room, setting a small stack of towels close by and turning down the heat on her stove so the water steamed, but didn't bubble. She arranged some of her strange, hinged tools on an old tea tray, then mixed another cup of her brew and brought it with her. I took the cup and sipped at it. I was still thirsty, and I wanted to do something other than just sit and endure.

"Have you ever heard of Black Jack Guillotine, Cathleen?" Miriam asked as she set out all of the necessities of her craft in the small workspace. I swallowed more tea, my tongue tingling from the heat, and shook my head.

"No," I managed. Miriam nodded.

"Most people on Headsman's Wharf won't speak his name. They fear it will draw his attention." Miriam touched my throat, her fingers against my pulse. "He's a black hooded ghost with a penchant for taking heads from those that won't be punished for their crimes. In life Black Jack was the city's headsman, and death hasn't stopped him from carrying out his duty. He brings law to the lawless, and it's said that for those who are willing to offer him sacrifice he'll take up his sword to avenge the wrongs against them. It's also said that he pays particular attention to women with red hair and women that are pregnant. You're both, and it's that fact saved your life tonight love, I have no doubt."

"So who's Katherine?" I shifted, trying to get comfortable. Miriam smiled again, but it was different this time. The smile was still beautiful, but it wrenched the heart and made you want to cry for the person that had to bear the weight of it.

"She was born Katherine de Veris, and she was a woman well known anywhere in the wharf," Miriam said, her words rolling like the tide as she found her rhythm. "The daughter of a shipwright, Katherine grew up playing in the dock yards and running through the market stalls. She was a free spirit, and she stayed that way throughout her youth. Until word of her beauty reached the ears of a man named Gerald Sullivan. Lord Sullivan was charged with marshaling the guard, and he was the last man who was given that responsibility by right of position rather than of merit. He came to Katherine's father, and in the way things were done then they agreed Katherine would wed the lord."

The words dried my throat in a way no drink would cure. I forgot the discomfort of cloth sticking to my skin, the pain of my belly and the slow struggle of life coming from me. The story struck a chord that reverberated through me. It was as if I was listening to someone telling a fairy tale about me.

"Her father was losing money." I licked my lips and drew a deep, slow breath. "And he offered his daughter's hand for the dowry so that he wouldn't lose everything. And because she loved her father, she agreed."

"She did." Miriam nodded. "She came to live with the Lord out on Docker's Quay, the place that housed his estate as well as the garrison for his guards and the dungeons for holding prisoners. The place is still there, but it was converted years ago into a records house. No one would live there after the things that gave birth of the Haunt of Headsman's Wharf."

"What happened to Katherine?" Miriam sipped at her own cup, and I wondered very briefly what she'd put in it—something to numb her, or something to wake her up? She looked thoughtful for a moment, and placed the cup very gently on a sideboard.

"Katherine gave her hand to Sullivan, but she had already given her heart to a boy named John Cutter," Miriam said. "John was on the verge of manhood, and he had just been accepted into the ranks of the city's watch. The two lovers spent almost every waking moment before the wedding together, tortured by the things they couldn't say and couldn't do. And though they tried to live their lives, they were always finding themselves near one another as if there was something bigger than both of them trying to ensure their paths were woven together. Some said that John stepped forward to take on the responsibility of the headsman for the express purpose of being able to come to the Quay to catch a glimpse of Katherine. And when the lord was away she sent for him in secret and told him the way into the Quay that only she and Sullivan were to know."

"And Sullivan caught them." My throat clicked like I'd swallowed an exotic bird that was trying to sing. I cleared my throat. "He found them together and killed them."

"Far from it child," Miriam said, a hint of amusement in her eyes. "No, Lord Sullivan was away on a tour of the ships for a fortnight. John visited Katherine every night, and storms masked their rendezvous. Thunder kept everyone deaf to the sounds of their lovemaking just as the rain kept all blind to what happened in the darkness. And so it likely would have continued, if Katherine hadn't had a little extra ballast from her lover."

"She had a child?" I groaned as another harsh twist corkscrewed through me. I went rigid, and sucked in a harsh breath that whistled over my teeth. Miriam didn't even hesitate. She pushed a stool between my legs and sat close to me. Her hands felt cool and dry where they rested on my thighs.

"Not yet Cathleen... but very soon now," she told me with a smile. "I give you my word this will all fade as soon as it's done. I think that if it didn't then very soon women would stop having babies at all."

Miriam stood and wiped my face again. She took my cup and hers to the sink, and busied herself keeping things as uncluttered as she could. She touched my neck again, and I tried to relax. It wasn't time yet. I just had to be patient. The pain was still there, and I shifted so I didn't feel the pressure when I breathed too deeply. I didn't want to hurt the baby, and I wished it would stop hurting me.

"Katherine tried to hide the baby for as long as she could," Miriam continued, sitting down near me again. "But Sullivan found out. He had her held in her chambers. He demanded the name of the father day after day, withholding food, warmth and sometimes even human voices from her. It seemed that, for all of his lust, Lord Sullivan was impotent and had never been able to lie with her, so he knew what she had done. He levied charges of adultery, witchcraft and a number of others of which she was, in time convicted. Every day John stood nearby, and every time he moved to speak, she shook her head no. Therefore, he waited and hoped until the day her daughter was born, and her final reprieve from the butcher's block fell screaming from her womb. Placed before the headsman, still bloody and weak from the birth, she whispered to John that she loved him. And John, unable to watch her suffering or her tears, brought his sword down on the woman he loved."

"My god." I tried to think of something, anything to say to that. Nothing came.

"Truly," Miriam said. "It wasn't but a fortnight after that the lord's body was found in his bedchamber, his head gone wandering. The baby girl was gone as well, spirited away from the nursery. Sullivan's head stood discovered hanging from the dock, but John Tanner disappeared forever. Some say he drowned himself, consumed by guilt, and now he has to levy proper punishment until he's wiped his debt clear. Others claim he swore an oath, and that he won't be able to rest until it's finished. Very romantic, but that's sailors for you. Hard men on the outside, but deep down every one of them still wishes he was living in a story book."

I thought of Michael, of his one bloody eye looking up at me in the rain, and hot tears came. They scalded my face and stung with salt. I wished, how I wished, I could banish that memory from my mind's eye and remember him whole. I wanted to remember him tender and smooth in the darkness. I could not. I could only see him with his beautiful face torn apart; something perfect ruined and made somehow uglier because it had once been whole. The pain grew inside me, and as it grew, it pulsed and squeezed my heart, clutching my breath in a vise.

"It's time," Miriam said. "Breathe steadily, Cathleen. Breathe in and then push as you breathe out. It will hurt, but have faith, you can do this."

The touch in such an intimate place surprised a breath out of me. I struggled to take another, but it was hard. My muscles contracted, and slick dampness dripped to the floor beneath me. I thought for a horrified moment that I was going to die, and panic made me open my lungs wide again. I pushed. I thought about Michael and the nights we'd stolen away in corners or on secret meetings. I pushed. I thought about Howard and his fury when I'd come home. I pushed. The bruises on my back and arms throbbed, remembering the beating that had given them birth. I pushed. I heard Michael's voice in my ear, telling me that soon we'd be away and I'd never have to be afraid of Howard again. I pushed. I thought of Michael hoping we had a baby girl as he rubbed my swollen belly. I pushed, and as my breath gave out, I heard a cry.

"It's a girl, Cathleen," Miriam said. I didn't look; I just tried to remember how to breathe without pushing. There was another tug, and a liquid rush that gave me a horrible sense of vertigo. Then I was staring at my daughter, swaddled in a clean, soft cloth, just a face with blood clinging to the corners of her eyes. She looked like she'd been through a horrible ordeal. She watched me, and her smile was a light in the darkness. I held up shaky arms and held her. I whispered, gently pressing my face against the wet, slick smell of her. I told her I was sorry about what had happened. Sorry about everything that had happened to us, but it was all over now. Even though I'd said that, I still jumped when someone pounded on the door.

"That's probably Samuel." Miriam blotted her forehead and wiped at her hands. "Showing up once all the hard work's been done, just like a man.

As soon as Miriam opened the latch, the door flew open. The edge struck her face, and spun her around. Miriam pawed at the wall, and as she fell, her hand struck the key. Before the lights went dark, though, I saw a tall, lean man standing in the doorway with a heavy blackthorn stick in his hand. A man who wore wealth like second skin and hung rage from his shoulders like a rain cape, a man I had once whispered the words "I do" to, even though they'd broken my heart. Howard stood there, back lit by the bloody moon, with the mist swirling around his legs. He looked like a thing being born from all the worst things in the night.

"You're a hard one to find, dearest," he said, spitting out the word like broken teeth. "But I am a man that finishes what he starts."

I was exhausted, and I still hurt like something more than a child was wrenched out of me, but I stood. My legs didn't want to hold me, but I backed away and put the chair between Howard and me, between the monster and my daughter.

"It shouldn't have come to this," Howard said, stepping over the bloody threshold and into the darkened room. He slapped the head of his cane into his open hand, a flat crack like a starter's pistol. "I offered to take you back, Cathleen. I offered to forgive your transgression and welcome you back into my home and my bed. Even after what you'd done with that poacher, even after you lied to me for so long."

I took slow, soft steps and tried to stay silent. I held my girl against my breast, and she pawed at me in the dark, as if to make sure I was still there, even though no longer connected by flesh. I reached for the counter. If I could find the boiling water, or one of those tools Miriam had left out, I would have something. My fingers found nothing except the wood stove. I gritted my teeth and jerked my fingers away from the searing iron. Whether she sensed my pain, or she felt fear as her first, true emotion, my daughter wailed. Howard's head turned, and the deep, ruddy light behind him, made his shadowed grin look like the mouth a fiend from the pit.

"Cathleen, dear, stupid, Cathleen;" Howard slammed his walking stick down and scattering delicate implements as he came on. "I told you that child would be the end of you. I want you to go to your grave remembering that if you had just listened to me, this wouldn't have happened to you."

I kept backing away. I couldn't run, I couldn't fight and both my and my daughter's lives were going to be too short. It was only when I was able to look away from the snarling wolf in men's clothing that I saw we were not alone.

Michael stood in the doorway, practically a part of the early morning dew that sweated from the night's fog. He stood whole, and looked at me with both his beautiful eyes. His lips quirked in that small, secret smile that always preceded a kiss. I stared at a ghost made flesh, and I crumpled, cradling my baby against me. I didn't want her to see anything of the next world when she'd only been in this one for such a short time.

"Any last words?" I had lived in terror of that voice for months, but now it sounded like the buzz of an angry insect in my ear. I watched Michael step through the open door.

"Michael," I said, and held out my one, empty hand toward him.

"Your Michael's been dead for months, Cathleen," Howard jeered, raising his stick up high above his head. "No matter, you'll be seeing him soon enough."

I saw him then as clear as I ever had. Michael held his hand out to me, but he didn't beckon me as a psychopomp might. He tried to speak the last three words he'd ever said to me, but no breath came to his lips. Michael raised his arm and pointed at Howard. He pointed, and when he did, something consumed him. I watched as a nightmare tore itself out of Michael; a hurricane of shadows and silent thunder. Out of the violence came something black and slick, like blood spilled in the gutters on a moonless night. A thing made of hunger; a swirling mass of funerary darkness that smelled of a charnel house and carried the cold of the grave like a mantle of office.

Howard didn't turn in time to see the bloody blade of Black Jack Guillotine raised up in a horrible mirror behind him. He didn't see the stained headsman's sword come down with terrible speed. I did, and it all took place in the space of a breath. Howard tried to turn, and as he turned his head came away from his shoulders. Blood frothed and pumped from the trunk of a body still curious about the happenings behind. The mouth moved as the head tumbled through the air, no voice and no breath to make his last words heard.

The shroud parted, and a hand reached out of that roiling blackness. The phantom headsman picked up the grim trophy by the hair. The thing paused, and looked at me. It had the eyes of a man who had washed his hands in blood for love, and who would drive the devil himself for redemption. There was an understanding in them, and knowledge of what I had meant to the man that had given his very soul as payment for the darkest of deeds. Black Jack Guillotine bowed to me, and to my daughter, before he turned away.

"Katherine," I called as he reached the doorway. I held my daughter tight and stroked her soft skin. I smeared the hot, slick blood back from her face, giving her a crimson mane. "Her name is Katherine."

Bloody Jack turned to us for a last, fleeting look. For a moment, I saw the ruined face of Michael staring out from inside the headsman's hood. Then his eyes snuffed out like candles in a squall, and the ghost left my daughter and me crying and covered in blood. Both of us were born again.

200

Alex S. Johnson

Amphantomine

Get away from the machine. Now. Just do it.
Hartford could not. The story demanded writing. A snake in his blood, incurved fangs sunk in the grey matter; lastly, the scene that scared him the most, in which the protagonist falls back on bad habits, ironically to bang the last nail in the coffin of his memoirs. Faked just enough to keep the lawyers and police away, but faithful to the soul of it; Her, Him, Betrayal, A series of words, no more, the pressure of his fingertips on the keyboard just as firm, or light, as that required of any other work.

He opened the bottom desk drawer. Just to see him through the final pages, a few rails. Two from the penultimate baggie, and one from the special mix, the rocks lightly silted with something special; something to ease the withdrawals and help him sleep.

Hartford lifted the inlaid metal box onto his desk and removed the two Zip-Lock bags, shaking the crystal pebbles from the bottom of one. The fresh razor lay next to them, still in its cardboard packing. Now for the Pièce de résistance and he would enjoy his rest, so well deserved, once he'd reached the end and saved the document. The last bag was marked "XX" with a red Sharpie. His heart thudding with anticipation, Hartford emptied the entire contents onto the silver tray. These rocks had a faint pink tinge.

He unsheathed the razor, whittled the rocks on the left to a single pile of powder, exchanged the blade for a plastic straw, and began working on the right-hand rocks. This pile was half again the size of the other. Using an old Citibank Visa card, he neatly formed three lines.

The rules—one from the left-hand powder to start, another line from the same once he'd hit the midway point, and the rail from the XX baggie when he'd finished.

A sour, metallic taste in his mouth, and then the speed hit. Hartford wondered that he could be such a hypocrite. The book tour already sold to stores and universities across the country pivoted on a clean, sober and healthy David Hartford, an author who had passed through the vale of addiction to share the tale of his triumphs with readers. His conscience offered appeasement by reminding him that he was a writer, and even his nonfiction was necessarily an illusion, the facts chosen deliberately, edited and shaped along a pattern that glanced at the truths it revealed while at the same time covering them.

Fuck it. Back to the machine. Job to do.

Hartford opened the document and slid the gray marker down to the place he'd left off. This was where he'd ordered the hit, a dingy bar in North Hollywood, patronized by the scum of the earth: hookers, dealers, down-on-their-luck actors, and him; no place for a best-selling writer of inspirational romance novels, even with a bad fake mustache, toupee and dark glasses. His contact was some scarred-up junkie asshole in a hoodie and ripped tennis shoes, obviously sketched out. A suitcase packed with non-sequential bills traded for a contract killing. A courier-delivered package upon completion of the job, containing proof, a proof that was undeniable, leaving him retching bile, his tailor-made Italian loafers spattered with the crab salad and champagne he'd treated himself to for lunch.

Her amber irises stared back at him from the bed of shaved ice. Alongside the hand, complete with the emerald wedding ring A small fortune recovered from the philandering bitch. The man's eyes were green, and his fingers bore no bands.

The back door man, as Hartford discovered, was his close friend, collaborator and business partner, Daniel Haggert. His pride lay wounded, and that affected his work, which affected his lifestyle. An inexorable logic led to the decision to punish the offenders, freeing him to imagine something other than his wife's panties in Haggert's mouth.

When he wrote this scene, of course, it only presented a path not taken, a dark fantasy eschewed. Nevertheless, every word of it was true, as the dwindling figures in his savings account attested. Silence was costly, very costly.

To recoup even a fraction of it, Hartford had embarked on the project before him. People loved confessionals, the viler the better, a book guaranteed to rocket right up the *New York Times* list and stay there. Hence his return-visit to the North Hollywood bar, this time to pack in supplies. The dealer was a dead ringer for the contract killer, but that didn't bother him. It was the blonde in the corner booth, staring straight at him through the lurid haze of neon-rippled smoke, who spooked him right the fuck out. The blonde who mirrored Samantha's features, her slight smile.

Her eyes.

"What's up, dude?" the dealer had asked. "You look like you've seen a ghost."

Hartford zipped shut the right-hand pocket of his black motorcycle jacket. "It's nothing," he'd said. "I just need to get straight. I'll be fine."

"Take it easy with that shit," the dealer replied. "Especially that last baggie."

And that was it, the final line . . . In two senses. Hartford pressed the "save" icon, then plucked the soda straw from the tray, bent down over his desk and plugged shut his right nostril with a forefinger.

The rush was incredible. Even though the quantity was small, this crystal was powerful, much too powerful for his heart, which exploded. Blood gushed from his nostrils and mouth.

As his eyes blurred, the lines of his home office decomposed; a strip of red neon blinked through the window of a darkened bar. Booths with tattered vinyl seating. A reunion with phantoms.

"Nice to see you again," said the blonde. She moved to the side, and Haggert stood up, extending his hand. "Join us. We've been expecting you."

J. C. Michael

Here Kitty Kitty

"For God's sake woman, do you have to make such a mess?"

The splodge of gravy sat on the white blouse like a brown teardrop, and the attempt to wipe it off inevitably served merely to worsen the stain.

"Keep your voice down please. It'll wash out."

"You'll be lucky. I don't know why you can't be more careful instead of eating like a spastic toddler."

"Pete, there's no need."

"I know there isn't. No need to miss that trap of yours at all, is there? It's sodding well big enough."

Ruth put her knife and fork down on her plate, the items of cutlery marking out twenty past four and the fact that she'd finished eating, despite half the meal remaining. "Shall we go?"

Pete glared at the woman he'd once found pretty, and now only viewed as pretty irritating. "No we shall not. If I'm paying for us to eat out then we can bloody well eat it. You can finish off," he said as he stood, "while I visit the gents."

"You've just moved 'ere then?" It was as much a statement as a question.

Although he kept his own eyes focused on the tiles directly ahead of him Pete knew that the old man at the urinal on his left was looking across at him. He had nothing to be ashamed of, but all the same, he was glad that the urinals were separate, and not the single trough type.

"Yeah, into Lowna Mill. We moved in on Friday."

Out of the corner of his eye he could see the old man shake off and begin to fumble around putting himself back into his pants.

"Friday flit, short sit,"

"I beg your pardon?" said Pete.

"It's what my old mother used to say. Means move on a Friday and you won't be staying long. The name's Percy." The old man reached out a hand even though Pete was yet to conclude his own business.

"Pete," said Pete, making no move to accept Percy's outstretched, and unwashed, palm.

There was a pause, and then Percy let his arm fall to his side where he wiped it on his trousers as Pete finished off with a shake of his own, and hurriedly tidied himself away.

"So how did you know who I was? Word's got around on the local grapevine has it?" said Pete as he moved over to the sink.

Percy made no move to follow suit. "Aye, saw you pull up outside and recognised the car as the one that'd been parked at the mill the past couple of days. Recognised your wife too, saw her taking a walk last night."

Pete winced internally at the way the old man's broad Yorkshire accent allowed him to drop not just letters, but almost whole words, from what he was saying. "Well, that's us. Like I said, we moved into the mill last Friday but if what you say's right, and I have my way, we won't be bothering you for long."

"You don't care for the mill?" said Percy in a contracted form that was nearer "Y' dearn't care f't'mill?"

"The Mill's nice enough," said Pete as he dried his hands on a rough paper towel. Dyson air blades obviously hadn't made it this far from civilisation yet.

"Things not so good with the Mrs?"

Pete screwed up the soggy paper and dropped it in the bin. "That's none of your business. Now if you don't mind I've a meal to finish."

"You don't want to be mistreating her is all. You don't want to be bumping into Kitty."

Pete had been on his way to the door as the old man had spoke but now he stopped, his fists clenched by his side. If the old man had been twenty years younger he'd have put the short-arse twat to the floor with a quick left hook, but he controlled himself. "How I treat my wife has fuck all to do with you, and fuck all to do with Kitty. Whoever the fuck she might be."

Pete's hand was on the door now, swinging it open. He stepped over the threshold, and heard the old man apologise. "Sorry, I don't mean to cause offence." The door was swinging shut, and he only just caught what the old man said next; "but you need to watch out for Kitty, she's the ghost that haunts the mill."

When Pete got back to the dining room Ruth was gone and, looking out of the window, he could see that their Audi was gone too. "Fucking bitch," he thought, as he sat down to finish off his steak and ale pie. "Fucking yokels," he thought as he finished off Ruth's chicken risotto, which, typically, was nicer than his own choice. "Fucking ghosts," he thought, as he headed to the bar to pay the tab.

"Enjoy your meal?" said Percy, who stood at the end of the bar.

"Lovely," said Pete.

The girl behind the bar smiled, and passed him the bill. Pete smiled back. She was attractive, in a rustic kind of way, but he didn't feel like hanging around to flirt. He felt like an argument. He felt like going home and showing Ruth the error of her ways.

"It's getting miserable out."

Upon hearing Percy's words Pete looked out of the window and could see the rain coming down, its intensity increasing with each passing second. The mill was a good ten-minute walk outside the village, and he only had a light jacket with him. Agreeing with Percy's next statement; "You should hang on till it passes over, have another drink," was a foregone conclusion.

"Pint of lager is it?" said the barmaid as if conspiring with Percy to keep him there. She had a nice smile, although one of her front teeth was set slightly forward of where it should have been.

"Go on then, why not, put it on the tab."

Pete's pint was pulled, but the barmaid wasn't going to be, not by him anyway. A group of young farmer types, all jeans, checked shirts, and waxed jackets, had come in and her attention was clearly focused on the tallest, and loudest, of them. The lad had ruddy cheeks and a wild mop of blonde hair, a stereotypical country bumpkin in Pete's eyes. He clearly belonged here in a small village on the edge of the moors. Pete didn't. He was a product of a purely urban environment, an environment he had only moved away from in an effort to save a marriage he had little interest in saving.

All he needed was a few more months to move some money around, a little while longer to build up a false trail of expenditure on untraceable commodities like drink, drugs, and women, when in reality the cash would be squirreled away for a new life post-divorce. Once his finances were in order his wife could go fuck herself as far as he was concerned. Ruth had bored him for a while at least the past twelve months, and now that she wanted a family, something they'd agreed wasn't for them before they'd even tied the knot. He knew it was time to get out. But he was damned sure it wasn't going to cost him a fortune to cut the bitch loose.

"I didn't mean to offend you earlier."

It was Percy, standing by the table Pete had moved to with a glass of what looked like whisky in one hand, and his flat cap in the other.

"Don't worry about it," said Pete. "I guess you locals always wind up newcomers for the first few decades they live here."

Percy smiled and took a seat, even though Pete had given no indication that he wanted the old man to join him. At least he could still feel the heat from the open fire, even with Percy now sitting between him and the dancing flames.

"I only thought it fair to warn you about Kitty, is all."

"Consider me warned."

"You aren't interested in the story?"

Pete looked out of the window. It was too dark to see much but he could see the rain hitting the glass. His own glass was still half-full. He took a drink, and considered telling the old man to piss off, but what would that achieve?

"Why don't we have another drink to welcome you to the village and I'll tell you the legend of Sarkless Kitty?" said Percy.

Pete looked outside once more, and then drained his final third of a pint. "Go on then, why the hell not."

"All of this occurred a good couple of hundred years ago," said Percy. "Kitty Garthwaite was from here in Gillamoor, a fair lass by all accounts, and she was courting a lad by the name of William Dixon from over in Hutton."

"So she's Sarkless, whatever that means, Kitty that haunts the mill?" said Pete.

"A sark's an old fashioned shift, like a long undershirt. She's known as Sarkless Kitty because she's naked when she appears. And strictly speaking she haunts the ford, not the mill itself."

Pete looked at him blankly, then smirked. "So she's a naked ghost? Sounds like the sort of spirit I wouldn't mind bumping into."

Percy smiled back, but the smile lacked warmth. "Perhaps I should finish the story first. Then you can decide if you still fancy meeting up with her, eh?"

Pete gestured with his glass for the old man to continue. The story seemed just the sort of rubbish a bunch of rural simpletons would peddle to tourists and incomers, but the old man was looking to hit his stride, and the rain continued to pour down, so he resolved that he may as well settle into his chair and hear the rest of the tale.

Percy sipped at his drink, and continued. "Well, there was Kitty, and William, whom everyone called Willie."

Pete suddenly spluttered into his pint. "Hang on, hang on, you're having a laugh right? A naked ghost, called Kitty, as in cat, as in pussy, and a guy called Willie? Is this the plot of a bloody Carry On film or what?"

Percy stood abruptly with a look of genuine anger on his face. "I can assure you that this is no joke."

"Oh, sit down," said Pete, gesturing once more with his glass. "Admit it, it all sounds a bit dodgy, but fair's fair and if you say it's a genuine local legend who am I to disagree? I can always google it when I get home. You have heard of google out here in the wilds, haven't you? The internet knows everything, even about backward little places like this."

Percy sat, a look of distaste etched across his face, but Pete was oblivious. He was far more concerned with waving his glass in the air to catch the attention of the girl behind the bar. He winked at Percy. "A sackless barmaid would liven this joint up, eh Perce?"

"Sark, not sack," muttered Percy.

The barmaid brought over another lager and a whisky and placed them on the table. Neither man spoke. Percy smiled, Pete leered.

"Crack on then," Pete said.

"Well, it was Whitsunday 1787 and the pair of them was due to meet at Lowna, by the mill. There was no bridge then, just the ford, and they always met there, as it's about two thirds of the way from Hutton to here, so a reasonable walk for the lad and a shorter walk for Kitty. Now for some reason they argued, and Willie stormed off back to Hutton. Nobody knows for sure what they fell out over, but most folk are of the opinion that she was with child. Willie rode to York not long after leaving her to get a marriage licence but, while he was gone, Kitty's body was found in the river."

"So he killed her because she was pregnant and then went off to York to cover his tracks?"

"Possibly, there've been a few theories over the years. He could have murdered her because he didn't want the responsibility, or he thought she was trying to trap him, or maybe even he doubted the child was his. Or perhaps he didn't kill her at all, and she committed suicide thinking he'd rejected her and she'd be shunned for sleeping with him, let alone falling pregnant, out of wedlock. There's even a chance that it was purely an accident. That she decided to take a swim after he left her and drowned."

By now Pete was wrapped up in the story, and so engrossed that it seemed as though he and Percy were the only souls in the pub. "So was she naked when she was found? Is that where this sack, sorry, sark-less bit comes into it?"

Percy sipped at his whisky. "Well, Kitty's body was dressed when it was found, but by the time Wille returned from York it had vanished. Some people think the Quakers' took pity on her and buried her in their own little burial ground not far from the mill. It would've been a compassionate act, to save her the ignominy of a suicide's burial in un-consecrated ground outside of the local churchyard."

"And people have seen her haunting the spot where she was drowned?"

"Oh, there's more to it than that," said Percy.

There was a twinkle in Percy's eyes and Pete shuffled in his seat. The heat from the fire was making him sweat regardless of the cold shiver the story was giving him, and the old man appeared to be having too much fun telling him about the ghost that allegedly lived, for want of a better word, in the river than ran right by his new home.

"When Willie found out that Kitty was dead he was distraught."

"Or at least he pretended to be," said Pete.

"Quite," said Percy, "and when he further discovered that the body was missing he went looking for it."

"Because he didn't want anyone finding out she was pregnant," said Pete.

"Perhaps, perhaps not, either way it did no good as he was found dead in the same pool the next morning."

Pete scoffed. "You tell a good tale but basically boy got girl in the club, either killed her or she topped herself when he told her he wanted jack shit to do with the kid, some helpful folks steal the body to bury it, and the lad tops himself out of guilt or grief. Oh, and then her ghost comes back but doesn't bother to dress for the occasion."

"I suppose you could summarise it that way," said Percy, "but I'm not quite done yet. Some local children were the first to see her after her death. It was about three weeks later and there she was, sitting naked on a branch and encouraging them to swim in the deeper side of the pool just off the ford. They ran home in tears. Others weren't so lucky. There were seventeen deaths in that pool in the following years, and all young men. And according to the legend the deaths only stopped once an exorcism was carried out right there in the middle of that cursed pool."

"Sounds like she was out for revenge, to me. Who'd have guessed it, a feminist serial killer ghost, no wonder the estate agent didn't share that little feature with us. Anyway, if she was exorcised what have I got to be afraid of?"

"You, Pete, should be afraid of her. The legend says the deaths stopped. Your internet will tell you the same; that an exorcism in 1809 did the trick and laid poor Kitty's spirit to rest. But Kitty only hid, and she still comes back on occasion to take her vengeance out on men like you. Rude, coarse, ignorant men, unfaithful men, men quick to temper of word and fist and crafty beggars like you who think they're smarter than everyone else." Percy's voice had begun to rise although nobody else paid him any attention. "You mark my words Pete, the way you treat that poor wife of yours, the contempt, the abuse, Kitty will come for you, and she'll have you. She'll bloody well have you."

With that, Pete slammed his glass down on the table, smashing it and cutting his hand. "Fuck the lot of you. Bunch of backward arseholes."

Everyone in the place turned to look at him; the barmaid, the young farmers, the couple in the corner.

"You need to repent, Pete, before it's too late. Accept your failings and resolve to change." Percy was almost pleading. "Look inside yourself Pete, see the darkness and reject it because though you'd deserve anything Kitty dishes out to you I'd rather see you become a changed man."

"Fuck you," said Pete as he thrust his bleeding hand into his pocket and pulled out his wallet. He ripped out a couple of twenty-pound notes and cast them down on the table, the paper stained red with fresh blood. Grabbing his coat, he stormed out into the rain, leaving everyone in the bar in stunned silence. The last thing they heard was Pete shouting "Bastards," as he walked past the window. They didn't hear what else he yelled into the darkness as he walked down the hill toward river in the driving rain; "Here Kitty Kitty, come show me your titties. Come on out and play you fucking tart. I'm not scared of you."

FROM THE MALTON STAR

The body of Peter Martins, aged 36, was found dead yesterday morning in the River Dove at Lowna Mill, between Gillamoor and Hutton Le Hole. Prior to his fatal accident Martins had spent the evening at the Rose and Crown in Gillamoor, with his wife, Ruth Martins. Mrs. Martins had returned home to the mill, which they had moved into the previous Friday, after what some witnesses have described as a "minor falling out," leaving her husband to carry on drinking alone. The same witnesses further stated that Martins consumed a number of pints of lager, along with shots of whisky, before leaving to walk the mile and a half home. Barmaid of the Rose and Crown, Joanna Jones stated that, "He seemed nice enough to start with, but appeared to grow more agitated as the night wore on. He wasn't too drunk, we would have refused to serve him if he had been, but he was definitely unsteady on his feet when he left."

The ford at Lowna is the focal point of the local legend of Sarkless Kitty, the naked ghost accused of luring young men to their deaths. Another local, who asked not to be named, said that, "It was likely a spirit that led to the accident with Mr. Martins, but it was the sort that comes out of a bottle, not some poor lass from two hundred years ago."

Today also sees the funeral of well-known Gillamoor resident Percy Windbert. Windbert, who had lived his whole life in the village, and whose family had lived there since the early eighteenth century, passed away peacefully in his sleep last week, aged 85.

213

Michael Thomas-Knight
The Obsidian Box

Frank Lucano walked to the entrance of his home office, looked down the hallway and pulled the door closed, locking both men in the room. He dropped several ice cubes in a tumbler, shook it around, and then poured some Dewar's whiskey over the ice. He swished it around and held it up to the sunlight.

"It looks like golden blossom honey," he said, then added, "How can something so beautiful be so God-awful tasting?"

"They say it's an acquired taste," Jimmy the Russian said.

"Acquired taste? Balls! The only reason anyone drinks this crap is it could calm the nerves of a three-legged cat during lunchtime in Chinatown."

Jimmy the Russian smiled, a genuine smile but cold and harsh. Jimmy's smile usually made people nervous, especially if the person owed someone money or had done someone wrong.

"Jimmy, I can't take it. I've been married to this woman for three years and I won't make it to the end of this one with my sanity intact."

Jimmy's eyebrows raised and he held his hands up in a halting gesture.

"Frankie, wait. I don't do that kinda thing. I don't get involved with marital disputes."

"Jimmy, just hear me out. I'm not asking you to do something bad."

"Oh, no?" Jimmy knew he was lying.

"Well, not exactly," Frank assured.

"I think I will have that drink," Jimmy said.

Frankie set up a Dewar's on ice in a rock tumbler and handed it to his old friend.

"She's suffocating me, Jimmy. She tells me no more gambling, and then has people follow me to make sure I don't stop at OTB. She demanded I move my office into the house. Now I can't have a lunch meeting with clients without her approval. I'm like a prisoner."

"Why don't you just get a divorce?"

"I can't. She made me abandon certain aspects of the business

214

for reasons that seemed good at the time. Now my business can't exist without the steady infusion of her money. She did this so she would have more control."

"I don't know, Frankie..."

"And that kid of hers; Autism, or ADHD or some other group of letters that don't make sense to me. He's a constant torment. Ten years old, he still acts like he's three. No one corrects him, teaches him right from wrong. He has no respect for others or anyone's property. I try to teach him or discipline him and Krista goes into a rage."

"It's not an easy thing dealing with a child with a handicap."

"But that's the problem. No one is dealing with it. The other day the kid goes on a rampage and rips every plant and flower out of the garden. Five minutes later the grounds crew is cleaning up the mess. There's a delivery from the local nursery and within the hour, everything is back to the way it was."

"You have to have patience. I don't know what else to say."

"Patience! I caught the damn kid killing a fucking chipmunk. He put a heavy rock on its tail and was whacking it with a stick just to see it bleed. I'm afraid one day I'm going to wake up with the kid standing over me, with an even bigger stick in his hand."

Both men sat for a few moments with no words passing between them. They finished their drinks. Frankie calmed down and lowered his voice before he began to speak again.

"There's a young housekeeper here. She started feeding a stray cat out back, a little black and white kitten. A plate of milk a day, nothing big. I loved to watch her with this kitten; somehow, it was peaceful, ya know? Last Sunday, I heard the power saw in the garage. I raced in to see what the commotion was...there was blood everywhere. The kid turned around with the buzz saw in his hand, blood all over his smiling face. Pieces of cat were scattered about the workbench. I was shittin' bricks. I grabbed a shovel and held it over my head. I told him, *you get the fuck outta here!* Thank God, he ran off. The blood, it was everywhere. I stepped closer to the workbench and there's this hunk of bloody meat, center of the bench. I walked up to it and an eye opened."

"Gees, Frankie." Jimmy's face distorted, as if he had drank sour milk. "What did Krista say?"

"I didn't tell her," Frankie said. "It's too ugly. How do you tell something like that to a mom, about her son?"

Jimmy sat there, shaking his head in dismay. This guy had

murdered people for the mob, a twenty-year veteran, but this story shook him. Frankie felt relief. Seeing his friend's reaction, he vowed he'd never tell the story again.

"I'm a prisoner in this house and this ten-year-old *retard* is the warden. I'm about to go mad."

"Frankie, I feel for you, but I don't know how I can help you. Women and children are off-limits for me. It's what separates me from the barbarians."

"I don't want or expect you to touch them. All I want you to do is attend to an item."

Frankie lifted up a throw rug, exposing a metal plate in the floor. He opened a flat panel to reveal a safe with a combination dial. Opening the safe, he pulled out a shiny black box made of stone and placed it upon the desk.

"What's in the box?"

"The culmination of many years of torment and suffering, wrapped in one entity, the most evil ghost-spirit known to the paranormal community—that's what's in the box. They say it was a man from Edinburgh tormented and tortured by the British Army. Soldiers had raped and killed his wife, then him. He haunted the estate house of the Scottish governor for a hundred years until was caught and trapped in this spirit box by a twentieth century spiritualist. Some say he's morphed into a demon, a ghoul that feeds on death, pain and suffering. The creature's hatred is only bound by the laws of this box."

"You know I don't believe in all this spiritual mumbo-jumbo."

Jimmy leaned forward and looked at the box, unsure. He did not attempt to touch it.

"Then this should be easy for you. You open the box and leave."

"When, now?"

"No, not now. One night when I'm not here."

Frankie pulled a manila envelope from the safe and locked it. He threw it on the table and sat behind his desk.

"I'm going to visit my mom in Jersey in a few weeks. You come here and open the box. Rumor has it that the thing inside is so scary, that whoever witnesses it dies of fright."

"What does that mean, 'dies of fright'?"

"I don't know, heart attack, I guess. Untraceable, natural. No weapon, no evidence. Certainly, no blemish on your reputation."

Frankie pulled out an age-worn book. He flipped through the yellowed pages and stopped at a page titled, *The Obsidian Box.*

"Here are the instructions for invocation. It's simple, a few words, a few movements of the box itself, and then you leave. You let the box do its dirty work. I'll make a copy of the pages for you."

Jimmy sat back in the chair, rubbing his forehead.

"I'm dismayed by this whole thing, Frankie. You were living the clean life. Five years. Straight and lawful. You were a beacon of hope for the rest of us. If you could make it outside the thug-life, then there was hope for us all."

This statement took Frankie aback. He tried to find the right words for the situation.

"Jimmy, it was all an illusion," he finally confessed.

Jimmy's head dropped in disappointment and his eyes averted from his friend. Frankie had no idea that parting from his old life had left a positive impact on his friends and associates. He thought the complete opposite. He had to make Jimmy understand his need for such a drastic measure. He decided to tell a story about a mutual friend.

"Did I ever tell you about Bobby Bags's death?"

"No, Frankie, you never did."

"It's a doosey, you're gonna love this," Frankie said. He started his story.

"Bags was hooked on the backroom poker clubs. Games were held in the backs of bodegas, cigar shops, and auto body shops throughout Seabrook. Seabrook was the Gagliardo family's turf back then. Bags was on a hot winning streak. When the game hosts couldn't pay their weekly *vigs*, Tony Gagliardo wanted to know why."

Frankie walked to his porta-bar and refilled his drink. He motioned to Jimmy with the bottle, but Jimmy waved him away. Frankie continued.

"So Bags is at Vincenzo's one night, winning chump change from the locals, when who do you think walks in, Tony Gagliardo himself. Bags is flush with cash from his winning streak and Tony G, the high roller, is always looking for a challenge. Next thing you know there's ten thousand dollar bets and two hundred *thou* cash on the table. Vincenzo is shitting bricks; he didn't mind some twenty-dollar bills exchanging hands, but this was ridiculous. Bags keeps winning and Tony G goes down four-hundred, eighty-five grand. So now, it's five in the morning and Bags has had enough. He gets up from the table, starts putting on his coat. Tony says, *where the fuck are you going, you gotta give me a chance to win my money back.* By this time, half of Tony G's crew is crowded into this back room of the Laundry Mat. Tony kept calling them to bring more cash. Vincenzo is chewing his fingernails because customers are coming in to do their laundry. But Tony G don't care, he says to get rid of them. So Vincenzo makes up some bullshit excuse, like rust in the water. He ushers everyone out and puts a closed sign in the window."

Frankie took a hearty swig of his Dewar's.

"How do you know this story, Frankie? You weren't there, were you?" Jimmy asked.

Frankie looked up, surprised by the tone in his voice.

"I heard it through the grapevine, ya know?"

"Why, there's a grapevine?" Jimmy cracked a little smile.

"There's a whole damn vineyard, Jimmy," Frankie replied, and both men chuckled. Then Frankie asked, "Can I finish my story, now?"

Jimmy nodded and gestured with his hand to continue.

"Tony G has no money left. He's down to betting twenty-dollar bills. Every time Bags wants to raise the ante, Louie the Bull gives him a cross look, like he's gonna break his legs. Bags realizes that, at this rate, it would take Tony a month to win back his money. So Bags tells Tony, why don't we forget about what you owe me? Tony G gets highly insulted. He pulls out his snub-nose and lays it on the table next to his cards. He says, *sit down.*

"Here's the dilemma, Bags can't leave the game with Tony's money. But no matter what he does, Tony keeps losing. He's a mush. The only way out is he kills Tony G, or Tony's thugs kill him. At four the next morning, after playing forty hours straight, Bags can't take it no more. He jumps up and grabs Tony's gun. The little ten-by-ten room explodes into gunfire. And that was the end of Bobby Bags."

Frankie paused, letting the story sink in.

"Krista is beautiful, but if she wasn't wealthy do you think I would have married her? I'm a rotten individual, Jimmy. I'm selfish and greedy. It was a gamble, I rolled the dice and it came up sevens. I married into a family with money beyond my dreams. Now I want out. Only they'll never let me out. Her father spent *a million* on the wedding. Dignitaries from around the world came to the event. The damn mayor came to the wedding, put ten grand in the envelope. Krista's father is not going to tell people we got divorced. His daughter doesn't get a divorce. She gets widowed perhaps, but not divorced. The gun is on the table, it's just a matter of who pulls the trigger first."

"Gees, Frankie."

Jimmy scratched his goatee.

Frankie hoped he had conveyed the dire situation he was in. It was just like the mob with these high society people. He hoped, being a loyal friend, that Jimmy would help him.

"I have thirty grand. It's the last of my money Krista doesn't know about."

Frankie pushed the manila envelope forward, hoping Jimmy would accept it.

Jimmy took the envelope and stuffed it in his coat pocket.

"Okay, Frankie, what do you need me to do?"

Jimmy didn't believe in any of that ghost nonsense, but he agreed to do this deed. He figured Frankie needed some time to get his head straight and probably wouldn't go to his mom's if this plan weren't in place. He knew Frankie had to come to grips and find a real solution to his problem.

Jimmy took off his leather glove and removed a pencil from his pocket to disarm the alarm system at the back door. He pressed the numbers with the eraser. His gloved fingers were too fat to depress only one number. When he was done with the numbers, the LED read, *Alarm System Disarmed*. He moved toward the door and stepped on something soft. His damn leather glove. He bent over to pick it up. "That's how OJ got caught," he said in a whisper, and placed the glove back on his hand. It was tight, but it fit.

The middle patio door was unlocked, as Frankie had promised. He entered the family room, walked through the hallway and entered the home office. He went straight to the hidden safe, and retrieved the Obsidian Box. He laid several items from his backpack across the desk. The ceremony called for two lit candles. This aspect bothered him most of all. The darkness was his friend, shadows his co-conspirators. Light got people in his line of business caught. He was tempted to skip this and several other aspects of the ceremony, but he wanted to tell Frankie honestly that he had followed the instructions, and the fact that there were no results was not because he mishandled the ceremony.

He lit the candles and noticed for the first time that the stone box had no keyhole, latches or hooks. There was no way to open the box without breaking it. It was like a coffin, Jimmy thought, once the lid closed, there was no further entrance.

The ceremony was simple, he had to repeat a Latin phrase six times and after each time, turn the box so a different side was facing up. He had to turn the box in a specific order: forward, forward, right, forward, right. Jimmy had Google-translated the Latin phrase out of curiosity, but also to get the correct pronunciation of the words. Loosely translated it read:

I set thee free, upon this night, to be rebound
by morning's light.

That was it, simple enough. Jimmy began. He placed his hand on the box, said the phrase, turned the box forward, and repeated the phrase. When he completed the phrase six times, he blew out the candles and stood. The final step was to turn from the altar and say another phrase. Then walk out without looking back.

When he turned around, a man wearing a gray flannel robe was standing before him, holding a knife. Jimmy had the good sense to complete the Latin phrase despite the unexpected change in events. He hated this, how well planned events sometimes spiraled out of control and into chaos. This was supposed to be a simple task. Now a witness had seen him.

Jimmy recognized the man from his few days of surveillance of the house. He was the head groundskeeper, Ricardo. He was not a stay-over worker, which only meant one thing, considering the robe; Krista was having an affair with this man. The man being here meant something else; Jimmy was going to have to kill him.

Ricardo looked at him, stupefied, questions written across his face. Jimmy knew it was better to deal with a surprise guest immediately, before they had time to think. *Here's the answers to your questions*, Jimmy thought to himself, and charged. Jimmy's left hand grabbed the landscaper's wrist and his right hand grabbed the man's throat. They both went down, Ricardo's body crumbling under Jimmy's weight. The knife skidded away from them, and settled into the corner of the room.

Jimmy concentrated on crushing the man's trachea. He expected a few blows from Ricardo, but got nothing. He was putting up no struggle at all. Jimmy's back ran cold with goose bumps. He leaned back a little to see Ricardo's face. Ricardo's eyes bulged from his skull and his bottom lip trembled. Jimmy released the grip on Ricardo's neck but the man didn't attempt to move. He let go of the man's wrist and all Ricardo did was point into the room. Jimmy didn't want to believe what that meant and made no attempt to turn around and look.

He watched the color drain from Ricardo's face as he stared at something behind them in the room. His eyes turned pale and his eyebrows whitened. The muscles in the man's face relaxed and his skin spread to a milky smoothness. Then the man's lips stopped quivering and as Jimmy watched, they turned blue. Jimmy had seen this similar sequence many times in his life, but this was the first time it terrified him. He ducked his head into the dead man's shoulder and shut his eyes. He lay still for a few minutes. An icy breeze swished over him. He waited a few moments longer.

Jimmy jumped up, collected the evidence of his deed, and jammed it into his black bag. A muffled scream upstairs was followed by the clumsy sound of a collapsing body. He headed into the hallway and back into the family room. A piercing scream shattered the silence, startling Jimmy terribly. A whining voice cried out, "No, no, no..." a half dozen times at least. The word was replaced by a gurgling sound, not wholly identifiable. Another body collapsed to the floor.

The blinking LED read, *A-Dapt Security is armed.* Jimmy fumbled in his pockets, looking for the paper with the de-activation code scribbled on it. He didn't know why the alarm reset, he was sure he had left it off. Jimmy pulled the code from his right pocket, feeling relief; he was almost out. Skeletal fingers reached from behind him and pulled the paper from his hand. Jimmy looked up at the reflection in the patio door. A face looked back at him, horribly deformed with black soulless eyes and jagged yellow teeth.

Then he felt the entity's subzero fingers close around his neck.

Frankie drove home from New Jersey late Sunday afternoon. He unlocked the front door at sunset and called into his home. He didn't expect an answer. He knew the house workers were off on Sundays and his wife, well...if everything went as planned, she would not be in any condition to answer. Frankie played the part, knowing the security camera at the front door would be watching and recording.

"Krista? I'm home."

No answer returned. He would make his walk through the home, and then call the police. First, he needed a drink, and detoured into the kitchen for his usual. He fixed himself a Scotch on the rocks. Standing by the fridge, he took a healthy swig before continuing on his way.

He entered the family room first. Jimmy's dead body lay crumpled at the back door.

"Jesus, Jimmy!"

Frankie held his heart as he stumbled into the room. Then he laughed, deep and heartily.

"You almost made it out, you fat bastard. You would've been lucky if you did. I only had this one shot and it had to work."

He sat in the lounge chair next to Jimmy's corpse.

"You rat prick, you. You let me tell the whole story about Bobby 'Bags' and never said a word. I knew it was you who pulled the trigger. I knew you were there that night. You let me keep talking like an idiot, like a jackass that didn't have a clue about who killed his own best friend. But the joke's on you Jimmy, I knew, I knew."

Frankie checked their bedroom first, aided by a bright moon shining blue light through the windows. Krista's nightgown was disheveled. Frankie bent, grabbed the left side of her nightgown and yanked on it several times until it covered her left nipple. Even though she was dead, she was still his wife and he didn't want those shit-head detectives ogling her. He couldn't tell how she died but suspected the dark bruises on her neck contributed.

Her son didn't fare as well. He laid flat upon his stomach, but his eyes were staring up, head twisted completely around until it faced the wrong way.

"Good riddance, you disrespectful little shit!"

Last step, he would go back to his office, close up his safe with the Obsidian Box in it. Then he would make his teary-eyed call to 911.

Frankie entered his office and found an additional dead body. He knelt beside it and recognized Ricardo immediately.

"Ricardo, you old prick. You should have spent more time concentrating on the hedges in the yard, rather than trimming my wife's bush."

Nothing that Frankie could do now. He worried that a dead Ricardo gave himself a motive to want his wife and her lover dead. However, he would have to work with the results he had achieved. He was lucky to get the bonus kill of Jimmy the Russian involved in his plan. No plan worked perfect.

When Frankie stood, he noticed an even bigger problem. His brows rose and his eyes widened. He gulped down the remainder of his drink.

"Shit," he said. "Shit, shit, shit!"

Even in the dark, he could see that the Obsidian Box was smashed. He walked to the desk and lifted a jagged piece of the broken stone. Next to the box was a hammer. He wondered who could've done this and why. Did Ricardo do this? The dread of realization washed over him; the ghoul was loose in the house. He dropped the black shard and rushed to the safe. He retrieved the book of spells and turned on the desk lamp. There had to be some kind of spell to make himself safe, to keep the evil spirit away. He clawed at the pages of the book, but no such spell became evident.

The desk light flickered. It became very bright for a few seconds then blew out. Frankie looked up into the room and his eyes blinked in rapid succession. His ears perked up as he listened and he held his breath to gain complete silence. He heard two voices whispering in a distant room of the house. It was faint and indistinct, but there. He became frantic, flipping through pages of the book despite not being able to see them in the dark. He threw the book aside. He heard a crash in the kitchen, perhaps his bottle of Scotch. The air in Frankie's lungs rushed out. Then he heard the wedding picture in the hallway crash to the ground and the glass shatter. The sound was loud and jarred his spine. He ducked down behind the desk, peering over the top, to watch the doorway. The room door, flung wide open and its knob smacked the adjacent wall. He watched but no one entered. Then he felt a tap on his shoulder. He twisted his head around and began to scream but the sound faded rapidly. Frankie blacked out.

Frankie regained consciousness, slowly opening his eyes and trying to focus. He was in the garage restrained by rope, sitting in a metal folding chair. The night's moon provided light through the windows. The ghoul stood before him, his hideous, smiling face tinted blue, his coal black eyeballs shifting with excitement. He clasped his boney hands together and twisted his arms up as if he had a wonderful idea that put him in a state of glee. He spoke something but it was from a fugue state and Frankie couldn't understand it. The ghoul stepped aside and Frankie saw the garage workbench with an assortment of tools lined upon it. The ghoul held out his left hand and a dark figure appeared from shadow next to him. He caressed the back of the shadow figure's head in a loving gesture. When the dark figure raised its head, Frankie saw it was the boy; it was Krista's son. He was dead but his spirit had stayed here. Why? But Frankie knew why. The ghoul's demented spirit, cast by years of torment, had somehow found a kinship in the boy's fragmented mind. The deal was sealed when the boy's ghost broke the stone box with the hammer. The age-old ghoul and the boy's shattered soul found a way to be together in the ethereal dimension, attending their nasty deeds and reveling in their blood-soaked mayhem.

That was when Frankie realized why *he* was still alive. The boy turned to the table. His wispy, ghost-like essence solidified. He picked up a power drill and a hammer and turned to Frankie. The boy liked to see things suffer. He liked to see things bleed. The ghoul squirmed with delight as the boy stepped forward. Frankie tensed and his whole body began to shake. His face distorted into a terrible grimace that resembled a crying baby. He cried aloud, but was cut short when he found himself choking on his own bloody teeth delivered by a perfectly aimed hammer blow. Frankie heard the piercing buzz of the drill fill his ears and he knew it was going to be a long, painful night.

Betty Rocksteady

The Sins of Our Fathers

Dearest William,

I awoke drenched in sweat this morning, the taste of salt fresh on my lips. The summer sun lit my room, but its warmth did not reach me. I shuddered, an icy chill reaching deep into my bones.

It is too late.

My father died soon after my birth. Upon his death, he left me a note, as I will leave this note to you. He pleaded I not make the same mistakes as he - never to allow alcohol pass my lips, and, never *to bring a son of my own onto this earth.*

Abstinence was easy. I had no desire to follow *his* example, not like that; I swore alcoholism and insanity was not for me.

Falling in love with your mother changed me. As a child, I had been denied the family I longed for. She made me realize we could create our own future. The happiest moment of my life was when the nurse placed you into my arms, your face red and wrinkled as you shrieked your arrival into the world. The greatest thing I ever created, you, my son.

With your first breath, something else awoke.

That very night the nightmares began, revealing to me my family's darkest shame: my great-grandfather, a failed lighthouse keeper who reeked of booze and sour sweat. His stench permeated my dreams.

Night after night, I tossed and turned, forced to bear witness each time I dared close my eyes. The lighthouse was stark against a sky purple as a bruise. My drunken predecessor was oblivious to his duties when clouds heavy with rain broke open. Thunder crackled and lightening spit, yet he lay in a drunken stupor, undisturbed.

Then the ship came, the crew filthy, exhausted, but finally home. My great-grandfather slept heavy. He never heard, but I do.

The crunch of wood and bone dashed against rock. A great ship in splinters, her proud crew reduced to bloody smears in the ocean, and then to nothing as the vast waters swallowed them whole.

He fell down the slippery steps of the lighthouse, smashing his skull on the cold stone. In death, he escaped his punishment and the townsfolk cursed my family name.

The dreams awoke something deep within me, a relentless, gnawing *need*. My family's guilt churned within me. I was powerless. A fire lit in my stomach and exposed the pits of misery.

Your mother does not understand, but the sins of our fathers can haunt us so.

With the first sip of alcohol, I awoke something else.

A different dream . . . *The night is cold as death. The ocean is strangely calm, the sky black as sin. A fog rolls in, enveloping me in its deadly embrace. I see a ship in the distance and the air crackles, electric with rage. They are coming for me. I tread water, and I wait.*

Dozens of hands yank, grab, and pull me under. The moon is a pallid mask, mocking, as my screams drown within the thrashing of waves. I gasp for breath, clawing at the sky as I sink for the final time. The ocean is alive with rage and I cough, sputter, and draw in seawater as I am pulled down, down, down.

I awoke this morning drenched in sweat. My lungs screamed for oxygen as I coughed salty water onto the bed. I sputtered and choked for a time, and it was when I was finally gasping in fresh, merciful air that I noticed delicate tendrils of seaweed wrapped around my fingers.

It is too late.

Death reaches for me across generations.

Will you indulge me in one last wish? My son, I beg you, allow the curse to die with me.

Father.

Justin Hunter

The Cistern

He had been chatting her up for hours now. Tom had never been happier to stumble into a dive bar more than he was tonight. He raised his glass and shouted to the bartender for a refill, bumping his hand against the overhead lamp, sending the light into a gentle rocking motion. The swinging light made the shadows play against the huddled masses at the bar. The other patrons gave him sour looks, which he didn't notice in the slightest. The girl was laughing.

"I think you've had a bit too much," she said, reaching out her hand, steadying the light. When she brought her hand down, she rested it on his wrist. His heart surged with delight. Her name was Pearl. He remembered it after having asked her what it was several times.

"I've had way too much," Tom said. "I had too much before I even came in here." Tom knew this to be true on many levels. Tom's night on the town started with friends after work several hours ago, at a completely different bar on the other side of town. Most of his friends only stayed for a couple drinks and then went home. Some decided to do a little bar hopping with him, but none of them lasted after the third bar. The last of his friends to leave, his best buddy Gavin, begged him to share a taxi with him and call it a night. Tom took the cab with Gavin, but just to get the guy off his back. As soon as Gavin arrive at his home, Tom told the cabbie to bring him to the nearest place of lubrication he could find. It wasn't a far drive.

Tom never only had a couple drinks. Once the alcohol started flowing, he didn't stop drinking until he blacked out. He never enjoyed the morning after. All he ended up with was a pocket full of receipts from bars he didn't remember going to and a bad hangover. No matter how upset the day after a binge made him, he never seemed to remember it while he was out. He felt fortunate that no matter what seemed to happen the night before, he usually ended up safe at home.

The bartender took Tom's glass, filled it with draft beer, and placed it in front of him. Tom thanked him and took a long drink, emptying half the glass.

"More," she said, drifting her hand along his inner thigh. "More."

Tom woke up, tasting dust and dirt. An earthy smell hung in the air. His eyes were fused closed with dried mucus and he rubbed them until they opened. His eyes felt so dry that his eyelids seemed to draw open like pieces of sandpaper scraping against each other. He sat up. A long string of saliva broke its connection with the floor and landed against his shirt. His mind reeled. Tom moved to his knees and dry-heaved. A thick wad of bile rose in the back of his throat. It tasted of bitter motor oil. He swallowed it back down.

Tom rolled back down on the floor. He clawed weakly at the ground. It came up in his fingers. The realization that he was lying on a dirt floor meant just one thing to Tom - he wasn't at home. There wasn't much he planned on doing about that at the moment. His sickness stole any panic he might have felt about waking up in an unknown place. He opened his eyes again and took a quick look at himself. He saw that he was clothed and thanked heaven for small favors.

A long repressed memory wafted through his consciousness. He saw himself waking up in an alley lying on his stomach with his pants around his ankles. He had trouble walking for more than a week. Tom had to use up all his vacation and sick time at work, and almost lost his job on top of it. Sick time required a doctor's note, and there was no way in hell that Tom was going to a doctor. He didn't want anyone knowing about the rape. After that, he stopped drinking. He made it almost two whole weeks before he fell off the wagon. It was the longest dry streak he had since he was a fifteen-year-old kid.

His mind drifted to thoughts of her. Not the whore he met last night at the bar. His wife was the woman he thought of. After they divorced, he thought of her every day for years. Now his mind only moved to her when he was waking up sick from a drunk. After all, his alcohol problem drove them apart. Tom thought about the old saying, 'time heals all wounds', and would have laughed if he didn't think it would cause him to puke. He knew for certain that time didn't heal shit. It only caused a person to forget or twist the past. The things he couldn't forget or rationalize, well, he drank until they went away. That was the first and last of it. Still he couldn't stop thinking about her. In his sickness and vulnerability – she was there. He remembered when he first met her. It was so many years ago.

He had been rummaging through the foul smelling second hand clothing at his local thrift shop. Whenever he found something that he thought would fit, he was disappointed to notice food stains or small tears that rendered the item unusable. There was nothing worth purchasing. He has been scouring the clothing for over an hour and was about to give up. The neighborhood was a poor one, so the thrift shop's second hand clothing was, in actuality, third or fourth hand, only donated when the previous owners deemed it lifeless.

"Couldn't find anything?" Tom startled by the soft feminine voice. The cashier was looking at him. A small smile drifted haltingly on her face. She wore simple, plain clothing that so matched the quiet drabness of the thrift shop that she could have been mistaken for a mannequin. She wasn't old, yet youth seemed to be a quickly fading memory.

"Nothing worth saving," Tom replied. The cashier gave a stunted laugh and put on a badly accentuated tone of the nouveau rich.

"You've got somewhere to go that requires clothing of a more upscale nature?"

"No."

"That's good," the cashier said. "I would have asked you to take me with you." Tom flushed at the thought. The four words he said to the woman were more conversation than he'd had with another human being in the last three months. He felt vulnerable and completely at a loss for words. The cashier laughed again. This time the sound came out clear and real. "You can unstick that tongue from the roof of your mouth. I wasn't asking you out on a date or anything."

"You have a pretty laugh." It was the cashier's turn to blush, but the rosy hue of her face couldn't begin to match Ted's scorched visage. The words had come out of his mouth unabated, dangerous, making him feel utter embarrassment and roguish at the same time. His hand drifted of its own accord to his sagging paunch, as if to display his inadequacies. The cashier put a hand over her mouth as if the sound of her laugh had betrayed her.

She dropped her hand and smoothed her hair away from her face.

"Thanks," she said. "You're quite the smooth talker, aren't you?" Her voice lost its luster, coming out rough and accusatory.

"No."

"Sorry," she said. "I don't take compliments well. I don't get many."

"I do like your laugh," Tom said. The words came easier this time.

"I like your taste in clothing," The cashier said. "Not buying anything, I mean. All we have here is crap." They both chuckled, looking at the floor.

"Would you mind taking a walk with me later?" Tom voiced the words into the abyss and felt himself falling after them. The moments that passed between reply felt like hours and he was lost within them.

"Alright," she said. "I get done here at nine."

Tom left the store, trying not to seem in a hurry. His steps quickened as soon as he hit the sidewalk. Life seemed to breathe into his body again. His soul swelled. He thought about how just a moment ago there seemed nothing in that store worth saving, including himself. Maybe there was something worth saving. Maybe they could save each other.

They didn't save each other. She had tried, but he just couldn't stop boozing. He couldn't even remember the night she left. She could have been gone for days, and he probably wouldn't have noticed. It was a long bender. He remembered that much. He had cleaned out the checking account and spent it all on rotgut gin bought from the bottom shelf at the local supermarket. He did remember thinking of what a good deal he scored. If you bought the booze by the case, you got a ten percent discount. It was like getting another couple bottles free.

Tom shook his head to clear the memories. It didn't matter. Nothing mattered. He cried softly and clawed at the earth beneath his fingers. When he woke up, she was gone. He looked for her for a while. Her family wouldn't leave him the hell alone. They thought he had something to do with her disappearance. The police did too, but they couldn't do shit. He didn't know where she went and they never found her. She disappeared. People do that sometimes. They just vanish.

A soft, feminine voice called to him from the darkness. "Are you awake?"

Tom jerked to his knees, an action that made him dry heave until he fell onto his back exhausted.

"I need something to drink," Tom said. He never felt so dry in his life. A glass of water would be heaven. He would kill for a beer.

"I love you, Tom," she said. A gentle hand rested on his chest. He was almost sorry about the vomit that covered the front of him.

"I need something to drink," Tom said. The hand that rested on his chest drifted up to his neck. Iron fingers gripped his tightly. He tried to rise but couldn't. His body was so sick and weak. He tried to scream, but the effort only made burning acid bile rise in his throat. He opened his eyes and saw his love, his wife, Pearl, her head caved in at the side. Her eyes were missing. She raised a mangled, maggot-infested arm and slammed his mouth full of earth.

"Drink," she said, teeth falling out of her mouth and pattering onto Tom's face like rain, "Drink."

Angeline Trevena

The Snow in May

May had worried that she wouldn't recognise her father, but when he came through the door, his eyes locked onto hers and she was six years old again. He sat down opposite her, just a small table between them. His eyes never wavered from hers. They were paler than she remembered and, of course, the skin around them had wrinkled over time.

"May," he said.

May pressed herself back in the seat. She hadn't heard his voice for more than twenty-five years. She opened her mouth, forcing "Martin" from it.

"You can't even bring yourself to call me Dad?" His eyes registered no emotion.

"You lost that right." Her heart was thumping so loudly she was sure he would hear it.

His eyes flickered from hers for a moment, and he clenched his hands into fists. His hands were still huge, powerful. May looked away, trying to shake the feeling of them tightening around her throat.

"I'm glad you came," he said. "I didn't expect you to."

"It was curiosity more than anything. I wanted to see you now, with adult eyes, not those of a child. You're just a man. Not the monster I remember. You're just a man."

He opened his hands, palms up. "Just a man," he repeated. "They're considering me for release."

The word sent bolts of ice through May's chest, and she bit her tongue to stop herself from showing it. The metallic taste of blood filled her mouth. "If it had been up to me I would have had you hung for what you did."

He picked at the edge of the table. "Your mother's death—"

"Don't you speak about mother."

"There are things you were too young to understand. Things I couldn't—"

May slammed her hand down onto the table. The officer

moved forward, but she waved him back. "My mother accepted me. You were jealous of the bond between us, scared of what we could do together."

"I was only trying to protect you."

"I needed protecting from you."

"You're not remembering things how they actually were."

"I remember everything just fine. I remember her standing between us, the knife in your hands, her telling me to run. And thanks to you I've never stopped running." She looked at the officer. "I'm finished." She stood and walked toward the door.

"That's not the way it was, May. I've always loved you. Probably too much even."

May turned. "You're dead to me."

May was still shaking as she carried her drink to a window seat. She leaned back into the faux leather chair and closed her eyes for a moment. A large vanilla latte was just what she needed to put the episode behind her and return to normal life. She checked her watch, wondering if it was worthwhile going into the office.

"May? May Everett?"

May looked up into the man's face, but it was a moment before she recognised the boy's face behind the beard.

"Olie Finley!" She stood up and wrapped her arms around his thin shoulders. "Look at you all grown up. Have you got time to catch up?"

He looked at his watch. "Well... no, screw it, yes I have." He sat down, placing his takeaway cup on the table.

"So how've you been?" May asked. "I haven't seen you since school."

"Alright, yeah. I'm an architect now."

"No way. All grown up and responsible. I remember flicking bogies with you in English." She laughed, but it sounded a little off, a little manic.

He raised his eyebrows. "Yeah, real man of the world now. Married, kids, the whole kaboodle. How about you? Don't disappoint me and say you're doing something boring."

She cocked her head. "Sorry, I'm in events management. Very normal I'm afraid. I even live in an average apartment, and I have an incredibly ordinary boyfriend who works in marketing."

Olie waved his hands at her. "No, my illusion is ruined. I

233

always imagined you becoming a funeral director, or a pathologist, or an entomologist or something. Remember how you were always collecting bugs in jars? Giving them all names? What happened to the weird little girl I knew?"

May shrugged. "She grew up I guess."

Olie leaned in, looking deep into her eyes. "Nah, I know she's still in there somewhere." He leaned back and grinned. "It's a crime that we lost touch. I've often thought about you, wondering where you were. I've missed you too, now I think about it. You're still the most interesting person I've ever known." He held his hands to his chest. "And my first kiss too."

May's hands flew to her mouth. "I'd totally forgotten about that!"

"I never have," Olie said dreamily. "It was in that den we made by the river. Our hands touched, our eyes locked, our lips met..."

May punched him playfully. "Oh shut up."

Olie raised his nose into the air, feigning insult. "Well it meant something to me."

"Oh please, I've kissed hundreds of boys since then. What would make you so special? Besides you got married, you weren't pining for me that much."

"Rebound." Olie covered his mouth and lowered his voice. "And if you ever tell my wife I said that, I'll kill you." He laughed.

"It's so good to see you, Olie. Especially today." She tapped her fingernails against the side of her mug. "I've just been to see my father."

Olie's face turned serious, and he slid his hand across the table, stopping short of touching her. "How was it?"

"Horrible. But I can't talk to anyone about it. I always tell people that both my parents are dead."

"Even your boyfriend?"

May shrugged.

Olie pulled his chair in closer, the legs squeaking boorishly across the floor. "And what about the other thing?"

May shook her head quickly. "The family curse? Would you?"

"I guess not."

May knelt down in the cool grass, gently laying a bunch of flowers against the gravestone. It held no inscription of how Cassandra Everett had died; people didn't want to see the truth in graveyards. They wanted to think their loved ones were at peace, watching over them, no matter how brutally they died. But May knew the truth. Death didn't release you from torture; it was just a completely new level of it.

"Hi Mum. I went to see him today. I didn't think I could do it, and I nearly didn't. So many times, I decided not to go. But I had to do it for me. And you know what, he looked smaller than I remember. I guess I'd built him up into something more. I just hope you're haunting the hell out of him like you do me."

May shifted, sitting down fully.

"He was trying to worm his way out of blame again. Telling me I had things wrong. How could he? I remember that day with more clarity than any other. I know what happened."

May watched as a single flake of snow, unusual for late spring, landed gently on the back of her fist. She smiled sadly.

"Remember when we used to make rainbows together?" She looked up at the grey sky. "I didn't even bring a jacket."

By the time she left, her hair was thick with snow, her clothes cold and wet, her muscles shivering.

"Can you believe this weather?" May called out as she went into her apartment. She tossed her keys onto a side table and ran her fingers through her wet hair. "Rhys, are you here?" She wandered into the open plan living room; the large window revealing the flat grey sky, snow spinning on the wind. "Rhys?"

Shrugging, she wandered into the bathroom and turned on the shower. The rushing water blocked out any other sounds, the steam gently rising. She pulled off her wet cardigan, and dropped it onto the tiled floor. May turned, startled by Rhys standing in the doorway.

"I didn't think you were here," she said.

"Where have you been?"

"Work. Can you believe this weather? I'm soaked."

"Don't lie to me." He stepped forward.

"I'm not." May ducked around Rhys and returned to the living room.

Rhys followed her. "I called the office. They said you had the day off. So where were you?"

"I don't have to answer to you," she said, backing up. She bumped into the back of the cream leather sofa—his choice.

"Who were you with, May?"

"I wasn't with anyone. You're paranoid."

"Paranoid?" He grabbed for her.

May quickly sidestepped his reach toward the kitchen, her back against the breakfast bar he had had put in.

"You disappear all day and then you lie about it," he said. "How exactly is that me being paranoid?"

"You don't need to know where I am every minute of the day. I needed to do something for me. I wasn't with anyone else. If you trust me you'll—"

"How can I trust you when you lie to my face?" He moved quickly and closed his thick fingers around her wrist.

She tugged, but his grip was too strong. "You're hurting me."

"Just tell me where you were."

"Rhys, please, let go of me."

He moved his face close into hers. She could smell curry on his breath. "Where were you?"

"Let go!" May screamed, wrenching herself free. Behind her, a plate threw itself at the wall, showering the kitchen with fragments of china.

Rhys backed up quickly. "What the hell?"

"Rhys, I'm sorry, I didn't mean to—" May reached out to him, but he moved further back.

"How did you do that?" His wide eyes locked onto hers. He stumbled into the side of the sofa, raising a hand to her defensively. "You just...just leave me alone." He scuttled out of the apartment, leaving May behind with the white noise of the shower.

May woke, the leather sofa beneath her cold and uncomfortable. It had grown dark outside and the orange glow of city lights bled into the room. She reached over and flicked on a lamp, the sudden brightness comforting.

Pushing herself upright, she stood and crossed to the window, peering down to the street below. The reflections of streetlights smeared across the wet road, but any other sign of the snow had disappeared.

The lamp flickered, dimmed, then brightened again. May turned from the window and watched it flicker once more. It finally died, leaving her in darkness. The room filled with the scent of stagnant water and wet earth. May turned back toward the window, watching a reflection of her mother waver and settle into focus.

She hung a few inches above the ground, her arms raised

slightly on either side, her head cocked awkwardly, as if an unseen hook suspended her. Some of her hair was matted to her face; the rest wavered like tendrils around her head. Across her neck, a deep cut began to bleed. Her pale dress began to darken in patches, marking each of the knife wounds that had killed her. Her blueish, aged skin hung from her skull, her eyes sunken into shadows.

"You're back," May said to the reflection.

"You lost your temper again," the image said, her lips still pressed together.

"I don't know what happened," May said, looking down at her hands. "I've been in control for so long now. I guess I became complacent."

"Snow in spring? You're nowhere near being in control. How many people are going to get hurt? How many more people are you going to lose?"

"Rhys will come back." May turned away from the window and sat on the sofa, pulling her legs up underneath her.

"I wouldn't count on it, and now you're all alone again." May's shoulder grew cold and damp as her mother touched her. "Remember what I taught you, remember how to hold back. When you let your emotions take over, you can't control it. It's not about stifling you, I just want to keep you safe. It's hard being different, but this is just the way things are for us. I thought I taught you better than this, May, all the lessons my mother taught me. Do you want to be alone forever, an outcast?"

"No."

"Do you want to be labelled strange, weird, freak?"

"No."

"Do you want to be feared, attacked, hated?"

"No." May looked down into her lap. "I just want to be normal."

"Then you must be perceived as normal. Act normally, be average, and normality will find you. You must avoid these emotional outbursts. Someone always gets hurt. I shouldn't need to tell you this."

"I'm sorry."

"Sorry doesn't bring people back. You need to hold your temper."

"But it's exhausting. I couldn't help it."

The lamp fizzed.

237

"You never can." The voice was fainter, and with it, the smell diminished. The lamp flickered into life and May closed her eyes against the glare. Outside, the snow began to fall again.

Olie walked toward her, an awkward smile on his face. May raised a hand and waved stiffly. The wind pushed through the small park, picking up leaves and discarded newspapers to throw at May's legs. She tucked her feet back under the bench, looking up again as Olie sat down next to her.

"Here." He handed her a bag of mini doughnuts, still warm.

She breathed in the sugary scent of them. "Mmmm, I could do with these today."

"You always did have a bit of a sweet tooth." He cocked his head to one side. "I'm sorry to hear about you and Rhys."

She waved a hand at him dismissively, and he flinched slightly. "It's my own fault. I can't control it anymore."

"So what's changed?"

May shrugged and turned away, watching a dog walker struggling against the wind.

"There must be something. Might it have something to do with seeing your dad?"

May looked back at Olie. "I suppose it's dragging things up from the past. Feelings. Anger. Things I'd rather ignore. Or try to, at least." She sighed. "It's just so good to be able to talk to someone about this. Other than my mother, I mean."

May felt Olie shiver next to her. "How often does she come to visit now?"

"It's increasing. Some weeks it's every day. And it's always the same conversation, like a recurring dream."

"And she's still...?" He gestured to his body.

"Still bleeding, yes. I wouldn't mind so much if she looked... like she used to."

"I remember how much it used to freak you out when you were younger." He shifted, turning toward her. "Remember those walkie-talkies we used to have? I kept a diary too, of every time she appeared, every time we talked. I was going through some old paperwork the other day and I found it." He pulled a folded notebook from his coat pocket and held it out to her. "It might help clarify some things."

May hesitated before taking it. "Do you mind if I read it later?"

"Not at all, and come on, share those doughnuts, the smell is killing me."

It wasn't the usual buzz of cell bells that woke Martin this time. As his eyes flickered open, he recognised the scent of wet earth. He sat up, rubbing his fists into his eyes, the darkness of his cell penetrated only by the sickly ginger glow of the perimeter lights, which crept in through the tiny, grubby window. As she appeared, she was bright, like the angel he always thought of her as.

She slowly came into form, smiling gently, sitting on the bed without disturbing the covers. She was beautiful, young, just like when they had first met. Her long, dark hair showed no sign of the grey that had come to pinstripe it, her eyes had none of the creases she always called her 'laughter lines'.

"Hello, darling," he said. "I've missed you."

Her smile fell away. "It's getting harder to come to you; it takes more energy each time."

"She's getting stronger," Martin said.

She nodded. "She's losing control. She's dangerous."

"She came to see me. I was shocked at how much older she looked, not our little girl anymore. But when I looked into those eyes, there she was, that little six-year-old girl with her temper."

"You have to save her from herself. She can't do this alone, you need to take control."

"I know what needs doing."

"You have to stop her before she hurts someone else. Before she..." She drifted off and her form flickered like an old movie. Flashes of stab wounds came and went across her body, blood staining her pale dress.

Martin screwed his thin blanket into his fists. "I'm so sorry I couldn't save you from her. She was just too strong." He snorted out a laugh. "A little girl too strong for me."

"She was never just a little girl. What she inherited... her abilities are way beyond anything I could ever do. I thought I could teach her the right way to use it, but she only wanted to destroy things." She sighed. "I know that you tried your best. Don't let the guilt eat you like this." She reached out and touched his face, leaving it damp.

"I did all this to protect her." He gestured to the cell around him. "Twenty-seven years of this, just to protect her. And now I have to end it all."

"You loved us. You did what any devoted father would do. You made the ultimate sacrifice to protect your daughter, and now you need to do it again. You can't let her live."

May slowly placed her mobile phone down on her desk. She stared at it, her hands balling into fists. Her entire body felt numb, cold, and she was sure her heart had actually stopped beating.

"Are you alright, May?" asked Kelly, the young receptionist, as she passed. "You're absolutely white."

May shook herself and looked up. "Yeah, just a headache coming on I think."

"You look terrible, maybe you should head home."

"Yeah, maybe." May grabbed her phone and crossed the office to the toilets, stumbling into a cubicle and pushing the bolt across behind her.

She flicked through her phone's contact list, dialling Olie's number. She listened to the ringing, willing him to answer. Outside the cubicle, the taps turned themselves on, water gushing into the basins.

He answered. "May?"

"Olie. It's happened. My dad's been released." She shuddered. "I need you."

"I'll come and pick you up."

May closed her phone and pushed it into her pocket. Water began to pool underneath the cubicle door.

It was dark by the time May unlocked her apartment door, her face streaked with tears, her clothes splashed with mud, her hair pulled loose from its usual style. She closed the door behind her and walked, dazed, through to the living room. She flicked on the lamp and looked up at Martin sitting in an armchair, a pistol resting on his thigh. A smudge hung in the air behind Martin's head, the smell of damp earth rich.

"I knew you'd be here," May said. "I knew."

"So why did you come?"

"Olie's dead. I don't even know what happened." She looked at her hands before clasping them behind her back.

"Then you understand why I have to do this."

"You killed Mum, now you've come to finish the job."

Martin shook his head sadly. "No. I loved her." He raised the gun, tears running over his cheeks. "You killed your mum. And now I need to save you from yourself."

Unfamiliar memories flashed through May's head. Her selfish, childish demands, her violent tantrums, the knives rattling in the kitchen drawers. With her father's quick temper, and her mother's abilities, it was a lethal combination.

"How could I forget?," she whispered.

Outside, thick snow swirled on the wind, blocking out the glow of the streetlights.

David Schütz II

The Moon Above Oak Road

Frigid was the Wyntersburg night.

It was colder there than it was in St. Louis. Cities of concrete and steel hold at least a modicum of heat in their bones; towns housed within the plains, with their empty, faded borders, do not.

The stark, punishing winds of southern Illinois rocked the blue Chrysler as it departed Interstate 70 and merged onto Little Belt Road. February, as is the nature of February, brought a bitter atmosphere upon the dark night and homes. The subtle plumes of chimney smoke ascended in an opaque rapture toward the beckoning sky. Life, in both its grandeur and tedium, is fraught with change. Wyntersburg is not.

Klaus Schtreicher gently depressed the accelerator. When he was satisfied that the vehicle was traveling at the rate of the speed limit so carefully designated by the appropriate committee, he relaxed the effort. He never exceeded them, as his pastime could not abide getting pulled over for speeding.

Police ask questions. Police could impede upon his charge. That, of course, he would not allow.

His perfect memory reminded him that once he passed State Route 9, he would see the familiar bent street sign, bearing the curt inscription, "Oak Rd." after a distance of about four miles. Indeed, he did see that landmark, and upon reaching it, he steered to his right and slowed, his shoulders tightening into unpleasant knots as the gravel lane grinded beneath his conveyance. He endured the vibration with frayed nerves for a minute or two, before passing the transparent husks of three houses that had, at one time, been quaint and simple, before they had been burned to the cold ground several Christmas Eves ago. He continued onward for one more mile and slowed pulled onto the rocky driveway of the lone standing house at the end of the road.

The structure stood tall and looked like a decaying disguise, displayed center stage, and bathed in the white beams of the automobile's headlights. Klaus gazed at his ancient boyhood home.

He switched off the ignition and the lights and exited the vehicle. Frozen brown grass lightly sounded its objections as he trod across its surface. Key in hand, he approached the threshold. Upon reaching the door, Klaus paused and listened to the world about him; it offered no voice, other than the rasping whistle of the racing wind.

That is good.

He turned the key and the portal yielded. Klaus leaned forward and inhaled rather deeply; the air within the house bore notes more rank than his previous visit. He stepped inside, and reached to his right. His seeking fingers grasped the flashlight that he kept upon the small table beside the door, and with a mere flick of his thumb, the room was cleft with a blade of light. He swept the beam from side to side and, finding nothing amiss, aimed the light before himself and walked to the fireplace.

He set the torch down beside the fireplace. He took a few steps to the left and retrieved some dust-laden wood from the kindling pile. Carefully, he placed pieces on the charred rack within the red brick alcove. He stood again and found the long wooden matchsticks within their box upon the mantle. He withdrew one and scraped it across the surface of the bricks. Spark became flame as the matchstick ignited like a shooting star. He inhaled once more before setting it between the lowest logs. He returned his gaze to the mantle and took the small canister of lighting fluid from it. He aimed the spout toward the wood and lightly depressed the sides of the canister, releasing a clear, pungent arc of liquid onto the logs. A brilliant light roared to life.

He returned the lighting fluid to the mantle and gazed about the interior around him. The living room sat sparsely decorated. A plush, indigo high backed chair flanked the fireplace. A frayed, woven carpet lay a bit askew, yet still centered upon the floor. Klaus strode across its tattered face as he exited the house. He left the front door ajar, crossed the lawn and returned to the car. The vehicle's trunk popped open with a resounding "thunk" as the key was turned within, its contents exposed to the shivering darkness. He reached within its shadowed contours and removed the awaiting cargo, a prize that seemed to shimmer in the

Midwestern winter's bitter moonlight. He reverently draped the young dead girl's form over his right shoulder. He closed the trunk and walked back to the house.

Once he had passed through the threshold and again occupied the living room, he glanced about the residence. The fire had doubled in breadth, offering a minute sunrise that illuminated its environs in a microcosmic dawn. There was a suggestion of warmth. He turned to the right and approached the dining table.

Flickering shadows danced about the chamber. The dining table, oval in shape, encircled by six ornate chairs occupied by three dark silhouettes. Upon his arrival, the visage of the inhabitants of three of the chairs became visible: a lovely, tall woman in a pretty, white blouse; a demure, stately lady of perhaps eighty years; a young man, his hair a bit too long, wearing a sweatshirt that bore the insignia of an institution called, "Highland Senior High."

All were exhibiting various stages of decay.

Each body contained a distinct marking, a unifying brand that they all shared: a smooth scar, which began beneath one corner of the jaw, descended in a brief, clean arc across the throat in a semicircular path that concluded below the opposite side of the neck. The wounds were carefully, lovingly stitched closed, sewn with precision and pride, reminiscent of the seams adorning a baseball.

Klaus carefully sat the young girl within the leftmost chair. He positioned her to face the others, respectfully, and gently swept her hair to one side. Her scar shone briefly in the nearby firelight. He smiled, and looked upon the pleasing tableau displayed before him.

"You're home."

Klaus started as the words. He whirled around, and beheld the breathtaking image that was Alyssa. She, too, was beyond change; even after all this time, she looked as though she'd just left the market where she'd once worked, the market in which he'd first seen her. She used to sing faintly as she operated the cash register, day after day. She was, all at once, mesmerizing and frightening. He had to have her.

He had followed her one evening as she left for home. She was walking, singing, existing in a life that was simple and free. Klaus offered a ride in the blue Chrysler, but what she had accepted was more than passage home to her small house in the city; it was a release from the bindings of life, the burden of years to come, and the privilege of wearing a lengthwise incision upon her subtle neck. He had opened her throat to let the sweet song out, to bathe in its blithe notes.

"Yes, dear Alyssa. I've returned. I've brought her to you. Isn't she perfect? Isn't she fine?"

"Indeed. Thank you."

She advanced toward the girl propped in the chair. When she moved, her legs did not. Upon reaching the child, Alyssa gazed upon her and smiled.

"She is very much like Hannah. She looked just like this, my little sister. See how she looks at the others as if they really are our family? Bobby, do sit up straight. Set a good example for our Hannah. Right, Mother?"

The woman in the white blouse stared silently at her, the empty caverns that once contained her eyes gaping in their eternal yawns. The woman had been the first one that Klaus sought, the ideal replacement mother for Alyssa.

Four months after he'd buried Alyssa in the back yard, Klaus returned to the old homestead in Wyntersburg. She had spent the idle time walking in the confines of the house, exploring that dead manor that once held a family that was not her own.

He sat in the plush chair beside the fireplace and marveled at her translucent brilliance, her sheer incomparable beauty. She told him of her fear. She told him of her lost dreams. She told him of the family that she missed, that she so dearly longed for. Over time, he had assembled a new one for her, to wile away the hours and months with her, between his visits. They were not those people that she grew up with, that she had adored and revered, but they were convenient and they sufficed, and they were all perfect; the perfect mother, brother, and grandmother. Tonight, the perfect sister returned home to Alyssa. The family was nearly complete.

"Is she not beautiful, dear Alyssa? Are not they all?" He found it difficult to contain his pride, his satisfaction in the successful pursuit of his charge.

"They are, Klaus. You have chosen so well."

"It is not only my honor, but my pleasure. They are lovely, all of them. Perfect. They cannot compare to you, Alyssa, but I pray that make you happy. I took them all; Of course, they had to be, their purpose be realized, and now that has happened. They have found their destiny, the reason for their being. They are here. They are yours, forever."

"Forever is a long, long time, Klaus. However, I fear they are not satisfied. They are not happy."

Klaus staggered back a step. It was difficult for him to believe that these people were not content. He had labored too hard, and he could not comprehend the possibility that they could be unsatisfied. He was forging the perfect family. For what reason would they not be cheerful?

"I do not understand."

"Silly Klaus, Can you not see?"

"Alas, I cannot. Have I displeased you, Alyssa? Have you pains? Are they not together, within the comfort of home, a fire alight to warm them? I took them from their small and insignificant lives and gave them their predestinate fates, as I did for you, dearest. You were too lovely for this cold world, so I plucked you from it, and gave you eternal life. I did so also to them, for you. Do they think that I failed? Dear God, do you, Alyssa?"

"No, my sweet Klaus, heavens no, you have not failed me."

"Then, what could it be?" For the first time in recent memory, he was worried.

"You have done so well. It is just... just that they, I, wish for something more. We are incomplete."

"What do you require? You have but to speak it and it is yours!"

"The father is desired, the one who is still missing; the one who must sit at the head of the table, the man of the house, to lead us in life and home."

"Indeed! Of course, I will find him. It will not take long, my dear Alyssa. I promise you."

"As I've told you, you have done so well. There is no need to seek, for our father is here."

Klaus opened his mouth to speak, to inquire as to what she meant, but before he could utter a sound, the ancient creaking of a nearby kitchen drawer silenced him. The faint orange glow of the fireplace sparked a gleam upon the surface of the knife leaping from its sanctuary. As swift as it was silent, the blade soared into his unsuspecting hand. His will was not completely his own. His fingers wrapped themselves around the handle. His brain objected to the sudden foreign occupation of his rising arm, and he fought with all of his might to stop the blade as it entered his neck.

"You, dear Klaus, will play the part. Welcome home, Father."

The corpses seated about the table turned toward Klaus and smiled. Alyssa drifted to him. Her lips curved into a smile as lovely and haunting as the moon over Wyntersburg. She grabbed his wrist and pulled the blade across his throat. He sputtered and gasped as he staggered backward, his jerky gait only ceasing when it deposited him within the chair beside the fire.

His eyes widened. His hands, once again his own, found the invading utensil and wrested it from his spraying flesh. He flung it away, the effort sending the knife toward the mantle, where it found the canister of lighting fluid. The impact caused the canister to leap from its station and collide with the fireplace below. The cap dislodged and the contents quickly emerged, engulfing everything in a rage of flame. The chair became an inferno.

Klaus wheezed and halted, as the world became a blinding star. The overwhelming pain eclipsed the surprise and shock he felt as his body transformed into a furious torch. The last image he beheld was that of his dear Alyssa, as she delicately pierced his open throat with needle and thread. Her family stood and walked, advancing to wait by her side.

The Wyntersburg night sky shined as the former Schtreicher home became an earthbound nova. The inconsiderate winds fed the starving flames as they reached toward the heavens like a martyr. The dawn brought a disquieting silence, and Oak Road endured, awaiting the promise of the coming spring.

Lori R. Lopez

burying the hatchet

A cloaked figure paced iron confines,
The ornate boundaries, a lonely private tract,
Like a wraith wafting among its stones . . .
Her shadow brushing weathered facades,
A jumble of grim shapes and dimensions
To mark their tombs with cryptic reminders.
She knew them by heart, having memorized
The names and dates, their epitaphs —
Walking here as a child, round and round
Uneven rows, hoping to spot a ghost.
She never did, yet returned many times,
For the somberness of the place did ease
Her troubled mind and soul.

Born in the house, the daughter of a maid,
She played at this cemetery, inventing games.
The dark gothic ruins now stood abandoned,
Though a village whispered it wasn't vacant.
Apparitions roamed the decaying halls
In company of spiders, dust and insects.
Unexplainable visions, moans and echoes
Remained of the family, a collection of bones
Twisted with agony, in terrified poses.
Looks of horror clung to withered faces
Buried underneath the mournful hill,
Where Amelia strolled to feel close to kin —
A mother she could scarcely picture.

It was rumored her father had been the son
Of the wealthy couple who owned the manor;
She might be their only living heir.
But gossip and tales were inadequate proof,

So she came to reclaim a sense of belonging
And pay her respects while avoiding a corner
Where the town had planted the family's bane,
A lady who killed them wielding a small axe,
Which was buried with her, locked in one fist —
The hand she had faithfully pledged in marriage,
Till a baby arrived with his striking gray eyes.
In a jealous rage she cut off her love's head,
And went after his relatives howling.

None cared to tread where Evangeline lay,
For she had been blamed, as witch hunts go;
Deemed vile and crafty — "An abomination!"
By men and women of upright bearing,
Fingers pointed to avert harsh scrutiny,
The disapproval of neighbors and friends,
Regarding their own misdeeds or failings.
The town enjoyed a good inquisition
For entertainment on a dull winter's day
And accused the girl's mother of enchantment.
She was hung alongside the unwed bride,
Whose vow was stained by blood and betrayal.
Soaked red, the fiancée had smiled in delight . . .

Executing them both would do her a favor;
She had intended to slay herself and the rival,
But Evangeline fled to hide with her baby
On hearing the screams and blows that night,
As a spiteful woman dealt a wicked justice
By chopping to pieces the flesh of her betrothed.
The hatchet was buried, yet without forgiveness
A murder must fester like a seed of revenge . . .
To rise from the soil in eternal conflict.
It was said these ladies nursed powerful grudges —
The other specters might flicker and wane;
Isabelle climbed out then dragged Evangeline
To watch her complete an atrocious act.

Their remnants were stark, the bones evident;
Dresses in tatters, smirched, unkempt
Like matted knots of manes. But their souls

Were donned as mantles to cover the ravages
Of time and punishment . . . straightening
Crooked necks that were broken by nooses;
Masking the defects and flaws of complexions
Tainted by rotting, by worms and beetles —
No doubt the lack of breath and a heartbeat.
Ghostly visages settled over the death-grins
Of skulls like Cinderella; Venetian masqueraders
Adorned by fanciful images, painted artifice;
The pretend facades of imitators at a ball.

Glowing and vibrant, dark and light vestiges
Regarded their enemy through determined orbs
And squared off in the graveyard, eerily pouting.
Amelia gasped at the sight of her mother —
With a shock of recognition. So familiar!
She could not forget such delicate features,
So much like the aspect she saw in a mirror.
Amie wished to embrace the lady once more,
Believing in her heart it was not possible,
Yet extending a hand to touch the shimmer.
Isabelle intervened and knocked her away . . .
A surge of force like a black thunderbolt
Crackled electric from a sweep of hand.

"You won't be so pretty when I get done!"
Isabelle raised her axe. A leer and a promise:
"Then I'll hack your daughter into tiny bits!"
Amelia had been flung, smacking a headstone,
And blearily watched a supernatural match.
Isabelle charging forth yelled in fury . . .
Her opponent sizzled with an aura of static,
Possessing no evil to counter the attack,
Relying on emotions as pure as white snow.
It was a cosmic battle, a spiritual contest,
The struggle for balance of two extremes —
Shades of love and hate. Illusion and truth.
One was death. The other represented life.

Defending her child, Evangeline flew forward

To embrace oblivion. Brightness wrestled umbra
In a wild somersaulting tangle of revenants —
Breath versus mortality; the risk of win or lose,
Victory or defeat. A clash of strident energies,
Perpetual foes. They were epic, catastrophic . . .
The ladies spun at odds, a virulent choreography,
A dance of contrasts, kinetically entwined
As currents jolted and popped, sparks exploded.
The phantoms skirmished, arcing, igniting;
A fierce and fateful combat that had to end,
Had to be resolved or utterly annihilated
In brilliant bursts of nullity or profusion.

The women tugged and pushed, give and take,
Unwilling to yield; refusing to be vanquished.
"You stole my life!" screeched Isabelle.
"And you robbed mine!" accused Evangeline.
"I will not let you have hers too!" swore she.
"This is not her crime! She was born without
Guilt, an innocent child. This is my burden.
I won't allow you to harm her!" cried a mother.
Love was her defense, her shield, her armor . . .
Hate was the tool for aggression of the scorned.
Wrath can be a formidable thing, a tragic weapon
Of the malicious. It might seem to overwhelm —
To dominate and crush the gentler side.

But when the dust clears and the score is tallied,
Virtues outweigh the cruel strokes of the vicious.
Growing impatient, Isabelle hurled the axe . . .
Beyond the reach of Evangeline's protection,
The blade tumbled through space and distance
To meet its target, the forehead of the spectator.
Evangeline would loose a horrendous wail
Of a grief so potent that it could shatter a heart —
Or destroy a fact. The flight of the hatchet
Would be reversed to sail with increased velocity,
Rebounding to its source, burying itself in the brow
Of the unwed bride. Isabelle would flop back
Inside her box and the lid of the coffin slam shut.

Dirt rained to replenish the hole; a tapestry of roots
Wove and fused to seal the grave forever and always.
Evangeline summoned to sleep at last,
Her soul to rest in peace, for she had lain awake
In a fitful torment. But Amelia dashed to her arms
For the hug she had craved and a final glimpse
Of the face that would be indelibly etched
Upon her mind, replacing the dent of an axe —
Healing the deep internal scar of a young girl
Who could not remember, could not be soothed
By a mother's smile, a maternal connection.
It was this that needed to be restored; ever after,
A girl could visit her mother . . . and feel loved.

Magenta Nero

Sleep Walker

Eyes flicker, then open. He stares up at the shapes that form and disperse in the fluid dark. He is like water or smoke, infusing the flesh, seeping into it, merging with muscle and bone. The body rises. Feet land quietly on the floor. He can feel cold skin resting on thin, worn carpet. Toes stretch and flex. Blinking in the dark, he knows where he is. He has come several times before. Slowly he stands up and begins to walk. Each step is rigid and reluctant; the body has not yet warmed to him. He can't be sure how long it will allow him to remain but for a little while it is his.

He stares down the long dark hallway, drawn toward the haze of light at the end. He walks along slowly, trying not to bump into things, finally coming to the kitchen. The dim glow of street lights seeps in through the window. He glances around, waiting as details become clear; the counter tops cluttered with appliances, cups stacked carelessly on an open shelf. The sink is full of unwashed plates and pots. A vase of crowded flowers sits on the windowsill. There is always so much work to do. Her housekeeping skills have not improved.

On the wall by the sink, a magnetic strip holds a collection of knives. Last time he came, they entranced him, and did little else but stare at them all night long. They are an exquisite set of knives with polished handles of dark wood. Expensive and stylish, they seem out of place in the tawdry décor. They are new, and he doesn't remember noticing them when he was alive.

The fraction of light in the room plays on the knives, illuminating the blades in soft focus. He approaches them and examines them closely, stepping back, stepping forward, until he finds the ideal spot from which to view them.

He can see the quality of the steel, thick and gleaming sharp, and the wooden handles sculpted to fit the palm with balanced, comfortable ease. Stunning artisanship. Mesmerized, he gazes at them. A long thin blade curves to a tip. Breath taking is the flat wide blade, a blade with which to cleave. Two smaller knives, daggers, light in the hand, for quick fast strikes, and a long serrated blade to saw through stubborn things. Tenderly he rearranges them in order of size. He feels a deep longing to yield one, a delicious craving uncurling. Nothing much, just a tiny little nip on the wrist, barely there, perhaps she would not even notice.

He selects one of the small sharp knives. In the moonlight, its skin is a pale shade of blue. Slowly he drags the blade over tender flesh, leaving faint trails of pink. He does this several times and, then, one final draw, a bit harder, makes a light incision. Blood collects quickly in tiny beads along the razor fine line. He feels nothing, no pain. Intrigued he stares at the wrist until startled by a sound. He carefully replaces the knife back on the wall.

The voice is faint in the darkness. It disturbs him. He can feel the body twitch in response, threatening to wake. He must find it and silence it. It is the little girl. He has glimpsed her before but has never come close to her. He shuffles back down the hallway.

"Mommy?" the voice calls, soft.

He enters the small bedroom. She is afraid. She is still asleep but she can sense him. The thick arc of sleeping lashes, paper-thin skin, stretched over eyeballs. She is restless. He reaches for her and lightly strokes the bony arc of her spine. The bodies are familiar and a sense of calm flows between them. The little girl settles and soon falls back into the breath of deep sleep.

He walks to the large bedroom window and looks outside. He would like to go outside. Wander in this beautiful body. Rain is falling gently and all is dark, quiet and still. Through the trickle of raindrops on the glass, he can see a row of bare trees along the wet glistening road, seemingly cut from the night, delicate and intricate silhouettes, everything enhanced when looking through another person's eyes. Then he notices his reflection: Her face.

She was his lover once. He never did let go. Even though they hadn't seen each other for some time he couldn't believe she didn't bother attending his funeral. Bitch. As if their relationship had meant nothing at all. She never understood how much he loved her. She even had the gall to accuse him of stalking. It gives him great pleasure to possess her body in this absolute way. Now she belongs to him, forever. Soon she will realize the truth; they were made for each other.

He turns slightly to admire the curves of her body reflected in the window. She is wearing a thin nightgown, her breasts visible through the sheer fabric. He touches the long blonde curls draping her shoulders and runs restless fingertips along her collarbone. He would like to touch her, really touch her, but he is afraid he may wake her. He can't be too careless. He is not sure how it works but he is able to possess her while she sleeps. There is no resistance as he slips in easily.

It was difficult at first and it took great effort to find her. He drifted through nothingness mourning her, willing himself to her side. He hovered above her, watching her slumber, wondering if she was dreaming. Pushing against her mind, falling into her thoughts, he discovered how to blend with her; returning again and again, he will claim her body and mind completely, little by little. Each time he goes a little deeper, a little further. Perhaps he may come to stay, he ponders.

Time passes differently here than on the other side. The laws of the physical body have become unfamiliar; it is like being born again. He seems to get trapped in thought for endless moments, fascinated by subtle sensations and glimpses of things.

He notices the darkness is changing hue, dawn is not too far away, and it is time to leave. He takes her body back to its bed and lays it down. Eyelids close and he is gone.

In the morning, she is standing in the kitchen drinking very hot coffee in rapid sips, burning her mouth but she doesn't notice. Her daughter is sitting at the table eating cereal. The loud crunching is an unbearable noise. It mingles with the fear churning within her. She keeps glancing at her wrist, bewildered.

Her panic builds as she glances around the room; the teacups on the shelf, that is not how she stacks them. The vase has been moved on the windowsill, she's sure of it. The flowers, there is something odd about them. She stares at them and realizes they have been rearranged in the vase. She is beginning to feel sick. This is not the first time these odd little things have happened. Things move around and order themselves in new ways. She is not imagining this. Her eyes fall on the row of knives mounted on the wall. They are aligned from smallest to largest, evenly spaced and perfectly upright. The sight of them is confusing and then terrifying. She glances at her wrist again, her breath catching. The cup slips from her hand. It shatters loudly; scalding coffee splashes her bare feet.

Tracy L. Carbone

Charlie's Garden

Shelly wiped her wrinkled brow as she moved among her orchids, dragging her bum leg. Since the stroke, her left leg only worked when it felt like it. And since menopause, the heat in the greenhouse left her sweaty and uncomfortable. If it weren't for Charlie and his lifelong dedication to the place, she would've given all the plants away and closed it up. But she couldn't do that to him. To his memory.

She adjusted a heating lamp above the carnivorous plant table. Charlie loved his carnivores. She'd never been able to keep the names straight, not the scientific names. But this section housed the flytraps, and that section the flypaper traps, so called, his sundews and butterworts. Charlie called them Jenna, Marley, all human names. Foolishness.

Charlie flashed in the midst of the plants. She reached through the hungry green arms, avoiding the tentacles, and retrieved his photo. Shelly looked at the black and white photo of her husband in the tarnished frame.

"You gave it all to them, Charlie. None left for me. You spent your whole life out here, with these, these plants, while I was inside and lonely. We never had children. You never had the need to take pleasure in me." She set the picture back, peered into the mouth of a pink flytrap. "Wouldn't surprise me if some of your seed went to feed these plants." She glanced at a faded sign next to the other variety, mere inches away, Drosera. Other words in smaller font followed but without her reading glasses, they were a mass of blurry letters. The plant looked like a skinny sugar cane with tentacles. Wet little fingers reaching out to trap life and devour. She shook her head, noticing gray dust around the rim of on the sundews. She dipped her fingers into it. "Oh Charlie, even in death you gave yourself to them. Even in death."

She scooped up more of her husband's ashes and flicked them toward the Drosera. "Here, take him. You're what he wanted."

But as she extended her finger, the tentacles of the plant grew, stretched, sticky and hungry, and pulled the ashes off her fingers, grabbed onto them. Shelly yanked her hand back and ran out of the greenhouse and the short distance to her home. Once inside, she locked the door and ran the faucet to scrub her hands. Welts formed where the plant had latched onto her. Drops of blood rose on her skin.

Tomorrow, she decided, as she gingerly blotted away the red and applied bandages to her fingertips, she'd sell the plants. So what if they were Charlie's whole life, and death. *She* was his wife. He was supposed to be devoted to *her*. Now that he was dead, she'd get rid of the plants, the dirt, and Charlie's ashes, which were deeply entrenched in the soil. All of it.

In the morning, Shelly awoke to raging hunger, a dry mouth, and sweaty armpits. She pulled her dentures from the bedside cup and fit them over her gums, which sucked in the cup water like a sponge. She started the shower. A few minutes later, as she lathered soap over her old wrinkled skin, the normally slippery bar snagged on her skin. Her armpits weren't sweaty; they were sticky. The soap wouldn't slide around, just stuck. She maneuvered her head to sniff. No smell. She washed the rest of her body without event.

After a hearty breakfast of eggs and toast and friend steak, she felt more herself. She looked to the greenhouse and sneered. Shelly picked up her keys and left the house to drive to the nursery. No doubt she could unload the whole lot to Jeff Briggs. He'd admired Charlie's collection for some time.

Shelly cringed when she walked into Briggs's Nursery. The smells of soil and chlorophyll and peat turned her stomach. Too many bad memories. The stench of her husband's mistresses. The stink that clung to him night after night when he fell into bed, spent and disinterested.

"I was out back when I heard the bell. How are you, Mrs. Cooper?" Gary Briggs asked, extending his hand. The flesh glistened with sweat and Shelly greedily shook it, drinking the juice into her dry wrinkles. Her heart began to beat erratically with a thrill, but her pacemaker pushed it back into rhythm. The teenager pulled his hand away and Shelly smiled in apology.

"I'm fine. Just fine. Is your grandfather around? I've got an offer for him."

"Sure," the kid said, wiping his hand on his jeans as if she'd contaminated him.

Shelly's stomach growled something fierce as she waited for Jeff Briggs to appear. It still roared when the old man tottered toward her. "Sorry about that, Jeff. I'm famished. Just ate a lumberjack breakfast and here I am hungry again."

Jeff laughed. "What do you say to a cup of coffee and some more breakfast then? I could use a break."

"I'd love it. Want to talk to you about my greenhouse." The two talked as they walked to Jeff's old Cadillac.

Jeff opened the car door and ushered Shelly in. Her stomach growled louder and her armpits were so sticky she had a hard time lifting her arms. *Great, some new old lady symptom,* she thought. When Jeff walked around and sat down in the driver's seat, Shelly got a whiff of him and grew hungrier. In the morning light, the white peach fuzz on his face called to her like shredded coconut on a pink cupcake.

"So what's this offer you came to see me about, Shelly?"

She had known Jeff most of her life and never once longed for him, but right now she wanted to gobble him up. "I thought you might like to take Charlie's plants off my hands."

He looked to her with surprise. "Which ones? I mean I'd take any but—"

"All of them. Tell you what; let's go to my place. You can take a look see in the greenhouse and I'll make us something to eat." Jeff swerved and did an illegal U-turn. He gunned the engine and in minutes they arrived at her house.

Jeff parked behind the house near the greenhouse then got out to open Shelly's door. Her fingers tingled as she watched his form approach. She looked down and gasped. Her fingertips were covered in dark red pulsating blisters. Clear liquid dripped from them. When he leaned in to take her hand, to help her out, her fingers elongated and grasped his forearms, attaching like suction cups. He screamed and pulled away, dragging her from the car and onto him. Two octogenarians rolling around on the ground, her tentacle fingers milking fluids through the pores in his arms, as he lost strength and his body withered to a husk.

Shelly rolled off the old man's shell, her eyes glazed. She felt sated. Finally. But what had happened? Her fingers shrunk to normal length. The welts remained but they were flesh colored. She looked to the husk. "My God, what have I done? Jeff?"

Shelly went into the house and poured herself some of Charlie's scotch. It tasted like bad breath but did the trick to calm her nerves. She sat in Charlie's smelly old recliner and closed her eyes for a few minutes to sort out what had happened. The last few years her mind had grown murky and sometimes she grew confused. Her daughter wanted to put her in a home but—And then she was asleep.

A smashing knock rattled her from sleep and she wrenched her head up. "Who's there!" she shouted. Her second thought was how hungry she was. Starving, and so thirsty. Next to her rested an empty gallon jug of spring water. When did she drink that? And why was she still parched?

"Open up, Mrs. Cooper. It's Gary Briggs. Is my Gramps in there with you?"

Shelly threw her head back, a rush of excitement filling her. Her stomach growled. Her fingers throbbed and darkened. Drops of dew appeared on her fingertips. Her mouth filled with sticky liquid. She tried to answer but gurgled her reply. She coughed and swallowed and managed to say, "Yes. He's here. Come in."

Gary walked toward her, just as she'd hoped. "Come here, dear. Help me up. I'll take you to him."

The young man approached her. "You don't look too good, Mrs. Cooper. Kind of splotchy."

"Help me up, dear." The fleshy young male arm reached out, sinewy and strong. Shelly's fingers stretched, darted out and wrapped around it in a death hold, paralyzing Gary, reducing him to dry fibers that skittered along the floor with the dust bunnies.

Sated again but less confused this time, Shelly looked down at her meal. She'd turned into one of Charlie's plants. A carnivorous flypaper trap. Would Charlie love *her* now, if he were still alive? Would he tend to *her*?

The door front door creaked open and the boy's father, Craig entered the room. He had been the spitting image of his son—until the boy lost all his fluids—but older. He shouted something, but all Shelly could hear was the blood coursing through his veins, the pulsating of all the liquid that could be hers if only he stepped a little closer. He looked down at his withered son, then at her, then at her fingers. She tried to speak but only gurgled.

Craig ran out of the house then returned. He smiled and moved toward her slowly. Shelly stood rigid, waiting to attack. But then Craig ran behind her and covered her with something dark and cold. A blanket, a tarp. She thrust her hands out but they wouldn't penetrate the fabric. Plastic. Cold.

Shelly awoke under a bright heat lamp. It felt good. She was hungry but the heat felt nice on her skin. She looked around her. Briggs's Nursery. Craig Briggs stood a few feet from her. She reached out her—arm? Like a sugarcane with tentacles. Where had her body gone? She felt the same, but—WHACK. Her tendril hit a glass wall.

"Shelly, hello," Craig said. "Welcome to my home. Welcome to your new neighbors." She turned her plant head toward the other plants. They turned to her as well. There was something familiar about—

"You do remember my mother, Jenna Briggs. Everyone thought she ran away but she was here the whole time. Not here of course. She was in Charlie's garden. She cheated on my dad with your husband but one of his other plants lashed out and, well, Karma. She turned like the others and Charlie kept her and all his ex-mistresses together. Dad waited so long to get control of Charlie's garden so we could get Mom back. I do feel bad that you're here now too but you did kill my father and my son. I could just let you starve but it wasn't your fault. Don't worry. You'll live a long time here."

Craig picked up Charlie's framed photo and faced it toward Shelly. "Here, I think my Mom has been staring at this monster long enough. He's your husband. You can look at him. That will be punishment enough."

Shelly's tentacles reached out for the photo, leaving a sticky smear on the glass. A lifetime of looking at her husband. That wasn't punishment. Finally, she had Charlie all to herself.

Doug Rinaldi

Bequeathed

His footfalls crunched with the weight of each step. The crusty, snow-covered ground revealed no other footprints other than his, and especially those of the little girl he could've sworn he saw running into the two-story Dutch Colonial standing old and stoic in front of him. Still, Tim felt confident about what his eyes had seen, despite the fog of windblown snow that rose up off the street as if the asphalt beneath were smoldering instead of slick with ice.

Tim glanced down at the antique tome of fairy tales cradled in his arm, the only remaining evidence—besides the contents of the urn—that his mother had ever existed. When he received a call from an attorney letting him know of her passing all alone in an assisted living home, he knew she had little of value, if anything, to leave to him. Not that it really mattered; even if he did remember her, harbored any of those special recollections shared between mother and son in his memory banks, he would never have *truly* known her, the maternal bond severed when she vanished decades ago with nary a mention of since. Yet, when handed her remains and the solitary book that she had bequeathed him in the attorney's office, he couldn't deny in good conscience her last wish of having her ashes scattered around her childhood home.

Why her attorney, for whatever reason, didn't have any pertinent information related to the home's whereabouts, Tim couldn't fathom. But it wasn't until he found an address scribbled on a scrap of paper and clipped to a ribbon of 35mm film negatives buried in the middle of the book, did he discover where she had once lived. Even though he generally despised lengthy trips and grumbled at how long he knew the trek would take him, he kept his promise. Maybe he'd even find some answers—or perhaps some closure to this door that just unexpectedly opened. Now that he arrived at last to this desolate and abandoned town in the cold of December, he fought the urge to jump back in his car and speed away, forgetting the whole ordeal inside a bottle of whiskey.

What about that little girl?

He read the address again before looking up at the faded house numbers painted on the door. This was it, his mother's old house rising up into the grayness of the sky. Through the snow he trudged, up the steps and across the porch. The front door stood somewhat ajar, hanging off kilter on its rusted, old hinges.

"Hello?" he called, suspiciously eyeing the house's interior. "Little girl? I saw you come in here. Are you okay?" After he crept inside, leaving faint footprints on the snowdrift that followed him in, he shut the door against the cold and carefully placed the urn on a shelf. The immediate silence deafened him and his eardrums popped.

He heard a faint sob and then saw a short blur of color race passed the threshold to another room. "Don't be scared. I'm not going to hurt you. This is my mother's old house." Silence answered his call. "It's okay." He tiptoed towards the next room. "Do you live around here?"

In the blanket of gloom oppressing the room, Tim bumped into one of the many sheet-covered pieces of furniture littering the space. He dropped the book and the resulting boom resonated, echoing through the walls. "Shit. That hurt," he said as he winced picking it up from the floor, the film negatives slipping out from between its pages.

With book and negatives in hand, he turned the corner into the next room where he saw the girl run. On the wall, someone had painted a mural of a flowery meadow. Though it was dull and had faded with time, he still found it appealing as it struck a chord of familiarity. Then he remembered. Tim stepped to the window and held up the film to the failing winter light. In one of the frames of the negative, the same mural reflected.

He heard the whimpering again.

Caught by surprise turning with the film still held up, he noticed that the scene caught on the negative moved, matching what he saw before him as if looking through a sepia-colored lens. He dropped the film, unnerved.

Tiny footsteps raced up a flight of stairs.

"Hey, don't be afraid." He scooped up the film and followed the sound. A wooden staircase led to the second floor as the dark began to overpower the pale light that filtered through the dirty windows. Gut instinct told him to look through the film again. He awkwardly closed one eye and held the film up to the other; everything before him took on the texture of old newsreel. As he moved, the scene within that single frame moved with him. He went back and forth—from film to reality—just to be certain what he was seeing was in fact really happening.

At the top of the stairs, a shadow lurked but vanished in the instant he stopped looking through the film negative. He continued upwards, minding his step and listening for any more sounds. On the landing, a lone table stood adorned with a tattered and stained doily. Yet, through the film, he saw a lamp smashed against the wall, fragments of it everywhere, and a freshly bloodied handprint soiling the once delicate, white cloth. He tore the negative away as a gasp caught in his windpipe.

He heard more movement from another room.

Awash with courage, he put the filmstrip back to his eye. Waves of dizziness claimed him from the ocular strain, but he kept moving, determined. The grainy tones and quality covered everything as he edged along down the hallway, yet, he couldn't mistake the wet streaks he saw on the walls for anything else.

A woman's maddening scream froze his blood. He tore his eyes away from the film and the house fell silent. "Hey! Is someone there?" Back through the negative, the screaming returned. Once more, he looked away to test his theory, and heard nothing. "Is somebody hurt?" he said, evermore confused.

Tim decided that somehow, with the film before his eyes, he had tapped into some ghostly radio frequency. He returned to the film and the shrieking reached a violent climax. He raced to the room at the end of the bloodied hallway. Seen via the otherworldly lens, the body of a girl, barely six years old, lay wounded and motionless on a bed; blood trickled from an impact in her skull and steeped the bed sheets in red. In the corner, a woman stood over a terrified little boy, who, younger than the girl, defensively held up a thick book in front of him. The raving woman, her face now marred by a twisted scowl, raised a hammer high. She began shouting obscenity-laced gibberish as she loomed over the cowering and crying boy.

"No!" Tim shouted, hoping to stop the woman from hurting another child. He leapt over a pile of toys on the floor with his mother's book his only weapon, ready to strike, yet unsure how he'd possibly be able to intervene. In the melee, he let go of the film on instinct, which threw everything back to darkness and cobwebs, but the momentum of his attack spun him off balance, sending him crashing into the wall.

Panicked, he fumbled around for the filmstrip, clumsily groping around in the dim room. He felt the celluloid with his fingertips and snatched it from the floor, putting it back up to his eye. Through the lens, a man rushed into the room, grabbing the woman mere seconds before she could unleash her rage upon boy. Tim stared, reluctant to believe, unable to reconcile what—and whom—he was seeing. "Dad," he asked.

He watched in snuff-colored disbelief as his father held the woman down as she thrashed about, hissing vulgarities. Another man, face pale with worry and fright, entered. Tim vaguely recognized the man as he watched him pull the big book from the boy's grasp and scoop him up. "It's all right, Timothy. You're safe, now," Tim heard him say as he rushed out of the room with the traumatized boy cradled in his arms.

Tim, dumbstruck, looked down at the boy's book now resting on the floorboards . . . then back to his own in shattering realization. All the energy drained from his body and he went limp while the commotion of the residual energy stored in the film's negative continued to unfold in the background.

He studied and compared the two books, one version rooted in the present and the other in the past, but both part of his reality. Disappointed with himself that he hadn't noticed sooner, Tim opened the front cover to an inscription only found in his bequeathed copy and began to cry for the first time in years.

"To my beautiful son, Timothy, I'm sorry.

Love, Mom."

Steve Berry

There's Someone in the Trees

"Dad, wake up, there's someone in the trees," Charlie whispered close to her father's face. "*Wake up!*" She looked back at the door, hoping she hadn't woken her sister.

He grumbled, tossing a hand at her.

"Please, Dad, wake up."

Eric opened his eyes and thought he saw his wife standing over his bed, her face half lit by the glow of the landing light. He leapt up, disorientated.

His wife was dead.

"*What's the matter?*" He sat upright and blinked his eyes.

"There's someone in the trees."

Eric reached for his cane. Charlie tried helping him but he brushed her hand away. "I can get it."

"Sorry." She stepped back while her father grabbed his stick. He wasn't an idiot, as he liked to tell people who wanted to help him -- just as he didn't need help raising the kids while his wife went off to war.

Charlie glimpsed the half-finished bottle of brandy on the bed stand. Eric caught her looking.

"I have a bad tooth," he said, feeling like he had to lie, even though he knew she wasn't stupid.

He grabbed the bottle, and said "Rotten molar." He unscrewed the cap and ran the bottleneck under his nose. Eric sighed and held the bottle out to admire the label. "Wake's you right up." He took a swig and gritted his teeth as the liqueur ran down his throat.

"Right, what the hell are you talking about?"

"The Christmas trees outside, someone is in there."

He pushed past her and swung back the curtains. The security light projected a wide funnel across the yard, which failed to the reach the Christmas trees sprawled across his property.

"Why's the light on?"

"I told you -- *someone's in the trees.*"

"Where's Beth?"

"She's still asleep."

He strode past her, flung open the door and padded down the hallway. Charlie chased after him, grabbing her coat off the banister.

Eric was already limping down the yard by the time Charlie made it to the porch.

"*Come on then,*" he cried, staring deep into the trees. A thick coat of ice lay over the branches like a white skin.

"Tell you now, Charlie, you best not have dreamt this."

They both looked at the barn as the door swung open with a slow, juddering creak.

"Get inside."

Charlie shuffled back, staring at the barn. "Dad, don't go in there."

Eric, treading carefully on the ice, paced as quickly as he could across the yard.

The barn door creaked again as Eric approached it, as if to warn him away.

He gathered himself and pulled the door wide open. He took a deep breath, as cold as the winter's voice. He hesitated at first, looking back over his shoulder at Charlie, and then went inside. He pulled a cord and the florescent tube stuttered at first before lighting up the barn.

A Volvo rested on axel stands, ratchets and spanners and dirty blue cloths littered the barn floor. He waited, watching.

There was nothing to see.

"Go back inside, go check on your sister." Eric was half out of the door.

"Is everything alright?"

"Everything's fine. Now go check on your sister while I lock this door. I can't have it swinging and making noise all night." He gave the barn a final glance. He caught something etched into the grime on the Volvo's windscreen.

"What the--"

You left us to die was scrawled on the glass.

"Oh Jesus," he said, suddenly feeling very cold, not the cold of the night but the cold of his past.

Eric stumbled back out of the barn and hobbled as quickly as he could back to the house.

"Jesus Christ," he muttered, pushing the door shut behind him. Charlie was right. Someone was in the trees.

The next morning carried snow. Charlie watched from her window as huge flakes fell from the dark, cloudy sky like countless white feathers.

She drifted away from the window and sat down at her writing table, a picture of her mother tucked into the frame around the mirror.

Charlie adored the pictures of her mother; but the military ones always gave her a warm feeling in the base of her belly. In this, she sat on a rock with a bright yellow desert behind her. Her lap supported a rifle. She looked invincible.

Charlie had asked her father why her mother had joined the army and not him. She hadn't realized he'd been drinking until he cast his narrow, sullen eyes upon her.

"What?" He banged his fists on the table. "Getting a bit of a mouth on you, aren't you Charlie. You think I'm not capable, is what you're saying. You think you can do it?" Spit hung from his lips. His eyes had exploded into huge, red moons.

"You wanna go do a man's job?"

Charlie shook her head and told him she was sorry. "I didn't mean to upset you."

Eric hobbled out of the kitchen.

Charlie couldn't understand why her mother going off to war had affected her father in the way it had.

Then that phone call came one spring afternoon when her father was having one of his better days. Everything was actually okay.

A roadside bomb had killed her mother. The look on her father's face would forever stay imprinted in her mind.

For just one afternoon, her father had been in good spirit; and then, in the matter of seconds, he was swept away forever.

Charlie hadn't been asleep long when she heard someone laughing outside. She opened her eyes and just lay still, scared to breathe, scared move.

A child laughed.

Charlie gasped as if a hand had locked around her throat.

She slowly climbed out of bed, willing the laughter to go away. She pulled back the curtains, biting down on her bottom lip.

A little boy sprinted off down the yard toward the Christmas trees, his blonde hair flowing in the wind like desert grass. His mother chased after him. The little boy bellowed raucous laughter, his head cocked back and his face tilted up to the grey sky.

Charlie intended on fetching her father but he was already pacing down the hallway, his stick going *clomp-clomp-clomp* against the floorboards. As he passed the doorway, he told Charlie to stay put.

Eric unfastened the locks and threw open the front door.

"*Dunno who the fuck you are,*" he cried, stomping down the porch steps.

The trees rustled. Eric lifted his stick and aimed it like a rifle. "You get the fuck off my property."

He watched with wide, unblinking eyes, pulling in fast cold breathes.

"Listen, just stay away from us."

The trees whispered in their sharp voices. Chunks of snow crashed off the branches. He stepped back. "D'you hear me?"

The little boy's face sprang out from the branches like a jack in the box. His eyes gleamed as blue as his frozen lips. Eric tried to scream but what came out was a cluster of muffled sounds. He lost his balance as he staggered back, his arms flailing.

Slender, pale fingers parted the branches. Eric gaped up at the woman stepping out of the trees, her eyes unyielding, grey as gun smoke.

"What the—" he said; his voice wavered. "*You're dead.*"

The woman and the boy stared at him.

Eric fell. He scrambled away, his fingers digging into the frozen dirt as he desperately pulled himself toward the porch. He looked back to find they had vanished into the trees.

Eric groped for the door handle, finally managing to pull it open. Eric fell inside the house and booted the door shut. He stared at up door, panting, tears trickling down his face. Eric squeezed his eyes shut and ran his hands up into his thin hair, unaware his two daughters were watching from upstairs.

"You can't be here, you're dead. I fucking killed you."

Charlie put a hand to her mouth and gestured for Beth to be quiet. She carried her back into their room.

Charlie didn't sleep for the rest of the night.

A few days later, Charlie woke to the sound of her father's drill outside, the clangs of a hammer, and her father's wet spluttering coughs.

She climbed out of bed and walked to the window, frosted with huge spider webs of ice. She craned her neck but she couldn't see him anywhere.

Charlie was happy he was up and out doing something. He hadn't left his room in days, but she had heard him mumbling to himself.

Charlie looked back at Beth. Her face was crumpled. Sweat added a shimmer to her usual pale complexion. Her closed eyes flickered as she grumbled and twitched.

"Beth, wake up, wake up," Charlie said, rubbing the sleep from her eyes. "Wake up. You're having a bad dream."

Beth's face puckered, adding a multitude of lines to her cheeks, making her look much older.

"*Daddy,*" she muttered, still asleep, though the wrinkles on her cheeks and around her eyes softened.

Charlie wondered what Beth was dreaming about, and as she continued to groan, Charlie tried shaking her awake. She would've succeeded if a scream hadn't almost lifted her out of her skin.

Her thoughts tangled and knotted as she bolted down the stairs, leaping two steps at a time. Had her father hurt himself, had he been drinking and drilled through his hand; she only knew that something terrible had made him scream that way.

"Dad, Dad, you okay?" she shouted from the porch, not understanding why her father was backing away from the front gates, gates he had fastened shut with a chain from the barn and a padlock the size of a dustbin lid. Her father had been fixing a *closed for the winter* sign above the front entrance.

Charlie didn't know much about cars, and she certainly didn't know what type of car was running idly in front of the gates -- only that it was blue with its bonnet crushed. A strong gale would likely turn that windscreen of crystals into a void.

The car door flew open and a woman collapsed out onto the fresh snow.

Charlie watched in disbelief as the car disappeared, dissolving into the depth of the atmosphere. Eric dropped on to his knees and sobbed into folded hands.

"What's wrong?" Charlie spun around. Beth's voice, sleepy and soft, made her jump.

"Beth, go in the kitchen now, I'll come and do you some cereal."

Charlie went back inside for a minute, kissed Beth on the forehead, still clammy from her bad dream, and guided her toward the kitchen.

"I won't be long."

After setting Beth down at the kitchen table, with the television to keep her occupied, Charlie put on her coat and shoes. She didn't fancy leaving her father out in that cold for much longer, regardless of not wanting to leave the house, not wanting to go anywhere near the yard.

His head snapped up to the sound of Charlie's feet crunching the ice.

"Is that you?" he asked, even though he was looking straight at her. "Is it you?"

"It's me, Dad."

For a moment, their eyes locked, until he returned his stare to where the car had vanished. Initially, he suspected his addled brain, doused in brandy, haunted by ghosts, was taunting him. What he had seen was just another customer with a similar car. No, it wasn't just another customer. It was the *actual* car -- a blue 2007 Ford Focus.

"I can't do this anymore."

"Do what?"

"They've come back to get me." His lips trembled. *"They're haunting me."*

Charlie thought about the car, the woman and the boy -- suddenly she felt eerily colder. It hurt Charlie to see him like this, and she felt useless not being able to help him.

"I didn't mean for it to happen. I had Beth with me. *I'm losing it, Charlie.*"

She forced herself to ask him, "What did you do?"

"Hit suh-someone. Luh-left em for dead."

Charlie's mind reeled back to the Volvo in the barn. It all made sense.

Thinking about all this, being around the barn, around the trees, hearing whatever her father was saying almost made her throw up.

Eric had patched himself together somewhat, wiping his face dry and clearing his throat. "You dunno what it's like for me, your mother leaving me alone to look after you and your sister. Just a fucking cripple, I am. It's all your mom's fucking fault."

"You need to go you inside. It's freezing."

Charlie helped her father up and walked him back to the house. His weight actually surprised her. He was all bones and skin and a breath stinking of Brandy.

Charlie sat him down in the living room where he sunk into the chair next to the radiator.

"I'll make you a cup of tea." He didn't say anything back.

Charlie kept checking on him, changing the tea even though he was letting them go cold. She made him a sandwich, which went untouched.

Her father never spoke a word to her for the rest of the day.

Charlie sat down on Beth's bed and watched her sister playing amid a pile of crayons and colouring books. She seemed happy.

"Beth, baby. I want to ask you something?"

Beth ignored her and continued colouring.

"Can you remember the night Daddy had the car crash?"

"Don't wanna talk about it. I'll have nightmares."

"You dream about what happened?"

She nodded, and for a second seemed trapped in thought. Charlie wondered if she was about to open up, but all she said was, "I see the little boy and his mommy."

"Do you have these nightmares every night?"

Charlie's smile began to slip down her face as she began to pin things together, connecting parts of the puzzle. "Tell me what happened?"

"I'll have nightmares, Charlie, stop it. Leave me alone." Beth turned her back to Charlie. "Stop forcing me."

Charlie left her alone. Knowing she was fighting an unwinnable battle, she decided now was a good time to check on her father.

Eric was standing at the top of the stairs. He was holding a bottle of Brandy to his lips.

"Dad, are you okay?" she said.

He turned to the sound of Charlie's voice but he wasn't seeing his oldest daughter, only the murmurs of a familiar voice. His lips peeled back, baring his teeth.

"Dad," Charlie said, "you all right?"

"I'm not your old man, I'm your husband."

Charlie's mouth slipped open in a gasp of horror.

"Gone quiet have you now, Sarah?"

"I'm not Mom."

Eric looked at her, his eyes nothing more than slits. He didn't know if to trust this voice. So much had deceived him lately. "Don't answer me back."

"Dad, are you alright?"

"I killed that woman and boy. Just like your mother. I sent her off to die. Now the dead have comeback." He lifted the brandy in both hands and slugged it back.

"Dad, go back down stairs, please."

"I might as well cut off my cock. I'm just a fucking cripple. What man lets his woman fight in wars?"

"Dad, go back downstairs. You look tired."

He grinned, and didn't look like her father anymore. "I've been tired a long time." He was looking beyond Charlie now, through the walls and upon those fir trees.

In the dim light, Charlie saw the monster in his eyes. Her father was lost; she had started to realize that, but as he rambled, speaking to the bottle, seeking answers, she wondered if he was lost forever.

She sunk back against the wall as he made his way down stairs, the Brandy hanging loosely in his one hand.

It was the middle of the night and Eric was standing in front of the window in Charlie's bedroom.

"They're back, that woman and the kid." He spoke quietly, slurring his words. "They're out in the fucking trees again." He grunted.

Charlie had heard him speaking but didn't want to open her eyes. She hoped if she pretended to be asleep that he might go away.

"Told ya, didn't I?"

Eric pulled his head back and drove it into the window. The glass cracked with a loud thud. Blood streamed down his face.

Charlie squeezed her eyes shut tighter, holding her breath. She thought about saying something but panicked at the thought she might trigger a sudden outburst of rage. She opened her eyes. Her father threw back another mouthful of brandy.

"What's brought them back now?" he said, the liqueur spilling down his chin.

Charlie slipped her feet out of the duvet, flinching at the cold floor. She checked to see if her father had noticed her tiptoeing over to Beth.

Her eyes were flickering again. That cute little face gleamed in a veneer of sweat, regardless of the cold.

Charlie pulled back the duvet and scooped her up. *Please don't look back, please, please.*

She carried Beth out of the room, treading carefully against the boards, praying they didn't creak, praying her father just stayed by the window.

"Where are you going, Charlie?"

She paused, briefly clenching her eyes shut. She had made it as far as the stairs.

Eric was standing in the doorway. His sullen, drunken eyes locked on her.

"I'm taking her down stairs."

"You scared of me?" He went for another gulp of brandy...

"—can't leave them, Daddy, they're hurt..." Beth cried out.

Charlie gasped. The strength in her legs abandoned her.

"What did she say?"

He dropped the bottle of brandy. Charlie screamed as the bottle shattered across the floor. "It's her," Eric said, his mouth twisting into a sneer.

"Don't be stupid." Charlie stepped back, holding Beth tight against her chest.

"Give her here. You don't understand. It was her all along. Give her to me."

"She's just a baby." Charlie began to cry.

"Give her to me, Charlie, give her to me."

Anger possessed him now, killing off any last shred of rationality he had left in him.

"GIVE HER TO ME."

Charlie screamed and bolted down the stairs. Eric roared as he slammed a fist into the wall, shattering the plaster to pieces.

Charlie ran to the kitchen. She flung the door shut, leaning her weight against it. She had bought herself a few minutes, maybe.

Her father's weight creaked on the ceiling, heading for the stairs. The back door leading to the yard was her only option.

The back door swung open.

Charlie froze. The little boy was standing a few paces away, a blanket in his arms.

"Don't let her wake up, she's our doorway,' he said, and offered her the blanket. 'If she wakes up we can't help you."

Charlie shuddered at the sound of her father's roaring voice.

273

"Come with me, we'll keep you safe." The boy's mother appeared behind him, tall and willowy; soft, crimson hair that waved as it descended on to her shoulders. "We don't have much time. We can't help you if she wakes up." A tight look of urgency constricted her face.

Charlie looked down at Beth's rolling eyes.

"Please," the woman said, and reached out for her. "I won't let him get you, I promise."

Charlie closed her eyes for a second and pulled in a breath. She considered her options. Her father's screams from the living room jolted her awake.

She passed Beth to the woman, who scooped her on to her chest. Charlie tried to hold back the gasp, but failed "Please don't take her away from me," Charlie said, crying now.

The woman smiled at Charlie. "I won't." She put a hand on her boy's head. "How could I?"

The boy said, "You need to keep warm, it's freezing outside, right Mom?"

The kitchen door exploded from her father's punch. Charlie screamed, slapping her hands over her mouth.

"We must go," the woman said, and rushed out of the house.

"Here, put these on." The boy pulled on Charlie's arm. He passed her a pair shoes.

"*CHARLIE. YOU DON'T UNDERSTAND. SHE'S FULL OF EVIL. BETH'S BROUGHT THE DEAD HERE.*"

Just silence now. She could hear the snow beating against the house.

Charlie screamed as her father's bloodied figure entered the kitchen.

"Hurry up, come on, hurry up," the boy cried, pulling on her arm.

"Oh my god," Charlie hurried her shoes on to her feet.

She ran out the house with the boy.

"How dare you do this?" He clenched his fingers into fists. Blood dripped on to the floor tiles. "Stupid little shit." He stepped out into the yard and screamed for Charlie.

Eric prowled after them, treading carefully as the ice was making walking difficult. The snow was thickening, but Eric continued his search for his daughters.

"*CCCCCHHHHHHAAAARRRRLLLLIIEEEEEEE.*" He circled himself, trying to see if he could spot them, but visibility was poor. The house had become a ghost lost in the blizzard. Eric wondered if Charlie had run back inside with Beth, unable to handle the cold, and considered going back inside to look.

Eric snapped his head around at a sudden crunch in the trees. He groped at the branches, ripping at them, trying to improve his view.

"*CCCCHHHARRRRLIIIIEEEE,*" he screamed, pulling the branches out of his way, ploughing through the trees, heading deeper and deeper into the plot.

Eric threw his hands up against the wind lashing him with ice and snow. The woman was standing in front of him. She was silent. The little boy appeared next to her, grimacing.

"Where are they?"

The trees began to tremble at the roots, shaking off their coats of ice. The ice cracked, its cry lost in the blizzard. A huge cyclone of snow was rising above the trees, spinning out of control, meandering back and forth like a gigantic albino serpent.

Eric threw his hands up against the whiteout, pushing himself forward somehow, one heavy frozen foot at a time. Ice crawled after him like long-stretched fingers, reaching for his bare feet.

"*You won't hurt your children,*" the woman cried.

Eric roared in agony as the ice locked around his ankles like shackles, creeping up his shins and thighs, casing his stomach, sheathing his body in a suffocating blue ice. Eric screamed, his hands wrapped around his head.

The cyclone swerved high into the night sky, dipping, leaning toward the house, threatening to swallow everything, consuming more snow and ice, sucking it up into is ever-building vacuum.

Boom.

The blast flattened the trees, ripped the gates of the front entrance and chucked them into the road, blew the porch door off its hinges, ripped tiles of the barn roof.

Charlie looked down at Beth on the barn floor, wrapped in a blanket. She was waking up.

"Everything's okay." Charlie leant in and kissed her. She got up and headed slowly to the door. She opened it a little and looked out at the yard, at the solitary figure standing out in the flattened trees, like a scarecrow surrounded by stumps of snapped frozen trees and dunes of snow and ice.

"Where's Daddy?"

Charlie looked back at her and smiled, even though she felt like crying. "He went into the trees."

T.S. Woolard

Ghosts: Revenge

□an acrostic⧄

G hosts of yesterday return,
H unting for stolen solice,
O bsessed with peace they can't obtain.
S pirits blow cold vapor from another realm,
T earing apart the sanity of their victims,
S topping at nothing to obtain one thing

R evenge on those who owe them reckoning.
E xisting only to quench its hunger,
V iolence, silence, and fear as weapons,
E verlasting.
N othing less will suffice.
G lance over your shoulder when you feel a chill.
E veryone owes an un-resting soul.

About the Authors

William Cook was born and raised in New Zealand and is the author of the novel 'Blood Related.' He has written many short stories that have appeared in anthologies and has authored two short-story collections ('Dreams of Thanatos' & 'Death Quartet') and two collections of poetry ('Journey: the search for something' & 'Corpus Delicti'). His work has been praised by Joe McKinney, Billie Sue Mosiman, Anna Taborska, Rocky Wood and many other notable writers and editors. William is also the editor of the anthology 'Fresh Fear: Contemporary Horror,' published by James Ward Kirk Fiction.

You can find him online at http://williamcookwriter.com

Mary Genevieve Fortier: Award Winning Author; Columnist, Editor, Reviewer and published Writer of Poetry/Prose of various genres. "Terror Train Podcast" Co-Producer, Character/Creator/Performer/Dialogue Writer of "Terror," The Disembodied Voice as well as author of both the opening and closing poems. "HONORED MEMBER" in "The Worldwide Who's Who Registry of Executives, Professionals and Entrepreneurs."

Mary's poetry has been described as mystical, melodic, flowing with a unique grace that at times has been likened to the old world poets.

Her horror poetry has been deemed as "Poe-esque" by many.

Most recent publications: "Terror Train," "Floppy Shoes Apocalypse,"(for which her poem opens and is used as the promo) "Axes of Evil II," "Bones," "Bones III," "Cellar Door III," "Spectral Hauntings 2," the James Newman Benefit Anthology, "Widowmakers" "The Ladies and Gentlemen of Horror 2014," "The Ladies of Horror 2014, "Temporary Skeletons"(for which her poem is the intro to the anthology) She can also be found in, "Satan's Holiday," "Welcome to Your Nightmare," "Blessings from the Darkness," "Shadows and Light Magazine, January

2014, April 2014 and July 2014 issues." In addition to being in print, Mary's poetry is featured in "The Wicked Library," Season 3, Episodes 307 http://www.hipcast.com/podcast/HpYfoSv4
307.1 Bonus http://www.hipcast.com/podcast/HCkVBt94 and "Christmassacre 2.
http://www.hipcast.com/podcast/HwkmTbw4
Hellnotes: "Horror in a Hundred." "Darkness on a Lonely Stretch of Road"
http://hellnotes.com/horror-in-a-hundred-darkness-on-a-lonely-stretch-of-road
"COLD" http://www.hellnotes.com/horror-in-a-hundred-cold-by-mary-genevieve-fortier
Mary is "The Terror Train Anthology Podcast" Co-Producer/Character/Creator/Performer/Dialogue Writer of "Terror," The Disembodied Voice as well as author of both the opening and closing poems.
https://www.youtube.com/watch?v=-GmmAY5EO-8
Other places to find Mary:
Mary has a position as a columnist, "Nighty Nightmare" for the horror website, "Staying Scared"
http://www.stayingscared.com/NightyNightmare.html
Named, "Woman in Horror" by Blaze McRob's Tales of Horror: http://www.blazemcrob.com/2014/04/mary-genevieve-fortier-woman-in-horror.html?spref=fb
A partner/editor/author for Black Bed Sheet Books, a reviewer for Hellnotes and Dark Regions Press.
RECENT AWARDS:
Mary is the recipient of the "Editor's Choice Award" in JWK's "Terror Train Anthology," and is the winner of both caption award contests in the January 2014 and the April 2014 issues of "Shadows & Light Magazine."
SOON TO BE RELEASED PUBLICATIONS:
The anthology, "Chunks," The opening and closing poems for "Fata Arcana Anthology," and the opening poem for "Doorway to Death Anthology
INTERVIEWS:
A featured guest: Viktor Aurelius' "Whispers in the Dark," on Blogtalk Radio:
http://www.blogtalkradio.com/viktoraurelius/2014/04/04/whispers-in-the-dark--episode-92

Staying Scared Interview with "Nighty Nightmare" (Mary Genevieve Fortier) and Thomas Scopel
http://www.blogtalkradio.com/viktoraurelius/2014/10/28/staying-scared-with-thomas-scopel-and-mary-genevieve-fortier-1
"A Knife and a Quill" http://aknifeandaquill.com/5-quick-questions-with-mary-genevieve-fortier/
YOU MAY ALSO FIND MARY AT:
Mary's column; Nighty Nightmare
http://www.stayingscared.com/Nighty%20Nightmare.html
For her complete bibliography: Facebook Writer Page.
http://www.facebook.com/MaryGenevieveFortierWriter
and... http://www.www.tupelohoneyhugger.com

Scáth Beorh is a Speculative Fiction writer whose books include the novel Black Fox In Thin Places (Emby Press, 2013), the story collections Children & Other Wicked Things (JWK Fiction, 2013) and Always After Thieves Watch (Wildside Press, 2010), the novel October House (Emby Kids, 2015), and the poetic study Dark Sayings Of Old (JWK, 2013). Raised in New Orleans and West Florida, with a visit to India, two years in Hollywood, and travel for a year through Ireland, he now lives in exile with his joyful and imaginative wife Ember in the village of San Agustín de la Florida.

Indiana writer **James Dorr**'s THE TEARS OF ISIS was a 2014 Bram Stoker Award® nominee for Superior Achievement in a Fiction Collection. Other books include STRANGE MISTRESSES: TALES OF WONDER AND ROMANCE, DARKER LOVES: TALES OF MYSTERY AND REGRET, and his all-poetry VAMPS (A RETROSPECTIVE). An Active Member of HWA and SFWA with nearly 400 individual appearances from ALFRED HITCHCOCK'S MYSTERY MAGAZINE to YELLOW BAT REVIEW, Dorr invites readers to visit his blog at http://jamesdorrwriter.wordpress.com.

Michael Tugendhat won the 2014 Dark Poetry Scholarship. He has a master's degree in creative writing from the University of Glasgow. His debut horror poetry collection is forthcoming from James Ward Kirk.

CS Nelson holds a BA of English and has appeared in US and Canadian ezines and anthologies. When not writing, he spends time with family, detains and releases what he believes to be alien life in the form of invisible dry-land giraffe-fish (after gentle interrogation and marshmallow peeps treats of course), and serves as a US Army Cav Scout out of Fort Irwin in the Mojave Desert. He also serves an Asian forest scorpion's and one Chilean tarantula's butler and chauffeur as part of his Tiny Tickles Scorpion Rescue project. He wishes bugs would paint more. That is all. His website is at www.nelsoncs.com.

K.Z. Morano is a beach bum and a blogger who writes anything from romance and erotica to horror and SF, F, and WTF. She is the author of the horror story collection, 100 Nightmares. Her stories have appeared in various magazines, online venues, and anthologies. She blogs at:

http://theeclecticeccentricshopaholic.wordpress.com/
Facebook page: http://www.facebook.com/100Nightmares

Guy Burtenshaw lives in a small town in southern England and has been writing horror stories for many years. He has published several horror and crime novels, a collection of short stories and his short stories have appeared in numerous magazines and anthologies.

Evan Dicken: My work has most recently appeared in: Shock Totem, Analog, and Daily Science Fiction, and I have stories forthcoming from publishers such as: Chaosium, Darkfuse, and Unlikely Story.

Brian Rosenberger lives in a cellar in GA and writes by the light of captured fireflies. He is the author of As The Worm Turns and three poetry collection.

Mike Jansen has published flash fiction, short stories and longer work in various anthologies and magazines in the Netherlands and Belgium, including Cerberus, Manifesto Bravado, Wonderwaan, Ator Mondis and Babel-SF and

Verschijnsel anthologies such as Ragnarok and Zwarte Zielen (Black Souls).

He lives in the Netherlands, in Hilversum, near Amsterdam. He has won awards for best new author and best author in the King Kong Award in 1991 and 1992 respectively as well as an honorable mention for a submission to the Australian Altair Magazine launch competition in 1998. In 2012 Mike won awards in the SaBi Thor story contest, the Literary Prize for the Baarn Cultural Festival and the prestigious Fantastels award for best short story.

More recent publications in various English language ezines and anthologies, among which several publications with JWKfiction.com, Encounters Magazine and others. For a full list please refer to Mike's site: http://www.meznir.com

Mike's debut novel, 'The Failing God', became available in English, during 2013.

Sheldon Woodbury is an award winning writer (screenplays, plays, books, and short stories) living in New York City, where he also teaches screenwriting at New York University. His books include "Cool Million" a how to guide on high concept screenwriting. His screenplay "The Book of Magic" won first prize in the Maniafest horror screenwriting competition. His latest short stories are "Bones in a City Graveyard" in Bones 2 (James Ward Kirk Publishing), â€œDirty Mindsâ€ in Serial Killers Quattuor (James Ward Kirk Publishing), "The Halloween House" in One Hellacious Halloween (Horror Novel Reviews), "Family Affair" in Clerics, Charlatans & Cultists (Gothic City Press), â€œLast Callâ€ in Shots of Terror (Angelic Knight Press), â€œPayback is a Bitchâ€ in We are Dust and Shadow (James Ward Kirk Fiction), â€œBetween Heaven and Hellâ€ in Demonic Possession (James Ward Kirk Fiction), â€œHoly Warâ€ in No Sight for the Saved (James Ward Kirk Fiction), and â€œA Beautiful Horrorâ€ in Hell II: Citizens (James Ward Kirk Fiction). His flash fiction stories have appeared many times on the website Hellnotes (JournalStone Publishing) and other stories on Popcorn Fiction (Mulholland Books)and Horror Novel Reviews. His article, â€œHeroes that Rockâ€ appeared in

Writer's Digest Magazine. "The World on Fire," his horror novel, was published September, 2014 by James Ward Kirk Fiction. His story, "A White Farewell with a Splash of Red" will be included in Once Bitten, a forthcoming anthology from KnightWatch Press.

E.F. Schraeder's creative work has appeared or is forthcoming in journals and anthologies including Voluted Tales, Dark Gothic Resurrected, Between the Cracks, Flashes in the Dark, Sirens Call, Carnival of the Damned, Babes & Beasts, The Kennedy Curse, and other places. Schraeder studied the humanities in graduate school, and is also the author of a poetry chapbook, The Hunger Tree.

T.S. Woolard lives in North Carolina with his wife and four Jack Russell Terriers. For more of his work look for The Grays, Indiana Horror Review 2014, and Cellar Door III/Hell II by jwkfiction, Floppy Shoes Apocalypse by J. Ellington Ashton Press, and his standalone short story collection, Solo Circus. To connect with him, follow on Twitter @TSWoolard, or visit tswoolard.wordpress.com

Ken L. Jones has been involved in the world of popular culture for over thirty years. He has worked as such places as Disney Studios and Harvey Comics. More recently he has become known for his horror poetry and has been published at many different companies.

Allen Griffin is a writer and musician living in Indianapolis. His work has appeared, or is forthcoming, in several cool places, including Innsmouth Magazine, the Splatterlands and Ominous Realities anthologies from Grey Matter Press, the Surreal Worlds anthology from Bizarro Pulp Press, and Our World of Horror anthology from Eldritch Press. He also has two chapbooks, "No Such Heaven" and "The Noxious Winds of Karmageddon", both available from Dunhams Manor Press.

John L. Sies has been a successful commercial graphic artist/cartoonist for the past thirty-five years. His work in advertising art has been published for companies throughout the Midwest, including Domino's and McDonald's. In 2010, he expanded his creativity into writing, starting with humorous articles for newspapers and magazines, quickly branching into fantasy, science fiction, and horror stories. He lives in San Antonio, Texas, where he teaches beginner computer skills to 3rd, 4th, and 5th grade elementary students, in addition to his creative ventures.

Flo Stanton's horror stories and poems have appeared in *Indiana Horror 2012, Traps, Studies in Scarlet, Whispers of Wickedness, Tales of A Woman Scorned, A Pint of Bloody Fiction,* and *Static Movement,* as well as online publications such as *Black Petals* and *Yellow Mama.* With her writer/photographer husband John she stalks Indiana's abandoned warehouses, factories, graveyards, and other haunted sites for inspiration. Find out more about them at www.3amblue.com.

Kenneth Whitfield A few of my credits include scripts in Unfashioned Creatures, Killer Queen, Death Rattle, and other comic anthologies. I have stories without pictures in Dark Visions 2, DemonMinds, Undead Dixie, and other horror print anthologies. I've also been online in Horror Garage and Dark Eclipse ezines.

William Peterson is a Missouri native and life-long resident who is either camping, fishing, sitting outside next to a fire or watching something about history, science or nature right now. He may even be writing... "I find endless inspiration within the natural world for science-fiction, horror and fantasy... Every story starts with 'What If ?' I strive to bring you with me as I attempt to explore that question." -W.P. Horror short "Wish Witch" included in "Twice Upon A Time" anthology from The Bearded Scribe Press - Feb. 2015

Sci-Fi flash fiction "In Plain Sight" included in "The Grays" anthology from the one and only James Ward Kirk Fiction - Jan. 2015

Four flash-fiction publications with Calamities Press Literary Magazine – 2014. Three runner-up spots at the WeBook monthly flash-fiction challenge. - 2014

Rie Sheridan Rose is the author of five chapbooks of poetry. Her poems have been published in Penumbra, The Voices Project, and Wolf Willow magazine, as well as the Boundless, Metastasis, Twenty: In Memoriam, and Di-Verse-City anthologies. She has had poetry in Terror Train, Bones II, No Sight for the Saved, and Abandoned Towers as well. Rik Raven writes what she would like to read stories that take place in our world, but where nothing is as it should be. Rik Ravens writing career began attending a writing course in a nearby village, where she was broke after the first assignment for copycat of Stephen King. This was not a criticism, but rather wonder at the intensity that she stopped in this little assignment. With this in her mind she could, after a lot of reading and writing, a few years later all start publishing short stories in the magazine Pure Fantasy. Of said blade, but also for Pure Thrillers, she is still a few years, she has been editor and rated stories, edited, authors and books guided reviewed. She also has been associated as a juror at the Unleash Award, the story contest organized by Jack Lance and Alex de Jong. When asked how she started writing there can Rik not the standard answer, "I've always wanted to write 'on display. Not at all actually, because it is true that they invented stories as a child, but it is also true that they lost all those stories after an accident. NAH was responsible for, among other things. aphasia (a language disorder), impaired concentration and memory issues. The recovery was difficult and she has almost twenty years no story had in her pen

Tim Jeffreys is the author of five collections of short stories, the most recent being 'From Elsewhere', and a novella, 'The Haunted Grove'. His short fiction has been published in various international anthologies and magazines. In his work he incorporates elements of horror, fantasy, absurdist humour, science-fiction and anything else he wants to toss into the pot to create his own brand of weird fiction. Tim is also a talented artist and gained a university honours degree in Graphic Arts and Design in 2000.
Originally from Oldham, UK, Tim moved 'down south' over a decade ago and now lives in Bristol with his partner Isabel and two young daughters. He remains a northerner at heart, misses the rain, and retains a stubborn refusal to suffer fools gladly. As a

result of this he has very few friends. Visit him online at www.timjeffreyswriter.webs.com

Stephen O'Connor is a writer from Lowell, Massachusetts, where he lives on the same street that Jack Kerouac once lived. He is the author of the short story collection Smokestack Lightning, the novel The Spy in the City of Books, and the upcoming novel The Witch at Rivermouth. He's published in The Massachusetts Review, The Houston Literary Review, Watchword, Three Candles and elsewhere.

Matthew Weber: I'm the author of A DARK & WINDING ROAD, a collection of short horror fiction published in October 2014. I published my first novel THE BULL (political satire) in 2012. My short stories and articles have appeared in CREATURE STEW (Papa Bear Press), WHEN RED SNOW MELTS (HNR Publishing), MICROHORROR, BEST OF DARK ECLIPSE, NEAR TO THE KNUCKLE, HAUNT JAUNTS, and ADDICTED TO HORROR MOVIES. I'm an affiliate member of the Horror Writers Association, and I've been editor-in-chief (and principle writer) of EXTREME HOW-TO home improvement magazine since 2003.

Nicholas Day currently resides in southern Illinois, where he keeps company with a small poodle and a lovely dentist. His undergraduate degree was completed through Southern Illinois University and he is currently working on his MFA in the Writing Popular Fiction program at Seton Hill University.

Steve Foreman is British, living in Entebbe, Uganda, with his South Sudanese wife, Hellen and two young kids, Sam and Ashleigh. He works as a security contractor in East Africa and the Horn of Africa, wherever tasks take him. As a freelance article writer between 1997 and 2005 he was published in several UK and African magazines, including BBC Wildlife magazine, Soldier magazine, Combat & Survival magazine, SCUBA magazine, Church of England Newspaper, African Travel Review magazine, Land Rover World magazine, Your Dog magazine, Travel News and Lifestyle magazine (Kenya), and What's Happening in Dar (Tanzania) Between 2002 and 2004 he was the Editor-in-Chief of African Travel Review magazine (Tanzania) and wrote articles for several magazines and official publications of the Ministry of Natural Resources and Tourism, and the Tanzanian Tourist Board. His short fiction has been published or accepted for publication in Twisted Dreams magazine (June 2011), Sirens Call Publications (2014 & 2015), James Ward Kirk Books (2014 & 2015), April Moon Books (2014 & 2015), Aphelion (Feb 2014), The Were-Traveler (issue 12 - 2014), Hellfire Crossroads (Vol 2 - 2014), and Blood Moon Rising (issue 56 - 2014).

Neal F. Litherland is a Northwest Indiana author whose work runs the gamut from high fantasy to Cthonian horror. New Avalon is the first book to feature his work alone, but it will not be the last. For updates on his new projects and news on appearances go to his author blog The Literary Mercenary at www.nealflitherland.blogspot.com.

Alex S. Johnson is the author of several books, including Doctor Flesh: Director's Cut, Wicked Candy, Bad Sunset and the upcoming Makami. He makes his home in Sacramento, California, where he works as Acquisitions Editor for the WetWorks imprint of J. Ellington Ashton Press.

Dona Fox began writing in 1988 and published stories and poems in Eldritch Tales, Haunts, Thin Ice, Cemetery Dance (Issue #1), Beyond, and New Blood. Recently, her work has appeared in James Ward Kirk Publishing, J Ellington Ashton Press, and Horrified Press anthologies. Dona also has a short story and a poem in JWK's Terror Train anthology; the Terror Train podcasts on YouTube provide the listener with an old-time radio show experience.

J. C. Michael lives in rural North Yorkshire where he works in the tourism industry. His debut novel, Discoredia, was published by Books of the Dead Press in 2013, and he has also had short stories included in anthologies from Fireside Press (Fireside Popsicles and Wishful Thinking), Books of the Dead Press (Suspended in Dusk), and Pen and Muse Press (The Dark Carnival).

Betty Rocksteady is an eclectic Canadian woman with a passion for horror. When she was a child, her grandfather led her to believe the Weekly World News was the only real newspaper, and that has influenced her entire life since then. You can check out her gothic pen and ink art or read more of her fiction at www.bettyrocksteady.com.

Michael Thomas-Knight is the author of numerous horror short stories, bending the scope of reality one word at a time. Michael's style ranges from classic ghost stories with violent conclusions to atmospheric Eldritch tales steeped in mysticism, cynicism, and irony. His stories have been published in publications, Dark Eclipse, Infernal Ink, SNM Horror Magazine, Fiction Terrifica, and Microhorror.com. His work has also appeared in numerous anthologies, Terror Train, From Beyond the Grave, Shadow Masters, Cellar Door II, O Little Town of Deathlehem, Journals of Horror and others. You can check Michael's Amazon Author Page for when new titles become available:
https://www.amazon.com/author/michaelthomasknight
You can find Michael at his blog, Parlor of Horror, which deals with all things horror: movies, books, and articles for the horror enthusiast.

http://parlorofhorror.wordpress.com

Justin Hunter has four published novels. JWK fiction has published his dark fiction novel, Nostalgia. Severed Press has published the black horror comedy series Chet & Floyd vs. the Apocalypse: Volumes 1 and 2. Severed Press has signed Mr. Hunter to a multiple book deal which will span several years. J Ellington Ashton Press will be releasing Justin's novel, The Book of Titus, in 2015. MorbidbookS released the novel What's Eating Keegan the Vegan in 2015. Justin Hunter has also been published in several anthologies. Anthology publishing houses include Emby Press, Strangehouse Books, JWK Fiction, NoodleDoodle Publications, and Great Old Ones Publishing. Mr. Hunter is also an ongoing contributing author to the flash horror anthology Demonic Visions series.

Roger Cowin (1964) was born in New Castle, Indiana. He has been working with the mentally ill for the past twenty-five years. He began writing poetry and short stories in high school before deciding to concentrate on poetry. His poetry is inspired by the wide expanses of the Mid-west and the inner landscape of its inhabitants. Balancing between the absurd and the rational, Cowin attempts to make sense of the complexities of our modern world. Equal amounts satire, anger and wry humor, Roger Cowin's poetry is both thought provoking and accessible to the general reader.

Angeline Trevena is a British horror and fantasy writer, and her short stories appear in various anthologies and magazines. The most unlikely of horror writers, Angeline is scared of just about everything, and still can't sleep in a fully dark room. She goes weak at the sight of blood, can't share a room with a spider, but does have a streak of evil in her somewhere.

David Schütz II: a former Shakespearean actor, spent many years on both stage and screen portraying a wide range of characters from Prospero to Richard III, as well as a Rogue's Gallery of villains in the world of independent film and television (playing serial killers, renegade exorcists, Mafiosi, etc.), besides screenwriting and producing independent projects. He retired from that realm in 2012, and his love of great works both in Shakespearean plays and classic horror has brought him to try his hand at writing short horror fiction. David has been published in several anthologies, such as: "Cellar Door III: Animals" and "Bones III" from James Ward Kirk Publishing; "Satan's Holiday," "Welcome to Your Nightmare," "Blessings from the Darkness" and "Temporary Skeletons," as well as in "Shadows and Light Magazine", Issues 1 and 2 and, three of his works have been published in the James Ward Kirk Publishing anthology, "The Grays." David is married to Mary Genevieve Fortier, a successful, published award-winning poet. They live happily together in Saint Louis, Missouri. His work has also been featured on Hellnotes.com's "Horror in a Hundred" series (http://hellnotes.com/horror-in-a-hundred-logan-street-by-david-schutz-ii). David portrays "The Conductor," and narrates James Ward Kirk Publishing's "Terror Train" podcast, presenting every story and poem in the anthology, "Terror Train." http://terrortrain.wordpress.com/
For more information, please visit David's Author page on Facebook: https://www.facebook.com/DavidSchutzIIAuthor

David's Amazon.com page: http://www.amazon.com/David-Sch%C3%BCtz-II/e/B00IGWAWAC

Magenta Nero is a fiction writer, poet and artist. She loves to spin grim tales of dark fiction, crossing genres of horror, fantasy and erotica. Her work has been published in Sirens Call EZine, Sanitarium Magazine and many anthologies by J. Ellington Ashton Press and James Ward Kirk Fiction. Magenta was born in Italy, has lived in the U.K. and Japan, and currently resides in New South Wales, Australia.

Blog: www.magentanero.wordpress.com.
Twitter: @Magenta_Nero.

Tracy L. Carbone spent most of her life residing in cozy New England, the backdrop of which is the setting of most of her fiction. Her horror and literary short stories have appeared in dozens of anthologies and magazines in the U.S. and Canada.
She is an active member of the Horror Writers Association, its Los Angeles regional group, and former Co-chair of the New England Horror Writers. She edited their Bram Stoker Award nominated anthology, Epitaphs, a creepy collection of horror stories and poems by the group's authors including a handful of NY Times bestsellers. To date, she has published five novels in genres including horror, young adult, medical thrillers, and mysteries, and also a collection of chilling cautionary tales aptly named, The Collection and Other Dark Tales. Tracy but has recently relocated to Southern California where the sunshine is plentiful and her dogs can go outside without sweaters.

Lori R. Lopez is the author of ODDS AND ENDS: A DARK COLLECTION, CHOCOLATE-COVERED EYES, AN ILL WIND BLOWS, THE MACABRE MIND OF LORI R. LOPEZ, POETIC REFLECTIONS: THE QUEEN OF HATS, DANCE OF THE CHUPACABRAS, OUT-OF-MIND EXPERIENCES, THE FAIRY FLY, MONSTROSITIES, JUGULAR and more. A resident of Southern California, she is an author, poet, artist, columnist, actress, songwriter, musician and activist for conservation, children and animal rights. Stories and verse have appeared on Hellnotes and Halloween Forevermore, in THE SIRENS CALL E-Zine and anthologies such as JOURNALS OF HORROR: FOUND

FICTION, DEAD HARVEST, TERROR TRAIN, CURSED CURIOSITIES, CELLAR DOOR III: ANIMALS, BONES II, WE ARE DUST AND SHADOW, INDIANA HORROR REVIEW 2014, MIRAGES: TALES FROM AUTHORS OF THE MACABRE, MASTERS OF HORROR: DAMNED IF YOU DON'T, DARLINGS OF DECAY, I BELIEVE IN WEREWOLVES, THIRSTY ARE THE DAMNED, and SCARE PACKAGE: 14 TALES OF TERROR. Fifteen of Lori's poems were published for an anthology titled IN DARKNESS WE PLAY. She unapologetically takes pride in creatively bending and reshaping the rules of writing when it suits her style.

Doug Rinaldi: In the winter of 1973, a young, pregnant woman planned an innocent night out with her husband. She was curious after hearing all the talk about what fans and critics alike were hailing as the "scariest movie ever made." The film's immediate notoriety made the decision for them. So, they took a chance, unaware of the outcome, absorbing the cinematic masterpiece of William Peter Blatty's The Exorcist. Never would they have fathomed what influence the movie would have on their unborn child or how the film would secretly manipulate the child for the rest of his life. To this day, Doug Rinaldi's mother insists that watching The Exorcist in such a vulnerable state had affected her son in such wicked ways that she blames it for his twisted and dark personality. Doug was born and raised in the bowels of Connecticut. Spending his younger years exploring the woods near home, Doug envisioned otherworldly scenarios that ignited his imagination. Art was life. Throughout adolescence, he created, inventing horrifying tales about devious lunch ladies and world-eating monsters. In 1995, he received his art degree in Computer Animation and Special Effects for stage and screen. However, writing dark fiction was his true calling. At the turn of the millennium, he joyously bid Connecticut a final farewell and relocated to Boston, Massachusetts where he's been continuing to hone his writing and artistic skills ever since.

Steve Berry: I am twenty-nine years old, and under my own name, I am unpublished. I had several stories published when I was much younger under the pen name Steven Blake. But, I have now killed him.

NOW AVAILABLE

NOW AVAILABLE

NOW AVAILABLE

www.ingramcontent.com/pod-product-compliance
Lightning Source LLC
Chambersburg PA
CBHW070833250626
47159CB00003B/754